A Temporary Forever

Merged

Maxine Henri

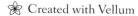 Created with Vellum

For all you, ladies, who dare to live your dreams.
You're fucking Queens.

Chapter 1

Caleb

The brunette sitting at the long bar across the dining room has been eye-fucking me for the past ten minutes. I should send her a drink, but my expected company—although very delayed—might interfere with any plans the beauty might have for us.

Still, I smile at her, and she licks her lips. From my table, I have a great view of her body, and it's giving me ideas.

I love a woman who carries her curves with confidence. When was the last time I hooked up with someone? The fact I don't remember is depressing.

Perhaps if she stays around long enough, we can pick up this game after my dinner.

Where the hell is Saar?

My sister is always late. I don't understand how she

keeps any of her modeling gigs if she extends the same respect to her employers that she does to the rest of us.

And it's not like she takes long to get ready. The woman hates makeup when she's not working. At times, I wonder if she comes late just to mess with me.

I tap my fingers on the white linen tablecloth. The plate setting glows in the ambient amber light from the large industrial ceiling lamps.

Around me, tables hum with conversation. The servers work with efficiency and the courtesy of a place that's well managed. Okay, maybe the bartender could prepare the orders—

Stop working.

Running hotels and restaurants globally, first under my father and now with my brother, Finn, instilled some habits that are hard to break.

I'm only here to eat, not increase their productivity and profit margins. Not that this Michelin-star restaurant needs my help.

Casa Cassi is as busy as always, but with my connections, I can get a table anywhere in the city.

Even though I hate what my last name represents, I'm not above reaping the benefits. Especially since Finn and I made a name for ourselves in the past year.

At least that one thing went well. I can't say the same for the other parts of my life.

The brunette raises the cocktail to her lips, and I

check my watch. Two more minutes, and I'll walk over to her and take control of my night.

Saar can eat by herself if she doesn't care to show up on time.

"Cal, I'm so sorry." My sister's breathy voice draws my attention.

I glance toward the bar one last time, and the brunette shrugs and, with an exaggerated pout, turns away. *Yeah, sweetheart, I'm sorry too.*

Standing up, I hug Saar and squeeze her extra hard. To rag on her, but also because I missed her.

Even at twenty-seven, Saar is the baby of the family, and since our parents don't speak to us anymore, I feel more responsible for her than ever before.

Especially since Finn and I could be blamed for the fallout.

Our parents might've had it coming, but it still isn't fair to Saar that she had to choose.

"Ouch, let go. I missed you too," she squeals.

"You're late."

She kisses my cheeks, beaming as if being late is a commendable achievement. "I'm sorry, but I had to pick up Celeste."

My smile falls as I realize the French dancer stands to the side. Celeste fucking Delacroix, the last woman I want to spend my evening with.

The woman is everything—curvy, graceful, radiant. That is, when you see her from afar, and she keeps her mouth shut.

I first met her when she choreographed Saar's fashion show almost a decade ago, watching her from afar, and she dazzled me.

She knocked the air out of me that first encounter. Not that she fucking remembers it.

At least I hadn't seen her for years until Saar insisted we have dinner together almost a year ago.

Little sis wanted to play matchmaker when Celeste lost work and needed a visa to stay here. I would have never agreed to dine with her, but it was my father's fault she lost her job, so I showed up.

Big. Fat. Mistake.

She even criticized the air I breathe. And while I enjoyed riling her up, I didn't particularly enjoy all her opinions.

There's something about this woman that makes me act like an idiot. And that pisses me off.

I charm. I play offense. And yet this woman puts me on the defense more than I'd like.

"Celeste." I nod.

"Prince Charming." She bows her head briefly and rewards me with a smile that would get her an Oscar. If there was a faking category.

"I thought it was just the two of us," I grumble to

Saar.

"I know, but Celeste has a big night tomorrow, and she needed a break and a distraction." Saar snatches the menu and starts reading.

"From what?"

"I have a lead role in a contemporary dance piece." Celeste says it with such pride, I can't help but smile.

"Congratulations."

Maybe this evening can play out amicably. The woman clearly takes pride in her work—something I can admire.

The server arrives, reciting the specials. Saar orders several items on the menu, like she hasn't eaten for days. And she probably hasn't. Her job annoys me.

"Sorry, guys, I feel like I'm living in perpetual jet lag." Saar yawns. She's just flown back from Europe, where she spends most of her time. "After I quit, I'll sleep for a year."

"And you'll finally live here," Celeste cheers.

"Talking about quitting, is tomorrow really your last day at Quaintique-Linden?" Saar turns to me.

Yeah, as if my life hasn't been turned upside down enough in the last eighteen months, I find myself exiting the career I always thought was my destiny. To my brother's dismay, I'm quitting the company we created together.

"Yep." I nod and take a sip of my drink. "So what is

the lead role?" I try to redirect attention away from me, because I'm not discussing my existential crisis in front of a woman who is a mere acquaintance. One that has been avoiding my eyes since she arrived.

Celeste looks at me now, her green eyes sparkling. She starts talking with enthusiasm. And I find myself lured by her words.

Not so much their meaning, but the melody. The longer she talks, the more prevalent the soft, lyrical intonation of her accent is. She elongates the vowels, and puts a charming emphasis on certain syllables.

The words flow from her lips—and fuck, those lips are puffy and kissable—in a uniquely elegant way.

When the waiter brings our entrees, the women dive into another conversation. The actual topic just glides around me as my eyes continue wandering to the woman across from me.

Celeste is wearing a tight red dress, with a cut that exposes and hides her cleavage at the same time.

On anyone else, it would look skanky and cheap, but she effortlessly gives the dress a sense of intrigue and refined elegance.

Her alabaster skin contrasts with the carmine satin. Add the perfectly coiffed chestnut hair, and she has the allure of a fifties movie star, a sexy kitten, and an elusive temptress. All those mix with a precision that draws you in, without the draw being the objective.

My gaze drops before I catch myself.

"My eyes are here." Celeste lowers her fork and points her fingers to her face.

Well, someone caught me. Fuck. But then, she hates me anyway, so why not have fun?

"Sorry, but your cleavage is inviting."

"Cal!" Saar swats at me.

Celeste scoffs and pushes her plate away. "That doesn't give you the right to blatantly glare at my boobs."

"Oh, sweetheart, why did you dress like this, then?" Yep, I went there. And I called her sweetheart, because apparently tonight's the night I completely lose my sense of propriety. Guess I left my manners at home.

Now Saar drops her cutlery. "Cal, what the fuck?"

But it's not like I have a chance to score any brownie points here, so I shrug.

"I'm genuinely interested." Not really, at the moment, but the issue is valid. "I mean, we're friends here. Frankly, I don't know any more when I can stare and when I can't. Sometimes it feels that just by looking at my assistant when I speak to her, I might get slapped with a sexual harassment suit."

And it's true. I've never in my life made unwanted advances, but I've been accused of things—usually by women who are after my money.

7

I'm not discounting the prevalence or the disgusting nature of sexual harassment, but it's annoying to be lumped in with my old man all the time.

I grew up with a father who routinely paid off women after he tired of them, or when they had no choice but to run to Human Resources.

My life is nothing like his, and yet often I'm judged for his actions.

Celeste raises her eyebrows slightly, but she quickly puts on the typical expression she wears around me. Like I'm an annoying mosquito.

"I wear this dress because I love it, and it makes me feel sexy and good. Because I love my body and feel comfortable in clothes like this."

Fuck, that throaty *r* when she speaks. My cock twitches.

"Obviously," I deadpan.

We glare at each other. I'm not even sure if I want to strangle her or bend her over this table and teach her a lesson. She dresses like prey, and I'm accused of being a predator.

I mean, I could have given her a compliment rather than stare. I didn't even plan to stare. The woman is bad news as it is. I don't need to pour oil into the fire.

"Okay," Saar says. "Let's go to the ladies' while Cal orders another round of drinks and thinks about his apology." She jumps up as if her chair has burst into flames.

Celeste drops her linen napkin on the table, her long red nails grazing the fabric. With the lithe moves of a gazelle, she throws her arm over the backrest of her chair.

I watch with fascination as the red nails disappear. She leans back in a fluid motion and crosses one leg over the other.

And now I desperately want to see her performance tomorrow night. What the fuck?

"I'm good." She smiles at my sister.

Saar groans. "Okay, but don't fight or kill each other while I'm gone." She stomps away.

Celeste tilts her head to the side, apparently expecting an apology. One that I owe her. But the stubborn bastard in me refuses to budge.

I lean forward, my eyes boring into her stony emerald gaze. "You're sexy, Celeste. So damn sexy that the man in me, the animal, can't help but respond. So if you choose to be sexy, then you need to understand your goddamn sexiness gets reactions."

She smiles. She fucking smiles. She never does what I expect. Fuck, I don't even know what I was expecting from her.

"No, Cal." She glides her tongue over her lips. "What I, and frankly, society expect is that the opposite sex is intelligent enough to tame the animal, to apply common sense and good manners, and not to let the drooling caveman direct his actions."

"So you don't want my compliments?" Obviously she doesn't, but playing this tug-of-words with her is more thrilling than I'd ever admit.

She throws her head back, her fake laugh drawing attention around us. "I've lived without your compliments for twenty-seven years, I'll do perfectly fine moving forward. But it wasn't a compliment you offered. You were ogling me, and not even trying to be subtle about it."

Fuck, why can't I admit my defeat here? I really should. *Just say sorry, Cal.*

Instead, I lean back, crossing one leg over the other, mimicking her pose. If she's the queen, I can be the fucking king. "It works." I shrug.

With another saccharine smile, she leans forward, making sure her cleavage is on display. I don't drop my gaze this time.

"I'm sure there are women who appreciate your behavior, but I like my men classy, with a dash of restraint in public places."

"And I like my women a bit more blushing, and less opinionated."

"Well, it's a good thing I'm not your woman."

Chapter 2

Caleb

It's a good thing I'm not your woman. The minute she said those words last night, something primal snapped in me. I wanted her to be my woman.

Probably just to prove to her she isn't immune to my advances. Or to prove to myself that... Fuck if I know.

I could smile at any woman, and she'd be mine. So why do I care about this particular one? She's hot as fuck, but her personality isn't my type.

Untamable. Unpliable. Unpredictable.

Un-fucking-forgettable.

Goddammit.

"Oh, Cal, I'm going to miss you." Reilly, my brother's assistant, pulls me out of my reverie. Or a downward spiral.

11

He gets teary as he hands me a card that could easily serve as a glitter bomb.

I keep it at arm's length. I don't need my suit to sparkle as I leave this office for the last time.

It's ironic how it took me thirty years to wake up one morning and finally realize that I was living a life planned for me by my parents—even by me—as I bought into the idea of this future.

That wake-up hadn't come suddenly, like a splash of cold water would cause. It'd crept in over the last couple of months.

And as much as I pretended thirty was too soon for a mid-life crisis, the restless feeling persisted.

"Reilly, at least you finally have a chance to win karaoke at the office party."

The boardroom and the reception area buzz like a bar on a Friday night, minus the cocktails. The table is laden with an assortment of bagels, muffins, and a ridiculously opulent fruit salad Reilly ordered, probably behind my brother's back.

Laughter that is slightly inappropriate for a Tuesday morning fills the Quaintique-Linden offices. It's for my benefit, and I enjoy seeing everyone relaxed.

It was important for Finn and me to create a culture diametrically different from what Linden Enterprises represented under its former CEO, our father.

"Yeah, if I ever blackmail Finn into renting a karaoke machine for us now once you're gone." Reilly huffs, sauntering away.

I make my way through the room, saying goodbye to my colleagues, coffee in my hand.

"So you're sure?" Finn catches my elbow, steering me away from the action.

I chuckle. "It's done, bro. Get used to it."

"You can always come back." The crease on his forehead deepens.

Finn not only spearheaded the hostile takeover of our father's company, and grew it significantly in the last year and a half, but also became a father and a husband.

The exhaustion shows on his face, but at the same time, I've never seen him as dedicated as he's been since he met his wife.

Seeing him might have planted the seed of discontent I've been dealing with lately. Not that I want a wife. No fucking way. But a sense of purpose has been missing.

I pat his shoulder. "I might not know what to do with my life at the moment, but I'm not that much of a loser."

"Asshole, that's not what I meant. I just... It's always been the two of us—"

"Jesus, having a baby made you sentimental."

Finn glares at me, shaking his head. "Dickhead."

"Look, I realized that fixing things was exciting, but running the day-to-day... I don't want to run his legacy," I confess.

By him, I mean our father. Not that I utter that name much.

"Fuck, Cal. It's our legacy. He's out. We got the company and its name back. Better, bolder... *ours*."

"Yeah, and you're the right person to run it. But after everything, and the shit that..." I still can't even name it, but Finn knows. "Anyway, I need to carve out my own thing. Something that isn't tainted with the memory of him."

"Yeah, but you could have stayed while you figured things out."

"Don't worry, bro, I won't be too far. You can always call me when you can't decide what tie to wear for a meeting." I smirk.

"Yeah, it's your invaluable fashion advice that I'll miss the most."

"You'll perish without it."

He punches my shoulder playfully. "Fuck. I don't know, I just always thought we were in it together."

"Well, I can't hold your hand forever."

"Fuck you."

I laugh and raise my coffee. "To new adventures."

Finn rolls his eyes, but can't hide the worried tilt of

his eyebrows. "Or your inevitable return," he retorts, the corner of his mouth twitching up.

"Thanks for the vote of confidence."

"I don't understand the rush. What's the plan now? You'll plunder your trust fund and fuck all the women who cross your path?"

"As if. I haven't partied properly ever since..." I put down my coffee mug, wishing this conversation could be washed down with something stronger. "Since Mia."

"Ironically, you're not dedicating much time or effort to her." Finn doesn't even attempt to hide his judgment.

"It's complicated." I look away, as if that made my poor excuse sound better.

"Bullshit. She just reminds you of another one of Charles's failures. You can't keep running away from your daddy issues, dude. You need to attack them head-on." Finn often refers to our father by his given name, disassociating himself in all ways possible.

"Yeah, how is that working for you?"

He shrugs. "A hefty bill from my therapist and still no closure, but at least I'm trying."

"Well, I'm the middle child. I sailed through without his notice, unlike you." That's a partial truth.

Finn, as the oldest, had been groomed to take over, growing up competing against an unattainable ideal our father harbored. While I was affected to a certain extent, my upbringing isn't something I lose much sleep over.

"And yet, you feel responsible for all his mistakes."

Fuck him for calling out my obsession to right my father's wrongs.

I just can't stand by and not address all of his horrible deeds. He negatively impacted the lives of so many others who suffered only because they crossed his path. I have the means to fix that, so I do.

"This party sucks."

I shoot him a grin, done with the conversation, and return to my now-former coworkers for a few moments before we break to get some work done.

Well, they do. I walk into my office with nothing really on my agenda. Collecting a few of my personal things, questions swirl, unanswered and unsettled, in my mind.

I really enjoyed fixing what our father fucked up in this company, but once the basics were covered, I kept looking for more things to solve.

I tried to satisfy that call outside of work, but that didn't make the days at the office any less dull.

Having grown up in hotels run by my father's company, I always pictured myself running one or more of them. And it came quite naturally to me. Like slipping on a well-worn jacket. A perfect fit.

Only underneath it, there's been an itch. A need to fix. To turn things upside down, inside out. For the better.

But fuck if I know what I'm looking for. And will I ever find it?

I pick up the small box of stuff I didn't even know I'd accumulated. A book, a stress ball, a photo of Finn, Saar, and me in Italy, and a few sentimental trinkets from our hotels across the world, where I worked for a few days or even a year in the past.

"Anna, could you please have this wrapped and ship it to my home?" I drop the box at the counter.

The receptionist looks up, sniffling, tears welling in her eyes. "Of course, Mr. van den Linden."

"What's wrong?"

"Nothing." She stands up, fidgeting with her hands. "I'm just sad you're leaving."

"Anna, I'll come and check on my brother. He and Reilly need you." I wink at her and call the elevator.

Multiple gazes follow me as I step inside the car, and I force one more of my signature smiles before the door slides closed.

I blow a raspberry. Fuck, this feels final.

My shoes pound on the belt as I increase the incline. Hitting the gym seemed like the best option on a Tuesday mid-morning, when most people are already productive in their careers or lives.

Deciding to leave Quaintique-Linden wasn't easy, but it felt right. I didn't envision that the actual physical act of stepping away would bring this much emptiness.

And it's only been two hours.

I guess I was supposed to plan for this. Why didn't I? Despite many people believing I'm the jester in the family, I have my life more organized than any of my siblings.

What does a person without a job do? Not that I need to work. My trust fund and my shares in Quaintique-Linden would more than cover me for the rest of my life.

But having money isn't the same as having a purpose. Only how does one find one?

Maybe I can have lunch with Saar before she leaves. That would cover at least two hours.

Fuck.

I missed the opening night of some exhibition at MOMA. Perhaps I can do that after my lunch.

The greenery shimmers behind the tall glass windows of the gym. Maybe I'll take a walk in Central Park.

That thought makes me chuckle. Last time I did that was with my nanny when I was in middle school.

"Laughing to yourself?" A man jumps on the treadmill beside me.

"Xander Stone. What the fuck, man? I haven't seen you since—"

"Shut up. I don't need the ladies around hearing we're old." He winks at a woman on a stepper next to him and she blushes, biting her lip.

I laugh. "What are you doing here?"

"Seriously, van den Linden, have you hit your head? I'm exercising. It's a gym." He wiggles his eyebrows.

I snort. "Dickhead, I meant in New York."

"I moved here a month ago."

"Seriously? How come I haven't run into you yet?"

He checks my screen and raises his incline by three more points. "Well, I've been busy flying back and forth between San Fran and here, no time for socializing."

"I never would've thought you'd grow up like that, party boy."

Xander Stone was my partner in crime during our time at Wharton. Three years younger than me, he was one of those kids too smart for his own good.

As a gifted child with photographic memory and an inherent ability to play the system, he skipped grades a couple of times, so we ended up in the same class in college. Not that he ever shows his intelligence, always the one stirring shit.

We lost touch after graduation. He moved to work in his family business in the San Francisco headquarters of their global developer firm, while I went to Asia to lead our flagship hotel there.

"Oh, that was just a temporary situation while I figured out the details of my relocation. I'm free tonight if you want to hit the town." He increases the speed.

For some reason, even though I was ready to slow down, I increase my speed as well. "We can do that."

"Let's catch up once I'm done, if you have time."

I have more time than I care. "I'll move a few things around."

An hour later, showered and sore—I'll feel that last uphill sprint for a few days—we walk into a small juice bar adjacent to the club.

"Are you in New York permanently, or just visiting in between the exotic locations where you pretend to work?" Xander slurps his smoothie, his blue eyes gleaming.

"Try to be a hotel manager for a day or two, asshole."

He throws his head back and laughs. "Don't be so sensitive. I'm happy to see you, that's all."

"Or you need hand-holding, being new to town and getting settled," I quip.

We take seats in the corner. The place is airy and light, with most patrons coming from the gym. Hunter's Clubs are state-of-the-art facilities, owned by celebrity trainer Hunter Stuart who owns similar gyms all over the country.

The businesspeople of Manhattan frequent this particular location, and a lot of deals get closed in this juice bar.

"I wouldn't mind an introduction to an exclusive club scene here." He raises his eyebrows suggestively.

The fucker wants my connections to get into a sex club. Some things never change. "I can vouch for you at my club, but let's go out first. I need to make sure you didn't turn into some sort of perv. I have a reputation to protect."

He laughs. "I doubt that, but thank you. We should go out, just like old times."

"Yeah, only the recovery takes longer." I shake my smoothie, the ice clanging.

He rolls his eyes. "I don't have that problem, old man."

"Sure."

"Congratulations on Quaintique-Linden. What you and Finn did there is commendable. Stealing the company from your father and turning it into a success so quickly took guts."

Shit. That's the last thing I want to talk about. How do I explain to anyone outside that I left a company that everyone in the industry and beyond has praised?

"You've been following me." I smirk. "That's touching. I'm sorry I can't say the same. What are you doing here? Has Stone senior finally let you out from under his wing?"

His features harden for a brief moment, but then he smirks. "Kind of hard *not* to follow you when you made sure your story was plastered all over social and traditional media. Papa van den Linden must be pissed."

"I wouldn't know. I haven't seen him in over a year."

"Shit. I'm sorry."

"It's for the best. His *legacy* has been haunting me with or without him." I air-quote around the word legacy, letting my friend know a bit without telling him the whole sordid story.

"You did what you had to do. I remember him. Charles was an asshole, if I may say so."

I nod and raise my glass. "And he probably still is. So, what are you doing here?"

He scratches his stubble with his thumb and index

finger. "I guess I didn't have what was expected to take over my family business, so I left."

"What do you mean?"

"My father sold the business without consulting me or giving me the opportunity, so I left. I joined a new financial group."

He explains the basic premise of the venture capital company he's starting with his friends, and something in me stirs. It's the familiar feeling of a challenge to be conquered.

"We're actually looking for someone like you— someone who can assess a business and make the necessary changes to improve its profitability and efficiency while maintaining the culture. We have several companies lined up to take over as silent partners or just buy it outright. And endless applications from start-ups. But at this point, it's just the three of us."

I take a generous sip before I put the chilled glass on the table in front of me. Leaning on my elbows, I look Xander in the eye and make a spontaneous decision.

"Today was my last day at Quaintique-Linden."

Chapter 3

Celeste

The cone of warm light hugs my body and isolates me in the dense darkness. My chest heaves with exertion and exhilaration. And a dash of anxiety.

My legs scream as I hold myself sideways on a chair, my heels in the air, the final notes of the sultry music fading.

It's premiere night, but before I let the worry set in, I enjoy the adrenaline from my performance pulsing through my veins.

Lingering in the pose, I surrender to the silence that cloaks the stage for a beat.

The familiar beat when the hard work of the past months culminates in the reward of performing in front of an audience. The beat just before we, on the stage, find out if all the pain, sweat, hard work, fun, creativity, and endless hours of rehearsals paid off.

I close my eyes, my head hanging backward in the sensual pose. In the still moment, the world feels paused, heavy with anticipation. I let out a shaky breath, inhaling the musk of the theater.

And just as a sliver of fear envelops the frantic rhythm of my heart against my ribcage, the applause erupts, washing over me with the audience's energy.

I jump to my feet, the pain forgotten, as my colleagues join me, and we bow to the people who graced us with their reception and accolades.

"You fucking killed it, darling." Jose, the male lead, hugs me as we rush to the edge of the stage and bow again.

The applause is deafening and electrifying. I continue the rehearsed curtain call in a daze, while Jose holds my hand, both of us beaming.

Merde, this feels good.

It's been a year since I almost packed it in and returned to France because I couldn't get a job. And then, out of nowhere, The Pulse Stage, a small off-Broadway theater, offered me a position, and shortly after, a lead role.

The standing ovations continue for what feels like another half of the night, but eventually we end up backstage.

"I booked the entire bar across the street. Let's celebrate!" Leon, the lead choreographer, hugs me with a suffocating force.

The changing rooms are a riot, all of us riding on the wave of our success. And as much as I love the spotlight, I also know how important it is to take care of myself after the performance and come down gently.

Because the highs of being on stage need to be managed carefully if I want to avoid addiction, or mental health issues.

But tonight, I might say yes and party to prolong the buzz. To enjoy it. To bask in it.

For once, I can be reckless and revel in my success with abandon.

"The first round of drinks is on me," Leon shouts from the hallway, and I laugh.

"You must come," Jose warns.

"Well then, get out of here so I can get changed." I shoo him away, laughing.

It takes me another hour to shower and change, since backup dancers and other colleagues keep coming up to me, and we hug, laugh, and congratulate each other.

I finally slide into an off-the-shoulder royal blue jumpsuit that falls down my legs in a heap of fabric, resembling a skirt. Most of my female colleagues are in comfy leggings, but that has never been my style.

Combing my still-damp hair, I fasten it into a tight bun and apply some lip gloss.

I'm exhausted, but I can't skip the party. Bonding with the rest of the crew is important.

And right now, I feel like celebrating. With tonight's success, my contract here will surely get renewed.

Perhaps over the next few months, I can reopen my dancing studio. Not that I'd be able to teach much with my current rehearsal schedule.

Still, I miss that connection with women who'd come full of doubt, with low self-esteem, who I helped to blossom through dancing. They'd find their confidence, and love their bodies and themselves, and on some level, that's more rewarding than the spotlight.

The hallway is almost deserted by the time I finally leave my dressing room. Instead of heading for the exit, I can't help but return to the stage.

The house is empty, the echoes of the night only a ghost now. I love the silence that swallows the theater after everyone leaves.

When I was a little girl, I used to sit in the pulsating darkness while my mom got changed after performing.

I dash across the wooden floor and jump down to sit in a velvet seat in the first row.

Closing my eyes, I let the events of the night settle inside me.

"I miss you, Mom. I wish you could have seen me tonight," I whisper, tears prickling my eyes.

I give myself a moment to reminisce, and then I leave the sacred place behind me so I can join the festivities across the street.

"Celeste, you're still here."

I freeze, groaning internally, but turn with a smile. "Mr. Reinhard, I was just leaving." *And so close to the back door*.

The theater director looks at me down his long, crooked nose. He regards me with suspicion, like I'm trespassing here.

The man is a bitter creature as it is, but he's taken a particular dislike to me ever since I joined the group.

I'm not sure why, and I never tried to investigate. Nobody likes him much, so I've never felt like I'm being singled out by his cold behavior.

He approaches me, his hands in his pockets, his lanky legs striding forward with a slight limp.

My heart hammers in my chest as I try to figure out why he's paying me any attention. He's been downright annoyed by my existence, so I stayed away, but it's not like I can turn and run now.

The silence I enjoyed just a minute ago spreads eerily now. We're probably the only two people still here. The realization coils around my spine, and I step back.

Goddammit. I square my shoulders and raise my chin, hiding my internal freak-out.

"Celeste, you know we're a small house, and a lot of admin work is on my shoulders," he says before he stops.

I swallow around the dryness in my mouth, but also to keep the words locked. Because if he didn't insist on a lot of unnecessary paperwork, he wouldn't need to complain.

Squashing my remark, I rake my brain for what I might have forgotten to log or sign.

"I still found time to fill out all the tedious paperwork to renew your visa, but I was too late, and you missed the deadline. As of tomorrow, your old visa expires."

I blink, my shoulders sagging slightly, but I quickly regain my composure and face him with a straight spine.

While my body is trained to perform on demand, my mind is misfiring in many directions.

"But I killed it tonight."

Yes, that's what I come up with. Amid losing my job, my ability to stay in Manhattan, my friends, the dream of reopening my school, I point out how well I danced tonight.

The irony of the situation is that I've been here already. After Charles van den Linden, Saar's father, got me blacklisted from work in New York, I almost lost my visa.

This gig saved me. I reminded Reinhard to fill out the paperwork on several occasions. Every single time, he made me feel like I was a nuisance. Merde, I shouldn't have trusted him.

"That's beside the point and, frankly, a loss to me that I really don't appreciate. But the situation stands. I can't employ you illegally."

I remain standing like a queen in front of him, forcing myself to postpone my breakdown. I can cry later, when I'm alone. When I can afford to be vulnerable. When I can lose it safely.

"What does that mean?" I really wish my voice came out with the confidence I fake in front of him. Instead, I rasp the words around the desert in my throat.

He huffs, annoyed with me or the situation, I'm not sure which. "Your understudy will have to take over quickly after tomorrow. At least the success of tonight might hopefully secure a sold-out house."

I blink.

I swallow.

I clear my throat.

None of it delivers any helpful thoughts.

"But I'm sure we can appeal. They must give me a visa if I'm employed here."

He shrugs. "Look, Celeste, I don't have time for all the red tape and paperwork, and you've been around long enough to know everyone is replaceable. By the time your visa is fixed, we'll be halfway through this season."

"But—"

"Spare me." He raises his hand to silence me. "Come back tomorrow, but you can't work here afterward."

Chapter 4

Celeste

SAAR

You were fantastic! Congratulations.

CORA

I wish I'd been there.

Let's have lunch today.

SAAR

My flight leaves tonight, so we're good. @Celeste?

CORA

She's probably still sleeping.

SAAR

Partying all night after that amazing performance.

Let's meet at one at your place @Cora.

CORA

(kiss emoji)

I groan as I turn around in my bed, my body screaming. It's no wonder, after dancing and then crying and raging all night.

I ignore the missed calls from Jose and all the messages from my colleagues. Missing the party last night is the least of my issues.

I don't respond to Cora and Saar, because if I canceled, they would come over. With it being Saar's last day here, she'll insist on meeting up. Getting out of that one is impossible.

I don't feel like dragging myself out of bed. Or across the town to Cora's bistro. Or to the theater tonight.

Or anywhere.

Ever.

My visa has always been tied to my work. A cabaret I used to work at had taken care of the renewals. I never needed to keep up with the paperwork.

Paperwork gives me anxiety.

Offices cause hives.

Officials make me want to curl into a ball and roll away.

Maybe that's why I didn't stay on top of Reinhard. Not that knowing why would help at this point.

Ever since the night my mother died and the police

barely acted, I don't trust the system. *Because ignoring it will make it go away. Magnifique, Celeste.*

My stomach growls, and I shuffle out of my bed and reach for the fridge in the kitchen corner. I can't afford more than a shoebox of an apartment. Everything is at arm's length. On a morning like this, it's a welcome problem.

The state inside my fridge is not as welcome. I bang my forehead against the door. With the busy rehearsal schedule, I neglected to grocery shop. Merde.

I force myself to stretch my limbs for twenty minutes, because I might be unemployed after tonight, but my body is still my only currency.

Dressing up in a white button-down shirt and dark green slacks that flare up at the waist, I decide to quit the pity party.

I was in a similar predicament almost a year ago, and an opportunity opened up. This time will be the same.

I smile at myself in the mirror. Fake as fuck, but it's all I have at the moment, so it will have to do.

It takes me another fifteen minutes to get to Chelsea, and when I enter Cora's bistro, I find the girls laughing at something.

Even Cora, who is usually very busy, is sitting at the table with Saar, relaxed. Her shiny ginger hair, usually tied in a ponytail, is blown out.

The scene pushes tears to my eyes. I'll miss this.

Stop it!

"Sorry I couldn't make it sooner." I walk over, and they jump up.

"The woman of the hour." Cora kisses my cheek, her red curls tickling my face. "I'm so sorry I couldn't be there last night. But things are looking up, and I might be able to take a night off and see you dance on the stage."

Cora took over her father's bistro after he fell ill, only to discover the entire business was in a very poor state. She's been working hard to help it bounce back.

Saar and our mutual friend Brook, who now lives in Portugal, started frequenting the bistro before their classes at my dance studio. Just before I had to close it, Cora became a regular in our tight group. Not that she has much time to see us outside of this little, charming place.

My dance studio used to be just up the street. Another dream that evaporated.

Stop it!

I quickly move to kiss Saar, because I don't want to break the news right away. It hurts that I can't even enjoy last night's success, because it's over before it even had a chance to settle in.

"I'm going to miss you." I squeeze Saar's hand before we sit down.

"I'm going to be back soon. I can't stand the hectocity of work for too long."

Saar is a model who works mainly in Europe, owning apartments in Milan and London. She misses Manhattan, but declines most of the offers to work here —a decision she made to avoid her parents as much as possible when she first started modeling at fifteen.

"Hectocity is not a word." Cora chuckles.

"It should be. The point is, we're going to hang out soon. All the time. Until you get sick of me."

"About that—" I start.

"What can I get you?" A woman I haven't seen before in a black apron with the bistro's logo smiles at me.

Her raven black hair is styled in a pixie cut that looks like it was shaped with children's scissors during a daring DIY moment. Her almost-black eyes draw attention.

But her glasses? They look like something you'd grab off a drugstore rack—cheap and not all that cute.

She is slender and so petite I immediately imagine her spending hours in front of a mirror practicing ballet.

"You're new." I smile.

Her tanned face turns red, and her eyes dart to Cora, who takes over. "Celeste, I'm proud to announce that I finally hired someone to help me here. This is

Lily. Lily, these are my friends, and they'll be getting on your nerves regularly. And Celeste always gets an oat milk latte."

"Nice to meet you." Lily fists her hands and turns.

"Actually, can I have two of your delicious croissants?"

"Of course." She dashes away.

"She looks a bit scared, but I'm sure you must be relieved to have hired her." I'm thrilled to see Cora relaxed for once.

"She is a bit nervous, but I have a good feeling about her." Cora takes a sip of her coffee and winces. Licking her lips, she adds, "I'm sure she'll get the hang of it."

"Of course she will." Saar crosses her legs, looking effortlessly beautiful in her jeans and a white tee, her blond hair in a messy bun. "Celeste, you must be exhausted and excited after last night. Congratulations. The whole performance was amazing, but you stole the show."

All for nothing.

Stop it!

"What's wrong?" She immediately picks up on my mood.

Out of my two friends here, I've known her the longest. We met when I choreographed a fashion show shortly after I arrived in Manhattan.

37

At that point, I hadn't picked up any jobs. I was all nerves, and we bonded together after I gave her a Snickers bar.

We lost touch and reconnected again last year, around the time I met Cora.

"I'm dancing for the last time tonight." I sag into my chair and blink rapidly. Merde, saying it out loud for the first time cracks the carefully forged no-more-self-pity veneer.

"That's bullshit. You were outstanding, they would be crazy to let you go!" Saar raises her voice, and several patrons look at us.

"What happened?" Cora frowns.

"My visa happened," I grumble.

"Wait a minute," Saar says. "You have a work visa tied to your job. That was the reason you needed a job last year. So if you have a job, the visa stands."

"Except that it needs regular renewals, and my boss missed the deadline for that. As of tomorrow, I'm a tourist here."

"Okay, so you'll miss a few shows, but you'll get back to it as soon as the renewal kicks in." Saar plays with a napkin.

"I was let go because the theater can't employ me illegally. They're giving the role to my understudy. They won't wait for me."

Lily, the new waitress, approaches with my order,

her hands trembling as she places the tray with my coffee and pastries in front of me.

The deafening silence around our table is probably not helping her composure, and as she pulls her hand back, she tilts the saucer, and some of my latte soaks my croissants.

"I'm so sorry. I'm so sorry," she chants, her eyes wide with horror.

Cora jumps up and rushes to the counter.

"It's okay. I was going to dunk them, anyway." I grab Lily's wrist and try to smile at her, to calm her down, though smiling is the last thing I feel like doing.

Cora returns with a rag and wipes the table. She walks Lily back to the counter and talks to her in a hushed voice.

No one speaks before she returns. "It's going to be okay," she says as she sits down.

"Lily or me?" I hate the defeat in my voice.

"What are the options to get your visa renewed, or apply for a new one?" Cora asks.

"This website is anything but user-friendly, but it looks like the process is lengthy and requires an employer to apply on your behalf." Saar speaks as she swipes up her phone screen with her finger.

With my bureauphobia, it hasn't even occurred to me to check the government website.

"My boss is glad to get rid of me." I sigh.

"Then he's an idiot, especially after last night." Saar puts her phone down. "Besides, there are other types of visas." She takes a sip of her drink, staring at me over the rim of her cup.

"Are you going to offer me your insufferable brother again?"

Saar means well, and I'm sure marriage might be a reasonable solution here. But Caleb van den Linden is the last person I would want to pretend to live with—or even like—in public. And I most definitely wouldn't want to owe him a favor.

As much as Saar thinks it's a good idea, Caleb dislikes me enough to refuse, even though he loves his sister and normally wouldn't say no to her.

"Yeah, it might be difficult after our last dinner, but Cal isn't planning to marry for real. Definitely not now, when—" she stops herself. "Never mind. He's available, and you know he's on a mission to fix all my father's mistakes."

"I never asked, what did your father do to Celeste?" Cora looks at Saar.

"My older brother Finn's wife used to take burlesque classes at Celeste's school. One night, Celeste asked Paris, my sister-in-law, to cover for a missing dancer."

"It was my key gig, and one of my dancers canceled, so Paris let me talk her into it. Only right after our performance, Saar's father barged backstage and wreaked havoc. He was upset about the mother of his grandchild 'stripping.'"

Saar rolls her eyes as Cora gasps.

"His words," Saar says. "The irony is that he was there because he was fucking one of the dancers. Who was younger than me. He almost cost my brother his fiancée, and the club fired Celeste."

Cora flinches. "Your father is—"

"A conniving, cheating piece of shit," Saar sums up matter-of-factly. "Yes, that he is, and worse."

"After I got the gig at The Pulse Stage, the problem was solved. I doubt Charles van den Linden even knows I was the casualty of his vendetta." I take a generous bite of my croissant.

"But his son knows, and he would want to help." Saar points at me, raising her eyebrows.

"I wouldn't go as far as *want*." I wipe the pastry crumbs from my lips. It could be a simple solution, but the price seems too high. The man is an insufferable playboy.

"What's with the two of you, anyway? I only met him a few times, but he's handsome, rich, and funny." Cora shrugs.

"I agree. A convenient marriage might be the best and fastest solution." Saar grumbles, "I'm sure he'd do that for me."

"I want to marry someone who wants to be with me. Call me a romantic. Your brother is one of those guys who asks for a number and never calls, and then pretends not to know the girl." I take a sip of my latte and stop myself from spitting it out.

Shit, Lily has a steep learning curve. I don't know the girl, but there's an aura of desperation around her that I sympathize with—I guess birds of a feather. I want her to succeed.

Saar snorts. "I doubt Cal has ever asked for a number. He just gets them. He oozes charm naturally, poor women. Though I don't understand why he's a dick around you. Perhaps that's a sign." Saar shrugs.

"What sign? That we should stay away from each other? I agree with that." I finish my second croissant.

"No, like, you know when we were kids, and a boy who liked you would bully you?" Saar stirs the spoon in her almost-full coffee mug. I guess she gave up after the first sip as well.

"That's the most fucked-up idea of romancing." Cora snorts.

"And we're not in kindergarten anymore," I add.

"I'm curious, though, why do you hate my brother?"

"Have you heard him talking to me?"

"I have, but I also heard you talking to him, and the razzing is mutual."

I don't know what to say to that. I'm usually not riled up that easily, but Caleb is a man who makes me feel challenged—and not in a good way. Besides, the last thing I need in my life is to be one of his women.

"Isn't that a good set-up for a fake marriage?" Cora pushes her mug away. "I mean, you'll get hitched with clear rules, and an expiration date."

I swallow around the lump in my throat. "And kill each other in the process?"

"You can minimize your interactions." Saar leans forward, propping her chin on her hand. "Think of your career, Celeste."

Chapter 5

Caleb

I pace the pavement in front of a rundown building, pissed. At myself. But mostly at Saar. I had to cut my second meeting with Xander short.

After I dropped the bomb that I left Quaintique-Linden, he told me more about his company, Merged, and fuck if I wasn't ready to invest on the spot. We agreed to meet today and discuss the topic more.

However, before we could get into it, I discovered seven missed calls from Saar and cut the meeting short.

And it's not even Saar who needs help. Seven fucking phone calls to help her goddamn friend.

Celeste Delacroix—even her fucking name is sexy —got under my skin. With her sass, her curves, her impossibly lithe dancer's body, those kissable lips.

Our encounters—and thank God there have been

only a few—never go well. The one a year ago ended with a cocktail in my face. The woman is certifiable.

Which begs the question, why the fuck am I here, pacing in front of the shabby brownstone in the East Village?

The fire escapes cluttered with potted plants present a stark departure from the neighborhoods I'm accustomed to.

The street is vibrant and loud, and probably safe. But I still feel like I might get robbed in my three-thousand-dollar suit. Why I fucking bothered to dress for the occasion is beyond me.

A lot about this is beyond me. Only my little sister could talk me into this level of madness. She had a hard time in high school and, topped off with our parents' recent estrangement, I can't help but try to make everything better for her.

I should just turn and leave.

Before I can execute the exit strategy, my phone buzzes. I check the display and groan. Fucking Saar.

"Are you there yet?" Saar practically screams into my ear.

"Remind me why it's a good idea?"

I turn my back to the building. A juice carton rolls alongside the curb. Faded graffiti adorns the facades of the businesses on the other side of the street—a small convenience store, a pizza place, and a nail salon.

I don't belong, but strangely, I have an urge to explore a bit.

"Cal, Celeste is my best friend. Her life is here. She has no other options."

"She also seems like someone who would rather fuck a cactus than spend time with me, so I fail to recognize why I am the one saving her."

"There will be no fucking, Cal." She sounds horrified. "Look, you're available—"

"How do you know? I could be in a relationship."

Saar snorts. Rightfully. I'd rather fuck a cactus myself than get tied up in a committed relationship—a choice I made a long time ago.

"Cal, you can divorce her as soon as she gets her visa. She can't lose this gig. She was spectacular in it. You won't just be helping my friend, you'll be enriching the cultural life of the city."

I roll my eyes. "You're shit at negotiating."

She sighs. "Please."

She might be a poor negotiator, but she is a master at blackmail. An easy deed, since I have never said no to her.

My sister went through a dark period when she was a teenager because of a man. Cormac Quinn became my enemy, even though to this day neither my brother nor I know what exactly went down. But we saw our sister hurt and losing her spark.

Enough to go above and beyond to make her life better. Her mental health improved, but the sentiment remained.

And as her plea echoes through the phone, I know I'm trapped.

"Look, I'm in front of her house. She better act amicably."

Because, let's face it, the first time I met Celeste fucking Delacroix, I learned women can't be trusted.

The irony of coming here to help her out is not lost on me. Neither is the nagging feeling that I'll regret this.

"She will. I promise, she will. I owe you, Cal."

"Yeah, I'll file it with all the other favors you owe me." I turn back to the building and take the few steps to the front entrance. "When are you back in the city, anyway?"

"I don't know, in a few weeks. Thank you, Cal."

I hang up, and before I can question my sanity, easily push the door open. What the fuck? Why does she live in such an insecure building?

The tiny foyer welcomes me with an odor of mildew and an obnoxious vanilla scent. The hallway is dark, with a narrow staircase leading up on my right hand side, and an equally narrow corridor along its side.

Half of the mailboxes are broken, barely hanging

on the wall with chipped paint. No woman—no human—should live in these conditions.

And where do I go now? I pull out my phone, hoping the address Saar texted me shows the unit number. Why isn't there a reception or a concierge here?

I find the unit on the ground floor. Thank God I don't have to walk upstairs. Not only because my quads still scream from my unofficial match with Xander, but because those stairs for sure fail all the codes.

Celeste's apartment is at the end of the gloomy corridor of carpeted floors and generic gray doors.

I knock with more enthusiasm than I feel. Probably best to just get this over with.

The door creaks open, and Celeste sticks her head out, hiding behind the door.

"What are you doing here?" she accuses.

Is she for real? I should turn around and go about my life. I don't have to save every victim of my father's lack of morals. Though based on this building, this candidate might need it.

I squint at the light seeping from behind her through the opening. "Are you kidding me?"

She raises an eyebrow. "Again, what are *you* doing here?" She doesn't fully open the door, eying me with suspicion.

"*Again*, are you kidding me?"

She widens her eyes and gapes with disbelief. And, perhaps, a dash of disdain.

"Look, Celeste, you need my help, not the other way around." I rub my forehead. This hasn't even started, and I already have a headache.

I briefly mourn the moments before lunch yesterday when I thought I had nothing to do and nowhere to be.

She rolls her eyes and sighs. "Saar sent you."

It's not a question, it's a realization. Fucking Saar. It's a good thing she would be on her way to the airport before I could get to her. Better for her general well-being. Because even my love for my sister has its limits.

A war wages behind Celeste's eyes, and then she steps back and widens the door's opening.

The long silky green robe she's wearing is tied fast with a sash, but the two sides still fall apart, giving me a better look at her cleavage than I want.

Or rather than I should have if I'm to leave this place with my balls still attached.

The emerald-green fabric matches her eyes. How can a woman dressed in a skimpy robe look so elegant? And why the fuck am I noticing?

I step inside and stop. For two reasons. There is nowhere to go, but I'm also shocked by the place.

It's smaller than my closet. She has a bed, a rack on

wheels with her clothes, and a sorry excuse for a kitchen.

That's all. It's clean and nicely decorated—if that can be claimed of a bed-only room—but it's minuscule.

"Is this your place?"

Instead of answering, she raises her eyebrows.

"You renting it?"

There's a decent person somewhere inside me—less snobby and more compassionate—but for some reason, it plays hooky today. Or anytime I'm around this woman.

"I own it."

She steps back and almost falls into her bed. And that gives me ideas and images I definitely don't need right now. All of them include that flimsy robe opening wide.

I force myself to focus on the task at hand. "Give me your passport."

"Excuse me?" She shoves the two sides of her robe together, fisting them. This is the first time I've seen her not flaunting her beauty around.

I clear my throat. "Do you want me to wait outside while you get dressed?"

She lifts her chin but ignores my question. "Why do you want my passport?"

"To send a picture of it to my lawyer."

"Why?"

"To see if we can fix your visa situation without tying myself to you for the foreseeable future. And in case of a negative answer, to prepare a prenup."

She snorts. "I don't want your money."

I chuckle. "Haven't heard that one before."

She jerks her head back. "Idiot."

She softens the d and accents the second syllable, and the melody of it stirs my cock. I'm like fucking Gomez Adams, aroused by a foreign accent. Fuck. My. Life.

"Okay, Celeste, do you want to stay in New York?"

"Not if the price is too high."

I laugh. "Most women would be delighted to marry me."

"I'm not most women."

"Clearly."

"What's that supposed to mean?"

Chapter 6

Caleb

"It means you're not most women. Far from it. You're the most elegant, classy woman I know, and I mingle in the upper class. You carry yourself with a confidence that is so damn attractive I have to tame the fucking animal in me."

Not sure why I'm referring to our last disastrous encounter. "But as soon as you open your mouth and spit venom at me, the attraction is void. So no, Celeste Delacroix, you're not most women. You're my sister's best friend, and I'll have to suffer your existence for a bit longer."

Her cheeks pinken slightly, and her lips part. And now I'm wondering what her just-fucked face looks like.

She glares at me, motionless. It's admirable how

she can be so completely still. It's also unnerving. The silence stretches, filled with loaded energy.

Why do I lose my manners every time I interact with this woman? Why can't I just help her out and go about my day?

She licks her lips, and I swear it's in slow motion. I shove my hands into my pockets and shift my weight from one foot to another.

Is she going to pretend she's a statue?

"You see, Caleb," she speaks like I'm five years old, "that right there is the reason we should not spend more time together."

We shouldn't spend time together. She's right, and not only because I keep insulting her. "I'm sure my lawyer can come up with a solution that will handle that concern for you."

She stares for several more beats, probably considering all the ways she could get rid of my body.

I stare right back, half wondering what the fuck I'm still doing here and half imagining what I can do with her pinned against the wall.

It's official. I'm completely unhinged around this woman. And the worst part is, I suspect my reasons for taunting her are simple. She doesn't fall at my feet like all other women.

It's like when I got my driver's license and I wanted

to drive Finn's red Ferrari, but he wouldn't let me. The challenge of getting him to relent was thrilling.

Only now I'm older, and I should be wiser. I should put my ego aside and stop fantasizing about a woman who clearly wants nothing to do with me. And yet the level of maturity I exhibit here is concerning.

She sighs, breaks our gaze, and turns to open a drawer in what I assume is her kitchen. It's really just a line of drawers below a sink and a stove with two cupboards above it.

She rummages through the drawer that houses all sorts of things besides cutlery. She shuts it and moves on to the next one.

"Merde."

Shit, that accent. I shift from foot to foot again. "What are you doing?"

"Looking for my passport." She scowls.

What? Jesus, this woman doesn't cease to surprise me. And not in a good way. "You don't know where your passport is?"

She doesn't answer, but continues with her frantic search. She opens the first cabinet, and my eyes widen. Instead of dishes, the whole cavity is stuffed with books.

Celeste pulls them out in stacks of three or four and shuffles through them before returning them.

They're not novels, as I would assume, but business and finance books.

The second kitchen cupboard is a library as well. This time, the shelves are stuffed with fiction.

I open my mouth to ask about the books, but I stop myself. Better let her focus on her task so I can get out of here.

After she's done in the kitchenette, she moves to a line of purses under her clothes rack.

As she squats to the ground, the ends of the robe slide back, exposing her legs. Even though the woman is soft in all the right places, the hours of dancing clearly molded her legs.

If those legs didn't belong to this particular woman, I'd love to dig my fingers into her skin and throw them over my shoulders—

I need to distract myself. "You're not very organized."

Again, such a gentleman.

Leaning back on her haunches, she gives me her best murderous look. Fuck, she's hot.

"I'm sorry I don't have the map." She tilts her head, her lips curling up.

"Map?" Is she high? I focus on her eyes, but they're as green as ever.

"So you could locate your manners. You're ogling again, Caleb."

"Well, it's not like I can look anywhere else in this shoebox." I glare, keeping my gaze on her face, but that doesn't help.

I still glimpse the rope opening slightly, a flash of black bra haunting me.

I need to get laid. Pronto. And get as far from Celeste Delacroix as possible. There must be some other way to help her that doesn't require our closeness.

Shaking her head slightly, she returns to her task. Like she's finally figured out there's no point in responding to my insults.

Which is a win. I think. It doesn't feel like one though.

I lean against the door and stare anywhere but at her. My gaze lands on a sketch framed on the wall. "You have an original Cassinetti drawing?"

She looks at the wall as if to confirm we're talking about the same thing. "Yes."

"Where did you get it?" These were auctioned by surprise at a charity gala. Was she there? I don't remember seeing her that night.

"Don't worry, I didn't steal it." She scoffs.

Our conversation is as delightful as ever. "I didn't mean that. It's just I see you also have a Philip Turner original." I refer to a painting on the other wall. "They probably cost more than this apartment."

"So? Art is a great investment." She turns around, grabs another purse, and shakes it.

"So is the real estate. Wouldn't you rather buy a bigger place?"

"Why don't you mind your own business," she retorts. "Enfin." She pulls her passport from the last purse.

She stands up and straightens her robe. Handing me the passport, she hesitates for a moment and pulls it back, clutching it to her chest. "Why are you doing this?"

I scratch the back of my neck. Fuck if I know. "I can't say no to Saar."

With wariness etched on her face and her brow furrowed, she tilts her head. "That seems a heavy burden," she says with sarcasm.

"Have you met my sister?"

"Hey, you can insult me, but not my best friend."

I chuckle. Celeste isn't just hot, she's loyal. The concept disturbs me, because the last thing I need is to notice positive traits about her.

"Look, I hate what my father did to you and many other people, so I guess I'm trying to fix some of it."

"Yes, but this is not on your conscience. I should have been on top of my visa."

I clutch my chest and pretend to stumble, finding

purchase with my other arm against the door. "A rare moment of self-awareness."

"Fuck you, Caleb. I don't have time for this. I'm due for my last performance" —her voices hitches as she looks at the small golden watch on her wrist—"in half an hour. I'm just wondering, what do you have to gain from this?"

Now it's my turn to stare in silence, because that question is valid. And the answer is *nothing*.

But that's what it looked like when I started helping others who my father wronged. At the end of the day, the opposite has been true.

I started fixing his mistakes because I was deeply ashamed of what he did—the lies, the cheating, the abuse of power—but to be honest, it was a selfish mission. I wanted to feel better about where I came from. And I gained way more.

For some reason I redirect the focus, because the pathetic hurt boy in me wants to know why she doesn't like me. Why she didn't like me when we first met.

"When was the first time you saw me, Celeste?"

She flinches. It's almost imperceptible, and she composes herself quickly. I can't say if she flinched at the sudden change of topic or because she does remember our first brief meeting, and all this time she's been pretending it never happened.

"I'm not a charity case," she snaps, ignoring my question again.

Guilty as charged, then. She must remember me.

"And yet... you're desperate for my help." Scoring points like a pro here. Christ. But if she can pretend we didn't meet ten years ago...

She winces. "Not desperate enough."

Stubborn woman. I want to help, but I won't force it on anyone. "Okay." I toss her passport to her bed and leave without looking back.

Chapter 7

Celeste

The door closes in slow motion, and in my mind, I can see Caleb walking through the building, probably worried his tailored shoes will catch fungus. Which legitimately might happen, but that's beside the point.

Snobby bastard.

Do you own this place?

Is it the home I always envisioned for myself? No. But it's what I can afford, and I made it mine.

I drop to sit on my bed and groan.

I'm angry at Saar for blindsiding me, at myself for always acting on impulse around Caleb, and at him for playing the guardian angel.

When was the first time you saw me?

He caught me off guard with that question. Hurt me, even. Why would he ask that? He's been pretending it never happened, so what's his angle?

Asshole.

But as I stare at the closed door, restricted by the size of my apartment, the realization crushes me.

My pride has just cost me my career.

Caleb van den Linden might be the only option to fast-track my visa, and I acted on my feelings.

When around him, I can't stop feeling *less*. Like I'm not worthy of his attention. Not deserving of his courtesy. Not good enough.

And that's not who I am. I am enough. I'm more than enough.

I was always too big to be a ballerina like my mom, but she helped me find my own form of dancing. She believed in me, and I carry that belief in her memory.

But that man makes me question everything. The moment he showed up and looked at this place down his nose, something in me snapped.

You're not very organized.

Fuck him.

Checking my watch, I soar into action and get ready to leave. My second and last night performing at The Pulse Stage.

I wipe a lone tear from my cheek. The makeup artist will have her hands full today.

I lock the door behind me and double-check that

it's secured. This neighborhood is safe enough, but that doesn't mean I should take chances.

I check my mailbox on the way out, and stop when my foot kicks something. The entrance doorknob rolls across the checkered floor toward the staircase.

Frowning, I look up and, sure enough, the building's main door is slightly ajar, the doorknob missing.

"I've been calling the super to fix that damn thing." The house gossip master leans her head down the railing. "The man in the pricey suit—was he visiting you, Celeste?—almost ripped the door off its hinges. Now I better keep watch since it doesn't close." She steps on to the landing, her arms folded over her chest.

"I'm sure now they'll come to fix it faster. Thank you for keeping guard." I smile, and she returns it with so much pretense I barely stifle a cackle. Instead of subjecting myself to further interrogation, I dash outside.

A boring subway ride later, I trudge through the abandoned alley that leads to the back entrance of the theater. I lift my hand to the door, but stall.

Do my colleagues know about my situation?

Has Reinhard told them already?

Or am I going to face inquiries about my absence last night?

Okay, Celeste, don't be a sissy. You're here to perform. Give them your best night.

I push the door open and merge into the familiar commotion. People are running around everywhere. The orchestra is rehearsing in the background. A dancer kisses me on the cheek as she dashes past me, whining about a torn bodysuit.

I make it to my dressing room without much fuss. I guess nobody knows yet. That's good. I can put everything to the side and focus on dancing.

I share the room with two of my colleagues, and they're already sitting in front of the mirrors.

"Celeste, where were you last night?" Matilde, the makeup artist, asks.

I put my purse down and rush behind the partition to put on my costume. "I'm so sorry." I stop myself there because I don't want to lie. But I can't say the truth either.

"Was there an admirer who drew you away from us?" Matilde continues, and the other dancers hoot with laughter.

I'm glad I'm hiding, because my face is probably an open book, tears welling in my eyes.

The last time I cried was the day I had to close my dancing school. Before that, at my mom's funeral.

This is hardly an occasion that matches. And yet the loss is like a lead balloon around my esophagus.

Can I even return to France? Nothing and nobody is waiting there for me. Only sad memories.

My life is here. Maybe not in this theater, but in New York. The city that never sleeps. The melting pot of cultures with such a rich tapestry.

The smell of the sewer and constant traffic delays. Theaters and the whole cultural scene. The congestion and the loud beat of the city. Its vibrant nightlife.

If I marry Caleb van den Linden, I can have it all forever. No more visa renewals, no more dependency. Well, if I don't count depending on him. But we could divorce, and then I could put it all behind me.

Reopen my school and rebuild my life. And perhaps meet a man who will complete me in the most caring and charming manner.

I walk backward from behind the partition and tap my colleague's shoulder while clutching the corset to my chest. She pulls at the strings and ties me in.

The only problem with that scenario is that Caleb has probably given up. I drove him away. His only motivation was Saar, and even that wasn't strong enough. I have nothing to offer him.

You carry yourself with a confidence that is so damn attractive I have to tame the fucking animal in me.

Can I lure the animal? Well, I certainly can, but do I want to? How would that make me feel?

He's clearly attracted to me, but not enough to treat me with respect. Would one night be enough for him to go through with the marriage?

I sit in front of the mirror, and Matilde gets to work.

Would I be able to erase it afterward? Would that be using my body to advance my life?

But that's what I've always done. Dancing. Using my body. This would be different, but what would be the downside?

It's a stupid idea, anyway. Why am I even considering it? As petty as it might be, I can't stand the fact that he had the last word. That he made the decision not to go through with it.

"You're quiet tonight. Are we not getting any scoop from last night?" Matilde shoves a pin into my hair, my head jerking to the side.

"Why don't you tell me how the party was?"

She sprays my hair, then purses her lips while she dabs makeup on my skin. "You should have come. Leon was looking all over for you. It seems the lead choreographer has a little crush on his star."

I snort. "Was he drinking?" *He'll be losing his star soon.*

"Close your eyes." She expertly smooths eyeliner over my eyelid. "Of course he was, but he was still disappointed by your no-show."

"Ten minutes," Leon's voice carries down the corridor.

"Shit." Matilde rummages through her makeup

case and stops talking, fully focused on the task at hand now.

She finishes with my lips at the same time as Leon's voice bellows, "Showtime."

The word has its magical effect, and in the midst of organized chaos, we all lean into our talents and skills and dive into the opening act.

The lights blind me as the first tones fill the house. And just like so many times before, I forget the ordinary to fully immerse myself in my art.

On the stage, there is no visa, no Caleb, no sadness. Only me, the music, and the freedom of movement. Full surrender.

Here, I can be someone else. Not better or worse than in real life. Just me, stripped down to the raw feelings while I portray someone else.

Without words. Without thoughts. Without censorship.

Just my legs and body, moving around with all I've got in me. For the audience. For my mom. But mostly for me.

Because every performance is a form of rebirth, the stage pointing a mirror at me, so I can bare my soul and rediscover pieces of myself.

The playful. The broken. The rebellious. The free.

When the curtain comes down, Jose pulls me to

him and hugs me tight. "Fuck, we did it again. Even better than last night, chica."

I swallow around the lump in my throat, tears of joy and regret pooling in my eyes.

The celebration backstage is even louder than the night before, despite yawns from the party or just from general exhaustion.

Leon knocks on the doorframe of our open dressing room. "You were magnificent, but let's not get over ourselves. Take a break, and let's meet at rehearsal tomorrow." His eyes meet mine, and I can't form a word through the loud echo of my heart in my temples.

"Celeste, don't forget to pack your things." Reinhard steps behind Leon, who jumps and pivots so quickly, the theater director almost topples.

"What do you mean, she should pack her things?" Leon's eyes dart between me and Reinhard.

Reinhard shrugs. "Today was her last day."

My face heats with the communal gasp that leads to complete silence.

Leon's gaze stops ping-ponging and lands on me. Fisting my clammy hands, I nod and look down. I can't bear the disappointment on everyone's faces. Or relief.

Whatever my colleagues might feel about me leaving, I have enough of my own emotions to bring me down, so I choose to stare at the linoleum as if it's the most interesting piece of art in the world.

"That makes no sense," Leon huffs.

Reinhard's voice makes shivers crawl across my skin. "I can't employ people illegally."

"What?" Leon snaps, a confused murmur in the background.

I look up, because hiding in plain sight is not going to fix the situation. I'm letting these people down, and I feel like shit about that, but I summon all my strength to own the fuck-up.

"My visa expired."

Leon jerks his head. "How is that possible? Have it renewed!"

I hug my arms around my waist. "We missed the deadline." I glance at Reinhard.

Leon whips his head to the manager, who looks completely unimpressed by all the drama.

"Are you kidding me?" Leon's words boom around us. He turns to me. "How could you?"

I flinch. "I didn't realize—"

"You didn't realize?" Leon flails his arms in the air. "You practiced with us for months, and didn't care enough to make sure you could actually deliver?"

"Hey, Leon, shut the fuck up." Jose steps around him. "Obviously she didn't do it on purpose."

I look at Reinhard, but he takes no responsibility, even though it belongs to him as much as me, if not more.

The muttering around me is soft, but I still catch the "how could she," "letting us down like this," "who will replace her," and "so irresponsible" comments swirling around.

"Our next performance is in a week. I'll have it fixed by then. You can terminate my contract officially, so I'm not an employee. Just let me rehearse in the meantime."

All heads turn to Reinhard. "I doubt you can manage that."

"I'll quit if you don't let her rehearse with us till next Wednesday." Jose folds his arms across his chest.

"Me too." Matilda steps forward.

"Me too."

"Me too."

Other dancers join in. I stifle a sob. What is happening? I spent months with these people, but never have I expected them to show up for me like this.

Everyone is staring at Leon, who says nothing, but looks at Reinhard.

The theater manager fidgets, his lips in a narrow line as he grinds his teeth. He pins me with an annoyed glare. "You better have a visa next Wednesday."

Chapter 8

Celeste

SAAR

@Celeste Are you engaged?

CORA

What did I miss?

SAAR

I unleashed Caleb on Celeste. I'm about to board the plane and neither of them is answering.

CORA

Celeste was amazing. I left Lily alone and went to see her.

SAAR

Was there a diamond on her finger?

Never mind. There was no time for that.

"Stop sniffling, chica." Jose hands me another tissue.

"We didn't mean it, anyway." Matilde bumps her hip against mine, and I snort.

"Celeste, you made this show a hit. You made a mediocre play into a divine art with your dancing. If you leave, we'll be unemployed anyway, so it wasn't even that much of a risk." Jose wraps his arm around my shoulder and squeezes.

"But you better have a solution, because Reinhard will sack us all, and I have children to feed," Matilde says.

My stomach dips as the depth of their unsolicited help sinks in. Reinhard would take revenge, maybe not firing the entire ensemble, but as he told me last night, everyone is replaceable.

"Interesting how Leon didn't join the rebellion, though. That was disappointing." Jose echoes my thoughts about our choreographer.

"Or smart. With all of you stepping forward, he didn't need to, and if it all goes to shit, he can still play nice with the management." My words ring true, but Leon's neutral stance was kind of disheartening.

Not so much for me as an individual, because I didn't expect any of my colleagues to step up like that.

But for me as a team member. I took him as a guy whose loyalty would remain with the team, not with the management.

"Frankly, if Reinhard hadn't hired you, he'd have sunk this theater already. I don't know why the new owner keeps him around." Jose takes a swig from his water bottle.

"I didn't know there was a new owner." I've paid little attention to the goings-on of The Pulse Stage beyond my performance.

"They're not new, Jose," Matilde says. "It's been a year, at least."

"Still." He rolls his eyes. "Why did they buy it if they don't care?"

Matilde shrugs. "I get my paycheck. Not my business." She looks at me. "So what's the plan?"

"I know someone who can help." Though just knowing him would hardly allow me to continue in this production.

I better figure out how to reach Caleb. I check my watch. Shit. Saar is in the air already. Can I call Finn's wife Paris and ask for his number? I can make some innocent reason for that, can't I?

"Ms. Delacroix?" A uniformed driver calls out when we turn to the main road. He stands beside a large black SUV polished to the nines.

"I wish." Matilde curtsies, and I laugh despite everything.

I'm overwhelmed by all of my conflicting feelings. The idea of offering sex to sweeten the deal for Caleb wars inside me.

A part of me embraces the decision as the best way to keep a level playing field with him. Quid pro quo.

The other part is protesting the use of sexual favors as if it's something dirty and tainted.

And the irony of it all is that I drove him away when he was offering his help for free. But then again, nothing is free.

"That's me. How can I help you?"

"Mr. van den Linden sent me to drive you home." He bows his head briefly and opens the door.

"So, there *was* an admirer last night." Matilde toots.

I quickly say goodbye to her and Jose, and cross the sidewalk to reach the car parked by the curb in a non-parking zone. I guess Caleb's employees are above the law.

But the legality of the matter is my last concern. I need to play this smart, because this is an unexpected, somewhat outlandish development, and maybe I can leverage it to my advantage.

"I usually take the subway." I stop by the open door, but don't get in.

"Mr. van den Linden wanted to make sure you got to your apartment safely. I'm instructed to walk you to the door." He beckons his head to the seat, his expression tense.

"Like a bodyguard?"

"Miss, could I perhaps answer all your questions during the ride?"

I stare him down, which doesn't seem to impact him at all, his expression remaining stoic. Like he's waiting patiently for me to get to my senses and do as I'm told.

"Why do I need an escort?"

He assesses me with a ghost of a smile. "To keep you safe."

"Does Mr. van den Linden routinely send his car to keep the citizens of New York safe?"

"That's something you'll have to ask him." He steps to the side but slightly forward. He isn't exactly crowding me, but subtly suggesting the direction of my next move. In other words, get in the car, woman.

I don't move. "But you know the answer."

"I'm just a driver."

"And a bodyguard."

He remains aloof, but I swear he growls softly. Since I need his help before I can take the next step in negotiating with Caleb, I get into the car.

I groan as my corset digs into my ribs the minute I dip into the soft leather seat. I didn't get changed out of my costume or wash my face. I couldn't stay there any longer with all the emotions threatening to spill out.

The compassion my colleagues showed me swirled warmly in my chest, but a part of me recoiled. I didn't know how to accept their kindness. I didn't deserve it.

"What's your name, driver-slash-bodyguard?"

His gaze meets mine in the rearview mirror as he pulls into traffic. "Peter."

"How long have you worked for Caleb, Peter?" Something tells me this conversation will be an uphill battle.

"Since he hired me." The corners of his eyes crinkle, but he looks back at the road immediately.

I smile. "Well played."

"We should be at your address in half an hour, miss."

I don't know if he wants me to shut up, or if he's giving me an estimate of how much time I have left to grill him.

Based on his initial answers, he won't share much with me, anyway. And he for sure won't give me Caleb's number.

"Actually, Peter, could you get me to Mr. van den Linden's instead?"

His eyes jerk to the mirror, but he says nothing. As he continues driving, he clicks something on the screen on the dashboard.

"Good evening, sir. Miss Delacroix asked to come to your place."

I slide to the middle of the seat to see Peter's profile, and I notice the white earpiece. He has Caleb on the line.

The silence seems to stretch to an unreasonable length. Is Caleb silent as well? Considering my request? Or is he giving Peter an earful for the outlandish suggestion?

"Yes, sir." Peter nods.

I hold my breath, but nothing changes. Peter continues to drive in silence. Is Caleb still talking to him? The screen on the panel remained black during the call, so I'm not sure if the call is still on.

Peter continues driving toward the East Village, so I guess that's my answer. Of course Caleb doesn't want to spend his evening bickering with me.

It's Wednesday night, but he probably isn't even home tonight. Or he has a woman there. That's the most likely scenario. Someone *blushing and less opinionated.*

Am I really going to let the whole production down? I slouch into the leather seat, my eyes set in front of me, the corset bruising my torso.

Funny how I don't feel its constraints when I'm dancing, but the minute I'm off stage, the thing becomes a prison. I should have changed.

"I can finally turn here, but it will take us another hour or so to get there in this traffic. There are water bottles in every door, miss."

I jerk my head to Peter and blink a few times. "He said yes?" God, can I sound more desperate?

Again, Peter says nothing. He just nods, which is great because at this rate, I'll be left with no dignity by the time I get to Caleb. And for this mission, I need every little smidge of it.

The drive takes more than an hour, that I spend fidgeting, lifting my hips off the seat to relieve my aching core, drinking all the water in the car, and rehearsing what I'm going to say.

In the depths of a dark garage, Peter escorts me to the elevator, swipes a card, pushes a button, and steps out before the door closes. "Have a nice evening, miss."

What? The lift jolts up and I close my eyes, breathing to calm my nerves. Why am I even this nervous?

Because it's not about me at this point. It's about the entire ensemble.

And because the success of this mission is in the hands of a man whose behavior and words bring all my insecurities to light.

In the hands of a man who—for the love of God—waits for me as the elevator door opens, wearing gray sweatpants that hang low on his hips and a white T-shirt that hugs the perfect V of his lean but strong body.

Caleb in a suit is handsome, but this casual version of him is pure foreplay. His light brown hair is damp and in disarray, as if he's just towel-dried it.

A five o'clock shadow covers his square jaw. His dark blue eyes are almost black as he pins his hooded gaze on me.

He stands there with the backdrop of the city glittering through the floor-to-ceiling windows that span the entire wall behind him.

His eyes rake up and down my body, and I feel so misplaced I freeze. God, I hate how this man makes me feel.

Before I find my mental faculties, the door starts closing. Caleb leaps forward and pushes a button, I think to reopen them, and I stumble outside.

Jesus. Could I have orchestrated a worse entrance?

Caleb eyes me, amusement dancing across his face. "Am I getting an encore performance?"

Yeah, I should've changed. And I shouldn't have drank all that water in the car. "Can I use your bathroom?"

He raises his eyebrows, but thank God, doesn't comment. He turns on his heel and points to a door, which I assume is the powder room.

I step in gingerly and let out a long breath behind the closed door. Jesus, this bathroom is larger than my apartment.

I sit on the toilet, engaging my muscles to void my bladder in a dripping motion.

The idea of starting this encounter while Caleb listens to my full stream is mortifying. Merde.

I finish my business and refresh my smudged makeup before I step outside. The powder room is in an alcove near the elevator. Both are on an elevated platform—the size of a ballroom—that opens up to a beautiful living room.

I find Caleb sitting on a sofa lining the wall of windows. A glass staircase leads up one side, and bookshelves line the wall on the other side. The room is cavernous, but also somehow homey.

And the king of the house doesn't hurry to offer any morsels of hospitality. He just sits there, waiting.

I take two steps down from where I'm standing, my heels clicking loudly on the wooden surface before they dig into the soft carpeting of the living room area. "You sent a driver."

In my frenzy to get to him, I didn't even get a

chance to evaluate what that was about. Why would he do that? Like a consolation prize? *I'm not helping you out with your visa, so at least I gave you a ride home?*

"You're Saar's friend, and your neighborhood didn't feel safe."

"My building was perfectly safe before you broke the door."

He shakes his head, rolling his eyes. "That door-knob was barely hanging."

I swallow the retort on my tongue. *Focus on the mission, Celeste.* "Thank you."

His eyebrow jerks up, and then he furrows it, studying me with suspicion. "What are you doing here, Celeste?"

I square my shoulders. Showtime. "I figured out what you can gain from the arrangement."

"I thought the price was too high." He smirks, throwing my words back at me.

"Well, maybe I realized I have more to lose, and that put a new value on the arrangement."

"So you came up with a counter offer?"

"Yes."

Why is it so hot in here? And why am I parched even though I drank the entire water supply in his car?

"I was trying to do you a favor, and you did every-thing to dissuade me. How do you know there still *is* an offer on the table?"

The bastard won't make this easy.

He sits there casually in those stupid sweatpants, his T-shirt straining across his chest. They should ban sweats for men. Especially when a man is built like God.

One arm casually thrown across the backrest, he rests the other in his lap. And suddenly I have an image of what he could do with those hands, and the whole transaction doesn't feel like such a sacrifice.

After the display of support from my colleagues earlier, I'm willing to go through with this. Push my pride and my feelings aside and take one for the team.

And considering the fine specimen in front of me, with his latent smirk and sparkling dark blue eyes, it might even be an enjoyable endeavor.

I step forward, placing one foot in front of the other, making sure my hips sway naturally. I'm a dancer, after all.

Caleb sits straighter, his gaze roaming down my body. I've never fucked with any purpose other than the joy of it, and my stupid head is offering all sorts of opinions, most of them judgmental, but I push them all away and saunter toward him.

I step between his legs. Caleb tilts his head up slowly. Very, very slowly, not letting the movement disturb him from his obvious appreciation of my body. Damn, the man is good.

Finally, his gaze lifts to meet mine. Full of hunger and heat. I smile at him and lean my knee on the edge of the sofa, grazing his crotch. Accidentally on purpose.

"What exactly are you offering here, Celeste?" he rasps, not moving. Other than his cock tenting the soft cotton of his sweats.

I plant both my hands behind him on the backrest, taking advantage of the tight corset I'm wearing, my tits practically in his face. I toss my hair. "Isn't it obvious?"

He takes a good, long look at my cleavage, his face impassive. I wish it was confidence that was running through my veins. Instead, my heart hammers with anticipation—not the good kind—and I wonder if he can see my thumping pulse.

But when his eyes meet mine again, the heat is a notch higher than before. "Sweetheart, I wouldn't be a good businessman if I acted on impressions."

Merde. He's going to make me work for it. "I don't think your dick shares that concern."

He gives me a smile that doesn't reach his eyes. "If you have an offer, use your words, Celeste."

I falter. *Fuck this*. I push off with my hands to straighten up. Before I can step back and look for my dignity, his hand moves to the back of my knee.

I gasp, and we both look down where his touch burns my skin. The oxygen supply in the room drops, and I can only get enough to reach the top of my lungs.

"So?" he taunts.

He can't know how sensitive I am behind my knee. Most of my former boyfriends took weeks before they found that particular spot, and yet, with an impulsive move, he landed right there. Goddammit.

"You marry me to help me get my visa, and I'll sleep with you."

He cocks his head and studies me, his finger tracing up and down, scorching my skin.

I invest all my acting skills into pretending I'm unaffected, but my underwear is soaked, and I'm sure he can smell it.

He shifts, leaning slightly forward, and inhales. Yep, he can definitely smell my arousal. He places his other hand on my other leg, tracing slowly up my outer thighs.

I stifle a moan. His touch is lethal, killing any inhibition or any restraint I think I still have.

He pushes up to stand, his height overwhelming as he looks down at me. I always knew Caleb van den Linden was handsome, but this close, I can fully appreciate his chiseled jaw, his full lips shadowed by the stubble on his face.

And his deep blue eyes. That gaze can melt panties, and it's a good thing I'm so wet because I'd burst into flames.

The pads of his fingers, soft on my skin, continue

their perusal up my torso, brushing the sides of my corseted breasts. Slowly, he trails up my clavicle to my neck. My breath hitches.

He squeezes my jaw between his thumb and index finger and tilts my head back. Is he going to kiss me?

Anticipation builds inside me, fluttering in my stomach, swelling in my chest, soaring in my core. Merde, this man is intense.

He stares at me for what feels like several lifetimes, his breath warm on my face. He smells of something earthy and chocolate, which is so unexpected and welcome. I want to bury my nose in the crook of his neck and feed my senses on his musk.

"I'll pass." He drops his hands.

I stumble backward, dizzy from the loss of his butterfly touch and confused by his words. "You'll pass?" I snap.

My legs hit the coffee table behind me, and I lose my balance, but before I can fall, Caleb snakes his arm around my waist and jerks me to him.

Now the light touch of his fingers threw me off, but his palm on the small of my back... *Dieu aide moi.*

"Yes, black swan, because I might be attracted to your beautiful dancer body, and my cock has a mind of his own when I'm around you, but I'm not going to sleep with you."

He lowers his mouth to my ear. "Not to save your

career or your stay in New York, not as a sacrifice or a bargain. Not until you want it, need it so much that fucking me is the only thought on your mind. Not until you beg me for it on your knees, because your pussy weeps for my cock."

Chapter 9

Caleb

The Merged offices take up two floors of prime real estate in a glittering skyscraper in the Financial District. Ironically, not too far from Quaintique-Linden.

"Mr. van den Linden." A receptionist with a headset in her black dreadlocks jumps to her feet and rounds the sleek white counter, eating the distance between us while talking to the mic.

"Mr. Stone will be with you any minute. May I offer you a coffee?" she asks me, gesturing to a spacious corner with white leather sofas.

The Monday morning commotion buzzes in the background. Who would have thought I'd find myself in an office only a week after I forever exited the last one?

Before I can sit or ask her for a coffee, Xander saunters in.

"Roxy, I'll take it from here. Thank you." He winks at her and extends his hand to me. "I'm glad you called, Cal."

"I'm still not sure four partners is a good idea," I say as we round the corner.

"Let me introduce you, and you can form your opinion then."

We walk down a hallway lined with glass-walled offices. The place reminds me of an ad agency or an architecture firm. It's nothing like the stuffy equity firms I've been to before. Most of the cubicles and offices are empty, their future occupants not yet hired.

"I wish you'd have told me who they are so I can be better prepared."

Merged is about to launch their operations officially, and there aren't public records available yet.

At this point, it's a true start-up before it even started, and the idea of being on the ground floor of something excites me even before I have all the details.

Details that I could have—and should have—dug up if I was operating at full capacity.

But my mind has been veering off. I haven't slept well since Celeste left on Wednesday night. The image of her standing between my legs has been driving me crazy.

When did I grow a conscience? Since when do I refuse a woman?

I keep telling myself it's because she is more trouble than I care for. My cock strongly disagrees. The boner her visit left behind needed several rounds of jerking off.

The result? Sore hand, partial physical relief, and my mind still questioning my sanity.

And the fucking hurt on her face. It was there for a blink before she put on her haughty mask and huffed.

When you beg me on your knees.

Fuck, I hope she will. Sooner rather than later. And the anticipation thrills me more than it should.

In the short span of a week, she's impacted me more than I care to admit. What was I thinking, sending a car for her? I blame the boredom.

Shit, I need to stop thinking about her, otherwise I'll walk into this meeting with a semi in my pants.

I miss the conversation between Xander and another woman before we enter what I assumed was a boardroom. It's not. It's a large corner office.

A CEO office, if my guess is right. And as soon as I see who's in there, I stop, ready to leave.

"Meeting adjourned." I scowl at Xander.

Cormac Quinn, my archenemy, smirks. "Really, van den Linden? Will you let some high school grudge

I've never understood keep you from the best opportunity of your life?"

He's leaning casually against the glass desk in his light blue suit, challenging me with his eyes.

"The value of the opportunity plummeted with you in the picture."

"What am I missing?" Xander frowns, his gaze darting between me and Corm.

"That's what I wonder." Another man whom I didn't notice before stands up from a large sofa in the corner. He walks to where I still stand by the door. "I'm Declan Quinn, Corm's brother. I've heard a lot of great things about you."

Brother? I'd never have guessed. While Corm has fair hair and his tan is probably hard-earned, the other Quinn is darker, with black hair and eyes.

I shake Declan's hand, glaring at Corm. "I'm assuming none of them came from that asshole."

Corm raises his arms in exasperation. "For the record, the grudge your family holds against me is one-sided."

"Fuck you, Quinn. My sister... Never mind. I'm leaving."

But I don't move, because at the mention of Saar, he flinches. And that's as good as a confession. He hurt her.

"Wait a minute, this is about a woman?" Declan scoffs and gets on my shit list right below his brother.

"I've never done anything to Saar." Corm approaches me.

The two other men in the room move—Xander toward me and Declan somewhere between us, getting ready to break up a fight.

"Really? Why don't we ask her?" I fist my hands.

Corm stops. "Why don't we? I'm not sure what you believe happened, but aside from ditching her on the dance floor, I always wondered where your overprotective act was coming from."

This stops me in my tracks. I can't fathom why he would lie about that, because he must assume I either know what happened or can easily ask Saar.

We've never gotten any details from her because we didn't want her to suffer through a confession.

Regardless, I still don't trust the man.

"Okay, kids, why don't we shake hands and get down to business," Declan says, returning to his seat in the corner.

"Cal, I think you're the right fit for this opportunity. Let us show you how." Corm gestures to the seating area where breakfast trays cover the table. Only then do I notice the smell of coffee in the air and relent. I'm tired as fuck.

There is no way I'm going to ever work with that

asshole, but I can at least listen to their plans. It's not like I have anything better to do at the moment.

I take a seat and let the first sip of coffee calm me while I glare at Corm.

"We'll need you to sign an NDA first." Declan pushes a stack of papers in front of me.

"I'm not signing anything without my lawyer." I drop the contract beside me.

Declan shakes his head. "Seriously, Xander, why the fuck are we having this meeting?"

"Not to piss him off right at the gate," Xander snarls.

"I trust him. We don't need an NDA." Corm leans back in the leather chair across from me.

"Me too," Xander chimes in, popping a strawberry into his mouth and looking at Declan.

Declan glowers at me and then shakes his head yet again—because, I agree, this meeting went to shit before it started. "Okay, let him steal our ideas."

"Merged will focus on streamlining mergers and acquisitions to ensure that both parties not only achieve financial success but also maintain or enhance their operational effectiveness post-merger," Corm starts.

"So like any other M&A firm." I take another sip of the coffee, which is probably a very particular blend of robusta and arabica because it's really smooth on my tongue. At least something about this visit scores.

"Yes, and no. With our combined experience and connections, we have an advantage of selecting the right opportunities," Declan says. "It's about the right people steering the ship. Besides, we'll have our own venture capital arm to foster startups that can be later merged with established firms." He goes on to describe the type of businesses they've already scouted and pre-approved.

The more he talks, the more I'm drawn in. This would be the exact kind of challenge I'd enjoy—take something new or nonfunctional and groom it to its full potential, but never stay bogged down by the day-to-day once the transformation is over.

I wish Corm hadn't extended his trust. Fuck, his involvement curbs my excitement. Declan talks about high-level financial projections, and I can see how they might need more capital. But I can also see the returns would be more than healthy.

"You may wonder where you'd fit in." Corm pins me with his challenging gaze.

"I'm not wondering anything. I don't sleep with the enemy."

Unfortunately, a particular enemy with emerald eyes comes to my mind, and I might need to adjust in my seat, but fidgeting is not the way to conduct negoti-ations. I'm not showing Corm any discomfort.

Corm sighs. "In case you were wondering... I'm the CEO of Merged. Xander is the Chief Strategy Officer. He focuses on scouting opportunities. Declan, the financial wiz, is our CFO. What we're missing is someone to run the operation, to focus on the integra-tion of the companies. Someone who can do what you've done with Linden hotels."

I'm not going to lie, it's flattering that someone noticed my contribution to what is generally perceived as Finn's company. I can't deny that this opportunity is intriguing.

"How much is your stake?" I turn to Corm. There are more questions I want to ask, but I'm not giving them the satisfaction of assuming they won this round.

"For now, I have sixty percent, Xander and Declan have twenty each. You would buy in and get twenty percent from me."

I snort. "Well, gentlemen,"—I put the coffee mug down—"and Cormac, thank you for the breakfast. I wish you all the best in your endeavors."

I stand up and walk away, shutting the door behind me. Taking my time to return to the elevator banks, I try to soak up the atmosphere in this yet nonexistent firm. Fuck, I wish the leaders were different.

After getting downstairs, I grab a coffee in the

corner shop in the lobby. Yeah, I need all the help I can get to shake off the lost sleep.

Pulling out my phone, I dial my sister.

"Hey, Cal, how are you?"

"Don't pretend you didn't trick me into visiting Celeste and blindsiding us both," I growl.

"Did it work?" She's too chipper for my current mood.

"That remains to be seen. But I'm not calling about your annoying friend."

By now, I'm well aware that the only annoying thing about my black swan is that she isn't mine. A fact I'll ignore for the foreseeable future.

Just because I want something doesn't mean I should have it. Fried food, sex in the middle of Times Square, Celeste Delacroix.

"What do you need?"

"What's the story between you and Cormac Quinn? What happened all those years ago?"

My question is met with silence. I exit the coffee shop and stop in the lobby at the glass wall overlooking the street.

Saar doesn't speak, and I almost regret asking her. What's the point in stirring up painful memories?

"I don't care about him. I practically forgot he exists."

That's an evasion if I've ever heard one. "Saar, I

ran into him, and I got a distinct feeling that perhaps the history between the two of you differs from what I always assumed."

"What did he say to you?"

"Tell me what happened back then. Too much time has passed, I'm sure you can explain."

"I'm not having this conversation over the phone. Besides, why do you care after all this time? It doesn't matter anymore."

"Fuck, Saar. I'll always put you first, but Finn almost lost Paris over this feud last year—"

"I fixed that."

"What? You knew about what went down?"

My brother forbade Paris to work with Quinn, which didn't go down well with his now-wife. Saar wasn't even in town at that time. Was she?

My sister doesn't answer. Fuck this shit. I feel like I'm in high school again.

"Look, Saar, I might have a business opportunity with him and—"

"Is it a good opportunity?"

"I'm not sure yet."

"If it's something you want to pursue, don't stop on my account. I'm not having Christmas dinner with Quinn anytime soon, but you don't have to protect me from him either."

"Are you sure?"

"Yes."

"Good, but you'll tell me the complete story when we see each other next time."

"Maybe. Cal?"

"Hmm?"

"Will you help Celeste?"

"And perish trying?"

"Cal, please."

Of course she'd ask this, just subtly feeding into my guilt over potentially working with a man who hurt her.

"I'll see what I can do."

"Thank you."

"Take care of yourself, sis."

These women will be the death of me. I down the coffee and basketball shoot the cup into the trash. Before I reach the revolving doors, Xander catches up with me.

"What the fuck, man? What did he do to your sister?"

"Why didn't you tell me you're working with the Quinns?" I hiss.

Xander looks around. "Because we're keeping everything under wraps before we announce the company."

"Look, I appreciate—"

"Cal, I can see you want to be part of it. What would it take to get you on board?"

"Twenty-five percent." Fuck. Did I just make a counteroffer on the spot like this?

"Okay, I'll take it back and call you later. Anything else?"

"Send the financial projections, the NDA, and everything else to Dominic Cressard, he's my lawyer."

Xander nods. "You won't regret it."

"I haven't committed to anything yet."

"Sure. Sure. Do you want to grab lunch?"

"No, I have to go and see my fiancée."

His surprised expression is the sweet cherry on top of the particularly foul cake this day has been so far.

Chapter 10

Celeste

I throw my vibrator to the side, sighing blissfully. I don't need to beg Caleb for anything. Even though I just imagined him while chasing my orgasm. And when I was doing laundry yesterday. And during my stretching session.

I pass, black swan.

The amount of humiliation that man has caused me would easily fill this apartment. But I can't spend the day hating Caleb van den Linden. I need to figure out how to save my position, my visa, and my colleagues.

I sit up and take a painkiller. I haven't slept well since Reinhard told me I'm fucked. And this morning, after tossing all night and falling asleep at dawn, some commotion and drilling in the hallway woke me up.

Someone must be moving in or out, because it's still going on.

I squeeze into my mini shower. God, that powder room in his house. Fuck, kill me for wanting something nicer in my life. Starting anew in France would set me even further back.

I let the hot water hit my skin and allow my tears to fall freely. If I cry in the shower it doesn't count, because I'm already wet.

I wallow for a few more moments, enjoying the hot water while it lasts, then step out and wrap myself in a towel before I pad to my room. I'm sure Caleb never runs out of hot water.

Stop it, Celeste. Forget about that insufferable man.

My ringtone distracts me from my pity party.

"Saar, how are you, babe?" I sound way too cheerful.

"I have good news. Cal is going to help you out, after all."

I freeze. "I don't think so."

"Celeste, stop being stubborn and take his help. I talked to him just now, and he agreed to try."

Try being the operative word here. I should rejoice, but after Wednesday night, when I couldn't get out of his loft fast enough, I can't imagine facing him again, let alone living with him.

"Saar, I doubt he means it. And even if he did, what if something happens? We both know it's bound to end poorly, and I don't want that to come between us."

She laughs. "I assure you, my brother's sworn off love, so there's no chance you'd break his heart. And the marriage would be fake, so I won't have to pick a side in the divorce."

"I offered to sleep with him," I blurt out.

"Oh my God." Her gasp carries over the line, shaming me.

"Don't judge me, I was desperate."

"I'm not judging. I'm just not particularly keen on imagining my brother having sex."

"Then you're safe. He refused me."

The line remains mute. Her lack of reaction makes me want to cry again. Yeah, that's how pathetic I am. The man who sleeps with any woman with a pulse rejected me. Kind of.

"Are you still there?" I ask.

"Yes, I'm here, I'm just... shocked."

"That I offered to sleep with him?"

"That he refused."

Not exactly refused. More like put conditions on it, but I'm not going to share that. My mind—and my pussy—are still riling from that statement.

Not until you want it, need it so much that fucking me is the only thought on your mind. Not until you beg me for it on your knees because your pussy weeps for my cock.

Even worse, now I'm attracted to him. His intense eyes, his broad shoulders, his feather-like touch, and those low-waist sweats. How casual and at-home he looked in his... well, home. Still his usual carefree self, but somehow with more substance.

The guitar in the corner, the books that looked used and not just for display, photographs on the shelves beside them. For some reason, I expected he'd live in a sterile fuck-pad.

While everything in that loft probably cost my yearly salary, it was all tasteful and didn't feel like it was picked out by a designer, it felt personal. Because somehow he fit in the place perfectly. I don't think a designer could have such an intimate touch.

Or one of his exes decorated the place. An unwarranted pang of jealousy swirls in my empty stomach. Merde.

"Yeah, which begs the question, why does he still want to help me?"

"He might feel he owes me, but... does it matter? Mid-life crisis adventure for all you care, as long as you can stay and dance."

Yes, that's the objective. I need to keep it in mind, and not get distracted by Caleb. Though the two seem to be well connected. "I guess."

"That's your problem, Celeste. You were surprised that your colleagues stood up for you because you never believe you're deserving of anything. And now you're questioning Cal's motivation because you don't trust someone would just do something nice for you. That they want to."

Someone in the background yells her name. "I have to go. Please let my brother fix this for you."

Someone doing something nice for me? Why? Why would they?

I still have three hours before my rehearsal, but I can't stand the ruckus outside my doors, so I decide to go to Cora's.

I'm about to text her when a message arrives.

UNKNOWN NUMBER

Meet me in an hour. Can you make it?
Caleb

He's attached an address, and a quick search shows it's a walk-in legal clinic. A legal clinic seems like the last place you'd find a man like Caleb.

I confirm without asking more questions, because the best strategy to not derail this is to not talk to him.

The smell of paint hits my nostrils as soon as I step out of my place. Two men on ladders paint the walls in the corridor.

I squeeze around, wondering what prompted the

management to spruce this place up. At the last owner's association meeting, we couldn't afford to fix the damn doorknob.

Of course, it's just my luck that the Karen from upstairs stands by the entrance.

"Can you believe it, Celeste? Apparently that snob who broke our door the other day is some hotshot millionaire who sent these nice boys"—she smiles at two handymen who are installing what looks like a camera by the main entrance—"to fix the door, install a security system and retouch the paint. All for free."

"How do you know it was him?"

"The super told me it's a rich man who visited his friend here and became concerned with the safety of our humble dwelling." She raises her eyebrows like she shared the biggest conspiracy. "That man's a catch, Celeste. Lucky you."

Yeah, lucky me.

"I didn't take you for someone who uses the services of a legal clinic." I sit across from Caleb in a small but tasteful boardroom.

"Oh, Miss Delacroix, don't get distracted by my pro-bono work, I charge him handsomely for my services." A tall well-dressed man saunters in and extends his hand to me. "Dominic Cressard, nice to meet you."

I like him instantly. There's a charming air about him that puts me at ease, which is an achievement in any official office. Though I must admit these offices are way fancier than any other legal clinic I've seen, even though I've only seen them on TV.

"Celeste. The pleasure is mine." I shake his hand. A Rolex on his wrist further confuses the legal clinic aspect.

Dominic takes a seat at the head of the table and opens a folder. "Let me get right to it."

"You usually stall to increase your billable hours," Caleb says dryly.

"I'll make them up on your next public indecency charge," Dominic deadpans.

By the way Caleb's jaw ticks, I wonder if the retort is based on actual events. Interesting.

I stare at him, hoping he'll look my way and confirm Dominic's statement. But Caleb has been avoiding my eyes since I entered.

I guess my no-talking policy meets his no-looking policy. What a great start to this union.

"Okay, so the process for a marriage-based green card is pretty straightforward. It takes ten to twenty-three months, but I can guarantee the shorter timeline. Maybe even shorten it further."

Twenty-three months? Merde. "Can I work while I wait?"

"You can get a work permit upon marrying a US citizen. The problem is, we can only apply for the green card with proof of a relationship." Dominic's gaze pauses at me, and then at Caleb.

"What does that mean?" Caleb looks at me for the first time and, if there was any heat or attraction there on Wednesday, it's completely gone now. His entire countenance is aloof today.

"Joint accounts, photos, utility bills, mutual residence." Dominic closes the folder in front of him.

Caleb sighs. "Okay, so we can't apply until we gather all of that? And Celeste can't work?"

"Well, we can try to cut the red tape if you don't tell my wife." He winks in a conspiratorial way. "But I'd suggest you marry quickly and open a joint account, kids."

Caleb's gaze meets mine and, for some outlandish reason, tears well in my eyes. I realize this is all fake, but the romantic in me is dying.

"If we get that all organized in the next few days, she can get a green card within a year? At the latest?" Caleb asks, talking about me like I'm not even here.

"That's the hope."

"So we can divorce within a year?" Caleb continues, and the words slap me.

A year of my life with this man? This man who's doing a favor for his sister but looks like he'd give his left kidney to be anywhere else, doing anything else.

"Well, not exactly," Dominic starts, and we both snap our heads toward him. "She'd get a conditional green card that's valid for two years."

I groan and drop my head to the table, tapping my forehead on the smooth surface.

"Three years?" Caleb's tone could cut diamonds.

"Yeah, and let me be clear." Dominic leans forward. "If they sniff out that this is just for Celeste to stay in the country, there can be serious legal repercussions. For both of you. Fines, or worse, jail time."

Silence descends on the room, heavy with ramifications, tension, and the finality of the sentence we're both considering.

Our gazes meet again above the polished table. My mind fires in all different directions. I think of my work, of the wonderful years I spent in New York, of my colleagues who would pay the highest price.

But I can't expect Caleb to sacrifice three years of his life. We're not even friends.

I wish I could read his mind, but he stares me down without so much as a hint of his thoughts. Just an unreadable mask.

"Do you want a minute to discuss this?" Dominic asks.

I'm about to nod when Caleb turns to his lawyer. "No, it's okay, let's continue."

Dominic raises his eyebrows, as surprised as me.

"Caleb—" I start, but he raises his hand.

"Shut up, Celeste. For once in your life, don't run your mouth."

I still open my mouth, but no words come out while heat spreads up my throat to my cheeks.

Dominic doesn't lose a beat and slides a folder to me. "Okay, so at Caleb's instruction, I took the liberty to prepare this prenup."

I hate that both of them can see how my hands tremble as I open the document.

"It sums up that you will get one million and an apartment of your choice upon your divorce, but no other claims can be made on my client's assets."

I gasp. "I don't want your money."

Caleb snorts and shakes his head.

"You may say that now, but three years with this one..." Dominic chuckles, ignoring Caleb's glare. "And I shouldn't be saying this, since Caleb is my client, but this deal is highly disadvantageous to you, given the current and future potential financial status of your husband-to-be."

Is this some sort of test? "As I said, I don't want his money, and I have an apartment."

Caleb snorts again. "You're not returning to that

hell hall."

Is this man for real? "That's really none of your business. I think the most important clause in the prenup needs to be my autonomy. You don't control my life decisions."

Caleb huffs his exasperation, shaking his head. "Celeste, just sign it so we can move on."

"Move on? What? Do you have more damsels in distress to save, or mistakes to fix so you can feel better about yourself?"

His jaw ticks. "Yes, my darling fiancée, I have an appointment at the courthouse to book. The sooner we get married, the sooner we can part ways."

"If you don't want..." My argument dies on my lips when I realize that this banter and bickering won't get me any closer to solving my problem.

Why is he doing this? Why do I care? His motivation shouldn't concern me.

For once, I can just accept someone's help. I owe it, if not to myself, then to my colleagues.

Probably making the biggest mistake of my life, I scribble my signature on the contract with the devil.

Only this particular devil wants nothing in return. And yet my heart and my soul are bleeding.

As soon as I lift the tip of the pen from the paper, Caleb stands. "Great. Only two years and three hundred sixty-four days more."

Chapter 11

Celeste

A shrilling sound pierces through my brain. What the fuck is that? I breathe to five counts, finishing my hamstring stretch. Yesterday's rehearsal was killer.

It's like Leon wanted to punish us for the rebellion.

And my understudy has been eager to take over, making everything more awkward.

To say that the atmosphere in the group has changed is an understatement. Perhaps some of my colleagues realized how much they put in jeopardy to save me.

And most of them probably regretted it. I hope to God Dominic Cressard can file all the paperwork and get me my work permit soon.

The screeching startles me again. The weird thing is, it's coming from my apartment. Did someone change my ringtone yesterday? Is one of the backup dancers pranking me?

My phone lies on my bed, its screen black. I look around, feeling like an idiot. Is it the front door?

I pick up the intercom receiver for the first time since I moved in. It's never worked. I guess the entrance truly is fixed.

"Hello?"

"Delivery."

"I didn't order anything."

"Are you Celeste Delacroix?"

This makes no sense.

"Yes." I don't move.

Should I let a stranger into the building? Ironically, I considered this building perfectly safe until an *unknown* benefactor improved its security.

Don't be ridiculous, Celeste. I chuckle at myself. "Come on in."

A minute later, I'm signing for a large white box. "Are you sure this is for me?" I glance at the bed where I put the package.

The delivery guy looks at me, his face impassive. "Have a nice day."

Closing the door, I stay rooted to the spot. Not that I'm expecting someone has sent me a bomb. Those don't arrive in soft boxes lined with silk on the outside.

Approaching my bed, I trace my fingers on the

glossy, cushy exterior. The lid is attached with ribbons on each side—not heavy-duty tape, freaking velvet ribbons.

I don't know who sent me the gift, but what I know is I've never in my life gotten something this expensive. Because the packaging itself is the epitome of luxury.

My hands shake with a mixture of anticipation and anxiety as I lift the lid and the softest golden tissue paper from out of the box.

I gasp.

And now I'm really hoping this is not a mistake, because I'm in love with the exquisite cream-colored dress inside it before I even pick it up.

Because it looks wonderful still folded. When I finally lift the dress, I almost drop it, fearing I'll soil the delicate silk, cold and smooth under my touch.

All my clothes are elegant and of high quality, mostly acquired in thrift stores after hours of searching. This dress is next-level.

I hold it against my body and turn to the mirror on my door. It's a true design masterpiece and, as shallow as it may seem, it makes my heart flutter.

The deep V neckline adds a touch of daring allure, beautifully complementing the modest long sleeves that end in a chic, slight puff at the wrists.

The skirt, oh, the skirt! It flares out in a perfect A-line that cascades in soft, smooth folds. It's one of those pieces that makes a woman feel powerful and feminine.

The number on the label says sixteen. It's my size. Only then, I remember to check for a card in the box.

We need wedding pictures.

The beauty of the dress almost wanes with the pang of disappointment. He didn't even sign the card. But he efficiently organized a dress for me. Just to *move on* with it, I guess. It's thoughtful, with a dash of insult.

I've half a mind to wrap the dress up and return it. I have nice clothes to wear for my fake wedding pictures.

I clutch the fabric to my cheek, savoring the smoothness. The girl in me who wants to hop into the dress grapples with the responsible woman who doesn't want to accept the gift. And there is no way I can pay him back for this couture.

Sometimes I hate my pride. I place the dress on my bed and put the kettle on. A woman I used to dance with years ago traveled to the Sahara desert, and she taught me that the Bedouins drink tea when faced with a tough decision. Their tea ceremony lasts hours, so by the end, they sort out their thinking.

I make my tea and, leaning against the counter, admire the dress. I take a sip. While it's been only minutes, not hours, I'm leaning toward wearing it. Keeping it.

Does it make him win?

But what's the competition?

My phone pings, saving me from the circle of useless opinions in my head.

> SAAR
>
> Did Cal get you a dress?

> How do you know?

> SAAR
>
> He asked for your size, I hope you don't mind that I gave it to him.

> I'm sure he knows by now I'm not size 2 (laugh emoji)

> SAAR
>
> Silly. How is the dress?

I snap a picture and send it to her.

> SAAR
>
> OMG, Celeste, that dress is you!!! (dancing emojis)

And therein lies my apprehension. A man who doesn't even like me, who is sacrificing himself to appease his sister and take revenge on his father, has noticed me enough to know my style.

As I put on my wedding dress, a constant *why* swirls in my head.

"Look at each other, lovebirds." The photographer, a woman in her fifties with short silver hair, beckons us together with her arm. "Groom, look your bride in the eyes and tell her how much you love her with your gaze."

The ceremony was uneventful, witnessed by Dominic Cressard, and truly more of a formality. Somehow Caleb's lawyer with his easygoing person- ality made the whole thing bearable.

I think I even managed to function properly, like a reasonable human being, despite my hammering heart, sweaty hands, and shallow breathing.

The entrance to the courthouse already put me on the verge of a panic attack, but luckily, the impersonal routine of exchanging vows happened so quickly that I was able to rush outside and breathe fresh air within ten minutes.

Dominic even got the marriage license expedited. That was great news, except it meant he left us to go file the green card and work permit application.

Caleb hasn't said a word to me, other than the scripted part in front of the city clerk.

"What's going on?" The photographer sighs. "The two of you look like you're coming from a funeral, not your nuptials. Do you need to take a break?"

"No." Caleb's response is so urgent, the photographer jerks her head in surprise.

He snakes his arm around my waist and yanks me to him. With his finger, he lifts my chin. I meet his gaze.

"Let's do this, black swan."

"Only two years and three hundred sixty-three days, after all."

He snorts. "That was a dick move." He holds me tighter, grazing my cheek with his thumb.

I chuckle. "A rare moment of self-reflection. Why, Mr. van den Linden, have you forgotten to take your asshole medicine?"

"But you, Mrs. van den Linden, never skip your sassing serum."

We grin at each other in a rare moment of... I don't know what. Camaraderie? A temporary ceasefire?

My skin tingles under his touch as my heart looks for an emergency exit. Caleb's gaze is on my face, but somehow, I feel it all over my body.

His Adam's apple bobs, making me realize my mouth is too dry. I lick my lips, and his gaze drops to them. He leans in, tucking a strand of hair behind my ear.

The brush of his fingers as they linger on my skin sends shivers down my spine. What is happening right now? Are we faking for the pictures? Because it sure doesn't feel like it.

And just like in Caleb's living room the other night, my body is primed for this man after his lightest touch.

"You look amazing in that dress." His tongue darts out to wet his lips.

It doesn't seem like a calculated move, but it still feels like the best erotic performance.

The dress fits me like a glove, and yet I find myself jailed in it. It constricts more than my corset.

"You didn't need to buy—"

Caleb puts his index finger on my mouth. "Hush, woman. Take a compliment like a good girl."

My breath hitches. Jesus. "Thank you." I don't know how the words pass through my throat.

He smiles at me with that boyish grin that makes me want to take his hand and skip across town. Because while I haven't had the privilege, I know Caleb knows how to have a good time.

"Who knew marrying you would make you blushing and obedient?" He winks.

I like my women a bit more blushing and less opinionated.

"It didn't make me yours."

Something dark passes across his face as his jaw ticks, but then he shocks me completely when his lips fuse with mine.

I'm caught so off-guard, I flail my arms in the air. The kiss is the right amount of soft and demanding. He's claiming me with the kiss. *It didn't make me yours.*

Despite the fact this is a ruse of a marriage.

Ignoring the reality of our less-than-amicable relationship.

Dismissing my protest.

Wait. I'm not protesting. I'm clutching his lapels, holding for dear life as he explores my mouth like it belongs to him.

Nobody's ever kissed me like this. Kissing me like it's a question of life and death. Like it's an Olympic discipline he's determined to master. Like he's been training all his life to deliver this kiss.

And I open up and welcome it, like I've been groomed to be kissed by Caleb van den Linden.

Because no kiss has ever felt this disarming. This essential. This carnal.

His tongue glides expertly as he sucks, nips, bites, and practically fucks my mouth with his tongue. It's a good thing he's holding me because I don't think my legs work anymore.

What works overtime is my heart—galloping like a spooked horse—and my lady parts—soaking my underwear.

God, I hope I charged my vibrator.

"I think I got it. That will be all."

The photographer's voice is like a jolt of electricity that snaps us apart. Frazzled, I turn, avoiding both people in the room. How did I forget about the camera?

With my thumb, I wipe the corners of my swollen lips, trying to compose myself. What has just happened?

Because I'm pretty sure I wasn't the only one forgetting about the camera.

"Right. Thank you. We'll need the pictures ASAP," Caleb says, his voice official and businesslike, not shaking like mine would, if I could manage to find it.

When I finally gather my wits and turn back to the room, smoothing my skirt like it got all dirtied up by that kiss, I'm met with the photographer's awkward smile.

It's just the two of us. Frowning, I look around the studio and, with an unspoken question, at the woman with a lens in her hands.

She shrugs. "He left."

Chapter 12

Caleb

I run to the street, loosening my tie. Fuck. Fuck. *Fuck.*

Why did I refuse her the other night? And in some fucked-up power move, I told her she'd need to beg for it.

Now I can walk around with blue balls.

It didn't make me yours.

And there I was, capturing her mouth like I had any business to do so. Because fuck.

Celeste Delacroix married me because she needed her visa fixed, but the only thing fake about me agreeing to the deal was my motivation.

Yes, she didn't deserve to be dragged into the mess my father always leaves in his wake.

Yes, my sister begged me to help her.

Yes, I never plan to marry, so giving her my name for a few years is inconsequential.

And yet, the twisted, depraved bastard in me enjoys being around her. Taunting her. Being sassed by her. Annoying the shit out of her.

But why?

Because she can take it. She can rise to the challenge, and fuck if that's not refreshing. And hot.

But she made it clear she wants nothing to do with me. Aside from that weak moment of desperation last Wednesday. Even then, she didn't want me. She wanted to save her job.

What a fucking twist of fate. I can have—and have had—any woman I want, and here I want the only one that doesn't care.

"Oh, you're here." Celeste's voice brings me back to reality.

The air still smells of last night's rain, its humidity heavier than usual for mid-spring. My gaze lands on her dress. It's perfect. She's paired it with emerald-green stilettos that match her eyes.

She looks like a movie star. Like a woman I want to parade around proudly, but also lock hidden away so nobody ogles her.

"Lunch?" I more bark the question than ask it. Always a gentleman around her.

Even if this woman had a seed of attraction for me,

I'm making sure as hell it doesn't sprout. What is wrong with me?

"Well, since you invited me so nicely, I guess we should have our wedding reception." She gives me a saccharine smile. "Lead the way, husband."

Husband.

The title has never had any meaning for me. Another side effect of witnessing how my father treated my mother.

He cheated and hurt her many times. And she suffered through it, until she gave up and leaned into their power play.

Because that's what their marriage had always been. I vowed to never get married. That institution doesn't stand for anything good.

I glare at Celeste, and she narrows her eyes. If she's wondering what my deal is, that would make two of us.

If she's wondering about that kiss and my exit, that also makes two of us. I'm completely unpredictable around this woman.

And I don't like that one bit. And yet the animal in me wants her so goddamn much.

Grabbing her hand, I march down the street like I know where I'm going, dragging her with me.

Luckily, there is a cozy, inviting Italian bistro on the corner, and we get a seat in the window alcove overlooking a quaint side street.

We don't speak, focusing on reading the menu and choosing our first meal as a married couple as if our life depended on it.

A chipper server in her twenties recites the specials to us. Celeste orders fish, and I ask for the same, because I have no idea what is on that menu.

"Will that be all?" the server sing-songs.

"I'll have a double whiskey. Do you have a Macallan?" I smile at her.

"Sorry, sir, we don't serve liquor. May I offer you our organic Sauvignon Blanc? It would go well with your halibut."

"Sure. Get us a bottle."

A ghost of a smile plays on Celeste's face. "Are we celebrating?"

"You'll learn, black swan, I excel at everything I do. And I plan to do that with this fake marriage as well."

And if I have my way, there will be nothing fake about the way we enjoy this pretend marriage. However short-lived it may be.

"Should I be scared?" She opens the linen napkin and places it on her lap.

Such an automatic motion, but not when executed by Celeste. She turns even the most mundane move into a graceful dance.

"More than it scared you to enter the courthouse?"

Earlier today, she looked like she was going to bolt,

like I was forcing her to be there. It made no sense, and I need to know what that was about.

Like I need—for some outlandish reason—to know more about this woman. Another mystery on my part.

I'd be better off staying away. Not speaking to her. And most definitely not kissing her again. Or maybe kissing her more.

That fucking kiss was like discovering the fountain of life. Okay, more like the fountain of pleasure. And that's a concept I'm happy to get behind. Any. Freaking. Time.

She flinches.

So, there was something that set off her hesitation.

Quickly, she puts on that daring expression like she's ready to fight with the world. "What can I say? It's scary to marry you."

I snort. A good save, but she's lying. "I'm sure you can do much worse, black swan." I decide to drop the topic. I'll find out, eventually. We're stuck together for three years, after all.

She lets out a chuckle. "I doubt that."

"And yet you pursued me relentlessly." I lean forward, grinning.

There's a table between us, but that flowery scent of hers assaults me, making my cock twitch. The woman puts an aphrodisiac in her perfume.

"I pursued a business arrangement with you. That's all this is."

But I'm not against mixing business with pleasure.

The waitress brings our wine, and we stare at each other while she serves us. The air is more charged than usual, but the charge is lighter.

We tease, we don't argue. And I can't say I hate it.

"You forgot that I have nothing to gain, so I wouldn't call it a business arrangement."

"Perhaps you're just a shitty businessman and I got a better deal."

I laugh. "Touché. Should we toast to this union?"

She raises her glass. "To not killing each other."

Snorting, I toast. "To getting you your job back."

Her eyebrows jerk up, like my wish surprises her. Like she wouldn't expect I would wish something good for her.

She takes a sip and puts the glass down in that signature elegant way of hers. "Why are you being nice to me?"

Her lips are slightly parted as she waits for my answer. The sad part is that it's a reasonable question. Somehow, somewhere, I made it my life's mission to be horrible to her.

This woman who has a tiny studio decorated like a true home. Who collects valuable art beyond her means. Who has books stuffed in her cupboards.

Whose body is made for sin, and whose wits are refreshing.

A woman I typecast at one point, and now I'm confronted with layers of her that don't match that mold.

"To be perfectly honest, when I agreed to help you, I didn't realize I was making a three-year commitment. So upon careful reflection, when I reviewed my calendar for the next three years"—I smirk—"I decided that keeping the peace with you is probably the best course for my—our—sanity."

She sighs with a dejected chuckle. "You could have backed out."

"Well, black swan, another thing you'll learn about me is that I'm a stubborn bastard."

She shakes her head, a smile lingering on her lips. "Is that why you organized everything overnight, so you're not tempted to give up before you commit?"

"No, that was for the benefit of your visa and your work."

Now she shakes her head, rolling her eyes like I'm full of shit. Okay, partially I am. I was hoping for a fast resolution—not that that's an option anymore, with the three-year-long red tape wrapped around Celeste's little problem.

"Besides," I continue, with another part of my motivation for the speedy resolution to her problem. "I have a business deal to close that requires my full attention."

The server places our meals in front of us, the scent of thyme and spices invading the air.

Along with anticipation. Or maybe it's just me who's hoping we'll continue that kiss after our wedding reception for two.

"What kind of a deal?" Celeste flakes off a tiny piece of fish and brings it to her mouth. Again, the movement is an art.

"I'm considering joining a business venture that interests me as an occupation, and would certainly make me richer."

"Why would you need to get richer?"

"Why wouldn't I?"

She takes a sip of wine, and I swear watching her is like an artful form of porn. What the fuck is wrong with me?

"Don't you have enough?"

"My *enough* redefines with the more I have."

"So you make more to spend more?"

"Wouldn't you?"

She eats for a moment, a line splitting her forehead. "I've never thought of it like that. But yeah, if I had more, I'd get a bigger apartment, new clothes, take a vacation."

"Of course. And you'd probably invest in more art,

support more causes. I spend only a small portion. I invest, so the money makes me more money."

She laughs. "You make it sound so easy."

"It *is* easy, but it's hard work at the same time, I guess."

The halibut tastes fantastic. I'd have never ordered fish on my own, but now I'm a fan. Just like that, two hours into my fake marriage, the woman is influencing my habits.

"So what is this new venture?"

"It's mergers and acquisition. I don't want to make you fall asleep."

"Because I'm just a simple dancer?"

I snap my head to her. Why would she assume that? "What the fuck, Celeste?" I saw her business books. I know she can discuss this.

"Isn't that what people generally think?"

"I sure hope not. Is that what you believe?"

"That's the opinion I'm faced with regularly."

I drop my fork, annoyance edging its way through me. "I'm asking if you believe it."

"I don't particularly care what people say, but it's not like any of your friends, or even you, would want to discuss anything substantial with me. Because I'm just a sexy dancer."

I grind my molars. She's trying to sound casual, but there's hurt in her voice, in her expression, as she avoids my eyes, suddenly dedicated to cutting a cherry tomato on her plate.

"For the record, black swan, if anyone makes you feel inferior, you remove them from your life. Or they'll have to go through me. Don't ever buy into that bullshit."

Chapter 13

Celeste

O h, the irony.

This man has been making me feel exactly that. Less than. Not enough. But I don't have the option to remove him from my life for the time being.

But his words... They melt my insides like a chocolate truffle, sweet and decadent.

"At least for the next three years." He smirks, jest crinkling around his eyes. God, he's infuriatingly handsome.

"Two years, three hundred and sixty-three days," I quip. "And yet you think I wouldn't be interested in talking about your new business venture. Because I wouldn't understand?"

He studies me for a moment. It's slightly

unnerving now after I experienced the explosion that kiss detonated, but I hold his gaze without wavering.

"I left my company because I realized I like fixing things. I like taking something that is broken, inefficient, and making it work. After Finn and I brought the company our father created into the twenty-first century and implemented—or at least planned—all the changes, I found myself at a loss. Like running a well-oiled machine became a chore. An unexciting existence. It must sound reckless."

He shakes his head, as if he doesn't like what he's saying, what he's feeling.

I dab the corners of my mouth with my napkin. "I mean, I enjoyed teaching dancing because there was variety. New people, and always some fire to put out. And I enjoyed when I danced in clubs because that was pure unpredictable chaos.

"In fact, my current job, that might seem like a pinnacle of success in my field because of its stability, and the triumph of the opening night, honestly feels a bit tedious. Don't get me wrong, I love the performance, but the regularity and familiarity of it is..."

"Boring," he finishes for me.

I smile. "Yes. I guess we're both reckless."

"Obviously, since we just committed a felony."

"Oh, my." I clutch my chest dramatically. "What

are you accusing me of? I married you because you're my one and only." A grin pulls at my cheeks.

"One and only idiot available at short notice." He raises his eyebrows, but the corner of his lips twitches.

I shrug innocently. "La fin justifie les moyens."

He groans and closes his eyes momentarily.

"Are you okay?" I drop my fork.

"Yeah." He gulps down his wine and refills his glass. "Anyway, I thought I'd take some time off and figure out what I want to do, but I ran into an old friend, and he has an opportunity that feels like the right fit."

Something like regret hangs in his words, which doesn't really fit the Caleb I know.

"Don't tell me you're one of those people who pass on an opportunity because they had other plans."

He laughs. "No, it's just one of the partners hurt Saar years ago."

Warmth spreads inside me. "You're very protective of your sister."

He sighs. "I love her, but she can take advantage of my affliction."

"Oh, I can totally see that. This time, it worked to my advantage."

I didn't mean more than my visa, but the air between us fills with meaning beyond that. Our eyes meet again in a silent conversation I don't understand, setting off butterflies in my stomach.

I fidget in my seat, rubbing my thighs together, because his eyes have arson-like side effects, setting my body on fire.

"I think Saar would understand." I swallow around the lump in my throat, and Caleb nods.

How does a conversation about a business opportunity get this hot? This makes no sense.

And how is it that in the course of twenty-four hours, his jabs are funnier, and my need to razz him is softer?

Have we both just accepted we're stuck together, so we're playing nicer? Did that fake kiss that felt so honest reset our chemistry?

Have we reached some sort of unexpected truce without even discussing it? And why do I want him to kiss me again?

I feel comfortable and uncomfortable with Caleb, all at the same time. It's like intellectually we're barely finding common ground, but physically? My ovaries and panties are melting. But leaning into that desire would be a disaster.

It's not like we can have a one-night stand where I'd leave in the middle of the night, itch scratched. Jesus.

"So how are we going to do this marriage? From what Dominic said, we need to prove this is real."

"I can get you pregnant." He tosses the napkin on his plate.

I choke on my fish, coughing and pounding on my chest with my palm. Caleb hands me a glass of water.

"Jesus, Celeste, it was just a joke. There's no fucking way I'd have kids."

"Never?" I blurt out before I can censor myself. Like I have any business to ask that.

"Never." The resolution in his voice is so final, I get a feeling this is not a pose, but a deliberation he's arrived at after serious consideration. "Are you okay?" He frowns at me.

God, why am I shocked? Visibly shocked. "Yes, of course. Could you stop joking and tell me how we'll prove we're together?" I retort, angered at myself but taking it out on him with my tone.

"Okay, black swan." He raises his hands in surrender. "I'll have a mover pick up your things tomorrow. You'll stay in my guest room. We'll take selfies and attend events together. I'll pick you up at the theater after the show occasionally, and I can't believe I'm going to say this, but I'll have my people tip off the paparazzi to snap a few pics. I hate those assholes, but la fin justifie les moyens." He throws my words back at me.

"You speak French?"

"Not really. Anyway, is that an okay plan? We can put your place on the market as early as tomorrow."

"As I said yesterday, I'm not selling my apartment. I'll return to it after the divorce."

He rolls his eyes. "That makes no sense. You'll get a better place in our divorce."

"*That* actually makes no sense. Why on earth would you give me anything?"

"Because I can, and I'm not going to treat you like..."

He stops and gestures for the bill.

"Like who?"

"Never mind. Let's go."

* * *

"I don't think we need to do it today." I step back, like the entrance of the bank is lined with poison.

"Yes, we do, Celeste. We need all the fucking evidence. We're getting a joint account."

Shit, after the ordeal of the courthouse, I can't possibly set foot in another institution. My head is spinning from the rushed ending of our lunch, and now he's pulling me into a bank.

Sweat trickles down my spine, distracting me. Is it going to show? Am I ruining this gorgeous dress?

"Celeste," Caleb groans, the automatic doors opening behind him.

"We can open an account online these days," I offer.

He makes an exasperated sound, grabs my hand, and pulls me inside. Fucking bully.

But even I can see how unreasonable my behavior must be to someone who knows nothing about my anxiety.

Caleb says something to a young teller, and we're immediately ushered through a door and into an elevator. Where are we going?

I should ask, but it's hard to formulate a sentence over the loud beat of my pulse in my temples. I wish this dress wasn't white and so precious, and I could wipe my clammy palms on it.

We follow a woman into a lavish office, I think, but it looks more like a living room. I let out the breath I was holding. This feels like someone's house. My mind relaxes a bit.

"Celeste?" Caleb's voice drags me from the fog of my near panic.

"Yes?" I blink a few times.

"Do you want a coffee?" he asks softly, and his voice wraps around me like cashmere.

I nod, and he puts his hand on the small of my

back. I almost recoil. He leads me to a large sofa, rubbing his thumb up and down my spine.

Calming me. Without being privy to the storm inside me, he knows what to do. Or at least senses what he should do.

"Have a seat." He helps me sit, like I'm a child, and saunters across the room to a fancy coffee machine.

"What is this place?"

The grinder echoes as I take in my surroundings: the soft carpet, the comfortable sofa, the glass table, the smell of coffee, the lavish decorations and expensive paintings on the wall.

"It's a private office to conduct business." He hands me a small espresso. "Milk or sugar?"

"No, thank you, I'm not a barbarian." I take the cup.

Caleb chuckles and looks at me with admiration in his eyes. Like I passed some coffee-drinking test.

"This does not look like an office." I take a sip.

Caleb shrugs. "They want their VIP clients to feel comfortable, I guess."

"Oh, you don't bank with the plebs downstairs." I down the best espresso I've had since I arrived in New York almost ten years ago. There are advantages to being rich.

I have rich friends and former clients. Saar, I assume, is wealthy. They never made me feel less or poor. And I've never judged them for their riches, but listening to Caleb earlier, I realized my view of rich people has been mostly negative.

Yet, he talks about money with knowledge and care. While he doesn't recognize his privilege, he also doesn't flaunt it around like it's his birthright. He's business-savvy, for sure, and takes for granted what was granted to him.

But I'm realizing his surprise about my studio, or about me questioning where we are right now, is more ignorance than superiority. And not even a pompous ignorance. He's simply never had the opportunity to see how the other half lives.

"Have you ever dated a poor girl?"

He jerks his head. "I don't date, but I don't ask women I hook up with about their net worth. I don't care. There's more to people than money."

No dates, only hookups. Why does that disappoint me? It's not like I would date him.

"Mr. van den Linden, I'm sorry to have kept you waiting. I'm Antonio Guerra, the personal banker here."

I startle, but don't look at the man who's just spoken. I'm still looking at my new pretend husband like he's a unicorn.

This will be a culture shock for both of us. I

thought I knew how the rich live, but clearly, I'm in for a surprise.

"It's okay, Antonio. May I call you Antonio? We didn't have an appointment. This is my wife, Celeste, and we'd like to open a joint account."

Not even half an hour later, I walk out of there, not only having a joint account with Caleb, but the proud owner of a new credit card. Approved and issued just like that.

I flip the black card between my fingers before I put it in my small purse. "Do you trust me that I won't ruin you?" I tease.

"Do you plan to buy several airplanes and yachts?"

I laugh. "As if I could—" My words die on my lips because Caleb wasn't really joking. "I could, couldn't I?"

He snakes his hand around my waist and pulls me to his side. "Since you don't even want the apartment I haven't bought you yet in our divorce, I think my assets are safe." He pulls out his phone, aiming the camera at us.

"What are you doing?"

"Say cheese, Mrs. van den Linden." He presses his lips to my hair, snapping a few pictures.

"You're very dedicated to collecting proof of this relationship." I jerk away from him, because his hand on my waist, his lips in my hair, his consideration of my needs, it's all stirring something inside me. And we can't go down that road.

He shoves his phone in front of my face. Even from his profile, he looks gorgeous, kissing the side of my head. I look stunned. "This will not sell it, black swan. You're a performer, try a bit harder. I'm too pretty to go to jail for you."

I roll my eyes and smile at the camera, and he takes a few more pics. This time, his lips stay away from me. The pang of disappointment is completely misplaced, but it still coils inside me.

"I guess if we're done, I'll go." I jerk away from him, as if it's his fault I'm feeling all conflicted about him.

"I'll drive you. Peter is here in two. What's the rush, anyway? Do you need your afternoon nap?" He smirks.

"I could use one, thank you very much, because someone decided to renovate my building."

He raises his arms in mock surrender. "Sorry for improving your living conditions."

This man with his savior complex.

"Has it ever occurred to you that not everybody wants to be saved by you?"

He shrugs. "Well, Grinch, usually people are grateful. You, on the other hand, have been fighting my willingness to help. I wonder why?" He steps forward, the fabric of his tailored jacket brushing against my dress.

"Why couldn't you imagine a fake marriage with me, black swan? What scared you?"

He dips his head, and now his nose is almost touching mine. I fight the urge to step back. Or to fuse my lips with his. Either would work.

"I've just married you, haven't I?" I croak.

"Don't sound so thrilled."

I step back. To keep my sanity. To cool down my body that seems ready to combust spontaneously in his vicinity. "The idea of three years with you is just so overwhelming."

"If we last that long." He turns and opens the door of his large SUV. I didn't even realize Peter had pulled to the curb already.

I did, however, notice how much his words smart. They shouldn't, because there is an expiration date on this sham of a union, but they do.

I slide into the car, and Caleb follows. The partition is up, so I can't greet Peter, but the privacy gives me the opportunity to set boundaries.

Because I need them. I need him to respect them, so I can hopefully survive the next three years unhurt.

And yet I remain silent. Sleeping with him would be amazing. But I'm sure that our marriage certificate wouldn't be enough to keep him interested long-term. And I don't think I can watch him bringing home other women.

A one-night stand is not an issue, but a one-night stand with your roommate would be a disaster.

The car pulls to a stop. Caleb gets out and holds the door open for me.

"I'll text you the time for the movers tomorrow," I say, leaning into the practicalities to distance myself from the salacious scenarios in my head.

"I'll get that organized. It's one phone call to my concierge."

I guess that's my life now. I nod and start to turn, but stop.

Boundaries.

"For the record, I enjoyed that kiss. In fact, if that was a fake kiss, then I can't possibly imagine what a real one would do to me..."

He cocks his head, and I continue before I find some stupid reason to give in to his charm.

"That being said, I don't think we should do that or anything else physical. It would complicate things between us, and this"—I point between us—"is only an arrangement. Besides, I'm not getting down on my knees for you." I refer to his rejection from the other night. "You haven't earned the honor."

Caleb smiles like he just won the lottery. "We'll see about that, black swan."

Chapter 14

Caleb

Roommates.

I've never lived with a woman before. I've never let a woman stay over. I love their company, but I love my autonomy even more.

I lived with my brother before, so it's not like I'm completely inexperienced in having a roommate.

Living with Finn, however, equaled gaming all night, bickering, farting freely, and taking turns to remove takeout containers from the coffee table.

Living with Celeste is not what I expected. Frankly, I had no expectations. In my crusade to help her—and I'm still questioning my sanity there—I didn't think past the actual formality of getting her a marriage certificate for her visa application.

That was a major oversight on my part. I might be marginally reckless in my private life, but I'm usually reasonably responsible in all my other affairs. Money, career, business—and I would file my arrangement with Celeste under that category.

But somehow it doesn't fit there because—*recklessly*—I didn't think about the perils of cohabiting with the fiery green-eyed swan.

My living room has fresh flowers on a console table. There are women's magazines forgotten on a sofa —and who the hell buys paper copies anymore?

A pink cozy blanket on my reading armchair.

Red scrunchies on the coffee table.

Fluffy white slippers by the entrance.

The list goes on. And it's only been a week.

The fucked-up part is, I should mind it. I would expect it to feel like an intrusion. And it bothers me, it's an adjustment, but—and I won't admit this to anyone— I'm not as bothered by it as I thought I'd be.

She's the epitome of a perfect roommate. Half the time, I don't even know she's here. She tidies up after herself—and after me. She brings breakfast when she goes for a walk in the morning. Not that I eat croissants.

She keeps to her room and doesn't sass me as much as before. It's like she's surrendered to the three-year sentence and wants to make sure I don't relent.

If someone suggested last week that I'd be living

with a woman, I would have given him a number for the best psychiatrist in New York.

Seven days into the exact living arrangement I've refused all my life, I have nothing to complain about.

Unless I'm the asshole who complains about a permanent boner. And I guess I'm that asshole. Because Celeste might be a perfectly respectful and easy roommate, but that doesn't change the fact that she's fucking here.

Her scent is infused in my furniture. Fuck, even my towels, and we don't share the bathroom.

Three times already, I've heard her shower running, and I can't un-imagine her being naked in there.

When music comes from her room, I practically see her moving that lithe body of hers around—stretching, dancing, just being.

I'm already attuned to her whereabouts by her shoes echoing on the floor. The clicking heels mean she's going to see her friends or to the theater. The slapping flats mean she's going for a walk.

She spends hours rehearsing in the theater or dancing at home, I'm assuming from the stomping in her room.

She works really hard. I don't know how her body takes it. What I know is that I'm constantly imagining what I could do to that body.

My schedule is practically narrowed down to a workout or a meeting here and there with acquaintances to secretly test the waters about the Merged promise. That doesn't take up much time.

All the rest is consumed by trying *not* to pay so much attention to Celeste. And failing miserably.

And I don't like to fucking fail.

The amount of porn I've watched to think of anything, anyone, other than Celeste while jerking off, would make me a respectable contender for a renewed teenager status.

Riding the elevator to my loft, I check my watch. She won't be home yet. Thank God. If I was my therapist, I'd see through the insincerity of my relief.

I kind of want her to be home. To stop politely cohabiting with me and finally give in to our attraction.

Because I see her checking me out. I notice the stolen glimpses and eye-fucking when she thinks I'm not watching.

The elevator dings and the door slides open, and I'm met with... fuck my life... an eyeful of a leggings-clad ass. A magnificent, begging to be kneaded and spanked ass.

She's in a forward bend for a glimpse of a moment. Too short to admire fully, but unfortunately—or luckily?—long enough to sear the vision into my mind. My cock strains against the zipper of my pants.

In a fluid, wavy move, she stands up, her weight supported on her legs. Fuck, she's strong. And flexible.

"Mon dieu, I didn't know you were coming home now."

She spins around, jumping backward and almost falling down the one step that separates the vast entrance hall from the living room.

I leap forward and snake my arms around her waist, jerking her to me. Her soft body molds to mine, and there's no way she doesn't feel the steel rod in my pants.

"It's my home, black swan," I grit.

Shooting daggers from her eyes, she lifts her chin. "I'm well aware."

Her arms flailed up in the almost fall and landed on my shoulders. We stand there in the spontaneous embrace with my cock between us.

My cock that is dancing in recognition of its closeness to a woman's body. Or is it this particular woman?

Celeste swallows.

She blinks.

She licks her lips.

All her motions, even the invisible ones, prime my senses, and make me want to spin her around and bend her over my sofa. Or at least kiss the shit out of her.

But I'm not a caveman. And if I keep repeating that

to myself, I might not act like one. *Might* being the operative word here.

"You were dancing." I state the obvious because apparently blood to my lower regions means no oxygen to my brain.

She widens her eyes, stifling a smile. "You're a genius."

"I'd call it observant," I deadpan. "But call me a genius if those are your standards."

She snorts and then swallows the laughter, stepping back, shocked that she showed me her genuine amusement.

Only she miscalculates how close we are to the stairs and almost tumbles down. Again.

And again, I pull her to me, and this time I scoop her up.

"Stop it. What are you doing?"

That's what I'm wondering as well.

She kicks her legs, but wraps her hands around my neck.

"I'm going to place you on the sofa, because clearly you are a danger to yourself. The last thing I need is to take care of you when you break your leg."

"But I'm heavy. You'll throw your back."

I stop, scowling at her. Heavy? My problem is she feels too good in my arms. "Hush, woman, and let me make sure you're safe."

I'm about to lower her to the sofa, but my cock still commands my brain, and instead, I plop down and settle her on my lap.

And now that perfect ass is rubbing my already interested member that grows harder still.

"What are you doing, Caleb?" Celeste squeals, but doesn't move. She freezes.

"Relax, black swan, you won't get pregnant from sitting in my lap."

"But you might get a black eye from it," she snarls, and attempts to wriggle away. She fails, but I grunt from the friction.

Why did I think it was okay to sit her in my lap? As if that one dance move I interrupted qualified for a lap dance, and I paid for the right to have her rubbing against me.

Fuck. It's official, I can't keep my dick in my pants around this woman. Even if said woman is perfectly correct in drawing the line, and assuming bumping uglies would only complicate our arrangement.

Because I have never had a woman sleep over—or in my bed—so living with one after having sex could only be a recipe for disaster. I'd rather become celibate. I wince internally at the thought.

"This is ridiculous, Caleb. Let go of me." Since she failed to push off, this time she slides backward.

Only the sofa isn't that long, so now her heels are in

my crotch. And at her softened *d,* my cock twitches again. Nobody says *ridiculous* with such sexy diction.

I grab her ankle, and by this point, I don't know what I'm doing anymore. I'm just accepting that sometime between this morning when I had a coherent, adult conversation with my brother and now, I lost my marbles.

"Isn't it hard to dance in these?" I take one stiletto off and then the other, dropping them to the floor.

"Not all of us are meant to wear ballet slippers."

Her quip ends in a moan as I push my fingers into the balls of her feet.

I expect her to kick me and run, but she relaxes and drops her head back, her lips apart. And now, just like in her apartment, I need to know if that's her just-fucked face.

"Did you want to be a ballerina?" I continue rubbing her feet, trying to avoid the blisters. Fuck, her feet are this battered, and she still walks around in heels all the time.

"Doesn't every girl want that?" She lowers her head to the armrest behind her, looking at me through hooded eyes.

"I think Saar wanted to be a princess."

She chuckles, but it turns into another moan as I hit a tense spot on her foot. "What did you want to be growing up?"

"A hotel owner."

"Really?" Genuine surprise is etched on her face. "And you became one. Not many kids are that lucky."

"I think they're luckier. I wanted to be a hotel owner because my father was one, and I really wanted him to like me."

"I only met your father once, and I can say with certainty he doesn't like anyone."

I snort. "And still, I used to take it personally."

"The fact he doesn't like anyone is his loss, but that doesn't make your loss easier. We want our parents to love us."

"I'm pretty sure I'm better off without them in the picture."

"And not being a hotel owner."

"I'm still a hotel owner. I only left the executive position. So why aren't you a ballerina?"

She snorts. "Have you seen me? I've always been too big to dance on my tiptoes. I can do it, but there wouldn't be a career for me in it. My mom was a very talented ballerina."

"So you wanted to appease your parents with your chosen career as well?"

"God, no. My mom would have supported me in anything, but when I'd cried about how I couldn't be like her, she did everything in her power to encourage my dancing. She'd taken me to different performances and clubs since I was six, so I learned that ballet isn't the only form of dancing."

"She must be an amazing woman."

Her silence draws my gaze to her face. Celeste is looking at the ceiling with a solemn expression while she plays with the golden watch on her wrist. "She was," she croaks.

"Shit. I'm sorry—"

"Thank you, but I had to learn to live without her a long time ago. I'm fine."

"What about your father?"

Now her jaw ticks as she searches for a response, her eyes darting around the room. "He loved my mom, but not in a healthy way. He was chronically jealous, and we had to leave."

"You don't have contact with him?"

She shakes her head, lost in memories or regrets, I'm not sure. She doesn't say anything else, and I don't think she will. Not yet, anyway.

While I found freedom when my parents cut contact, I can sense that Celeste is on the opposite spectrum of feelings about not having them in her life.

Or at least her mom, because it feels like her relationship with her father is about as complicated as mine, if not more so.

I don't know when my hands' movement slowed down, or when I stopped massaging her soles. I'm now tracing through the soft fabric of her leggings, up and down to her knee.

It probably started as a mindless move, but somehow the contact penetrated into my awareness, like everything about this woman.

And now I'm so hyperaware of the feel of her under my fingertips that I can't stop. She closes her eyes, and I take that as encouragement. Drawing circles up her legs until my thumbs graze between the thighs.

She grips my wrist. "Caleb." Her warning is tentative. Or maybe that's what I want it to be.

"Yes, black swan?"

She swats me away, pushes up to her elbows, and swings her legs over the edge to sit beside me. With a gap for two more people between us.

Fuck. I better go take a cold shower and paint the tiles with my cum, yet again, to prevent a severe case of blue balls.

How is it I can seduce any woman with my smile, and here I am, rubbing my cock against her like a horny adolescent, and she's immune?

The woman has some amazing willpower. It would be rewarding to break it.

But behaving like a desperate idiot?

"Sorry, your ass greeted me today and—"

"No need to explain. I'm sorry I submitted you to

that. I needed to practice one part of the choreography, and there's carpet in my room. It's not a good practice surface. Sorry."

"Don't apologize. For the record, it was a welcome sight."

I wink at her as our gazes collide. There's a softness there, and a lingering smile on her face. Heat colors her cheeks, and in the light coming from the window, she looks angelic.

We stare at each other, suspended in an intimate moment that feels significant. Deep. Almost tender.

The world ceases to exist, fading into the background, while Celeste is the focus of all my senses. Her subtle flowery scent infuses the air. Her chest rises and falls in the rhythm of her faintly audible breathing.

We are frozen in this moment of attraction and restraint. Of connection and distance. Of desire and reluctance.

And then she looks away, and the spell is broken. "Look, Caleb, I'm not saying you're not attractive—"

"Why do I feel like this is a consolation speech? You won't believe it, but I've never gotten one."

She laughs. "Oh, I believe that. But you and I... it's not a good idea. I'm sure you agree."

"Well—"

"Caleb," she warns. "You really want to be living with a woman you bang once?"

"Why once?"

"Be serious about this. We might be trapped together for three years. If we shag now, it will be a very long three years."

"Or we would get it out of our systems."

"I don't think I would be able to pretend like nothing happened. Besides, I'm friends with your sister, and it feels weird. I wouldn't be able to tell her, and I don't know how I feel about that."

Fuck. The last thing I want is Saar discussing my sex life with her friends. "I'm sure she'd be okay not knowing. Nobody needs to know."

She puffs out a breath, blowing away the hair that has fallen into her face. "Clearly, we're both experiencing sexual frustration. Why don't we come up with a system that will allow you to bring women home?"

"I don't bring women here."

She snaps her head to me, her eyebrows shooting up. "What do you mean?"

"You're the first woman, besides Saar, who's been to this apartment."

She stares at me like I've just presented an irrefutable argument that the Earth is indeed flat. "Where do you take your hookups?"

"One of my hotels, or Finn and I have a place for that."

Her eyes almost pop out. "You have an apartment for fornication?"

Every time she's flustered, her accent is more dominant, and I have to restrain myself from grabbing her throat and pulling those leggings down to her knees. "Fornication? Have you just arrived from the eighteenth century?"

"Forget my vocabulary. It still doesn't make your admission about a fuck pad any less ridiculous."

"I'm not judging your lifestyle." How does every conversation we have end up completely derailed?

"I don't have an apartment dedicated to..." Her eyes widen like she's had an a-ha moment. She smiles at me. "We can share it."

"So you don't want to fuck me here, but you don't mind doing it there?"

She rolls her eyes. "Don't be silly. Bringing someone here would be awkward, but we can use your apartment to take care of our needs. I'm sure you had a system figured out with your brother."

She's pulling my leg. She must be. The corner of my mouth curls up, but she's looking at me with an expectation that doesn't resemble mockery. "You're serious?"

She stands up and walks to the stairs. Taking each step with her usual grace, she smiles at me, leaning over the banister. "It's a perfect solution. You can even have the place for more days a week. I'm generous."

Dumbfounded, I plop down to lie on the sofa, watching her ascend. Is she for real? I don't want to know she's fucking some loser. I'm not enabling that.

That's preposterous. She must be teasing me, the little wench.

But what if she wasn't?

Why am I concerned about her sex life?

Because as much as I hate to admit it, I envision Celeste's sex life to be intricately entangled with mine.

Now I have to get her on board.

Chapter 15

Celeste

SAAR

How is married life? LOL

(eye roll emoji)

CORA

I'm sure it's better than my work life.

What's wrong?

CORA

Lily is a disaster.

SAAR

No surprise there. Back to my inquiry:
is my brother still alive?

Disposing of his body now.

@Cora I'll come to have a coffee later.
Moral support.

CORA

Love you.

SAAR

I'm stuck in Stockholm.

CORA

Not feeling sorry for you at all (kiss emoji)

I jerk my hand to lock the portafilter in Caleb's fancy espresso machine that has more functions than a cockpit's control panel.

The two weeks after our wedding have been the longest in my life. And I've been through some shitty times.

Like when I moved to New York and lived on the streets. And that was an improvement compared to my life in France.

Never would I have imagined I'd be more unsettled living in luxury, with no care or need in my life.

Actually, therein lies my problem, because all those tough situations before sparked the strength and desire to improve my living conditions.

There's nothing to improve about my gazillion thread-count sheets, the most comfortable mattress, or the space in my room that could double as a dance studio for my practice, if it wasn't for the soft carpet.

And yet... anytime I'm out of my room, it's like I'm

walking on eggshells. Because my roommate/husband is everywhere.

In his low-hanging sweatpants and a tight tee on the sofa.

In his bespoke suits before leaving to negotiate his deal.

In his running shorts going to or from the gym.

Naked in his shower.

Okay, that one's only in my imagination when I hear the water running.

Caleb's ocean breeze aftershave assaults my senses, mingling with the freshly ground coffee. I'm almost afraid to turn, because my vibrator is currently charging, and I can't alleviate my lust once I get an eyeful of the sex personified who is my husband.

Especially since our last bonding encounter on the sofa. To my dismay, Caleb somehow became more sexy, more delicious, more seductive after I suggested we take care of our needs in his other apartment. Separately.

Not that I have anyone to take there. Or that I want him to take someone else there. The idea spreads through my stomach like acid. But what did I expect, that my sexier-than-God husband would simply quit sex for the duration of our marriage?

"Good morning." I can hear the smirk in his voice.

He's enjoying this taunting. But I'm not getting on my knees for him. He had his chance. Oh, who am I kidding, I would get on my knees and beg at this point.

If only I could return to my apartment and never see him again after.

No awkward moments, no disappointment.

I spin around. "Good morning."

I swallow. Jesus. Holy. Christ.

There he stands.

In his underwear.

Damn, the man is built like a Greek god, a physical perfection. His broad shoulders and sculpted chest lead to a taut stomach. His abs are so well-defined, my hand almost shoots out on its own to trace the delicious ridges and panes.

The ripple of his muscles with his every breath is mesmerizing. With his shoulder propped against the fridge, he watches me with a smirk.

"Like what you see, black swan?" He winks and saunters to the coffee machine.

Too close to where I stand. As he leans forward—or I imagine he does—I barely stop myself from gasping.

His freshly showered skin is still a bit wet, and he smells like... well, like a wet dream. And I know because I've been having them on repeat since we've been living together.

I brace myself for what's coming. Why is he crowding me?

"What are you—" I start.

He hits the button to stop the filtration and steps back. Sure enough, my mini cup is overflowing.

"Could you"—I flail my hands in the air like that will give me a better command of the English language —"could you just... merde... cover up."

He pours the coffee into the sink and starts preparing a fresh cup. It's coffee-making porn. I should sell the idea.

"Why would I cover up in my own house?" He looks at me with fake innocence.

"It's just... it's—"

The words die on my lips. Or they were never born, because my brain clearly stayed in my room today.

But even if I could still speak, my voice disappears as Caleb steps closer again. Even closer than before, I think. His scent envelops me, his breath fanning my face.

I step back, hitting the counter, and he follows, dropping both his hands on the surface behind me.

I'm caged, suffering from the lack of oxygen, language, or common sense. While drowning in an abundance of desire.

I meet his eyes. They're darker than usual. He

lowers his face closer to mine, a mere inch away, and drags his nose across my cheek, inhaling indulgently.

My heart contends for a world record in the number of beats per millisecond. I lick my lips and part them, but still no voice. Or the willpower to push him away.

"It's—" I stammer. Apparently this morning, *it's* is the only phrase in my vocabulary.

"Making your pussy weep for my cock?" He whispers in my ear.

Not until you beg me for it on your knees because your pussy weeps for my cock.

All this time, he's been teasing me. His behavior has been deliberate. To make me beg.

The bastard. Game on then.

I push at his chest, ignoring how his skin burns and invites me, or how his muscles mold under my touch. "I'm not getting on my knees."

Even his smug smile is sexy. "Maybe we can amend that. You don't need to get on your knees."

I duck and slide under his arm to gain some distance. "I've never agreed to any conditions. I offered sex, you refused. I don't beg as a general rule, let alone when I don't need something."

He snorts and folds his arms across his chest, his biceps bulging. "Don't you? Are you telling me if I checked now, you wouldn't be soaked?"

"No," I lie. "Don't worry about me. My pussy is well-serviced, thank you very much."

* * *

I take a sip of my latte and spit it back into the cup. "I'm sorry, Cora, but you need to let her go."

Cora puts her hand over her mouth, tears brimming in her eyes. "No wonder she agreed to minimum wage. But I can't afford anyone else. Besides, I feel sorry for her. She needs the job."

"Maybe I can ask Caleb to come around and advise you on how to increase the profitability of this place. He ran hotels and restaurants, so he understands these kinds of operations. There must be a way for you to increase your revenue enough so you don't have to slave here constantly."

"I don't know. I'm sure he has his hands full. It's been two years. If I haven't figured it out by now, I don't know if I can."

"Hey, don't give up. Do you want me to look at your books and see if there's room for improvement? I used to run a viable dancing studio." I shrug.

"Would you?" Cora smiles. "I really need a break."

"Of course, but you need to let Lily go."

Cora whimpers. "I know."

Abandoning our drinks, we watch Lily work. Or

163

rather, we wince every time she drops, spills, or breaks something.

"I can't do this. I'm going to help her." Cora stands, but then she hesitates and sits again, this time with her back to her fumbling employee.

"You know what, I'm going to enjoy ten more minutes of freedom before I'm chained to the counter again. How are you? Are you back on stage now?"

"No, we didn't get the paperwork sorted in time, but Caleb's lawyer promised it should be any day now. He even had a conversation—I wish I was a fly on the wall for that one—with my boss, and my job is safe until I get the permit."

"Caleb really stepped up, helping you like that."

And driving me mad with his allure. "Yes, he's been really great. But it's such a different life. I need milk, so I just punch it into an app and it gets delivered. I was searching for a yoga class near me, and he laughed, called his *concierge,* and within minutes, I got an email with options and schedules. And he gave me a credit card."

"For household expenses?"

"No, he put no limitation on it. I haven't used it, and I don't plan to. It shocks me how anything essential is hard work and optimizing for me, and easy for him. Like he can focus on what matters to him because his money takes care of the rest. I could buy into that concept."

"Couldn't we all? And Saar worried you'd kill each other."

I snort. "We still may, Cora. We still may."

I consider telling her about my attraction to Caleb, but decide against it. I trust Cora, but I can't risk her telling Saar.

That doesn't stop me from thinking about Caleb that way. Especially since he makes sure I do. The confident bastard thinks he can win this game.

"Maybe it's just a pent-up unresolved attraction the two of you feel." Cora dives into the topic I'm trying to avoid.

"The man gives me whiplash. There's something about him that attracts me, besides his body"—I practically moan—"but he can be so infuriating."

"So a typical man?"

I chuckle. "I guess."

"You should just sleep together and get it out of your system."

"And then live together for three years like nothing happened?"

"Three years? That's how long it takes to get a green card?"

I nod. "I can't just sleep with him. What would Saar say?"

"What do you mean? Saar would be happy for you. But if you're worried, then she doesn't need to know. It's just sex."

"I think my vagina is connected to my heart. I'm not saying I'd fall in love, but feelings would be involved on my part. I'm sure for him I'm just a convenient hook-up."

"Yeah, but what is your other option, ignoring the attraction for three years? He's been driving you crazy, so even if you feel more connected to him after you sleep with him, you're safe. If history has shown us anything, it's that he'll piss you off soon after."

Cora shrugs, kisses my cheek, and leaves to take care of her business before Lily destroys it all.

Her words ring true—in theory. Only Caleb hasn't pissed me off since our wedding.

* * *

I trudge out of the elevator and find Caleb on the sofa on his tablet. He shed his suit jacket and tie, his gray button-down sleeves rolled up.

He must have just arrived because he usually showers and changes before lounging around.

"Hey." I drop my handbag on the console table.

He doesn't look at me, nor greet me. Standing up,

he throws his jacket over his shoulder and starts toward the stairs. "There's Thai in the fridge."

I stare at the empty staircase a while after he disappears. What was that about? Is he mad at me? That was the most lukewarm, downright aloof, welcome I've ever received from him.

Definitely a three-sixty from this morning. But then, a man like Caleb can have any woman he wants. Of course, he's tired of chasing—not that he was chasing—me. That's for the best, anyway.

And yet, the idea of other women spreads bitter poison inside me. Merde, I hate jealousy. And now I'm annoyed with Caleb for sparking such a rotten emotion.

I warm up a coconut curry, and sit in the kitchen at the breakfast table by the wall of windows overlooking Central Park.

Eating mindlessly, I think of my conversation with Cora. Can I just have sex with Caleb and move on?

Not that he looks like he's interested anymore. It might have just been a shitty day, and his behavior has nothing to do with me.

His footsteps mobilize me into action. I jump up and start tidying the kitchen, so I can go to my room and avoid him.

I sense him behind me without even looking. As I

push the dishwasher door closed and straighten up, he steps to my side and hands me a sheet of paper.

"Have a look and let's put it on the fridge."

"What am I looking at? A cleaning schedule?" I squint at the squares with dates and our names alternating in them.

"You suggested we come up with a system to use my other place, so here you have it." He drops a set of keys and a key card on the counter and storms away.

I let go of the paper like it burned me. What the hell? This morning he was still seducing me, and now he wants to fuck other women?

He gave up so quickly. I follow him to the living room. He opens a cabinet in his bookcase and pours himself a whiskey.

"What's going on?" I can't blame him for deciding to cut his losses and take care of his needs, but something is off here.

He looks at me like I'm an annoying insect. "Nothing's going on. You asked for a system. Every second day, you can bring your boyfriend to the fuck pad. Just be discreet for your own sake. I'm already committing a felony here, so let's not get caught."

There is so much to dissect in his statement, starting with the cold and detached delivery. My mind latches on to two words. "My boyfriend?"

He takes a gulp. "Or whoever *services your pussy*."

My pussy is well-serviced, thank you very much. I laugh. "Are you jealous?"

"Don't be ridiculous." He passes me, heading to the hallway under the stairs that lead to his office. "I have a business call to make."

Chapter 16

Celeste

Boyfriend.

I roll my eyes and fasten the black fishnet to the garter and admire the result in the mirror. I'm wearing a short, silky black camisole that barely covers my ass, and a pair of lacy panties.

Okay, the garter and the stockings might be overkill, but if Caleb can walk around in his underwear, I can wear mine. I'm classy, after all.

And a bit slutty.

I decided to approach our little tug-of-war pragmatically. We—well, only I—have been fighting the attraction, but it's only made everything worse.

So if one approach didn't work, I'm going to try the exact opposite. We'll scratch the itch, and I'm not going to overthink the aftermath. Mostly because the current frustration is at least as taxing as the potential regret and awkwardness.

Never before have I let my fear of what might be dictate my actions, and I won't start now.

I throw on my green silk robe. Caleb ogled me in it at my apartment, so I know he likes it. Let's see who will beg whom now.

His business call must have ended because I hear him downstairs. I toss my hair, put on some lip gloss, and pad my way down the glass stairs.

This outfit really requires heels, but this is just a casual evening at home. Barefoot will do.

I almost giggle. This is going to be fun.

Caleb isn't in the main living space. He must have returned to his office. Goddammit. Now I feel ridiculous. My grand entrance was spoiled.

Before I can consider my next move, the door of his office clicks open. "No, Corm, I'm not fucking ready to bite the bullet for the team. I'm not on the team yet. I told you, I want twenty-five percent."

His voice approaches quickly. I randomly pull a book from the bookcase and plop in the armchair, sideways, with my legs swinging over the armrest.

Caleb emerges from the hallway and stops. I look up from my reading quickly and mouth *hi*.

Score.

He's gaping at me, but I quickly return to the page

I'm reading. Well, pretending to read, because all my senses and attention are focused on the man across from me.

"No, this is not some misguided revenge for Saar. You want my expertise, and I want an influential seat at the table. Simple."

The person on the other side is arguing loud enough for me to hear his voice, and I forget my character for a second and look up.

My eyes lock with Caleb's. He's leaning against the arched doorway under the stairs, a cunning smile dancing on his handsome face.

He lets his gaze run up and down my figure, and I swear my skin burns.

"Quinn, make it happen or find someone else. I've got to go." He disconnects the call.

I return to the book. He moves toward me. I think. I'm so engrossed in my pretend reading, I can't be sure.

A soft click, and his watch drops to the coffee table. His phone follows. I can sense him closer. I can smell him closer.

"What are you doing?"

I close the book and meet his gaze. "Isn't it obvious? I'm reading."

"I didn't know you were starting a company." He folds his arms, his head slanted to the side.

Frowning, I glance at the cover of Zero to One: Notes on Startups, Or How to Build the Future.

Merde.

"Because a dancer can't be interested in business?" I snap, abandoning my femme fatale character.

He lifts the book from my hands and sits on the coffee table, flipping through the pages.

"Oh, I'm pretty sure you're business-savvy. It's just that your attire at the moment is more of the *chilling with a romance book* kind."

He puts the book aside and rests his arms on his legs, leaning forward.

"I used to run a successful business." For some outlandish reason, I'm defending a point that is not the point here.

"Is that what you want to talk about?" His gaze is heated as he calls me on my bullshit.

I lift my legs and spin round to sit up, crossing one leg over the other as I lean in. "I wasn't planning on it. In fact, I wasn't planning on much talking."

"What would your boyfriend say?"

I roll my eyes. "I wasn't planning to talk about that either." I coil a strand of hair around my finger, smiling. I'm not going to tell him there is no boyfriend. The man has enough power over me already.

He licks his lips in slow motion and drops his hand to my knee. The touch is electrifying. I push up off the sofa and stand between his legs while his touch skims up my thighs.

Ironically, this is similar to my first attempt to seduce him, but while then I felt like I was selling myself for a visa, this time... I don't know, it's just the two of us consenting to having a good time.

Caleb doesn't break our gaze as his hands move higher. My knees buckle when he squeezes my ass. My hair cascades around my face as I lean forward, lowering my hands to his thighs while sinking my ass into his hands.

He cups the back of my neck, and our lips connect. It's not a heated kiss, it's an exploratory one, just tasting each other, finding a rhythm, taking our time to play, to seduce, to enjoy.

Snaking his hand between my legs from behind, he finds my sensitive bud, rubbing it through the flimsy fabric of my panties.

I'm glad I didn't wear my heels, because there is no way I could stand here like this and take his ministrations. Even barefoot and used to physical activity, I'm barely able to hold myself.

"I can't wait to taste you, black swan." He shoves two fingers in me, not bothering to push my underwear to the side, and the freaking fabric intensifies the friction.

Without much fumbling, Caleb crooks his fingers

and finds the spot like he's always had a map of my pussy.

He continues pumping his fingers in and out, my panties stretching painfully around my thighs as he shoves more of the fabric into me.

"Mon dieu," I moan. "I'm going to come."

"That's the point. Let go and scream my name."

The explosion that follows his words is spine-tingling. Mind-blowing. Heart-stopping.

Thank God I don't sing in the theater, because I'm sure I lost my voice with the scream. And while his name was on my tongue, I swallowed that.

"Merde." I sink into the armchair behind me, spent. Fuck, how do I go back to my vibrators after this? But that's a problem for later.

Caleb stands and yanks me up with him. Holding me around my waist, he pinches my chin between his finger and thumb. "I said to scream my name."

"I can't give you everything." I try to sound casual, sassy, but the deep truth behind my words comes across loudly.

His face hardens for a moment, as he stares me down with an intensity that makes my heart try to escape from my chest. I fully expect him to drop me here and leave, but then a crooked smile tugs at his lips.

He shakes his head and drops his mouth to mine in

a punishing, bruising kiss, sealing the deal. Accepting the challenge.

I didn't mean it like one, but clearly there are no boundaries to his cockiness. I'm not going to complain. My vibrators will get a well-deserved rest while he's trying.

He slides the silky fabric from my shoulder, and I moan into his mouth. The elevator ding penetrates through my dazed mind, and before I can make sense of what's happening, Caleb jumps away from me like I just burned him.

"Fuck, I'll have to bleach my eyes now." A young woman—no, a girl—at the elevator covers her eyes, dropping her backpack to her feet.

"Mia, what did I tell you about swearing?" Caleb reprimands her.

She snorts, rolling her eyes. "Fuck is literally the first word you ever said to me."

I pull the two sides of my robe together as if I can scrape together some decency here. What the hell is going on?

Dressed in a simple black T-shirt and ripped jeans, the girl's makeup might be an attempt at a goth style or just a case of absolute lack of experience in making herself look pretty.

"Who are you?" Instinctively, I step away from Caleb, almost toppling onto the sofa behind me.

The girl jumps down the step and assesses me with distrust. "Who are *you*?"

Caleb's eyes dart toward the elevator, and then to the hallway that leads to his office. Is he looking for a fast exit?

I put my hands on my hips. "What the fuck, Caleb? She's too young, even for you!"

"Ew, gross." The girl scrunches her nose.

"Celeste, this is Mia, my daughter. Mia, this is Celeste, my wife." Caleb recites through his teeth, like uttering the words is the last thing he's ever planned to do. Or like one of us got him into this situation.

"Daughter?" I ask incredulously.

"Wife?" Mia asks at the same time.

"Mia, why don't you go to your room and order pizza? I'll come talk to you in a minute." Caleb goes to pick up her backpack while Mia stares at me.

My mind fires in so many directions that I can't settle on one. He has a daughter. A teenage daughter. How did I not know that?

Goosebumps sprout on my skin, and I sigh. Because out of all the ways I could have met this girl, I'm half-naked.

She snatches her backpack and dashes upstairs.

"Sorry about that." Caleb rakes his hand through his hair.

177

I belatedly grab a blanket from the chair and wrap myself in it. "Why didn't you tell me?"

"Only Finn and Saar know about her."

"How can you hide a daughter?" I hiss my words.

I don't know the girl upstairs, but I don't need to traumatize her with my tantrum, and I sure as hell feel like throwing one. Especially since her father isn't offering an explanation.

"I only found out about her three months ago." Caleb sits on the coffee table across from me again.

The scenario from earlier flashes through my mind, and I almost chuckle at the absurdity of the situation.

"How come?"

"I'd much rather continue with our previous activity." He cocks his eyebrow. Extending his hand, he traces a line down my cleavage. "I think you were ready to beg me."

I swat his hand away. "Nice avoidance tactic, but you're getting zero action until you explain."

"Fair enough." He props his arms on his knees. "I got her mother pregnant when we were seventeen. Mia will be twelve this summer. When Reese, her mother, found out she was pregnant, she came to see me, but my father intercepted and paid her off. To get rid of the child and to disappear, so I'd never find out."

My heart sinks. "That's terrible."

"That's my father." Sounding detached but also deeply affected, he studies his hands for a moment. "Reese decided to keep the baby, but I guess she ran out of money and decided I'd be an easy bank machine."

"Jesus." I cover my mouth.

"Mia showed up three months ago, and an expedited paternity test later, I became a father. And added another offense to my father's list of fuckups."

"But I've been living here for two weeks."

"Yeah, Mia's here every second weekend. Her mother didn't care to face me, so the whole arrangement happened over text message. Mia begged me not to involve my lawyer, and a part of me wanted to pretend this wasn't happening, so I just accepted it."

"What do you mean? Jesus, Caleb, you need to meet with Mia's mother and discuss some proper custody."

He sighs. "I know. But I... I don't want the confirmation she's only after my money. Once I involve lawyers, that's what's going to happen."

"So you're just, what? Spending two weekends a month with your child without being her official guardian? What if something happens?"

"What could happen? She spends her weekend in her room on her phone, and then goes back to her mother at the end of it. I gave her a credit card, so I don't know why either of them would be upset with the arrangement."

I stare at him, unblinking, but no... the scene is still real.

"For a smart man, you can be really stupid."

"What do you want me to do? It's not like there's a manual on how to become father of the year to an eleven-year-old. She doesn't really want to hang out with me. I tried. And yes, you're right, I should make it all official, but I needed a moment to grasp reality."

"You tried? Wow, I didn't take you as someone who gives up. You're being so selfish right now. A child needs their father. And I'm sure you don't have to be father of the year. Simple interest goes a long way."

"You've met her for half a minute, and you know what she needs? She barely talks to me. Her mother only sent her here because they needed money."

I jump up, the blanket falling to my ankles. "So what? You have so much to give them. You practically gave me a credit card to buy an airplane."

He stands up too, towering over me. "That's not what I said. Please do not buy airplanes on credit, that's not a smart decision." He smirks.

"Are you seriously joking now? This makes no sense. You can support them and wouldn't even notice it, so why are you putting your head in the sand?"

"Because I don't trust her mother. And having

someone reminding me of what an asshole my father is—"

"You're behaving like him right now. Maybe not as ruthless, but equally selfish."

His jaw ticks, and I fear he'll shut down. And probably divorce me, but then he bows his head. "I don't know what I'm doing here."

Two things happen in the aftermath of his admission. One, I realize my husband just showed me a vulnerable side of him. It scares me and thrills me at the same time, and it shouldn't do either. I shouldn't care. It opens up my heart, and that is not a good idea.

And two, as much as I want to pretend it's none of my business, no part of me is on board with that notion. And that's a much bigger pile to unravel.

I came down here today to seduce the man I married. Instead, I gained an instant family.

Chapter 17

Caleb

"**D**o you have any questions?" I tap my fingers on the dresser behind me as I lean against it.

I gave Mia a redacted version of my sudden marriage, because when push comes to shove, I don't trust this girl not to rat us out to the immigration officers.

Sitting on her bed, with her back against the headboard, she drops an uneaten slice of pizza back into the box. "Is your wife okay with me being here?"

She doesn't look at me, her gaze on her duvet as if the stitching pattern was the most fascinating thing in the world.

Explaining—really lying about—my marriage to Mia was the longest conversation we'd had since she showed up and told me who she was.

Celeste is right, my behavior around Mia is shameful. But Celeste saw Mia for thirty seconds. And I know the girl is hiding something.

Along with the fact that her mother doesn't even want to see me... As sad as it is, I don't trust this girl—who I should feel some connection to.

"Celeste doesn't mind. Though sometimes I wonder if you want to be here." I push off the dresser and walk to the door.

She rolls her eyes. "What's not to like? You feed me, I have a comfortable bed here, and you don't nag me about being on my phone twenty-four-seven. And your donations to my lifestyle are great." She plops on to the cushions, narrowly avoiding the pizza box, and stares at the ceiling.

I don't know what to say to that, but clearly she comes here for perks, not for bonding.

"Good night, Mia."

"Night, Daddy," she says, mocking me.

Fuck. My. Life.

Ever since this girl showed up at my office, everything has been spiraling. I question my work. My hate for my father has doubled. And I have no sense of purpose or action. It's like I'm drowning in this shitload of doubt.

Doubting what I want to do. Doubting everything I grew up believing since it's tainted by the man who sired me. Doubting Mia's intentions.

Come to think of it, Celeste is the only thing in my life that makes me tick. That makes me feel like me, even when she drives me crazy. But even with Celeste, the seed of doubt around her motivations took root.

I make my way to my bedroom at the end of the hallway, stopping briefly at Celeste's door. The vision of her sprawled in the armchair downstairs *reading* brings a smile to my face, and I raise my hand to knock, then freeze.

Crossing the threshold of her room would offset the delicate balance of our arrangement. She was right when she pointed out that a one-night stand isn't an option for us.

With an unexpected jolt of regret, I drop my hand and retire to my room. Plopping into my bed, I turn on the TV and mindlessly click through the channels, while my mind circles through the mess my life currently is.

Maybe I should take Xander up on the offer to go clubbing. It might not put things into perspective, but it might help reset my brain, and stop the thoughts of Celeste.

Corm Quinn doesn't want to budge on the additional five percent, and I might need to pull out of the negotiation. Failing.

Mia would rather watch paint dry than bond with me. And I have no idea how to be a father to her.

And then there's my wife, who I don't hate as much as I used to. Who is a welcome distraction from all the other shit. And who I still failed to fuck.

I turn on my phone's screen. Great, I've been organizing my thoughts for almost an hour, and I'm nowhere close to resolving anything.

I swing my legs over and decide another whiskey might help me fall asleep. I go downstairs and enjoy two inches of the amber liquid while watching the city flickering below me.

The house is silent, but my mind remains focused on the two people upstairs. A graceful femme fatale who I would very much like to devour, and an aloof almost-teenager who I simultaneously wish I still didn't know about, and hate that I didn't for so long.

What a fucking twist of fate that these two are my family now. At least on paper.

When my mother joined my father in the vow to never speak to any of their children, I didn't consider it a loss. But with Finn having a baby, and Saar being abroad most of the time, something was missing.

Not that I used to hang out with my parents much, but there was a sense of belonging to a family, an obligation to show up.

I wish I knew how to transfer that obligation to the two women sleeping upstairs.

Putting my glass down, I make my way up and stop on the last step, catching a glimpse of green silk.

Celeste is standing in front of Mia's room. I approach carefully to find the door is slightly ajar, Mia sleeping peacefully.

My wife came to check on my daughter. Given our real circumstances, the scene is outlandish. And yet a warm feeling spreads across my chest.

Celeste slowly closes the door and turns to leave when she collides with me and yelps. I cover her mouth, and we stare at each other for several beats before I'm sure she won't scream.

She fits so well against me that my cock salutes, having a mind of its own. She's not wearing makeup and it makes her eyes shine brighter, the emerald in them glimmering.

The hallway is dim, the city lights coming through the large windows above the glass banister overlooking the living room. But even cast in the shadows, her beauty is somehow more obvious, the lack of makeup giving her an air of innocence.

I crash my lips against hers, and she tenses at first, but then grants me access and joins in the wild dance of our tongues. The woman is an excellent kisser.

Kissing has always been a required part of foreplay for me, but I can stand here and kiss Celeste Delacroix for hours and thoroughly enjoy myself. Enjoy us.

The thought hits an emergency button in my head, and I pull away. Celeste is flushed and breathless, staring at me with enough heat to set us on fire.

Before I can apply any form of logic, she cups my dick and hums. Like a man possessed, I drag her to the door of her room, then halt. I might be ready to explode, but I'm not crossing that threshold.

I pin her against the wall, jerking my hips against her. I cup her throat, angling her to me. Her breath hitches, her heartbeat pumping against my palm.

"Okay, black swan, you won this round." I drag my nose across her cheek, inhaling the aphrodisiac this woman is.

Yanking the sash of her glimmering robe, I find her wearing that flimsy camisole from earlier. Only she shed the rest of the outfit, no longer wearing the garters and stocking. And no bra.

I groan, cupping her heavy breasts. Fuck, she is perfect.

"What did I win?" She pants the whispered words.

"I'm the one getting on my knees this time." I pinch her nipple through the camisole and kneel.

I smirk when her eyes widen. "Caleb, let's go to my

room," she hisses, pulling the sides of her robe together in some unreasonable quest for modesty. "We could wake up Mia."

"You just have to be quiet, black swan."

She almost falls as I lift her leg over my shoulder. My actions might be unhinged and reckless, but the minute her nails graze my skull as she fists my hair for support, I forget where we are.

Because if I thought no bra had turned me into a caveman, the encounter with her naked pussy just undoes me. No panties.

Flattening my tongue, I have a first taste of my wife. *My wife*. Fuck.

She moans. Not too loud, but in the silence of the apartment, the breathy sound booms. I lean back on my haunches.

"You taste like the garden of Eden. I need more, so be a good girl and keep quiet, or I'll have to gag you."

"Or we can just go to my—"

Her words die on her lips as I dive back in, teasing and playing with her sensitive bud before I sink two digits into her heat.

Fuck, I could feast on her forever and die a happy man. The thought shakes me, and I almost recoil, but her whimper draws me in.

Never have I given pleasure with such dedication.

Never have I felt so much satisfaction from a woman's reactions.

It might be because she resisted for so long. Or because I persisted in teasing her when we were forced to share space. Or just the prolonged anticipation.

But simply having her like this feels like the endgame. My dick hardens in protest, reminding me this is just foreplay.

It doesn't take long before I feel her clenching around my fingers while she pushes her hips forward shamelessly.

I look up and, fuck, the sight is worth half of my assets. Celeste is moaning into her fist, her hooded gaze sultry.

I reach to squeeze her breast and twist her nipple, and she clenches, gripping my fingers in a vice-like hold as her climax takes over. I keep pumping my fingers and massage her clit as she rides the wave, but soon I have to use both my hands to support her because her legs give in.

Standing up, I push the neckline of the camisole down, exposing her large breasts. "I need to taste these as well."

I take one pebbled peak into my mouth like it's my only lifeline. Her soft gasp gives me an unreasonable jolt of satisfaction.

I rise to kiss her mouth, still holding her for support.

"I can't believe I let you do this," she whispers.

"Complaining, black swan?" I nip at her earlobe.

"Oh, I want more, but here? What were you thinking?" She holds the back of my neck, berating me, but keeping me close at the same time.

"I was thinking you're my wife, and I have the right to fuck you."

"Now who is from the eighteenth century? Your right is limited by my consent."

"I don't remember you stopping me. Or was pushing your hips into my face, almost suffocating me, an attempt to escape?"

Even in the darkened space, with city lights flickering on the wall around us, I can see her cheeks color. "Asshole."

"There she is." I smirk, and I know I should leave it at that, but my cock is painfully trying to burst through my briefs and my sweatpants.

Tonight's encounter started recklessly, so why would we tone it down?

"Wait here."

She's about to say something, but I kiss it away from her lips.

"Stay fucking here, Celeste, or I'll punish you." I take her lips again. "With or without consent."

Okay, clearly my dick took over my brain yet again, but by the flash of excitement in her eyes, it didn't take it too far.

Dashing to my room, I return with a condom in my pocket. A normal person would move the events to one of our bedrooms, but I'm me.

And if I'm going to finally enjoy Celeste Delacroix, I need it with a dash of daring carelessness.

"What are you—"

I kiss her again because I'm done with banter. "I need you to be silent for a little longer."

I yank her across the hallway, then whip her around and push her against the banister, her back to my chest.

"Caleb—" She moans as I squeeze her breasts and sags into me. "We really shouldn't. Not here."

"Tell me you want me to stop, black swan." I move her hair away and kiss her neck, nibbling my way down to her shoulder while I play with her nipples.

She melts into me, raising her hand and fisting my hair again, holding me in place. I guess that's my answer.

"Caleb, she can't find us like this."

"She won't if you keep quiet."

"This is madness." Her words ring of protest, but her body tells a different story.

I've always been an unhinged bastard, avoiding

bedrooms because they brought on boredom, but this is next-level recklessness even for me. But I can't stop.

I rip the wrapper with my teeth and sheath my engorged length. "Celeste, tell me the danger, the anticipation of being caught doesn't thrill you, and I'll stop."

She pants, her breasts heaving in my hands, but she doesn't say anything. I fist my cock with one hand, and with the other, I push her between her shoulder blades. She bends slightly, her arms landing on the railing and her hips pushing against me.

I lift her robe and lean over her, whispering in her ear. "What's it going to be, black swan? Should I stop?" I nudge my tip between her folds.

Her head falls forward and she stifles a moan. "I'm going to divorce you for this. Be quick."

I chuckle, and in one thrust I plunge into her. Fuck, she's tight. I pause, allowing her to adjust.

"Merde," she gasps and bites her forearm.

Her robe slides and covers the spot where we're connected. As much as I'd like to watch, the silky green cover softens the threat of our location, adding a touch of privacy.

Or that's what I'm trying to tell myself. Because as much as I enjoy sex with a dash of risk, this feels different.

Firstly, my daughter is behind the door. Our

nonexistent relationship would certainly get derailed if she walked out. A part of me knows that's not probable, but an unfamiliar, newly born conscience sprouts guilt.

And guilt has never invaded my mind before. Even after reckless liaisons that Cressard had to bail me out of.

"Harder," Celeste hisses.

And therein lies the second novelty. This woman isn't like any other. She takes with abandon, chasing her own pleasure.

Most women in my life try too hard to please me. To make sure they earn a chance at a second time or more. My affection. My commitment.

Celeste isn't like that. Perhaps because she's stuck with me, so she doesn't have to perform to get that next-day call. But it's not just that.

Every move. Every thrust. Every touch. She takes them without inhibition. She welcomes them like she deserves them. Like she knows her value.

While I have her in this position, at my mercy, I still sense her autonomy. And fuck if that isn't the hottest thing ever.

"Your pussy takes me so well." I dig my fingers into her delicious hips.

I move in a frenzy, drowning in this woman who has been getting under my skin for weeks now.

With my hand, I trail up her spine, her soft skin

like silk under my fingertips. And since when am I noticing details like that?

Suddenly, I'm annoyed by the spell she cast over me. I fist her hair and pound into her like she's my enemy.

Because with all the feelings sex with Celeste stirs in me, she is an enemy. I don't need her uprooting my deeply encoded habits.

Sex is just sex. I keep repeating the mantra, the city lights blurring in front of me.

Celeste stifles a cry, her walls clenching around my cock. She sags against the banister, coming, and chanting something French into her forearm.

"Bend over, fingers on the floor," I order.

She looks at me over her shoulder, and fuck, I wish I could take a picture. She's breathtaking, with her dazed gaze, swollen lips, and the background of the city that never sleeps.

"Show me that dancer body of yours, black swan."

She smiles languidly and then bends forward, her fists touching the floor by her feet. Fuck, she's flexible. With her folded like that, my cock sinks so deep I grunt, and it takes me only a few frantic thrusts before an explosion of pleasure rages through me.

"And still you didn't scream my name," I say, mostly to distract myself from the assault of thoughts and feelings pouring through my mind.

She pushes away, glancing at Mia's door while she tries to cover herself, pulling the sides of her robe together. She spots the sash where it dropped earlier and dashes to pick it up.

I tuck myself into my pants, feeling strangely lonely as my arousal slowly evaporates. Fuck. My legs move before my brain decides.

I open Mia's door softly. Lying across her bed, she has her arms and legs sprawled like she's making snow angels, her covers on the floor.

An unfamiliar feeling nudges me forward. I tiptoe into the room and pick up the duvet. For the first time in my life, I tuck my daughter in.

Careful not to wake her, I watch her for a beat. Deep in her sleep, she looks innocent and much younger. And so fucking like me.

When I turn, Celeste stands in the doorway, a ghost of a smile fighting with a scowl on her face. I close the door behind me.

"That was reckless," she hisses.

"And yet you didn't stop me."

Pulling her to me, I nudge her chin to turn her face to me. I seize her lips and kiss her.

To thank her for playing this lewd game with me.

To apologize for dragging her into a conflicting situation.

To ensure her that I've got her back, even though my behavior tonight contradicts that.

And most importantly, to enjoy her for a short moment longer before I let her go.

Because having sex with her was supposed to be the endgame. And I'm sticking to that.

Chapter 18

Celeste

> Caleb has a daughter? WTF!

SAAR

> Sorry, it wasn't my story to tell. Have you met her?

> Yes.

SAAR

> I haven't.

> Shit. He struggles with his role in her life.

SAAR

> He struggles with our father's role in her life.

> That's not Mia's fault.

SAAR

> Protecting your stepdaughter already:-)

> Don't joke, he treats her like she's here to con him.

SAAR

> We don't know what her intentions are. He's being cautious.

> God, you're all fucked up.

SAAR

> I told my therapist to send his bill to my parents.

> (kiss emoji) That sounds fair.

nd yet you didn't stop me.

I've been up for a while, but I can't muster the will to get out of my bed. Caleb thinks I unleashed the animal in him, but he was right. I never stopped him.

I never stopped him.

There were parts of me screaming to run to safety, to behave, to protect myself. But equally loud—no, louder—was a wild part in me Caleb found and released.

A part I didn't even know I had.

Dark.

Spellbound.

Raw.

Perhaps I'm a dancer because there's an exhibitionist in me. Perhaps the pent-up sexual tension between us had to erupt just like this.

And perhaps this is what I haven't discovered about myself before. I enjoy sex with a side of danger. Not physical danger, but danger nevertheless.

What if Mia had walked out of her room? Jesus. Uneasiness swirls in my stomach, bidding its way to my conscience. The girl doesn't need more emotional scars than she already has.

But she didn't. Nothing bad happened. Nobody discovered us. Our twisted liaison was... ours.

It leaves me with a smile lingering on my face. Caleb van den Linden knows his way around a woman's body. To think I judged him for his man-whore ways, only to realize that reaping the benefits of his experience is the next level of bliss.

I avoided sex with him because I feared the next morning, and how we would live together for months after we succumbed to our attraction.

Now, as the sun shines through the windows, coloring the new day warm and vibrant, the only thing I fear is that he got fully sated and won't be interested in me again.

I only had a brief, clandestine, stolen taste of Caleb van den Linden, and I need more. Even if that means I'll get hurt.

Because let's face it, the opposite scenario isn't in the cards. The man doesn't want marriage—a real one —or children. At least not more than he already has.

He doesn't want a monogamous future. Or a committed relationship. He's not husband material and, color me naïve, but I still believe in happily ever after.

And still, I can't drop it. Not just yet.

After my half-hour stretching routine, I shower and dress casually in a simple brown dress with a V neckline teasing my cleavage, a flared skirt, and a large satin ribbon at my waist. I comb my hair into a simple ponytail tied at my nape.

I don't bother with makeup, since I don't know what I'm doing today.

I can't perform yet, so I have the day off. I hope to have plans with Caleb, but I don't want to assume. If last night was the final destination for him, I'll just go to Cora's and avoid him until I shake it off.

Opening my door, I stop, surprised. Something— probably vanilla and definitely burned—permeates the air.

The scene I find in the kitchen downstairs is unexpected. And somehow endearing. Caleb—in his stupid low-hanging sweats—and Mia are making pancakes.

"Good morning. I didn't know you could cook." I lean in the doorway, grinning.

Mia snorts. "He can't. I'm trying to teach him."

Caleb shrugs, but doesn't look at me. I guess that's my answer. Last night was a one-off. I swallow my disappointment.

"What are you making?" I ask Mia, trying not to look at his ripped back while he dedicates unreasonable effort to washing a dish.

"Well, it should be pancakes."

"Hey!" Caleb flicks water at her, and she jumps to the side.

The domestic scene warms my heart. The two of them bonding doesn't match what he told me about their relationship yesterday.

The two of them bonding also makes me feel like a third wheel. I can't even be jealous, because they have the right to spend the day together without my interference.

The two of them have the right. All I have is a memory of last night, and a bit of hope. One that dissipates with Caleb's ignorance.

"Caleb made the batter before I came down, so—" Mia almost smiles as she pours the creamy liquid into the pan. "And he burned the first batch."

Caleb finally turns off the faucet and wipes his hands. "The YouTube tutorial was shit."

Our eyes meet, and his face hardens before he

looks away. Yeah, I guess dealing with last night's conquest isn't something he's experienced before.

That's what I deserve for giving in to stupid attraction.

"Does this look good to you, Celeste?" Mia doesn't pick up on the energy between her father and me.

I approach the stove and peek over her shoulder. I'm pretty sure there is no way that the mass in the pan can turn into a pancake. "Well—"

She looks at me sideways. "I don't think this is what a pancake should look like," she murmurs.

"Fuck." Caleb groans. "Let's go out for brunch."

I tense, unsure if the invitation extends to me as well. No way am I spending the morning with him. Nowhere close to him. I need time to lick my wounds and find my strength.

Because it's one thing to hope he would want more and be disappointed, but I was also hoping that scratching the itch would clear the air between us. But as I feared, it only made the next almost three years feel even longer.

Mia turns off the burner and pushes the pan away. A moment of silence stretches as she lowers her head, her hair hiding her face while she pulls at the sleeves of her shirt.

Caleb shrugs with resignation on his face. And despite everything, I can't help but interfere. They had such a good start, I won't let them retreat into their shells.

"That's a wonderful idea, Mia, isn't it?" I wrap my arm around her shoulders, but she recoils and steps to the side.

"You don't have to take me with you. I can stay here. Or I'll go home."

Oh, shit.

Caleb sighs. "Not taking you with us, Mia. Going together. Come on, I'd like to spend some time with you." He puts his hands into his pockets, pleading.

Jesus. I wish he didn't look this sexy.

"You do?" She frowns.

"Of course," Caleb says, smiling hopefully.

Mia chews on her lip, looking at us through her tresses. "Okay. All three of us together."

Caleb jerks his head to me. And I glance away. If I excuse myself, she might think I don't want to spend time with her. Which is the last thing I want on her shoulders. It's her father I don't want to spend time with.

"All three of us, of course," Caleb says, smiling at Mia, who relaxes visibly.

I can see how she'd feel more comfortable with someone else on their first outing together. So I put on a brave face.

"Great." I smile at Caleb who looks somewhere

between pleased, full-blown freaked out, and annoyed. "Mia, I need to do my makeup. Would you like me to help you with yours?"

Her eyes pop out. "Really?"

"Of course. Let's go."

Mia dashes to the staircase, and as I pass Caleb, he mouths a reluctant *thank you*.

And the hurt me can't just let it slide, so I smirk at him. "We need pictures for my application."

I trace my finger over the fine china, the taste of poached eggs lingering on my tongue, mingling with the hint of truffle in the hollandaise sauce. And a dollop of discomfort from my current company.

The restaurant exudes a sense of refined elegance, and it should make this moment feel wonderfully indulgent, but Mia has been obviously uncomfortable.

And Caleb has been trying too hard with her, and is even more aloof toward me. He's behaving like I wronged him somehow.

A car stuck in traffic moves more smoothly than the conversation has gone at our table.

We sit by the window, the lazy weekend unraveling on the street. Mia excuses herself and runs to the bathroom.

Of course Caleb took us to a popular, upscale place, but I don't think he realized the girl might be overwhelmed by the polished marble floors, the chic décor, and every other detail, including the delicate scent of blooming orchids in the middle of our table.

This place is amazing, but it's not a family restaurant.

"Thank you." Caleb takes a sip of his water, and I'm not even sure if I heard him right.

"Whatever for?"

"We wouldn't be here without you. Mia doesn't look thrilled, but she's here, which is an improvement."

His gaze focuses on the street. Like after last night, he can't even look at me. I want to tell him his distance is unwarranted, and we can just pretend nothing happened.

I'm a big girl. I can protect my feelings and, as much as I wish for it, any commitment from his side isn't expected. There's no need to act like an asshole.

But then again, he always has. Unfortunately, this is not the time or place, so I push the feelings deeper and try to ignore the foul taste of this outing.

"I think this place is a bit..." I hesitate.

"You don't like it?" He snaps his head to me. Oh, wow, now I got his attention?

Chapter 19

Celeste

I roll my eyes. "I think an eleven-year-old girl not used to your kind of luxuries might be a bit over-whelmed."

He lowers his head, playing with the spoon in his coffee. "I keep fucking this up."

Another rare moment of honest fragility from this man. And I don't know how to take it. Because on the one hand, he's confiding in me, thanking me for being a buffer between him and his child.

On the other hand, it's quite clear he'd rather be anywhere but near me. I'm sure if it wasn't for his hopelessness around Mia, we wouldn't be sitting here. It stings, but again, I'm a big girl.

"You're not fucking anything up. It's new for both of you. You'll figure it out." I fold my arms across my chest and look outside.

This feels more like a forced meeting between two divorced parents. Bound by the need to discuss their offspring, but utterly uncomfortable spending time together.

I've only just met Mia, but shit, she deserves better.

"You seem to know what you're doing." His words ring like an accusation. Fuck him.

"She seems to like her makeup." I address my words to the window, just like him.

I suggested a natural look for her, and to my surprise, she accepted. I had a feeling the goth style wasn't a phase, but more a mask or a cry for attention.

"That's definitely an improvement. You changed her from a ghost to a girl." He taps his fingers on the table.

Where the hell is Mia? Without her around, the awkwardness between us grows.

"She asked why I'm staying in the guest bedroom?" I don't even know why I'm sharing that with him. I guess anything to prevent the heavy silence from stretching.

"Shit. What did you tell her?"

"I told her we're remodeling the master closet and bathroom, so I have my things in the guest room, and that I use it because you snore."

"I don't snore," he scoffs.

Is he for real? That's the fight he wants to pick. I abandon my resolution not to poke into things.

"I wouldn't know, would I?" I quip, and he fixes his eyes on me.

We glare at each other, the air between us filled with the remnants of last night. What are we doing?

I sigh. "We should talk about last night."

"I'm sorry I got carried away." He looks away again, and I'm not sure if he's talking about this conversation or last night. "You were right, sleeping together isn't wise, given the terms of our arrangement. It won't happen again."

"Fine by me." I spit the words, practically defying their meaning, but I can't help it.

He looks at me, unimpressed, but before we can say—and regret—anything else, Mia returns.

She plops into her seat, her eyes darting between the two of us.

"Shall we order anything else?" Caleb asks, and she shrugs. He sighs and turns to me. "Do you have a rehearsal today?"

So, now we pretend to get along. It's none of his business, but I remain civil. "No, I have the day off."

And why does he care? I guess just making sure I won't be around all day.

"Rehearsal?" Mia looks up, her eyes void of indifference for the first time.

"Celeste is a dancer," Caleb says, and if I wasn't annoyed by his behavior, I'd think there was a tinge of pride in his voice.

I whip my head to him. "Have you ever seen me dance?"

With his napkin, he wipes the corners of his mouth, then drops the linen on the table. "Yes, I have." He rolls his eyes.

"A rehearsal at home doesn't count," I murmur, and turn to Mia. This bickering about inconsequential shit doesn't make any sense. "I dance in an off-Broadway cabaret-like production. It's a play about a burlesque dancer who falls in love with the club owner."

"And it's all just dancing?" Mia puts her arms on the table, leaning closer. "Like a ballet?"

"A contemporary dance, but in this one, we incorporate different dance styles to move the plot forward."

"Wow, that's so cool."

"Maybe you can come when I'm back on stage." I grin at her, enjoying how this girl finally unveiled a bit of herself.

"Maybe." She shrugs, looking away as if she realized she had shown more warmth than she planned.

"Do you like dancing?" Caleb asks.

"I used to be in a hip-hop crew in school, but then... I quit." She shrinks in her chair, hugging herself around her midriff. "I'll wait for you outside." She springs up and disappears before we can react.

Caleb gestures for the bill. "And I thought we made some progress."

I want to tell him to be patient, to let her open up on her own terms, but I'm not a parenting coach, and he doesn't deserve my opinions.

We pay, then find Mia leaning against the wall, drawing circles with her foot like it's the most riveting thing in the world.

"Would you like to go to the *zoo*?" Caleb asks awkwardly.

She rolls her eyes. "I'm not five."

He rakes his hand through his hair, sighing.

Our lukewarm relationship is one thing, but I can't watch the two of them falling out before they even have a chance to grow together.

Both clearly want—even if they don't admit it—and need this connection. I look at Mia, and then at Caleb, and for the second time this morning, I decide to facilitate their bonding.

As uncomfortable as it may be to spend time with Mr. I-freaked-out-after-I-fucked-you.

"I have an idea, but it might not be available." I hold up one finger, silently asking them to hold on a minute, already dialing my friend's number.

Mia and Caleb look like they're having the worst day in history while I make arrangements.

"We're in luck. I booked us for therapy."

They both glare at me, probably considering whether they can just leave me here and run away.

* * *

Mia throws a glass to the floor and immediately follows with several plates, stomping her feet over the shards.

In the other corner, Caleb swings a baseball bat to smash a mirror. I lunge, bringing the hammer down on a vase before I demolish the table it stood on.

Forty-five minutes later, we're drenched in sweat and thoroughly relaxed, laughing.

At the front desk, we take selfies, get disgustingly sweet blue slushies, and hit the street.

"How do you even know about this place?" Mia slurps loudly through her straw.

"The owner used to work at a club where I danced, and then he opened these smashing rooms for corporate team buildings. He invited us to test it before the opening, and I've been coming here occasionally. It's my form of therapy."

"I don't think training for a half-marathon helped me release this much stress. I'm fucking buying the place." Caleb basketballs his cup into the garbage bin.

Mia's eyes widen, and I laugh. "He's probably not kidding."

Smashing was the best therapy for me as well. Fuck his aloofness. Soon we'd both forget last night, and we'd learn to cohabitate.

The visit lifted the veil of hostile energy between us, like we seized the opportunity to exorcise our frustration.

My disappointment lingers, and so does Caleb's distance, but somehow the fun exercise and Mia's presence showed us we can put the night behind us.

Not that I've stopped thinking about it. His hands on my body, the reverence of his touch, the expert manhandling. The way he took care of me before he chased his own release.

Like my body had been waiting for him and came alive under his ministrations. Flashbacks of his fingers digging into my hips, him filling me to the hilt, the flickering lights of Manhattan, my breasts heavy in his hands... and his words.

Merde, his words. *Show me that dancer body of yours, black swan.*

Caleb's phone rings. He glances at the screen and groans. "Sorry, I have to take it. Think about what you want for supper." He winks at Mia and takes a few steps away before answering.

"This was fun. Thank you." Mia swirls her straw through the crushed ice, watching the motion.

"We can come again." I smile at her, even though she's avoiding eye contact. Even though I can't promise we will. "Or you can come to a rehearsal with me next time if you'd like."

I understand this girl landed in my life by chance, and that her father probably doesn't want me bonding with her, but I can't help it.

She stops stirring, but doesn't look up. "Okay."

"Did you enjoy hip-hop?"

Maybe I'm pushy, but there was something behind the girl's response earlier, and I know how hard it is to find a place in the world of dancing.

"I loved it," she murmurs.

We sit on a bench by the small parkette while Caleb paces the sidewalk, arguing with someone.

"When I was little, much younger than you, I wanted to be a ballerina. I took classes, but I was too clumsy and big for the delicate dance. There were girls who used to laugh at me."

"I'm good. We won a competition, but..." She fidgets, her shoulders slouching.

I worry she won't continue, but I don't want to make her more uncomfortable.

Caleb has his head down, listening to whoever's got him all riled up.

After a moment she continues. "My group still competes and performs, but it costs money to travel and buy costumes and..." She stands and dunks her cup into the garbage bin.

"But you could afford it now. Caleb gave you a credit card, didn't he?"

She spins around. "Yes, but I already use it for... Never mind. I don't want him to cut me off because I overspend."

"Oh, Mia, have you bought an airplane?" I decide to lighten the moment, because the tortured face of that little girl is breaking my heart.

She chuckles. "An airplane?"

"Don't do that, but I'm sure you can put your dancing expenses on that card. It would make Caleb happy."

"I don't know. I heard him talking to his brother on the phone and telling him I only come to get his money, so I-I don't want to..." She looks away, chewing on her bottom lip.

"Mia." I sigh, wishing I could take some of the heaviness from her shoulders. "I know the two of you are just starting to find your way, getting to know each other, and unfortunately, a lot of people try to get money from your dad, so he sometimes assumes—"

"Sorry about that." Caleb joins us.

"Is everything okay?" I ask, forgetting I don't really want to talk to him.

He shakes his head. "Don't worry about it." He turns to Mia. "So, where are we getting supper?"

Fuck him. "We're thinking kebabs, but Mia wants to tell you something," I decide to push my luck one more time.

"Do I?" Mia looks at me with horror.

"Do you?" Caleb asks, intrigued.

"Mia is joining her hip-hop crew again," I announce.

Mia's eyes flick to Caleb, who smiles. "That's wonderful. I can't wait to watch you dance."

And for the first time since I've met Mia, a wide smile stretches across her face. I bask in her happiness for a moment, but when I turn to Caleb, I freeze.

He's glaring at me.

Chapter 20

Caleb

I throw my phone across the office. It bounces off a bookshelf and lands on the wooden floor. It doesn't break, which is a good thing, but it doesn't alleviate my agitation.

Celeste spent Saturday with me and Mia, but left for some friend's celebration this morning. It felt like a made-up excuse to get away from us—me. And I can't blame her.

Though I nearly panicked at the idea of being alone with Mia, it turned out to be a good day.

Still a lot of awkwardness and missteps, but

yesterday helped us to forge a path in the right direction. The annoying part is, we wouldn't have gotten there if it weren't for Celeste.

Watching her interact with Mia, witnessing how she stepped up and helped me with my daughter, and how easily Mia connected with her, was an eye-opener.

I freaked out after we had sex. I've never wanted a commitment, and I still don't. They always turn into transactions, and I'm not interested in those.

But as I was falling asleep on Friday night, the idea of *more* with Celeste lingered on my mind. I don't know how to do more. I've never tried, and frankly, with Merged negotiations and Mia, I have enough on my plate.

This is not the time.

She seems determined to dissuade me, anyway. Like on Friday morning when she made the comment about her pussy being serviced. For half a day, I was pissed she'd been fucking someone behind my back all this time.

Only it wouldn't have been behind my back. Half the day, I hated the asshole she was banging, and the other half, I was pissed at myself.

She doesn't owe me anything. For all she knows, I'm hooking up with other women all the time. Only I'm not, and that cemented my foul mood for the second half of the day.

But then she surprised me with her wanton *reading,* and I couldn't pretend the option wasn't finally on the table.

I couldn't have anticipated that she would become the first woman I'd want a second serving with. She bewitched me.

So in the morning, I created a boundary to help deal with my confusion. I couldn't even look at her without wanting to pin her against the wall. Which would be the worst idea.

It was just sex.

As much as I keep repeating it, it doesn't ring true. Especially in the light of the day we spent afterward. With my daughter. Like a family.

Fuck.

Only while I'm fighting my attraction, she goes to fuck someone else.

How dare she? When she suggested we share that condo—fuck, I don't even remember when I was there the last time—I thought she was bluffing.

And then she tells me her pussy was well-serviced. Goddammit. When I made the roster, I was sure she would abandon the idea. But I guess whoever services her is worth the risk of getting caught.

I stand to pick up my phone and flip through my contacts. There must be someone I can hook up with. The apartment is mine tomorrow, after all.

Only I don't feel a spark of desire to even call any of the contenders, let alone meet with them.

Annoyed, I dial Xander.

"Hey, man, ready to sign?" he answers cheerfully, and I want to hang up. The last thing I want is negotiating.

"Are you ready to give me twenty-five percent?" I quip.

"Fuck, Cal—"

"That's not why I'm calling. What about hitting the town tonight?"

"Sorry, man, I still have a presentation to work on."

"Christ. You used to be more fun." Can I sound any more desperate? Or maybe I sound like I always used to, and I just feel desperate.

Is she going to stay there all night? Or is it just a hook-up and she'll come home afterward?

"Well, I'm starting a company, and I wouldn't be this swamped if you got on board. We would get work done and have more fun. Sunday isn't a good time to go clubbing, anyway."

"What's Quinn's deal? He won't budge, and that doesn't give me confidence that I can work with him."

Yes, be a reasonable person and focus on business. Fuck, I hate how off-balance the woman makes me.

"Why don't we have breakfast tomorrow and talk?"

I consider. I'm sick of talking about this. I want in,

but we're at an impasse. Frankly, I don't mind if my share's twenty percent, but I can't give in because that would set the tone for our future collaboration. We'd be better off not working together at all under those circumstances.

"Okay, let's talk tomorrow. Why don't you come over to my place? I'll text you the address."

"Sounds good, but don't overdo it tonight. I'll wake you up at seven because I have a nine o'clock."

"Okay, Dad." I roll my eyes and disconnect the call. I text him the address and add his name to the approved guest list.

I dial Finn, but he doesn't answer. It's too late to call Saar, so I sit behind my desk again and review the last quarter's financials for Quaintique-Linden. I might not work there anymore, but I'm still a shareholder.

Staring at the numbers—or trying to—for what feels like hours, I check my watch. It's only been ten minutes. Molasses flows faster than this evening.

I sigh, refocusing on the numbers again, but they blur together in an indecipherable mess. I snap the laptop shut and stand, stretching my stiff muscles.

Making my way to the kitchen, I ignore the feeling of loneliness. This used to be my kingdom. I lived here alone and loved every minute. Now, the space seems foreign without the green-eyed wench.

Fuck.

I take fried rice from the fridge, and without heating it up, I sit behind the breakfast counter bar. I puncture the dish with the chopsticks a few times and then promptly throw it in the garbage.

I trudge to the living room and pour myself a glass of whiskey. The night lights flicker behind the window, the city full of life.

Never have I found the view so dissatisfying. I down my drink and pour myself another one. By the third one, I decide to go to sleep, but for some reason, I can't make it upstairs.

I want to see her face when she comes home. The sick bastard in me wants to see if she looks as satisfied as she did on Friday night.

For hours, I alternate between pacing and sitting on the sofa. I doze off for a few hours, but as the morning sun peers through the windows, I'm wide awake and even more... What? Am I jealous?

I laugh out loud. That's preposterous. Ignoring the lingering headache, I pour myself another whiskey, because that's the way to start a day. I freeze when the elevator dings open.

I whip around, and my gaze collides with hers. Something perverted in me rejoices, because she definitely doesn't look better than yesterday, or more satisfied. More like she slept about as much as me.

Fuck. Have they fucked all night?

She walks across the large room gingerly.

"What's wrong?" Her voice trembles.

"Where the fuck have you been all night?" I bark before I can stop myself.

She flinches.

At the question.

Or at my tone.

I'm past caring. I've been up all night, waiting for her.

Why am I so caught up with this? It's like the less I can have her, the more I want her. What the actual fuck? By now I should know the farther I am from Celeste Delacroix, the better.

And yet here we are, glaring at each other like it's an athletic discipline.

"I texted you my whereabouts," she says through her teeth.

"I didn't expect you to stay over. What were you thinking? What if someone saw you leaving there in the morning?" I'm full of shit.

She frowns and then cocks her head, assessing me like I'm a wild animal. And frankly, I don't blame her. Even I can see that my behavior is way out of line. Way beyond normal. Or reasonable.

And I'm the one who made it clear that we wouldn't repeat Friday night.

Under any other circumstances, I would have

moved on already. Quickly and with no fuss. Maybe a bit of wining and dining, but often that's not necessary.

So why don't I do just that? Why is this woman like a high I'm chasing? Like making her mine is the only fucking thing on my mind. Like I'll get some reward for breaking her will.

I won't.

But it might make the next three years easier for both of us. But that's water under the bridge, since she goes and fucks God knows who.

She keeps staring at me in that eerily still way. Her ability to control her body in this way, or any other way, is such a fucking turn-on.

Stop. This. Shit.

Finally, she takes one step closer, then another, placing her feet on the ground with caution like she isn't sure it's not quicksand.

"Why don't you tell me what this is really about, Caleb?" She enunciates each word with the precision of a chainsaw, cutting right through me.

If I grind my molars harder, I might spit enamel soon. With another step, her scent hits me, and I hate that another man has...

Fuck. Fuck. Fuck.

I don't get jealous. Is this a case of me hating to lose? There wasn't a competition, but the taunting game between us was enticing enough to keep me interested.

More than I've been interested in anything for a while. And then Friday night just seared her into my mind.

"I'm talking about you being reckless." Now I take a step, because that perfume of hers pulls me in like she's the only woman on earth. My temptress.

Only she isn't mine.

She takes another step, invading my space completely. The fabric of her skirt brushes my knees. "What is *this* really about, Caleb?"

The daring tone in her voice, and that French r of hers cloud my judgment completely, and I grab her wrist and pivot her.

With her hand pressed against the small of her back, between the two of us, I pin her against the window.

The city blurs below us, but my senses are crystal clear, focused on the woman in my hold.

Or the hold she has over me. Against my will.

Fuck, gentleman am I not this morning. Her soft behind molds against me, and my cock stirs.

Yes, I blamed my fake wife for not taking the threat of felony seriously enough, but here I am, practically assaulting her.

Her breath comes out in short bursts, just like

mine. But she remains still, not fighting me. The caveman in me takes that as an invitation, and I lower my head to her neck.

My own breath bounces off her delicate skin, the whiskey reminding me of the night I had.

What am I doing? Like she burned me, I step back.

She spins around and steps to the side. Fuck. Have I scared her?

She glares at me as her lips part, but no words come out. She shakes her head and glances over the city. Either she's trying to find her composure, or she can't even look at me.

"What's bothering you, Caleb? You fucked me, and then you made it clear that you're done with me. So what is your fucking problem?"

"You want to know what this is really about? Well, black swan, what I don't understand is why you trapped me in this marriage if you have a fuck buddy to lean on. What happened? He wasn't available for three years?"

She laughs. She fucking laughs at that.

"Are you jealous?" She steps closer, taunting me with her essence, with her glare, with her no-nonsense attitude.

My nostrils flare. "Of course not."

"Okay, then what is this little tantrum about,

Caleb? You said you don't want a repeat, so why does it bother you if I spent the night with someone else?"

Because I fucking want a repeat.

The minute the thought materializes, I lose my mind completely and claim her lips. She yelps, but immediately wraps her arms around me, pulling me closer.

The kiss is savage. Full of frustration and hate. But even full of agony, her taste is intoxicating.

Her taste. I remember it's mingled with another bastard. And I almost step back, but something primitive in me snaps, and I need to erase him from her.

I walk her backward until her feet stumble on the glass stairs. She loses her balance, but recovers quickly, dropping to a step and pulling me with her.

She bites my lip and moans. The tangy taste of blood mixes with our saliva. With one knee between her legs, I reach under her skirt and cup her mound roughly.

She arches into my hand. "Fuck me, Caleb."

"I'm nobody's seconds," I growl, but I rip off her underwear. "Not that he took care of you, your pussy is drenched."

"Idiot," she says in French. "Do you really think I'd have married you if there was someone else? I went to sleep at the Park Avenue place to get away from you, after you made it clear you were done with me."

What? A boulder that had no right to weigh down my chest dislodges. I pinch her jaw between my thumb and index finger. "I'm so going to punish you for that."

"You should punish yourself for the way you behaved the morning after." She pulls me to her and kisses me, her kiss even more aggressive than mine.

She reaches into my waistband, and as soon as her hand wraps around my cock, we both groan. And the time for words, while still very needed, evaporates as we frantically seek each other in the most primal way.

Celeste tugs down my sweats and boxers to expose my cock. She reaches for her purse that fell beside her and rummages through it.

"What are you doing?" I swipe my fingers through her folds. Fuck, she's so ready for me.

"I have a condom here somewhere." She pulls out a shiny square. "Voila."

She rips the wrapper, and we both watch as she slowly, delicately sheathes my engorged hardness. The moment is in stark contrast with the previous turmoil. It's like we need this reprieve to make sure we're on the same page.

When she's done, she circles her palm around my girth and squeezes gently. Her gaze finds mine, a challenge and a mild threat in her eyes.

And I take her wrath. I take it because I deserve it.

I take it because even though I'm not ready for it, I can't not have her.

But that's the only still moment before I hike her legs over my shoulders and plunge into her, like I can really punish us both.

Her for making me believe she was with someone else.

Me for caring. For fucking wanting her.

We fuck like we hate each other. And at this moment, we probably do. We might have gotten married on paper. But neither of us signed up for the complications.

For the onslaught of desire that has robbed us of common sense and self-preservation skills.

The room echoes with our slapping bodies and moans. Unlike the first time, Celeste doesn't need to be silent, and she expresses herself with abandon. And I can't get enough of it.

"Come for me, black swan," I growl, because I'm so close I teeter on the precipice.

It only takes one flick of my thumb over her clit, and she clenches, all her muscles tensing around me.

A few more thrusts and I follow, tilting my head and roaring my last tendrils of frustration into the ceiling.

We pant and glare at each other before I withdraw. She opens her mouth, but her eyes widen as the elevator dings. I pull my pants on, the full condom sagging awkwardly.

Leaning over the banister, I spot the visitor and swear under my breath. I slide Celeste to the side, as if that will help the situation.

"Wow, Cal, the view is spectacular!" Xander saunters in, two coffees in hand.

Fuck, he really got here early. He stops at the edge of the living room, squinting at me. Hopefully, the sun blinds him enough to hide what's just gone down here.

"You're here." I step further into the living room to give Celeste some privacy. She remains there without moving, and if he has noticed her, he doesn't let on.

He checks his watch. "Am I too early?"

"No, no. Why don't you go to my office? It's through that double door, down the hallway to the right. I need to grab something upstairs." I put my hands in my pocket and cross one leg over the other, feeling the condom sliding down.

"What? No tour?" He takes a step.

"Later," I snap. "Let's talk business first."

He narrows his eyes, then shrugs and moves to his left. I puff out a long breath.

I dash to her as soon as he disappears toward my office.

"Are you okay?" I help her stand up. Fuck, I hope the stairs didn't scratch her.

229

"Yes. Who is that?"

"Xander Stone, one of the partners at Merged."

She giggles at that. "Dieu merci he didn't come a minute sooner." Her gaze drops to my crotch. "You better get changed."

Sure enough, there's a stain on my sweats. "Yeah, I'm glad the condom didn't drop to the carpet in front of him."

She laughs and bends to gather her things. I slap her ass, and she yelps. "Hey!"

"You deserve that." I take a step up and turn to kiss her. "This is what you do to me. This is who I became after you cast your spell on me. My wild grew unhinged. My carnality has turned deviant. When I'm around you, my animal breaks all the cages and destroys all leashes. I hope you're ready for the consequences."

Chapter 21

Celeste

CORA

I really need to fire Lily.

You haven't done it yet?

CORA

She moved to NYC to become an actress and she has no other prospects.

Shit, but she can't be destroying your business.

SAAR

I'll talk to Finn, he might be able to help.

CORA

And fast, please.

"**O**kay, I think we can add that number at the beginning of the second act. See you tomorrow," Leon bellows, while we all yawn and groan from the rigorous rehearsal he's just put us through.

"The tyrant is grateful today, we should toast to that," Jose whispers in my ear as we move backstage.

I chuckle and yawn again. "I'm exhausted. I can't possibly go out tonight."

"Traitor." Jose bumps his hips against mine, but winks.

I shrug, stifling another yawn. I might have spent my night at the Park Avenue condo, but I certainly didn't sleep. It felt like a good idea to get away from Caleb.

I didn't mean to taunt him with that. In fact, I was sure he would welcome having me out of his hair. Out of his space. Out of his sight.

But the out-of-sight didn't work for me, because he remained on my mind. The. Whole. Fucking. Night.

At dawn, realization hit me. I've been acting like a victim. It took me that long, sleepless night to acknowledge Caleb made no promises.

Yes, he could have acted with more courtesy the following morning. But we both needed time to adjust and process, and with Mia around, we didn't have the space.

Still, I was wrong about it all. He didn't turn his charm down because he was done with me. He freaked out—even hated—that he wasn't.

I hope you're ready for the consequences.

Am I? The question has been on my mind all day. Would I willingly dive into a situation that screams heartbreak? I shouldn't.

And therein lies the problem. I want to.

It's like Caleb's orgasms robbed me of my self-preservation skills, my sanity, and my reasonable judgment. Like having fun with Caleb van den Linden is more important than protecting my heart.

Like we somehow connected, and he's now willing to play longer than usual, and I'm content to let him.

Could it work?

Perhaps, if I go into it without hope.

After my colleagues and I get changed, all of us file out and round the corner.

"Oh, look, your secret admirer is back, Celeste." Jose jerks his head to the other side of the street where a familiar SUV stands, just like that night when Caleb refused my *indecent* proposal.

My heart flutters, a smile stretching across my face. Caleb sent Peter to pick me up. Even though he's done that before, the gesture spreads warmth through me.

"I'll see you tomorrow," I call after my colleagues, and skip across the street.

The passenger window rolls down, and my husband's handsome face makes my heart stop and restart.

Our eyes lock, and butterflies flap between my stomach and my chest. *Don't catch feelings, sotte.*

The swooning is concerning because it threatens to break the boundaries I'm barely managing to keep up. Let's just have fun.

"I didn't expect a ride." I lean on my elbows in the window.

"Well, I need you to ride my cock, and it's a matter of emergency." He smirks. His gaze increases my temperature, sizzling and inescapable.

"An emergency?" I drawl, straightening up.

"Get in the fucking car now," he commands, opening the door.

Holy shit. I throw away all notions of a gentleman or feminism, because his demands might not speak to my intelligence, but they are a siren song to my body.

"What about Peter?" I whisper when I slide to the seat beside Caleb and the car moves.

"That's what the partitions are for." He cups my neck from behind and yanks me to him.

His kiss is urgent, almost desperate, like he really

couldn't wait a moment longer. His hand finds my breast while our tongues dance together.

My body responds to his closeness and his touch, goosebumps tingling across my skin while desire pools between my thighs.

We move with frantic urgency. My hands in his hair. His hands roaming, prodding, squeezing. Moans and grunts echo through the small space as we devour each other with insatiable hunger.

He hoists me and spins me round so I straddle him.

"What are we doing, Cal?" I cup his face, panting.

Like I already forgot my vow to just have fun. One kissing session pushed me close to that useless hope I promised to avoid.

He blinks a few times and then smirks. "Not fucking... yet."

Why am I pushing this? As if by laying it all out, I could control the outcome? I can't. And talking about it won't protect me either. People fall in love. People fall out.

The problem is, I can see myself easily falling for this man. While before he instilled insecurity in me, now he empowers me. Yeah, people fall in and out, but let's hope my fall won't be fatal.

"You know what I mean." I groan as his hands continue their exploration under my skirt, slipping into my panties and squeezing my ass.

"Why do we need to label it or name it? We're both enjoying this physical connection. We cleared the morning-after awkwardness, so let's just ride the wave."

His words pierce through me like poisoned arrows, while he returns to kneading my behind and kissing my neck.

The poison spreads through me, tearing my insides apart, melting them in a pang of disappointment.

Did we clear anything? Apparently, this morning's hate fuck cleared things out. *I hope you're ready for the consequences.*

But like an addict, I can't stop him.

Maybe it's seeing him warming up around his daughter.

Or the new level of sexual experience he pulled me into on the landing of his loft.

Or something unknown—unreasonable—that my awareness doesn't yet understand derails my survival instincts.

"But—"

He puts a finger over my mouth. "We can worry about tomorrow, or we can enjoy today. With the first, we'd only worry. With the latter, if tomorrow is shit, at least we had one day of fun."

I snort. "Is that your motto?"

He winks, moves his hands across my hips, and

shoves my underwear to the side, sliding his fingers between my folds.

"Looks like your pussy is on board with my life's philosophy. So wet for me, Celeste. Such a good girl."

I must be an undiscovered glutton for praise, because I push away any thoughts and grind my hips against his hand.

"Greedy." He chuckles.

He's right. What's the point in worrying about what might happen tomorrow, or a week from now? *Your heart might disagree*, a devil on my shoulder reminds me. *This is just fun.*

He plunges two fingers into me, and with his other hand he grabs my neck and pulls me to his lips.

The kiss is searing, fervent and so raw, it doesn't match his casual 'let's ride the wave' comment. I had meaningless sex before, and either Cal is a man who does everything with the utmost passion, or he's hiding his true feelings.

The first is a probability, the latter is only my hope. *No hope, sotte!*

I'm a performer, and I can pretend this is just a show. And like after any show, I'll step out of my role and decompress. That's the only way to survive him.

"You're so fucking gorgeous," he murmurs against my skin, licking, biting, kissing my jaw, my throat, my clavicle, all while lazily sliding in and out of me.

His words, his talented tongue and fingers do their tricks, and my arousal builds up, coiling around my spine, making me forget the conversation.

"Mon Dieu," I gasp, riding his hand like this is my last ever orgasm. And it might be. Because who knows what our expiration date is, and Caleb van den Linden ruined all other men for me.

"Let go, swan," he whispers, and crooks his fingers. *Merde.*

I fall over the edge so fast and hard I completely forget my surroundings.

Caleb withdraws his fingers and holds me tight, his nose buried in the crook of my neck. Another van den Linden contradiction. If this is just sex, the aftercare isn't necessary.

And yet here we are, the man holding me like I'm precious cargo. I can't stand it. We either play his game, or we lean into the one I'd like to explore. But we can't linger in between. Can we?

It's just fun. For as long as I can do this without getting properly hurt. I'm just a performer.

"I thought you wanted to fuck," I tease.

"I just fucked you with my hand... and you got orgasm-induced amnesia, apparently."

"Stop talking, pretty boy, and get that impressive cock of yours to work." I cup his hardness, slipping into the role of a playful lover. As casual and temporary as my husband wishes. It's in my best interest, after all.

"Impressive?" He drawls, smirking.

"Oh, no," I groan. "That was a slip."

He laughs. "Sure it was."

"Yeah, and now we'll die here, suffocated by your growing ego."

I crush my lips to his, and we grin and kiss at the same time. "Would you like my cock in your pussy, your ass, or your mouth, black swan?"

"Hmm, so many options." I unbuckle and unzip him, taking my time. I slide my hand into his waistband, and he groans.

"Choose now," he grunts, but before I can respond, he flips me, props me on my knees sideways on the leather seat, hiking my hips up.

It's uncanny how easily he manhandles me. It's concerning how much I love it.

Pushing up the hem of my dress, Cal rips off my underwear.

"Hey," I protest over my shoulder.

"You don't need them."

"I most certainly do."

"I'll buy you the manufacturer." He rips the condom wrapper with his teeth.

"But *I* can't buy an airplane?" I tease, and gasp immediately when he drives into me, shoving me forward. I plaster my hand on the window, holding on for dear life while he pounds into me, bruising my hips.

"Your pussy takes me so well, black swan. So tight, so right for me. Fuck. Are you going to scream my name finally?"

"Still—haven't—earned—it." I pant the words, the pleasure building up my spine.

My words push him into a frenzy of violent thrusts, like he's punishing me. I guess he doesn't have people denying him often.

And while it's not an upper hand in the partnership, it somehow gives me a minor consolation that I still hold some level of control.

Caleb wraps his arm around me, and his fingers find my clit. It doesn't take much until I feel myself clenching.

"That's my girl. Milk me dry." Somehow, he increases his piston-like tempo. Soon, I'm coming, and he follows me shortly after.

My cries are an incoherent chanting of French invectives, but his name is at the tip of my tongue.

Merde. I almost slipped.

* * *

Do you want to buy an airplane?" Caleb cuts off a small piece of his rare steak.

After we enjoyed the ride from the theater, he instructed Peter to take us to Modigliani's in Tribeca, because that's the only place with a decent steak, apparently.

"What?"

"In the car, you said you can't buy an airplane."

I only narrowly avoid spitting out the sparkling water I just drank. "I was teasing you. You know, when a man rips someone's underwear, he usually offers to replace the ripped pair, not buy the producer." I can't believe I need to explain this to him.

"It would be more efficient than buying you a new pair every time."

I burst out laughing as he grins at me. "You planning to rip off more of them? That's such a waste. What about the environment?" I tease.

"Says the woman who wants to buy an airplane."

My laughter is sudden and loud. "Are you ever serious?"

"Whatever for?"

"I don't know this side of you."

"Wrong. Swan, you've been so pissed at me all the time, you didn't get to acknowledge it." He makes a point of staring at my boobs when he says it.

"You're a pig."

"And you're finally enjoying every minute of it."

We eat our dinner without talking for a few minutes, but the fluid communication continues.

Intense glances, shared smiles, accidentally intended grazes of a knee, touched hands. Our silence is filled with a delicate bonding.

Physical-only arrangements shouldn't feel like this. I dismiss the thought as soon as it's born, and remind myself I'm still in my role as Caleb's casual lover. And I'll play that role with Oscar-worthy conviction.

"Talking about buying shit, did you know Mia dropped her dancing group because she couldn't afford it?"

His shoulders tense, and he grinds his teeth. "I gave her a credit card."

"What has she used it for?"

"I don't know."

"You don't know? You believe she's after your money, but you didn't check how much of it she's taken?"

He snaps his eyes to me, the former warmth visibly cooled. His jaw is set so rigid, he might need to visit a dentist if he doesn't relax.

Way to kill the moment, Celeste. "It's none of my business, sorry." I refocus my attention on my half-eaten fish, flaking it mindlessly.

Caleb squeezes my knee. "Don't be sorry. My relationship with Mia improved one hundred percent this weekend, and it's all thanks to you. You were right, I'm behaving like my father. The problem is, I don't really know how a father should behave."

"She just wants to be loved, and I know you can't switch it on just like that, but your attention is important."

"I'll check with my accountant what she's been spending money on. Thank you for telling me."

I smile at this man who is so confident in other parts of his life, and completely lost as a parent. But he can admit that, which is way more than many other parents would.

Certainly not my father. I shiver at the thought of him.

"You're welcome."

"I know you didn't sign up for an instant dysfunctional family..."

"You're lessening my hardship with all the orgasms. And I didn't sign up for those either."

He cups my nape and pulls me to him, his lips grazing mine. "What can I tell you, black swan? I deliver."

"And so humble."

We kiss, and I forget about the world, my visa, the fake marriage, and lose myself in the feel of this connection like it's just a normal date. Like this is a legitimate romance.

After dinner, we walk outside, and Peter opens the door for me. Before I slide into the back seat, Caleb stops me.

He pecks me on my forehead. "Peter will take you home. I have a late meeting. Don't wait up, get some rest."

He steps back, and Peter takes his place, like I'm a celebrity in need of a bodyguard. Probably he's just doing his job, or helping Caleb get away with this sudden bullshit.

Stunned, I drop to my seat. Before the door closes, a glimpse of Caleb's face leaves me completely unsettled.

He has a late evening meeting while guilt mars his face. Merde.

Chapter 22

Caleb

A piece of shit.

That's what I feel like.

The sun peeks through the slits of my blackout blinds. I stare at my ceiling instead of going to the gym. But it's not the lack of workout that's making me feel shitty.

Last night, at the restaurant, I had a thought. I saw myself arriving home with Celeste and taking her to my bedroom.

Simple? Yes.

Exciting? Yes.

Normal? No. Not for me.

I didn't lie when I told her no woman had ever visited my place. And no woman's ever slept in my bed. I don't do beds. Unless I'm alone.

For some fucked-up reason, I wasn't ready to admit that. Or to break this little rule of mine. Which left me with only one option—send her home alone, wait till she fell asleep, and then tiptoe to my room like a thief.

There are several firsts that happened here.

First time I actually would have invited a woman to my bed. If I wasn't a coward.

First time I'm more concerned about protecting someone else's feelings. Because I couldn't just drop her by her room's door.

First time I'm actually ready to grovel. Because fuck, we have a good thing going, and I'm not ready to give it up just yet.

I don't like any of these novelties.

Even though I'm not sure if she's even pissed. Or hurt. Or indifferent.

The last option churns in my stomach. Fuck.

Another thing churning inside me is the unequivocal realization that I'm a hypocrite. I want the woman, but only on my terms.

Having Mia appear in my life and then letting Celeste in... It's too much at the same time. No time to adjust, to reconsider my values.

My lifestyle has been uprooted, and I need time to digest. Hence the upset stomach.

Fuck, this will give me ulcers if I don't pull my head out of the gutter. Or pull the plug on all of this.

The latter stops me in my tracks. The idea of going back to the begrudging cohabitation with Celeste lies heavy on my chest, restricting my oxygen supply. What the fuck?

The doorman calls me about a delivery, and I make my way downstairs. Celeste is in the kitchen.

Her chestnut hair is in a tight bun, and she's wearing one of her casual dresses, though Celeste's casual is quite formal.

The dress is black, not her usual color, but it hugs her waist and shows her curves in all the right places. She doesn't see me, and I savor the moment for a bit.

She opens a cabinet. Always so graceful.

She rises on her tiptoes. Always so feline.

She takes a cup. Always so... uniquely Celeste.

She rubs her fingers against her neck, massaging her nape while she taps her foot, waiting for her coffee.

I lean against the post that brackets the entrance. "Good morning," I rasp when the elevator dings.

She swirls around and my heart rate spikes, pulsing on high alert. Dark circles shadow her eyes, her face bare of makeup.

She doesn't really acknowledge me, her gaze lifting above my shoulder toward the elevator.

"Good morning," the concierge calls out.

"You got a delivery." I turn slightly, so she has a better view of the enormous bouquet of red roses.

Shit, I might have overdone it. The concierge wobbles as he puts the large vase on the ground and turns to retrieve my other gift from the elevator.

"I haven't ordered anything," she scoffs.

"I did the ordering." I saunter over to her. "A gift."

She glares at me, her face set in a hostile facade.

When neither of us moves, the concierge clears his throat. "That'll be all, Mr. van den Linden."

"Right." I reluctantly leave her to cross the living room toward him. "Thank you." I give him a fifty-dollar bill and take the box from him.

He departs. Finally.

Though judging by Celeste's stormy expression, maybe I need a human buffer. When I look back, she's standing in the entrance to the kitchen, leaning where I was before.

Her green eyes gleam with something I can't quite understand, but it sends chills down my spine. She looks like the version of her from before we got married. When she hated me. When she had walls up all around.

Okay, time to grow up and own the shit. I approach her, my gaze not leaving hers. There's a challenge in hers, and I hope she can see the determination in mine.

"I think I caused some damage yesterday." I hand her the box.

Her eyes travel from my face to the box, but she

doesn't move, cradling her coffee. Okay, if I thought she might not be pissed, I now know she certainly didn't appreciate me leaving her behind last night.

A part of me recognizes that explaining why I did what I did would be the right thing to do here. But I'm not ready for that. *Coward.*

In the tense moments that follow, when she simply stares at the box in my hands, I can practically hear my heart beating in my chest.

I have no experience with groveling, but even without prior firsthand knowledge, it's obvious I'm not succeeding.

"Come on, open it." I try to sound casual.

A war brews behind her eyes, but then she sighs. A heavy, loaded sigh, like I'm an annoying sibling she doesn't want to deal with.

She puts her mug on the breakfast bar behind her and finally takes the box from me. Placing it beside her coffee, she opens the lid gingerly, like I might've laced it with poison.

Under the tissue paper, she finds thirty pairs of delicate panties.

She cocks her eyebrow. "I'm no longer getting the company?" She purses her lips, no muscle on her face suggesting she's joking.

I swallow. Fuck, I'm really not good at this.

"I wanted to make you happy." Christ, I need to stop talking if this is the shit that comes out.

She snorts. "Flowers and new underwear? Having a guilty conscience, pretty boy?"

The ice in her voice could fill all the slushy machines around the city.

"I'm sorry I left you alone last night." I step closer, but she folds her arms across her chest.

"Please, Caleb, you have no obligation to babysit me. I hope you had a nice *meeting*."

She snaps the lid closed, takes her cup, and walks into the living room, giving me a wide berth.

"Come on, Celeste. Talk to me."

She whips around at the foot of the staircase. "Look, Caleb, you don't owe me anything. You're free to have other liaisons. It's not like we discussed exclusivity, but it's shitty form to fuck me and then ditch me out of the blue."

Fuck, she thought I went to see another woman. That didn't even occur to me, but of course that would sound like a plausible explanation in the absence of facts.

"I had a meeting with Xander." I hate myself for lying to her, but I just can't bring myself to tell her the truth.

I went to the Madison Club and had a drink and

talked to a few people. All of them men. And that's not even the pathetic part of the truth.

We already broke all the boundaries of this arrangement, so what difference would it make if I took her to my bed?

But this is also about my personal boundaries, my basic principles. Ones I set up to protect myself.

From unnecessary complications.

From deeper connections.

From close dependence.

From deception.

Besides my siblings, everyone else I got close to betrayed me, starting with my parents. I'm the typical cliché of a rich boy with trust issues. Fuck. My. Life.

She sighs. "As I said, you don't owe me an explanation, but next time, could you give me a bit of a notice? I didn't beg you for your time. *You* came to pick me up." She extends her thumb, counting. "*You* took me for dinner." She points up her index finger. "*You* threw a tantrum when you thought I was with someone else." She adds another digit. "We spent hours together, and several times during that time, you could have mentioned that you had a meeting later and Peter would drop me off."

"I get it. I know I fucked up, hence the gifts." I shrug, not daring to approach her. Yet.

"I would prefer it if you didn't need to apologize

for your actions. You made me feel used and discarded."

Her bottom lip quivers, but she wipes the weakness away and squares her shoulders.

Fuck. Fuck. Fuck.

I close the distance between us. "I'm new at this. I have no point of reference for keeping a relationship alive. I fucked up, and I promise to try harder."

It's not lost on me that I'm still lying to her. But one step at a time. And have I just labeled this as a relationship?

"Look, Caleb, if this—whatever it is—is too much, too fast for you—"

"No, black swan. It's not enough." I step closer, crowding her. Her back hits the glass balustrade. "I thought getting a taste of you would be enough, but I was a fool. One nibble." I do just that, lowering my lips to her throat. "One bite." I sink my teeth into her warm skin.

Her chest heaves, but her body remains tense.

"One handful." I cup her breast. "One pinch." I twist her nipple between my thumb and finger. "One swallow of you, black swan, and I'm an addict."

I grind my hips against her as I lift my gaze to meet hers. She glares, but she doesn't protest.

And it might be just my wishful thinking, but her body relaxes a bit, engulfed with mine.

I lean down to pick up the hem of her dress and trace my fingers up her thigh. A whole-body shiver rakes through her and, fuck, I love her reaction, and that's before I skim the fabric of her panties.

"Look at you, all wet and ready for me."

"And still mad at you for ditching me."

"Let me make it up to you." I seize her mouth in an arresting kiss.

With my lips, I try to tell her what I can't yet with my words. I kiss her so she knows I didn't mean to ditch her. I had no intention of making her feel used or discarded. That I'm lost in her, and also lost in this arrangement.

Cupping the back of her neck, I pull her closer to me, trying to kiss away her worry, her anger, her indignation.

My worry. My panic. My distrust.

She moans into my lips. "Don't fucking do that again. Just tell me you have a meeting. You don't have to give me your schedule or whereabouts, but don't drop me like a used toy again."

I press my forehead to hers. "I promise." And I mean it. I might not be ready to take her to my bed, but I never want to make her feel the way I did last night.

She snakes her arms around my shoulders and pulls me to her, crushing her lips against mine before asking, "How many panties are in that box?"

"Thirty."

"Then rip off the pair I'm wearing. Now."

"You don't have to ask twice." I turn her around and pin her against the railing, her back molding against my body. "And one more thing, black swan. We. Are. Fucking. Exclusive."

Chapter 23

Celeste

SAAR

I got a job for Lily.

CORA

Does it include handling anything breakable?

Or anything edible?

SAAR

No, don't worry. I think she can manage this one.

CORA

I really hope so, I like her.

You shouldn't get too attached to your employees.

CORA

She is really, really nice.

You still have to let her go.

C aleb and I lie sprawled on the couch, neither of us in a hurry to move on with the day. It's moments like these, or the seamless conversations we have been enjoying, that take root in my chest, spreading content, warm feelings I don't want to dissect.

He pissed me off on Monday night, and I'm still not sure if I believe he had a meeting scheduled. It looked like a spur-of-the-moment decision.

All night, I wondered if he went to see another woman. Not that I had any right to wonder about that, but my mind took the idea for a spin like it was a shiny new car.

And one more thing, black swan, we are fucking exclusive. And that naive girl that still lives somewhere in me rejoiced.

The week after that carried in a fever of work and fucking on repeat. We've yet to make it upstairs, but I don't mind the urgency with which he devours me. Every. Single. Time.

I believe him when he says we're exclusive. I'm also quite aware of the expiration date on this. Our convenient arrangement morphed into an exclusive relationship, but Caleb has made it clear several times he would rather spend Christmas with his father than commit.

His infatuation will run its course eventually. So as his hands run mindlessly through my hair and down my back, stroking lazily, I let myself enjoy the languid quiet of my post-climatic daze, while I regroup to step out of the role and regain my independence.

Caleb's phone buzzes, and he groans and pats the floor to find where it landed at some point.

"Yes."

I hear a male voice, and then Caleb continues, "Send it up. Thank you."

"Another delivery?" I ask as we both scramble to straighten our clothes.

I get a gift every day. I don't need them, but they work their magic like his praise does. They've been thoughtful, like he got a manual to everything Celeste. I got a massage. A box of croissants. A small but valuable painting. A beautiful vintage watch. I'll never wear it, but it's the thought that counts. The fact that he noticed the state of the one I wear.

"Cookies."

That's all he says, and I swear his cheeks color pink a bit. There's always a jar of homemade cookies in his kitchen, but I assumed the housekeeper stocked them.

I tried one before, and quickly stashed the jar into a closed cabinet because those things are addictive, and I couldn't have them on display at the breakfast bar.

Caleb tips the concierge and carries the jar to the

kitchen. This is so bizarre. "I didn't know you had such a sweet tooth."

"They're just a gift." He drops the jar on the counter and busies himself with the espresso machine. "Do you want coffee?"

"No, but I would like to know who sends you cookies. Regularly." I open the cabinet and point to the other glass jar with identical goods.

The grinder's rumbles fill the room while Caleb casually walks to the box with my new underwear.

It's quite ridiculous it still lies in the kitchen, but Caleb insisted he needs access to it. And we usually get too *busy* to tidy anything up.

He inspects the contents and pulls a pair out. "Wear these today."

"Stop deflecting. Who bakes for you?"

Leaning down, he shoves the panties into my cleavage and breathes—just fucking breathes—at the sensitive spot on the side of my neck. "Are you jealous, black swan?"

His warm breath sprouts goosebumps all over my skin, and I shudder. This man can direct my body like an award-winning conductor.

"Well, since baking isn't something I can compete with..." I tease.

Stepping back, he feigns shock and puts his hand

where his heart is. "You didn't disclose your lack of domestic skills before I wed you."

I laugh. "It's a good thing you can hire a chef, but don't try to distract me from this. What's the cookies' story?"

He groans. "They're from my former nanny."

I don't know what I was expecting, but it wasn't this. "Your former nanny still bakes cookies for you?"

"It's not what you think." He shakes his head, picks up his coffee, and takes a cookie from the jar. After taking a bite and downing it with his shot of java, he sighs. "I found out recently that my father fired her when she didn't reciprocate his advances. He refused to give her a reference and got her blacklisted from working as a nanny for pretty much anyone in New York.

"She ended up on welfare. She's been struggling for years. I got her a job, and I bought her a small apartment last year. She insisted on at least baking for me."

He tells the story devoid of emotion, like the whole thing is an embarrassing nuisance.

On instinct, I reach to take a cookie and step closer to him where he's leaning against the counter. I bite into the scrumptious disk. "You're a good man, Caleb."

"Not really. My father is a terrible man, so I trade fairer." He snakes his arm around me and cups my nape before he claims my lips.

It's a lingering kiss, no urgency or raw desperation. Just two people sharing a moment in the kitchen. The languid spell of it stretches, along with my heart.

This man surprises me daily, and I don't quite know how to reconcile that with the image I've always had of him.

His phone shrills to life again, and he groans.

"God, I hope it's not another delivery." I laugh, but tense when Caleb shows me the display before answering. *Dominic Cressard.*

"Be fast. I'm in the middle of something." Caleb doesn't bother with a greeting.

I swat at his chest, rolling my eyes while he taps the speaker icon and drops the phone on the counter.

"I can call later," Dominic says, unimpressed.

"Or you can get it over with now." God, how is this the same man who turned his former nanny's life around?

He fists my hair and guides me to him for another kiss. He eats my protest with his greedy mouth, running his hands up my ribcage.

"I tried to reach your *wife*," Dominic laces the word with sarcasm, and it's a good thing my mouth is otherwise occupied because I would tell him what I think about his attitude. I might not be able to claim a loving relationship, but on paper, I'm. The. Wife. No sarcasm warranted.

But I forget my indignation when he continues, "Her work permit came through."

We pull away, and I can't help it. I bounce on the balls of my feet, shaking my hips in a celebratory dance.

"Thank you, Dom. That's good news," Caleb says before he kisses me again.

"My bill is in your inbox." Dominic hangs up. No one ever praised lawyers for their bedside manner.

"Congratulations, you can dance for the audience again."

"Finally. I'm sure Reinhard will not be happy."

"What do you mean? You're the star of the show."

"First, you haven't seen the show. But despite its success, the theater director has been treating me like I'm the bane of his existence pretty much since I started."

A frown passes over his face, but it's gone before I'm even sure it was there, and his signature sexy smirk settles over his handsome features. "I went to your premiere. That asshole should be happy he got you to dance there."

"You were at opening night?"

"Sure." He shrugs and takes another cookie. "I have something to show you." He grabs my hand, but his phone pings loudly again.

He came to the opening night? The night after we

261

spat words at each other during dinner with Saar? Before I needed his help with the visa? *Sure. Sure?*

"Jesus Christ," he murmurs and swipes at his screen, pulling me closer.

XANDER

Sorry, man, I fought him on this.

I'm still stunned by his casual revelation, and perhaps I shouldn't see the message, but he holds me close and doesn't hide it. "What does he mean?"

"I have no idea. I'll call him later." Pocketing the phone, he drags me from the kitchen.

"Are you sure? It must be about the deal." We cross the living room, and my mind is misfiring in so many directions.

I have no time to digest any of it—the week of a very real-feeling relationship, him buying apartments for struggling former employees, attending my premiere, all his gifts, my work permit. And now he just casually, but with determination, wants to show me something, ignoring his potential business partner.

Give a girl a whiplash, anyone?

"They have been jerking me around long enough. I'm sure a few more minutes won't change much."

"Caleb, this is your future career," I protest as he pulls me up the stairs.

"And this will take only a moment."

At the top, the hall splits to the right where our bedrooms are, and to the left where Mia's room is across from a guest bedroom.

Caleb leads me away from our rooms, his hand warm around mine. He stops in front of the spare bedroom. "Have a look."

I frown. "Are you moving me to a separate *wing*? You'll still run into me, you know that, right? This place is enormous, but it's not that huge."

He scoffs, "Stop talking and open the door."

What is so interesting in a spare bed—?

I gasp.

Mirrors cover one entire wall, reflecting the soft glow of the natural light streaming in from the large windows. A pristine wooden floor stretches out, inviting, begging for the touch of dancing feet.

The sound system tucked neatly into the corner completes the simplicity of the room. It's all perfect, every detail thoughtfully arranged.

What was once a luxurious guest room has been transformed into a dancer's haven.

My heart pounds against my ribcage while my eyes well up. "How? When? Why?" I can't seem to form a coherent sentence.

"How? I hired people who came when you were at rehearsals."

"How do you even coordinate a construction crew

with my schedule?" How does he even know my schedule?

He shrugs, leaning against the door frame. "Do you like it?"

I twirl around, the wooden panes smooth under my feet. "But why?"

"You mentioned the carpet in your room was a problem."

"I could have practiced downstairs. You practically have a ballroom stretching in front of the elevator."

"Sure. I love coming home to an eyeful of your ass, but I'm not bleaching the eyes of the concierge and delivery boys. Especially with all the deliveries we get." He smirks.

His phone steals our attention.

"Fuck. I better take care of this."

My fake husband walks away, leaving me in my new personal dance studio. The potent cocktail of emotions shuddering through me almost brings me to my knees.

Elation. Joy. Appreciation.

Shock. Confusion. Fear.

We're just having fun. My mantra is becoming harder and harder to believe.

I'm drunk with all my conflicting feelings. Because I'm a performer, I can try to slip in and out of my fake wife's role. But that role feels less and less fictional.

I glance around the room once more, unsure how to shake the foreboding feeling. Because my husband can disperse gestures of kindness like candy, but where does that leave me?

Am I a convenient lay?

Am I more?

Or am I another charity case for him? Caleb to the rescue, solving everyone's problems.

But the biggest problem is that at the end of the day, I know that I'm irrevocably destined to have my heart broken.

Chapter 24

Caleb

"What the actual fuck, Cal? Out of all people, you leave to work with that motherfucker?" Finn didn't even want me to come to our—his—offices.

The server at the Madison Club bristles, halting three feet from our table, the two plates with our lunch wobbling in her hands.

I smile at her, and she looks at my seething brother, then takes one more step.

He notices her and gestures for her to bring the food to our table. I've never seen someone serve food so fast, and I grew up in the hospitality industry.

"Can I get you anything else?" she asks, maintaining a professional and very forced smile.

Finn scoffs at her, clarifying that the only thing we

want is privacy. The poor woman scurries away, leaving me alone with my brother's wrath.

I'll be sure to tip her generously, and I'd laugh at the scene. But my current situation is not humorous.

"Calm down, asshole." I put a napkin across my lap as if I have any appetite.

"The only asshole here is you, Cal." Finn tears apart his salmon with a fork like it offended him. "What will Saar say?"

"Saar knows."

This stops him in his violent food attack. He pins me with a look of disappointment and, fuck, I think hurt. "I see."

"No, Finn, you don't see. You called me here to throw a tantrum while you know shit about the situation. And you judge based on some forgotten feud without giving me the benefit of the doubt."

He inhales to protest, but I stop him with my hand. "You're not my fucking father, so don't act like him. You, out of all people, should understand."

Closing his eyes momentarily, he sighs, his jaw still ticking with frustration or perhaps with a bit of regret. "Fuck." He drops the fork and pushes his plate away, the salmon thoroughly cut and uneaten.

"You should get some protein in you, so you don't get cranky." I smirk.

He glares at me, but I push my plate away as well because eating is the last thing on my mind.

"Fuck, Cal. So Saar is okay with this?"

Of course he's concerned about her, and I'm glad his anger came from that protective place. But as much as I hate to admit it, I wish he was concerned about me.

"She's okay with it."

Finn nods and leans back in his chair, observing me.

I guess if I want to discuss it more, he's not going to initiate. "She is, but I'm not."

Finn flinches. "What the fuck, Cal? Did he manipulate you? Blackmail you? Why didn't you come to me sooner?"

"Finn, I swear to God, cut the fucking parental routine or this conversation is over. I need your advice."

He plays with his wedding band, a new habit of his when he's thinking, and then he nods. It's all he does, but we've known each other our whole lives, and I know I've got his attention.

"I've been in conversation with Merged, the three partners, since the day I left—"

He opens his mouth, but I stop him again. "Chill, it's not the reason I left. I wasn't planning to launch into something new, but fuck, Finn, their concept just speaks to me."

I give him a top-line overview of the Merged mission and vision, and he listens intently, interrupting with a question here and there.

"Okay, I see how the company is a good fit for you. But the partners?"

"That's where it's all screwed up."

After I left Celeste in her new dance studio and called Xander, it was too late to pump the brakes on Cormac fucking Quinn's plans to lock in my involvement. The asshole announced the new company and its partners with a press release.

"Not surprising with Quinn involved. What happened?" Finn asks.

"I wanted to secure my position, and we've been negotiating my share."

"That's smart." Finn picks up his glass of water.

"We haven't agreed on anything yet."

Finn stops with his hand halfway to his mouth. "The announcement named you as a partner."

"Yep. I guess the answer to your question—if he tried to blackmail me—is yes."

"That motherfucking piece of shit. But what does he gain? You can simply announce he made it up and he'll look like an idiot."

I play with my lunch like that will help me time travel, or kill Quinn without consequences.

"Cal? What did he have to say for himself?"

"I haven't spoken to him yet."

"What?"

"Mostly because I'm too pretty to go to prison for manslaughter."

He crooks his eyebrow, unimpressed.

I blow out the air from my cheeks. "I wanted your advice."

"Talk to your lawyer. You can potentially slap him with a slander suit."

And this is the part where I struggle. "You're right, but at the end of the day, I would be the one losing. The opportunity was something that I wanted to do because it just made me tick. Not because Daddy dearest groomed me for it all my life. Not because it was expected from me. But it was something I could see myself enjoying."

"Cal, it was your first opportunity to pop up after you left. There will be a gazillion more. There always are. If you like the concept, consider your negotiation with the fucker market research and invest in a similar project. One that will be your own. Beat him at his own game."

"I don't have enough available capital to pull that off. Besides, I don't want to be a CEO. Too many fucking responsibilities in that job that I hate."

Finn checks his watch. "Shit, I have a meeting now, but think about it and let's talk again. And I'd be happy to invest in a company that would go into direct competition to Corm fucking Quinn."

"Good to know."

He stands up, but pauses. "How's married life?"

God, I want to wipe that smirk off his face. "Fuck off, Finn."

He laughs. "Just play it nice. If you hurt Celeste, Paris will cut your dick off. She's very attached to her former dance teacher, and frankly, I'm attached to the moves she learned from her."

"TMI, I don't want to know about your wife's moves. And rest assured, I can't hurt Celeste. It's a fake fucking marriage."

But as I watch him leave, I wonder if that's still true.

I wonder about it even more when, dejected by the lack of resolution for my problem this meeting gave me, I pull my phone out and call the one person who I instinctively know might not have a solution, but will give me some comfort.

Celeste shows up half an hour later, her beautiful figure clad in a pencil skirt and a blouse with a plunging neckline. She's delicious.

"You got changed." I kiss her cheeks when the club hostess leaves her at my table.

"I needed a shower after testing my new amazing dance studio." She shimmies her shoulders, beaming, but then turns serious. "Don't worry, I'm wearing the underwear you requested." She takes a seat beside me and a shiver runs down my spine.

"Thank you for coming on a whim like this." I take her hand, kissing her knuckles.

She smirks. "Don't get used to it. I'm still buttered up after you changed an entire room for me."

Fuck, I did change a room for her. Like she's there to stay. I shake my head. Mia can practice there as well, after all.

Craning her neck, she scans the large members-only restaurant through the arched opening of our private dining area. "So this is where the most powerful men of Manhattan meet?"

I chuckle. "Some of them are the most powerful in the world."

"Don't say that, because you'll have to get me an unlimited guest pass."

"You can come anytime as my guest." I run my hand up her back, enjoying the subtle shiver my touch elicits.

"Good. Imagine who I can meet here. I plan to marry up after our divorce."

She's teasing me, but the idea curls my fingers into fists. Oblivious to my reaction, she gasps. "Is that Andrea Cassinetti?"

I turn in the direction of her gaze, and sure enough, the famous artist is glaring at the man across from him.

Celeste is all giddy beside me, like the fucker's some kind of celebrity. Enough is enough.

"Eyes on me," I growl.

She whips her head to me, and I expect her usual sass, but instead, her eyes shine with something I can't quite name.

It's raw. Primal. Full of heat.

Like my claim aroused her, but also surprised her. We stare at each other for a moment, the room fading into the background, my current problems turning frail, a distant vexation.

And then her face transforms into the brightest, warmest, most radiant smile, and it hits my chest with a spellbinding intensity.

She is irresistible with her cheeks flushed, the green in her eyes glimmering, and wearing the underwear I selected for her.

She hasn't screamed my name yet, stubborn woman, but right now, in this moment, she feels like mine. And for the second time today, I wonder just how fake this marriage is.

The implication of that thought seems to fill the space between us, because Celeste blinks and recoils—it's a brief change in her facade, but I notice.

And a part of me is grateful she broke the spell.

She squares her shoulders. "Is this a booty call, pretty boy?"

"Don't give me ideas." I glance at the room outside our little enclave. Private enough.

The server comes to take Celeste's order, and I take the interruption to set my head straight.

Pulling my phone out, I find the Merged announcement and show it to Celeste. She scans the page, her eyes widening, and then she frowns.

"I didn't know you signed the deal."

"I didn't."

"But—" Quickly, the implications dawn on her. "Merde. What are you going to do?"

I shrug and grab a carafe to fill our glasses with water, just to do something. "Finn thinks I should sue him and take his concept to start a competing company."

"Wouldn't that be unethical?"

"It's not like venture capital, mergers, and acquisitions are copyrighted concepts..." I take a sip of my water, wondering why I haven't ordered something stronger.

"But you don't want to do that, do you?"

"A part of me was settled on the idea. I was pushing for a bigger share, but I was almost ready to cave. But if I accept this under the current circumstances, it will taint anything I do there. I would basically be giving in to blackmail."

It's so much easier to let my thoughts run in front of Celeste than it was with Finn, which is refreshing but also weird.

Finn has always been my sounding board. Celeste, however, seems to slide into that role effortlessly.

"You didn't like the guy to begin with, so after this move, can you imagine working with him?"

I sigh. "I'm not going to be someone else's doormat."

"Of course not." She puts her hand on my thigh and my cock springs to attention. "I can only draw from my own field. Dancers often hate each other. The competition is fierce, the number of leading roles limited, and everyone is replaceable.

"Over the years, I've worked with people who would stab me with their high heel, but the minute we hit the stage, we all pull together for the common goal—to create an entertaining, lasting performance. You don't need to like Cormac or trust him in general, but do you trust he'll put the company and its success first?"

I've never thought about it, but I wouldn't have discussed the partnership with him if I'd sensed he was there to fuck it all up.

In fact, him forcing my hand proves he wants to hit

the ground running and lock down all the leads we have. And I want to close the deals I've been working on in the background.

"So you think being a doormat is justifiable for the greater benefit?" That part doesn't sit well with me. Because business is one thing, but I can't put my pride to one side.

"He blindsided you, but he played his hand and has no cards left." A smile lingers on her face.

And it hits me. I really have been so blindsided and pissed about Corm's betrayal that I didn't think straight. How did I not see that? Fuck, she's smart. And fuck if it doesn't make her a hundred times more sexy.

I stand up, my chair balancing on its two back legs. "Let's go." I pull Celeste to standing and drag her across the busy restaurant.

She gasps, her heels clicking in a distorted rhythm as she tries to keep up. "What's the rush? I wanted to meet Andrea Cassi—"

"Celeste," I warn, and the wench laughs.

And the sound—however mocking—reverberates in my chest with an unfamiliar, but not unpleasant, feeling.

But I don't have time to dissect that.

Chapter 25

Caleb

"I don't understand why I'm coming with you," Celeste grumbles.

The elevator stops on the sixteenth floor, and the last person in the car finally exits before we move up to the twenty-seventh where the Merged offices are.

I turn around and crowd her, pushing her into the corner. Before she reacts, I kiss her like she's the last source of oxygen on earth.

She whimpers into my mouth, and I want to fucking hit the emergency stop button and force her to finally scream my name.

But the door dings and I have to jerk away. Her lips swollen, she glares at me. I don't blame her. I've been acting like a madman.

"Just bear with me, black swan. I'm having a shitty

day, and you're making it better." I take her hand and we step outside.

Roxy is waiting there. She flinches, her lips setting into a straight line as she assesses Celeste. Okay, maybe bringing your wife to your future workplace isn't the best idea.

Roxy recovers quickly and puts on her welcoming smile. "They're waiting for you, Mr. van den Linden."

"Call me Cal. Could you please get my wife something to drink, Ro?"

"Cal, I'll certainly make sure your wife is comfortable while she waits for you. Please don't ever call me Ro."

"My apologies, Roxy." Okay, I like her. "I won't take long." I smile at Celeste.

She glares at me. Why I brought her is beyond me, but somehow I needed to know that she'd be on the other side of the door when I exited the battleground.

I wink at her, and she rolls her eyes. Chuckling with renewed energy, I march toward Corm's office.

"At least one of them is taken. If one more candidate swoons over the rest of them during their interview, I'll claw my eyes out," Roxy says, I'm assuming to Celeste, and I turn to look back.

Celeste looks like she'd rather walk barefoot on broken glass, but she smiles at Roxy, and I leave them there, almost certain the two of them might assume world domination while I'm gone.

I don't bother to knock because Corm is expecting me. I'm not even surprised Xander and Declan are in the office with him.

They must be waiting for my move since they've pulled theirs. Besides, the security from downstairs gave them a heads-up. Hence Roxy's *warm* welcome.

"Caleb." Corm greets me like I came for a friendly visit.

"Asshole," I respond, and don't bother to acknowledge the other two men in the room.

"Oh, come on, it's not like the outcome would be different if we waited for you to come around. I respect the fight you put up, but I needed to move things along." He gestures to the coffee table.

Xander and Declan are sitting there. Xander looks pissed—I'm guessing he really fought against the announcement. Declan looks bored, which I think is his regular countenance.

I sit down in the same chair I occupied when I first came here. The level of intrigue is very different.

Corm sits across from me and pushes a folder in my direction. Pulling a fountain pen from his pocket, he places it on the folder without saying anything.

I push his pen to the side and open the folder. The partnership contract includes everything we discussed, and it names me a partner with twenty-three percent in the company.

"I met you halfway," Corm drawls.

If he's in any way nervous about how this will go, he doesn't show it.

My gaze turns to Declan. "Did you agree with his blackmail tactic?"

Declan doesn't move. He doesn't shift in his seat or clear his throat while he holds my gaze. He takes his time before he answers. "We have several deals at the point of signature. We couldn't afford any further delays."

That's almost like admitting he was on board with Corm's backstabbing. My research revealed very little about Declan's relationship with his brother, but I assume he agreed with the plan too.

The older Quinn seems to be kind of a recluse since his wife left him, but he's a financial wizard. Will these two always gang up against me?

But then Declan adds, "That being said, I read the announcement in the news probably at the same time as you." His gaze flicks to Corm, his jaw set.

So Corm didn't even tell his brother. I turn to Xander. "What about you?"

I don't think it's a secret I talk to Xander outside of this office, but I don't want Quinn to know the extent of our friendship.

"Frankly, I'm considering cutting my losses and pulling out after this."

Corm almost fucking rolls his eyes. "Okay, I apologize to everyone, and I promise I'll respect your opinions in the future."

That makes me laugh. "Your promise is worth shit, since nobody in this room trusts you."

"I couldn't afford to wait any longer, Cal, so I gave you a little nudge. I can guarantee you won't regret this."

The dark circles under his eyes run deep. The man looks exhausted, but I doubt a guilty conscience is at fault here.

"Good, you can guarantee by amending this." I tap my finger on the paperwork in front of me. "I want thirty percent."

Corm bristles, but to his credit, it only takes him a moment before he realizes his move might have been a check, but I came to deliver a mate.

"Either I walk out of here with thirty percent, giving me the same level of control you have, or you can let everyone know the first deal Merged ever announced—its own inception—was just a joke. I'm sure that'll bode well for any future deals." I lean back into the comfortable cushions of the chair, not even trying to tame my gloating.

"Actually, I'd feel more comfortable with such a

distribution of influence and control." Xander nods, smirking.

Declan remains bored-looking, like this has nothing to do with him.

And my lifelong nemesis, to his credit, knows when to own his fuck-up and admit defeat. He stands up and walks to his desk, picking up the landline.

"Roxy, can you please print the partnership contract again with the following change: Cormac Quinn, CEO, thirty percent, and Caleb van den Linden, COO, thirty percent." His gaze is on me while he talks, a mixture of loathing and respect. "Roxy, if I cared about your opinion, I would have asked. Bring the paperwork ASAP." He slams the receiver down, the pen holder beside it toppling.

He sits back, and a sense of accomplishment and anticipation descends on me. I trust only one other person at this table, yet my gut tells me I won't regret my decision.

"So should we pop champagne?" Xander relaxes in his seat.

Both Quinns look at him like he's just suggested karaoke at a funeral, but then Corm shakes his head. "Fuck it."

He walks to a sleek white cabinet in the corner and produces a bottle of Macallan 1926 and four tumblers.

"I can't believe I'm opening this with you assholes, but the occasion calls for a respectful celebration."

He pours an inch from the bottle that cost more than a million dollars for each of us to toast our new partnership. The mood in the room is an outlandish mixture of excitement and frustration.

There's a knock at the door, and Roxy walks in before anyone answers. "I don't get a taste, *boss?*"

"Of course, you're a valuable team member." Xander jumps up and takes the paperwork from her. "Isn't that so, Corm?"

Corm's gaze lands on the bottle in his hands. "Of course," he mumbles, and pours for our office manager.

He glances at each of us and raises his glass. "To the best company ever."

I can toast to that, because something tells me we might have had a bumpy start, but this ship will take us places.

* * *

"Sorry it took so long." I smile when I return to the front desk with Roxy.

Celeste stands up, glaring, but then her curiosity wins. "So?"

"Roxy, will you please show me my office," I drawl,

and the smile that spreads on Celeste's face is probably as rewarding as the win.

Funny how such a simple, silent show of support can make my chest swell. It might be because I never had anyone cheering for me. Our parents considered any win just an opportunity to move to the next target.

My father, while I worked for him, was always more focused on pointing out failures.

Or maybe it's just that this woman's support makes me feel like I'm a better man. Like earning her approval is what makes me or breaks me.

"Of course, Cal."

I lace my fingers through Celeste's and navigate the hallway, following Roxy. She stops in front of a corner office.

"Welcome aboard." The office manager opens the door. "I'll ask the interior designer to come by tomorrow, so you can design it properly. Press o on your landline if you need anything, and I'll schedule a proper onboarding with you for later today."

"Thank you, Roxy."

I pull Celeste inside and close the door.

The office contains a desk, a standard set of cabinets, and bookshelves, making it sparsely furnished. All from a quality dark wood that lends a stuffiness to the space, but the two connected walls of glass overlooking Manhattan soften the feel.

"I'll make sure to frame one of our wedding photos for your desk." Celeste crosses her arms across her chest, probably still annoyed I dragged her here for nothing.

"Come on, celebrate with me." I pull her to me and capture her mouth.

"You got your twenty-five percent?" she murmurs against my lips.

"No." I thrust my tongue, savoring her. I can't believe I had her only this morning and it wasn't enough.

This morning? Fuck, it's like a lifetime has passed since.

She moans and we stumble, her ass hitting my new desk. She pulls away. "What do you mean, no?"

"I got thirty."

Her eyes widen, and maybe I just want to see it, but I could swear a jolt of pride flickers in her eyes. "So you'll be even richer," she drawls.

I pinch her ass. "That's where your mind goes?"

She gyrates her hips against me, smiling. "I'm with you for your money only, pretty boy."

I've only known two kinds of women. The gold diggers who would never admit out loud that your bank account is what they love, and the proud, independent kind who make too much fuss about me spending on them.

I didn't care either way, because I was in it for my fun and selfish satisfaction, but with Celeste, it's different. She isn't annoyingly fighting me about what I spend on her. But she also teases me about my wealth, and it's so refreshing.

She doesn't need my money, but she takes it when I offer a gift or help. Like she knows her value and doesn't need to play on greed or overt modesty.

I quirk up my eyebrows. "I thought it was for your visa."

We grin at each other, refusing to admit this is about more than her visa or my money, but feeling it, nevertheless.

A Hollywood smile, a politician's promise, or Monopoly money in a real estate deal—those are all fake. What's sprouting between me and this woman feels anything but.

"Congratulations."

One word that hits me in my solar plexus and continues to creep into all the darkened crevices of my soul.

Her praise. Her approval. Her support.

I'm like a child starved for a hug or a kiss. She gives them freely and genuinely, and I can't see myself letting go of this. The little boy in me is validated.

The man in this room wants to lock down the fluttering feelings and never revisit them again. Getting

Celeste's approval is like having one taste of her. Devastating.

Because I can't have just one.

And I don't need it.

I want it. I desire it. I crave it.

I don't need it, but going on without it will leave a permanent scar.

"I have you to thank for it. If you didn't point out earlier—"

"You would have realized it yourself. You were just too distracted by your initial—justified—reaction to the betrayal."

"Still, you fast-tracked that process."

"What can I say, I'm not just a pretty face," she quips, her nails scraping up my back, sprouting goose-bumps in their wake.

"You see, black swan? And you were worried I have nothing to gain from this arrangement."

I don't tell her I'm gaining way more than I ever imagined. And while my expectations were pretty low —even on the negative side—the reality's snuck up on me with a vengeance.

The most unexpected, fiery, green-eyed surprise I never knew I needed in my life. And I'm going to make the best of it.

While it lasts.

Chapter 26

Celeste

SAAR

I'm quitting my job.

CORA

Oh, no, is the shoot that bad?

SAAR

I don't mean the shoot, I mean I'm done with modeling.

Do elaborate.

SAAR

I hate it. I'm hungry, angry, exhausted, and most of the time abused.

What happened?

CORA

OMG What's going on?

SAAR

Sorry, I'm just tired I think. I miss you.

"Y ou really didn't have to drive me, Peter."

"Mr. van den Linden insisted you use the car when he doesn't need it, which is happening a lot lately."

It's been four weeks since we christened Caleb's new office thoroughly. I will never look Roxy or anyone at Merged in their eyes again. And yet, I don't regret any moment, touch or moan.

Since that day, however, Caleb has been working. Working more, and stealing too few moments with me.

I wish we had more time for each other, but with my renewed work permit and his workload, we're both too busy.

To Caleb's credit, even under immense pressure to announce his first win at Merged, he's found time to see me—and fuck me—at least three times a week.

Either he sneaks into my shower in the morning, or sends Peter to pick me up and get me to wherever he just finished a meeting, or we squeeze in a lunch in his office—no food included.

The evenings when I don't perform can sometimes feel lonely, but I'm usually so tired I fall asleep as soon as I hit the pillow.

And even when he's not there, Caleb always sends me my favorite takeout or a bottle of wine. Or a gift. The man really has no spending brakes.

"I'm glad I have something to do," Peter says as he pulls into the slow Manhattan traffic.

A pang of guilt swirls in my stomach. I've been complaining about being driven while I didn't realize that Peter's livelihood depends on it. Especially now when Caleb doesn't use him as often as before.

"How long have you been working for Caleb?"

"Only a year, but I've known him for much longer."

"How?" I perk up and lean forward. I don't suppose Peter would betray Caleb's trust and share much, but I don't want to waste the opportunity to learn more about the man.

Peter flicks his gaze at me in the rearview mirror and then back to the road, shifting in his seat.

I guess I got excited too fast. I slide my butt back on the smooth leather and smile. "Sorry, I didn't mean to pry."

Peter doesn't acknowledge my apology, nor does he answer my question, which only piques my curiosity. But I don't want to make him uncomfortable with my interrogation, so I pull my phone out to check my messages when he suddenly continues.

"Young Mr. van den Linden is a good man. He has a wild side to him, but neither he nor his brother are like their father." His words are laced with contempt.

"You used to work for the senior." It's a statement

as I read between the lines of what he said. "Did he fire you unjustly?"

"That's not how he would see it." Peter snorts. This is the first time he's exhibited any emotions. The man is the epitome of stoicism.

"And Caleb found out and gave you an opportunity," I conclude with certainty.

I've always thought it a rich boy's whim to be driven around, even though he doesn't really need it in the city.

Especially since Caleb is a man who doesn't mind taking an Uber. And he despises status because that's the only thing his father values.

But employing a man who was probably abused by the older van den Linden and the power he loves to misuse, that's a different story.

A story that spreads a warm feeling through me, leaving me oddly conflicted about everything Caleb.

"Yeah..." Peter looks like he wants to elaborate, but instead he studies me in the mirror while we wait on a red light. And then he decides, I think, that he can trust me. "One might think he does all the good deeds to spite his father. But every time I do the pharmacy pickups for their old housekeeper, she tells me stories from his childhood when he would fight for every bullied kid, bring home every stray pet, or help her behind his parents' backs."

As much as I would like to laugh at this, because the playboy I know doesn't seem to bode well with the kind memories, I believe all of them.

But why does Peter... "You do pharmacy runs for their old housekeeper?"

"Only when Mr. van den Linden can't." Peter flinches. "I'm sorry, Mrs. van den Linden, I shouldn't be talking about his personal business. My apologies."

"I won't tell on you, Peter, but I appreciate you sharing with me."

It sheds more light on the man I married for a visa, crumbling my desperate efforts to keep my heart at arm's length.

* * *

> Cora added +212 658 7487 to this conversation
>
> SAAR
> Who is that?
>
> CORA
> Lily. I hope you don't mind.

"I'll be right with you." Cora hugs me when I enter the bistro.

There's a young man behind the counter, and Lily sits at our usual table.

Cora rushes over to the man who is polishing glasses, and I take a seat across from Lily.

"I hope you don't mind that Cora invited me to join you today." Lily smiles tentatively.

"Of course not. I'm glad. How are you?"

"The new job at the concierge service is great. All day long I'm helping people to book appointments, make reservations, research things, and simply organize their lives. I think I'm better at it than... " She looks at Cora and her new employee.

"That's good to hear." I laugh. "I'm sure your clients keep you busy. Sometimes money comes with an unhealthy dose of eccentricity."

"Or misguided entitlement," she whispers, and looks away like she's just imparted a trade secret.

"As someone married to a rich guy, I can attest some of them are normal. Equally fucked up as the rest of us."

"That's good to know." Lily worries her lip, lost in her thoughts.

Even though she's a few years younger than me, she is still older than I was when I arrived in this city. But I guess it's hard to start from scratch and follow one's dreams with empty pockets.

I want to encourage her, but Cora plops in beside me. "How is married life treating you?"

I let out a loaded breath. "It's too good."

As each day passes, it's harder to play the role of a fake wife with benefits. It's becoming impossible to step out of that role. It's getting easier to slip into it and enjoy the fairy tale like it's real.

"The words sound positive, but the way you say them..." Cora eyes me.

"He's been attentive, caring, hot and irresistible, and I don't know what to make of it. He demanded exclusivity, sends me gifts, and we fuck like rabbits."

"That sounds perfect. What am I missing?" Lily frowns.

Cora tenses beside me, and my heart rate speeds up a notch.

"Shit. I'm sorry, I forgot—"

"What's going on?" Lily's gaze darts between me and Cora.

Cora groans. "I believe we can trust this one." She smiles at me, biting her lip.

I sigh. "I married my friend's brother to secure my visa. For all intents and purposes, we're pretending it's a genuine marriage."

Lily makes a zipping motion with her hand across her mouth. "Your secret is safe with me. But based on what you said, it feels like a real marriage, too."

I puff out the air from my cheeks. "I wouldn't say a real marriage, but a real relationship nevertheless. Only it isn't."

"Why do you insist on saying that? Why don't you both admit things have evolved and see where they might go?" Cora plays with the plastic sign holder on the table.

"We're talking about Caleb van den Linden. A man who swore off marriage and has been a playboy until now." I turn to get the attention of the new guy, because I really need my coffee.

"That's romantic." Lily sighs.

I chuckle. "What's romantic about that?"

"A playboy that insists on exclusivity. Obviously you're special to him." She grins.

"Or I'm convenient for him and his busy schedule, and his entitled ass doesn't like sharing." I sag into my chair, deflated.

Not that anything in Caleb's actions would confirm that. But then, nothing's refuted it either.

He's been as playful as ever. Attentive, yes. But that might just be his game. The man takes care of his father's mistakes, for fuck's sake.

"Since when are you so cynical?" Cora huffs, stands up and talks to the new server before she returns. "Your latte is on its way."

"You hired new help?" I ask, hoping to move the attention from me. But I'm distracted by her comment. Am I being cynical?

I've been holding back, reining in my feelings,

because from the get-go I knew Caleb doesn't do relationships. That's why our arrangement should have worked—in theory.

But nothing in his behavior since we started sleeping together suggests he's not in it fully. God, we need to have a conversation.

Though having *that* conversation might mean I'd find out I'm just a convenient lay, and that would throw us into that uncomfortable 'morning after sex with your roommate' zone. I wish my green card was sorted already.

"Are you even listening to me?" Cora interrupts my train of thought. "The new guy is significantly better than Lily"—she looks at her former server—"no offense, babe."

"None taken." Lily raises her mug as if her lack of skills is a reason to toast.

"Anyway, Sanjay is my new server. I took your advice and set clear boundaries, and now I think he fears me. That's why he didn't come to take your order."

That makes me chuckle. "I can't possibly imagine anyone fearing you."

Cora is a decade older than me, and she is a no-nonsense, down to earth woman with a big heart, but sometimes she can come across as abrupt, controlling, and a bit intimidating.

Lily snickers, and Cora's eyes widen. "Were you afraid of me?"

"At the beginning, yes."

"Oh shit, and I was being kind to you." Cora turns and watches Sanjay for a moment.

"I'm sure you're kind to him as well. Setting boundaries doesn't mean you're a bitch to someone." I poke her ribs with my elbow.

And as to my own point, Caleb is kind to me, but that doesn't mean he reset his initial boundaries. He just stopped being a jerk because having sex with me is more fun.

"Maybe I'm just not built to be a boss." Cora folds her arms across her chest, sliding lower in her chair.

"You're a great boss, and besides, you won't ever grow this business if you keep working the counter, the kitchen and the floor," Lily points out.

"Which reminds me, I looked at your numbers. There's some room for growth, I think," I say, as Sanjay brings my latte. I take a tentative sip and sigh, savoring the beverage with closed eyes for a beat.

Lily giggles. "Definitely better than mine."

"When you say growth, all I hear is more work." Cora puts her head into her palms.

"Not necessarily. I'm not an expert, but I think with some additions to the menu, happy hours and more promo, you can draw more of a crowd without too much effort."

"I can't pay for expensive marketing," Cora mumbles into her hands.

"It doesn't have to be expensive," Lily says. "I can help you with social media."

Cora looks through her fingers, but says nothing.

"I'm better at that than I am at making coffee. Let me help you."

"I think it's a great idea." I take another sip.

Heaven. This latte is even better than anything Cora made herself. Caleb would love it.

The thought makes me pause. When did I start considering his opinion even when he's not around?

It crept up on me unexpectedly, but it's there. I think of him when I get a standing ovation, wishing he was there to celebrate with me. When I drink my morning tea alone, because he left at the crack of dawn. When I see a meme and almost forward it to him.

When I add walnuts to my salad, just like Caleb always does.

When flipping through an online gallery, I want to ask him his opinion on a piece of art.

When I dance in the home studio he had made for me.

Merde. I'm truly fucked.

Cora drops her hands, her gaze dancing between us. "Okay, let's do it, but I'll start paying you as soon—"

"Three months. I'll do it for free to make up for all the mess and breakages I caused here. And because you deserve help. After that, we'll talk." Lily lifts her mug again to seal the deal.

Cora turns to me. "Thank you for giving me the push, and looking at my numbers. It's a shame you don't have your school anymore. By now, it would have been the largest and best dance school in the city."

"That's still the dream."

I haven't thought about my studio lately, but that doesn't mean my desire to reopen it has weakened. With my work permit and the show income renewed, I can finally start saving again.

And after my divorce, thanks to Caleb's insistence on a prenup with a nice payout, I might be able to fast-forward those dreams.

The thought saddens me, and a part of me wishes I could have it all. But that's too good to be true, as the next few days will prove.

Chapter 27

Caleb

"Knock, knock."

I look up from my desk, my vision blurry from hours of staring at an acquisitions report.

Corm stands in the doorway, holding whiskey and two tumblers. My jaw ticks. We've reached an unspoken truce. As much as I hate to admit it, he brings a lot to the table. A lot of useful insight and strategy, aside from his assholeness.

I lean back in my chair, stretching my arms over my head. "What do you need?"

"I need to take a month off and lie on the beach." He saunters in without invitation and sits across from me.

"Fuck off, Corm, I don't have time for your daydreaming."

This is the first time in over a month since I started here that *he's* come to my office. But that doesn't mean I'm going to bow and chitchat.

For one, I may trust and respect his business instincts, but otherwise I don't trust the air he breathes.

For two, I want to finish this report before Celeste finishes her show tonight, pick her up, and fuck her six ways to Sunday.

And then take her to breakfast and listen to everything she has to say about her friend's bistro, her manager being an asshole—I need to do something about that—or her colleague's child, the applause she got the night before.

Frankly, at this point she could recite her shopping list and I'd listen with reverence.

And therein lies my biggest problem. I'm infatuated with my wife.

A concept that is highly inconvenient. I've been telling myself to back off, but her spell on me is irresistible.

Corm doesn't seem perturbed by my lack of welcome. He pours me an inch of his expensive whiskey and another glass for himself. The liquid sloshes languidly into the polished glasses.

"Cheers." He passes me the tumbler.

I don't particularly want to drink with him, but I'm not going to pass on his Macallan 1926. It must be a special occasion since he opened this bottle again. "What are we celebrating? You learn how to masturbate?"

"Ha, ha, I can jerk off just fine, but I don't need to. Plenty of women out there to take care of me. How's married life?"

I take a sip of the amber liquid. "What do you want, Quinn?" The idea of talking about Celeste with this douchebag makes the hair on my nape stand on end.

"It's been a month since you joined us, and next week we're announcing not one, but three mergers. I wanted to acknowledge that having you join us was a brilliant decision."

Is he taking the credit now? "You mean black-mailing me into it?"

I've been working a lot since I signed the partner-ship, but I've been enjoying every moment. I'm not telling him that though.

"Semantics. You're here, and I just wanted to acknowledge your contribution." He swirls his whiskey in his glass.

"Careful there, or I might think you like me."

"Let's not get carried away." He raises his glass and I snort.

"Well, for what it's worth, I enjoy my role at Merged."

He tips his glass to me and then takes a sip. "I know we didn't start off on the right foot, but I respect that you put our differences aside and made a smart business decision."

I swallow a quip, because if I got to know this man a bit better in the last few weeks, I know this is a rare moment of honesty with a dose of humility on his part, and I'm going to enjoy it along with my Macallan.

"My wife told me how cutthroat the entertainment world is, but at the end of the day, everyone pulls together for the best performance."

"I guess I have your missus to thank." He stands up.

"Don't go anywhere near her," I warn.

"Protective. I never took you for the marrying kind."

He isn't wrong, and I'm not really married. "You don't know me, Corm. And as much as I appreciate the celebratory drink, I'm not interested in bonding with you over my private life."

He chuckles. "Fair enough. I promise not to charm her when I finally meet her. Xander and Declan are across the street at the bar. We were hoping you'd join us."

I check my watch. Goddammit, Celeste is probably on her way home already. I text Peter, who confirms it.

If I go home now, I won't be able to avoid her bed.

Or mine, but either way there would be me in a bed with a woman.

First, that kind of sex feels boring.

Second, if we were in her room, would she expect me to stay? And if we were in mine, I wouldn't be able to send her away.

That would certainly hurt her. And I promised her, and myself, not to make her feel used ever again.

"I need fifteen minutes to finish this report. I'll join you then."

Bonding with my partners is overdue anyway, especially after our rocky beginning. And it would solve my Celeste dilemma.

Somehow, due to the sheer demand of our schedules and a bit of careful planning on my side, we've avoided evenings at home together, essentially solving my little problem.

But I was looking forward to seeing her tonight. Fuck. I finish my whiskey, not savoring it anymore. If there was someone I wanted to celebrate my one-month anniversary with, it was Celeste.

So why do I fear her in my bed so much? Waking up beside her might not be such a bad thing. Not that I'd know, since I've never done that.

But having her in my bed, as opposed to in places where we could get discovered, might bring the novelty and excitement factor down a notch.

It would be a sure way to get bored, and fuck, I don't want that.

Goddammit, this is such uncharted territory.

"Are you joining us?" Roxy pops her head into my door. "You know they accepted you already, but it wouldn't hurt to join the fun sometimes."

I slam the laptop closed and swipe my jacket from the back of my chair. My phone vibrates on the table, and I glance at Roxy. "I have to take this, but I'll be there in a few minutes."

Her heels echo down the hallway as I pick up my glass and my cell. Walking to the wall of windows, I hit the green icon.

"Has Quinn screwed you over already?" Finn asks, a hint of gloating in his voice.

"Fuck you. You'd be the last one to find out."

We might tease each other ruthlessly, but it's always good to hear from him.

"Just call me to bail you out after you kill him."

"Is there a reason you're calling, or you just didn't get your dose of harassment today?"

He laughs. "I'm sure you miss it, bro. I'm on my way home, and I almost stopped at your old office to chat with you."

"Aw, you miss me." I grin, looking at the flickering lights of the city, my old office just a distant memory. I got settled here fast. The thrill of something new and different hasn't waned yet.

"No, I went to make sure you hadn't come back crying."

I snicker. "How are you, asshole?"

"I'm good. I'm taking a week off, believe it or not."

"Did Paris threaten to leave you?"

"She might have made a few valid points, and I realized a week won't shatter the company."

"That's good. At your age, you need to take it easy."

"I'm only three years older than you. How are things over there?"

"Decent."

"That's a raving endorsement."

"You'll hear some announcements soon, and you'll see all is good. Can I ask you something?"

"Do I think you made a mistake partnering with Quinn? Yes."

"Fuck you, Finn." I don't mind his razzing. We grew up like that, and I know it's his weird way of making sure all is okay.

"Okay, okay, talk to me."

"You've been with Paris for almost two years now..." Fuck. I don't even know what I want to ask.

"Good math skills, Cal. Are you angling for rela- tionship advice? Fuck, are you involved with Celeste? Have you—"

When I say nothing, he continues, "I told you not to hurt her! Paris will cut off your balls. And probably Saar too."

"Who said I fucked it up? I just... I don't know. Do you ever get bored being with the same woman?"

"Do I look bored to you?" He doesn't even have to think about his answer. "The past two years have been the best years of my life, and I'm a sleep-deprived father of a toddler. Every day is a new adventure. Even on the days when we just nap on the sofa, exhausted."

I play with my empty glass, considering his words. Can his situation apply to me and Celeste? Finn is in love with his wife. I'm trying to have a relationship with a set expiration.

"Are you catching feelings?" Finn asks.

"I just don't want things to get awkward between us, since we're stuck together for three years."

The words sound like a repeated mantra I subscribed to a while ago, but they feel outdated now.

Music seeps into the darkness, pulling my mind into painful reality. I squint at my watch. Ten o'clock.

I sit up, my dark silky cover sliding to the floor. I haven't slept this long in weeks. Also, I haven't been this hungover in... months. When did I stop partying?

The bonding with my partners last night didn't go as expected. I thought I'd have one obligatory drink. Instead, I came home at three in the morning after drinking gallons and playing pool.

Even Declan loosened up, and he's definitely the most reserved of us. It was a much-needed team-building exercise, but I'm fucking paying the price now.

I get up, pull on a T-shirt and take two Tylenol in the bathroom before I wander out of my bedroom.

The music is coming from the room across the landing. Celeste must be practicing. As I approach, giggles surprise me. Shit, I forgot this is Mia's weekend.

Squinting to subdue the headache pounding behind my eyes, I peek in, and Mia freezes partway through a move.

"I forgot you were here today," I growl, the headache talking.

Mia flinches.

Fuck. Fuck. Fuck.

"Good morning to you too, Mr. Grouch." Celeste glares at me.

And just like that, I won the biggest asshole award. "I didn't mean—" I step inside, and Mia instinctively steps back.

Her reaction is like a punch to my gut. What was I

expecting? That I lash out and don't get what I deserve? But she doesn't deserve any of this.

I run my hand over my face, hoping to wipe away my hangover. "Sorry, let's start again. I'm going to have a shower and find my personality, and then we can go for brunch. Okay?"

They both glare at me, Celeste probably considering how to claw my eyes out, and Mia hoping to be anywhere else but in a room with me.

I don't know if I look as bad as I feel, but my look must be pity-inducing enough that Mia finally nods.

Well, good morning, everyone.

I trudge back to my room. The painkillers kick in by the time I finish showering, and I feel marginally better.

I don't find them in the studio, so I knock gently on Mia's door. Soft voices direct me toward Celeste's room.

Since her door is slightly ajar, I see them in front of the vanity mirror. Celeste is braiding Mia's hair. My wife is taking care of my daughter.

The image hits me with a feeling that is warm and sappy, but not unwelcome. I stop to watch them for a beat.

"You have a great sense of rhythm, and with a little practice, you'd be really good. You already are, but practice makes perfect." Celeste squeezes Mia's shoulders.

"Do you think Cal is upset I paid for my dancing classes and rejoined the crew?"

What? Fuck. A part of me understands this is a private moment between them, but I can't walk away now. Neither can I step in and tell her I don't mind at all.

And then an irrational sensation crawls up my spine, akin to envy or jealousy. The two of them have grown closer, while I'm standing on the sidelines, avoiding this kind of intimate moment.

With my wife. Or with my daughter.

What's the worst that could happen?

"Of course not, Mia." Celeste shakes her head.

"Just... he hasn't been around much, so I thought he was mad at me."

I stumble, propping my hand against the wall. I'm worse than my father. He at least gave me negative attention.

I'm running away from this responsibility. And there is a young girl who's the victim of my actions.

"Oh, Mia, he's starting a new company, and that takes a lot of work. His current absence has nothing to do with you. I promise." Celeste bends and gives her a hug from behind, the two of them a picture of beauty and affection.

I lean against the wall and close my eyes. Within all the lows I've experienced in my life, this single moment is the worst.

The two of them deserve so much better. And without another moment of hesitation, I bolt.

Chapter 28

Celeste

I hold Mia in my arms for a few more beats, my heart breaking for the girl. She's so strong and self-sufficient, but in this moment she feels so fragile and innocent.

Merde. Caleb might fear commitment with me, but he can't do this to Mia. She didn't have a father in her life for a decade, she deserves one who cares beyond his credit card.

The shitty thing is, I know he doesn't want to hurt her. He just doesn't know what to do. And he doesn't realize how his absence impacts her. I didn't realize it either.

"Come on, let's wait for him downstairs. Where would you like to go eat?"

Mia drags her feet behind me like I'm forcing her to attend a broccoli-eating contest, taking each step gingerly.

Caleb rushes out of the kitchen with a smile. "I called the smashing place. We're booked in an hour."

Mia stops and eyes him, an unsure ghost of a smile tentative on her face. "I thought we were going out for brunch."

"Change of plans. We're having street hot dogs on the way." He winks at her and her face lights up.

I don't know what happened between his earlier behavior and now, but seeing Mia's hesitant responses puts a grin on my face.

"Look, Mia, he did find his personality in the shower." I hold my hand out to high-five her.

She scoffs, but hits me back. Grabbing her hand, I pull her toward the elevators.

"Okay, I deserve that." Caleb shrugs. As we walk past, Mia extends her other hand in his direction.

He looks down for a moment and takes it, his throat bobbing. My chest swells with warmth for these two wounded souls who, despite my efforts, found their way into my heart.

My fake marriage might end sooner than I'd like, but I will forever cherish this moment.

We pile into the elevator like a normal family going out on a Saturday. We might be an unconventional group, but this morning we feel like a family.

* * *

Sun rays tickle my face as we stroll down the bustling chaos of Times Square. We smashed an entire room, and we ate hot dogs, sauce dripping down our forearms.

I pretended to take a call a moment ago, to give them some alone time.

Their heads angled toward each other, they share a laugh about something on Mia's phone screen. I wish I could hear them over the honking cabs and chattering tourists.

But even just seeing it, experiencing it, I feel we've turned a page after the awkward morning. Seeing them like this tugs at something deep inside me.

Thumping bass music fills the air and Mia stops, her feet already finding the beat. A street performer is throwing down some impressive hip-hop moves on the pavement in the middle of the square.

I can't help but snap a picture of the two of them. While Mia is completely enthralled by the young man with a boombox, Caleb steals a glance at her, his expression softening.

"Go on." He winks at her, nudging her forward. "Show them what you've got."

Her eyes go wide, gaze darting between the jamming dude and Caleb. Excitement and shyness etched around her face, she bites her lip, and instead of forward, she steps backward, bumping into me.

I'm about to tell her she doesn't have to do it, even though it's clear she's just shy, when Caleb steps forward.

"I'll join you." He shrugs, a dare in his eyes.

Mia glances at me, and I nod as if it's my place to give her the okay. Her face lights up, and she angles toward the makeshift stage area.

The performer, sensing an opportunity, cranks up the volume and steps back, giving them the spotlight. The crowd around us gathers, curious about this unexpected twist.

Caleb stomps his feet awkwardly, his movements stiff and unsure, and I stifle a laugh. Mia grins as she takes the lead. Her body flows to the rhythm with grace and confidence.

Caleb watches her, a proud smile spreading across his face, and then, something incredible happens. He mimics her movements, his initial awkwardness melting away as he lets go of his inhibitions.

The crowd cheers them on, and Mia's laughter rings out, pure and joyful. She reaches for his hand, and together they spin and twirl, a beautiful, unrestrained duet.

I clap along with the crowd, swelling with affection, watching them. As I stand here, witnessing this beautiful scene, my heart opens up, embracing this new, unexpected family.

Caleb's eyes meet mine for a moment, and I see a spark of something raw and real there—an openness that wasn't there before. Or one that I didn't want to see because of its possible meaning.

It's like the wild, unfiltered joy slowly chips at his defenses. And I know this is about his daughter, but I can't help but hope. Because there's no way I could have ever exited this arrangement without hoping for more. As much as I wanted to protect myself.

His gaze locked with mine, we travel into another world. Music and noise fade away as we remain in our own bubble in the middle of the vibrant city. His feet stop, and the hectic energy around us freezes.

Something passes between us that is deeper than the usual heat. Greater than our fears. Truer than our misconceptions.

The performance ends with a flourish, the crowd erupting into applause. Caleb's gaze breaks away and he joins Mia in taking a bow, their faces flushed and beaming.

Caleb wraps his arms around her in a first sponta-neous and sincere display of affection. After a tense beat, Mia snakes her arms around his waist.

I wish I could document this, but it's their moment and I don't want to disturb it with my phone. As they return to me, Caleb pulls both of us into a group hug, his laughter echoing in my ears.

Mia giggles as she turns and chats with some of her audience, a woman showing her a phone screen.

"Did you see that?" Caleb asks, breathless and grinning.

"Oh, I saw it all. I knew Mia was talented. But you've got some moves."

He leans in, his lips by my ear. "I've got moves, black swan. And you already know some of them."

An involuntary shiver shudders through me, all my emotions crashing into this moment, and I know beyond a doubt, surrounded by the bustling heart of the city, I belong right here with them.

If only that was reality.

* * *

"Are you sure you don't want us to drive you?" Caleb asks Mia for the tenth time.

We had the best afternoon, but Mia got a text from her mother and announced, rather anxiously, that she needed to go home.

"I'm fine. I've taken the subway lots, and it's faster." She bounces on the balls of her feet.

"Just please let us know you got home all right." I give her a hug.

"And if I can do anything to help..." Caleb offers, a veil of awkwardness creeping between them again.

"I will." She turns and skips down the stairs, but stops halfway. "Thank you for a great day, Dad."

Caleb squeezes my hand so hard I worry about my bones, but the significance of the moment directs my attention away from the crushing force.

He swallows. "I'm looking forward to the next one already, Mia."

Seeing this proud man choked up cracks another barrier I created around my heart. We stand there motionless long after Mia disappears underground.

"Caleb van den Linden, it's hard for me to admit it, but I've been swooning all day." I turn to face him.

The grin that lights up his face is warm, but also the one I know well by now. Full of heat and desire. "Does it mean I can pull you into the alley here?"

"Wow, who are you, and what have you done with my deviant husband? He would never stop to ask." I feign horror, mostly to mask my excitement.

I never knew sex in public could be this thrilling. Be something I crave.

"In that case." His long legs eat the few feet across the pavement, and he drags me with him, holding my hand.

The alleyway is narrow and dark, filled with humid

air. But it's also abandoned. A square of light leading to the street on the other side of this block is far away. It's not a completely secluded area, but it gives us some privacy.

I think.

Or rather, I don't think at all. Because my back hits the brick wall, and Caleb captures my mouth with such ferocity, I lose my mind.

I only feel, drowning in this man's desire, in his need, in his willingness to please. To take and to give.

"Hike up your skirt, Celeste," he demands.

Aw, the player is back. My gaze jumps in all directions. For a brief moment, I consider the question of safety here, but I dismiss it immediately.

I trust this man completely.

Trust? The idea sneaks up at me so suddenly, I want to bolt, hide, and deal with the implications.

Instead, I pull him in to kiss him. All in, teeth clashing, tongues dancing, biting and sucking like this is the only kiss I'll ever give.

"Skirt. Now," he growls.

It's a testament to my absolute lack of common sense or self-preservation instincts when I'm around this man, because I grab the fabric and shimmy my hips to pull the tight material up my thighs.

Merde, why did I wear a pencil skirt today?

As soon as he glimpses my underwear, Caleb grabs

my wrists and looks around. "Don't ever wear this skirt again." Frustration laces his voice.

"I like it. What's your problem? It's up." The humid air sticks between my bare thighs.

"Yeah, and you're exposed for everyone to see." He steps closer, covering me with his body.

"Jesus, then hurry up so I can lower it." I'm wound up with my need for him.

He growls and yanks my skirt back down. "Not here."

Before I can even process the situation, he drags me back to the street. The man who enjoys sex in all the weird, not discreet places, cares about my modesty?

I stop. "What just happened?"

Caleb groans. "You wore a stupid skirt." Someone bumps into him, and he pulls me to the side.

"That's never stopped you from wetting your dick before," I snap.

We glare at each other, our chests heaving. It doesn't bother me that he changed his mind about sex in the alley, but this caveman act is redundant.

"Fuck." He shakes his head slightly, closing his eyes.

"That, we didn't," I quip.

He opens his eyes and studies me for what feels like an eternity.

During that pause, I consider telling him that I feel

this relationship is getting out of hand, and we need to talk about it. Define it. Or just agree that we're still on the same page.

Because if our story started with a deep dislike, I've certainly moved on from that. And even without discussing it, I know he has as well.

The question is, are we on the same chapter? Or has the plot changed, and now we're each living in a different book?

"Talk to me, Caleb." I put my hand on his chest.

He keeps shaking his head, like he's trying to rid himself of something. "Someone could have seen you there... I don't want anyone to see what's mine."

My breath hitches. *What's mine?* "What are you saying?"

"I don't know what I'm doing, Celeste."

The statement is full of anguish and frustration. But it's also a moment of self-reflection. One that he decided to share with me. Like he trusts me as much as I trust him.

We stand there while the pedestrian traffic flows around us, like the two of us have our own world. Where I'm truly his, and he's mine.

I keep my hand on his chest, his heartbeat pulsing under my palm, and I weave my other hand through his fingers. Holding space for him. For me. For us.

He sighs. "It's all too much. I don't do commitments, and suddenly I'm partnered with three other people founding a company. And at the same time, I'm trying to figure out how to be a father. It's all happening at the same time. And then this..." He bows his head, closing his eyes briefly.

His torment vibrates through our touch, and as much as I want to hear him say it, declare something about the two of us, I can't make any demands, because he's right. He's got his new company and Mia to focus on.

"You worry about Mia and Merged. I'll be here until the visa." My stomach sinks at the liberty I just awarded him.

But I can't cause him more stress. Everything in his life is new, and as much as I want to be his constant, that's not who we are.

He cups my cheeks and lowers his forehead to mine. "Just give me some time, black swan. I'll figure it all out."

"Okay, pretty boy. In the meantime, I won't wear a pencil skirt."

He chuckles and takes my lips.

"Sorry about..." He beckons his head toward the alley. Then he smiles, quirking his eyebrow. "You told me you like your men with a bit of restraint in public," he says, reminding me of our hostile exchange from what feels like a lifetime ago.

"I think you changed my mind about that." I grin. "Besides, do you expect me blushing and less opinionated now?"

"It wouldn't hurt," he teases. "But you're perfect the way you are."

Oh, my poor heart. I kiss him, and pretend his kiss is all I need.

That his kiss is more than him reassuring me. Telling me things between us are real. Are bigger than our physical attraction. Are beyond the visa application.

I take his kiss because that's all he can offer now. And more than my demands, he needs space.

I take his kiss, and hope despite myself that its sweetness will heal my heartbreak.

Chapter 29

Caleb

"**O**kay, woman, we're past fashionably late. Hurry up."

I adjust my tie for the hundredth time, pacing by the grand windows at my loft. This gala is an important event for the Merged partners.

While advertising awards are usually a bore, crucial business players will be there, and we have a strategy in place for some important conversations.

And now I might miss some of them, goddammit.

"What's taking so long?" I down my whiskey.

The sound of her heels draws my attention. When I turn, my breath catches in my throat. Celeste places her foot on a step, her delicate hand on the balustrade, and she descends like an apparition.

Her hair is in loose waves, pinned over one shoulder. She's radiant in her dress. That fucking dress. Kill. Me. Now.

The deep emerald satin clings to her curves, the slit revealing a tantalizing glimpse of her leg with each step.

The plunging neckline and the delicate cap sleeves emphasize her elegance and allure. She looks like a goddess, every inch of her demanding attention and respect.

Fuck. I must have tightened my tie too much. I'm suffocating suddenly.

She smiles at me when she gets to the bottom of the staircase, and I'm still standing here like an idiot.

She's stunning.

"What's up? You were in a hurry and now you're just standing there." She checks her watch.

"That watch hasn't been working for a while now," I grumble.

She moves her hand behind her back in a protective gesture, but rolls her eyes. "I guess now we know why I'm late."

She takes my glass from my hand and puts it on the coffee table.

Leaning in, I can practically see her stomach in that neckline. Yeah, she's stunning, and it drives me crazy.

I swallow hard. "Is this what you're wearing?"

She flinches and runs her hands down her hips, like the flowing fabric needs smoothing. "Yes, genius, this is what I'm wearing," she snaps.

That's my girl. Always finding her sass when I act like an asshole. "God help me," I murmur, and without another glance at her, I pass her and stomp to the elevator.

"Well, I'm really looking forward to this evening." Bitterness laces her voice. No wonder. Fuck, I need to get my shit together.

"Let's go," I growl, putting my foot between the sliding doors.

She picks her skirt up and saunters slowly—extra slowly—but with her natural elegance to the elevator, while I stand there like her butler.

A butler to the queen.

Her flowery scent tickles my nostrils when she breezes past me, and I swear I have half a mind to cancel the night. Fuck business. Fuck my business partners. Fuck all the assholes that will ogle her.

Peter waits for us in the garage. "You look lovely tonight, Mrs. van den Linden."

"Thank you, Peter." She smiles at him and gives me a death glare before she slides into her seat.

Even my driver's behaving better than me tonight. Maybe I should really stay home.

The minute I sit down, Peter starts raising the partition.

"I'd prefer you kept it down, Peter. Thank you." Celeste scoots to the furthest end of the seat, as far from me as possible.

We drive out to the street in silence, the loaded energy filling the air, suffocating me. I adjust my tie. Yet again.

Celeste is staring out of the window, her skin glowing from the streetlights. Fuck, the woman is a vision.

"I'm sorry. You look great tonight. I've been on edge. This is an important event." I reach to squeeze her hand.

She swats me away. "You have no right to comment on my appearance. I can wear what I want. And while we're at it, don't fucking give me compliments either. That way, you don't get confused."

"Celeste..." I hit the partition button, because Peter doesn't need to be privy to this.

"I said partition down. I don't feel particularly safe with you right now."

"Don't be dramatic."

"Don't be an asshole."

"Peter, stop the car right now."

"Good idea. I don't think I want to go anywhere with you tonight."

The car comes to a stop. "Peter, please wait outside for a moment." I glare at her.

"Is this supposed to make me feel better?" she scoffs.

"I'll be right outside, ma'am." Peter gets out.

"I don't quite know what's just happened," I say.

"I love this dress, and I love the way it makes me feel. I spent enough time when I was a teenager fighting my body image. With others and with myself. And I don't need you to comment on my appearance. To con—"

She turns her head away and doesn't finish. I have no idea what she was planning to add, but it's like she decided I'm not worth sharing her feelings with.

It's like a punch to the gut, but I don't have time to dissect that, because there's enough to unpack in what she did say.

Fuck, she got it all wrong. I wasn't... fuck. Fuck. Fuck.

"Look at me, Celeste."

Several beats pass where she doesn't move, her hands trembling in her lap. I yank at my tie's knot, lacking oxygen.

"Look at me." I take a chance and scoot closer.

She recoils, but she doesn't open the door and run, so I take it as a win.

"Celeste, I might be confused and unprepared for

what is growing between us... but let me make one thing clear for you. I fucking love your body."

She finally turns her head to me, her eyes glistening. I reach tentatively and run my thumb along her jawline.

She shivers and swallows, her eyes full of hurt, but something else too. Something that looks like... But that can't be.

Is she truly scared of me? No, that must have been just part of the heated moment.

"This dress, black swan, makes my cock hard. The problem is, I'm pretty sure it will have the same effect on other men."

"The question is, what will you do about it?"

Her question rings with importance. I'm thoroughly fucking confused as to what I've triggered in her. But it's clear she won't give me the complete story tonight.

I'm at a loss on how to move past this, whatever *this* is, so I lean in to what I know works between us.

"Since I can't make them not look at you, I'll just have to finger fuck you during the dinner to make sure everyone can smell who you belong to."

The words come out naturally, but the need to execute them is stronger than ever. Like claiming this woman is a question of life and death.

Fuck, this arrangement grows more complicated every day.

A flicker of heat passes through her eyes before she sighs, "Idiot." Like always when she is upset, she says it in French.

I lean in and she tenses. "It turns me on when you speak French."

She stifles a snort and pushes me away. "Now you're just cheesy. We better go. You have work to do."

Shit. I forgot about the event completely. In light of Celeste being upset, it didn't matter. I don't even care that she overreacted, or why, as long as she feels better now.

And as Peter gets back in the car and pulls into the traffic, Celeste puts her hand on top of mine.

She doesn't look away from the window, but it still feels like the world rearranges itself to its regular, comfortable rhythm.

My mind is spinning from all the information and fucking small talk. More importantly, my head isn't in it, as my gaze keeps trailing Celeste. Not so difficult since she's the most beautiful woman here.

"If you'll excuse me..." I try to extricate myself

from the banker who's droning on about capital interests. "I need to find my wife."

My wife. If I could bottle up the feeling behind the word, the ICE would expedite Celeste's visa.

"I didn't know you got married, Caleb."

And I wish I remembered your name.

"Your father hasn't mentioned anything."

And now it's obvious why I don't know who this man is. He's been living under a rock, because everyone knows about the fallout of the van den Lindens.

I turn away, done with this loser, and locate Celeste. She's laughing at something at the bar, but I don't see the source of her entertainment.

"Here you are." Xander appears by my side. "Art Mathison's wife was saying goodbye to someone just now. If we want to get a meeting with him, we better find him."

Mathison is the best in surveillance and security. Rumor is he made his money hacking, but nowadays his significant riches come from information gathering. Information is money in our world.

Celeste angles closer to whoever she's talking to, but other guests still block the person.

"Okay, let's find him quickly," I growl.

"What's up your ass?" Xander shakes his head.

I don't bother to explain myself. Mostly because I don't really like the answer.

We need Mathison on retainer, but the fucker is as elusive as a taxi in rush hour. We haven't been able to secure a meeting.

He comes to these events only if his wife forces him. It's as if she's socializing her stray dog. I have yet to see him enjoying himself at a function.

"There he is." Xander gestures toward a large man. He's glaring at someone who talks to him while his hand rests on his wife's back.

We weave through the mingling guests in the ballroom, my stomach growling. I can't believe that we were late, I've been networking for an hour, and they haven't even started the dinner or the awards ceremony.

As we approach the Mathisons, the person they're talking to leaves.

"Violet." I bow my head to Mrs. Mathison. The blond with unusual brown eyes is a gallery owner.

"Caleb." She smiles, and her husband gives me a murderous look. "Art, this is my client, Caleb van den Linden."

Mathison nods, but doesn't bother extending his hand until his wife looks at him. Not sure what her look tells him, but he shakes my hand and mumbles something unintelligible.

"Pleasure's all mine." What's this fucker's problem? "This is my business partner, Xander Stone. We were hoping to have a chat with you."

His features rearrange into something akin to constipation, but before he can refuse us, Violet chimes in, "I'm going to the powder room."

She pats his chest, and another silent communication passes between them before she leaves.

"Art, you're a hard man to track down," Xander says.

He doesn't say anything, just glares at us.

Xander shifts from one foot to the other. "We were hoping we could—"

"We want to hire you," I interrupt. Clearly the man hates small talk and is above social etiquette.

"Merged?" he asks, obviously knowing who we are.

I nod, again hoping no words are the way to win this man.

"Tuesday at ten a.m. Casa Cassi." He lifts his gaze and his features smooth slightly before he takes a step and leaves us there.

"What the fuck was that?" Xander snorts.

"We just got a meeting." I watch Mathison join his wife. Something in the way he looks at her bothers me. Or intrigues me.

Like the petite blond can bring this powerful man to his knees, and he would stay at her feet gladly.

333

A few months ago, I'd have said he was completely pussy-whipped. Now, it just seems like he has his safe harbor.

"What is Casa Cassi?" Xander interrupts my train of thought.

"A Michelin-star restaurant that opens at noon," I say absentmindedly, my gaze already looking for the woman in the green dress.

I spot her at the bar and move before I think.

"Hey, where are you going? He said ten in the morning," Xander calls after me.

"That's a problem for Tuesday. I have an evening to finally enjoy."

It's like she's transmitting a siren song that draws me to her. Knowing all night she's been around but not on my arm has been driving me crazy.

Whatever happened earlier is still in the back of my mind. I need to make sure she's okay. I finally make it to the bar.

Her laugh carries to me like a tune that I loved when I was a boy, and every time it's on the radio, I can't help but hum along.

"Are you having a good time?" I snake my hand around her waist from behind.

Celeste tenses at first, but relaxes immediately. "There you are." She sounds all cheerful and genuine, which differs greatly from earlier.

But I'm distracted by her companion.

"I see you met my wife, Corm," I bark.

"She's lovely company, and yet you managed to ignore her all night." The shit-eating grin on his face would not rile me normally. When it comes to Celeste... I don't even want to finish that thought. Or its implications.

"I was working. Unlike you." I step closer to her, feeling her body hum beside me.

Corm pops an olive from his drink into his mouth. "I got things done faster."

Fucker. "I got a meeting with Art Mathison."

And that wipes the cockiness from his face.

"Boys, play nice together." Celeste leans in to me and hiccups. "Oops. I think I need to eat something. When is dinner, Cal?"

She's drunk, and she calls me Cal all of a sudden.

I barely stop myself from punching Quinn in his fucking nose when they luckily open the doors to the adjacent ballroom, and everyone moves.

Celeste turns to get a water. Good girl.

I take the opportunity and hiss at Corm, "Stay away from my wife." My voice is low, so she doesn't hear it, but it doesn't leave any room for interpretation.

"Relax, I just wanted to find what got you to tie the knot so suddenly. Or rather, who."

My jaw ticks. Fuck, did he get her drunk to find

out...? Did she tell him the truth? Is he going to use it against me?

I put all my effort into not showing my thoughts on my face. "It's none of your business, Quinn."

"I'm just being friendly." He lifts his arms in surrender, a cocky smirk on his face.

"He's been friendly." Celeste puts her hand on my back, and the rush of ownership that boosts through me should be concerning. But it isn't. "I hope you don't mind I told him the truth."

I snap my head to her. "What?"

"That it was love at first sight." She winks at Corm.

Little minx. I pull her closer and kiss her temple, inhaling the feel of her. And for the first time tonight, my nervous energy dissipates.

Celeste lets out an adorable moan. Fuck, she's a cute drunk.

"I'm sure Corm appreciated your candor. Let's find our table."

Corm leaves us, presumably remembering that he came with arm candy of his own and should find her before we get seated.

"Drink your water, black swan," I demand.

"I was pissed about your 'I hate your dress' comment, so I had two martinis."

I don't hate her dress, but I'm not going to argue that now.

"Only two?" I look at her skeptically. That makes no sense.

"I never told you this, but I can't hold my liquor. At all." She stumbles, giggling.

Wrapping my arms around her, I let out a laugh.

I steer us toward the ballroom entrance, and my gaze collides with steel-blue eyes. My laugh dies on my lips.

Chapter 30

Celeste

The one time I met Charles van den Linden was up there as the most embarrassing day of my life.

The man destroyed my career once, and the way he glares at me right now sobers me up. Caleb tenses beside me.

"Merde," I mumble.

When I got my dress for this event earlier, I was excited about spending a glamorous night out. I hoped Caleb and I could just have a blast, without thinking about work, our entanglement, our growing unnamed feelings, his daughter, or my visa.

Just two people having fun.

But his question about my dress triggered the deepest wounds in me, and I overreacted to his offhand comment. I kept repeating to myself that

Caleb is not my father, but the memories still streamed in.

I know, deep down in my marrow, he isn't like my father. But his comment... the motivation behind it... it unleashed so many fucked-up insecurities.

And speaking of fathers.

The brunette on Caleb's father's arm is definitely not his wife. She's probably younger than me. Beautiful, tall and skinny. I never feel threatened by women who look like supermodels. My best friend is one, for fuck's sake.

But the way her stare fixates on Caleb... *that* I find threatening. I mean, she's here with another man, but...

I look at Caleb, whose gaze is on her as well. With contempt, I assume. I hope. I have no real claim on this man, and perhaps it's just the aftermath of my insecurities, but the tall brunette sparks something inside me.

A flicker of self-doubt grows in intensity, consuming me faster than I can regroup.

"Father." Caleb gives them a curt nod. "Carly."

So it's not some random arm candy for the night. Caleb knows the woman. Against my better judgment, that prompts me to step away from him.

Caleb looks at me, frowning, and then takes my hand and squeezes. "Celeste, this is Carly. Carly, meet my wife."

My wife.

Those two words spread through me like a much-needed confidence potion. I don't even bother to question their unresolved validity.

Squaring my shoulders, I give Carly my best performance, smiling like this introduction is a true highlight of my night.

"I'm pleased to meet you, Carly." I don't bother extending my hand, because I know she'll just ignore it.

Carly's—whoever she might be—face falls. She eyes me with suspicion, and a generous dose of contempt.

Caleb's father doesn't acknowledge us, but takes Carly's hand and kisses her knuckles. "We should get to our table, darling."

Carly scoffs. "In a minute." She turns to Caleb. "Your wife?"

"Enjoy your evening." Caleb's voice is clipped as he tries to move past them.

Carly grabs his biceps. "She's not your type."

Caleb takes a long breath in and closes his eyes briefly. "And how do you know my type?"

Now, a smart woman would remember she's here with another man. Perhaps the other man would interfere. But Carly seems set on debating the topic, and Caleb's father doesn't seem interested in moving on. It's like he enjoys the impending drama.

Drama that might get out of hand if the bitch

doesn't remove her hand from my husband. Drama that's getting contained only because, unlike her, even drunk, I know I'm here to support Caleb, not embarrass him.

Her behavior, however, helps lessen my insecurity. She's definitely not attractive.

"Well, she's..." Carly vibrates with indignation. "You know." She rakes her haughty gaze down my body. Is she really going to compare our body types here and now?

Caleb smiles at me, and then turns to her. "Do you mean graceful, elegant, and smart? Exactly my type."

My heart swells in my chest. I have defended myself against snarls like this many times, but having someone give me a compliment to rebut the venom? It shakes me to the core. God, I don't need a knight in shining armor, but it feels good to have one.

Carly doesn't read the room and gasps. "But she's—"

"She wants to say I have more fat on my bones." I shrug.

"Carly," Caleb's father warns.

"Carly, if you have nothing nice to say about my wife, then shut the fuck up." Caleb swirls me around and leads us to our table.

"So?" I can't help myself, and my drunken, unfiltered mind wants to find out how he knows the woman.

"Not now," Caleb growls, as he moves the chair for me to sit. My retort dies on my lips as the lights dim, and the host takes to the stage.

The ceremony unfolds, with boring speeches interrupted by dinner courses. The conversation at our table flows, mostly thanks to Xander's efforts at meaningless chatter. His companion has a bubbly laugh, but absolutely no personality.

Cormac looks bored the entire time while his lady converses with us. And Declan, who—according to Caleb—comes to these events only with a hired escort, plays with his food and keeps checking his watch.

Caleb is his usual charming self, but tension radiates from him. I don't think anyone else notices, but I do.

His jaw is set, and he seems distracted.

"I saw your old man earlier," Corm says, and Caleb's foot bounces.

It's a slight movement, but I sit close enough to feel it. Merde, I was so wrapped up in my own world, I didn't even realize what impact our earlier run-in might have had on Caleb.

"Corm, I hear you own a nightclub." I pretend his question never happened. "It must be challenging running so many businesses." Praising a man has never failed.

Corm's not an idiot, though. An asshole for sure, but not an idiot, and I half expect him to throw me under the bus and continue his taunting.

"I love clubbing," Xander's plus one chirps.

Corm ignores her and pins me with his glare. "You know a lot about me, Celeste."

"Only fair, given the interrogation you submitted me to earlier." I smile at him.

"It was just a fun, friendly conversation." He shrugs, leaning back.

"Oh, I had fun, but I wouldn't go as far as counting you among my friends." I lace my sarcasm with honey, beaming at him.

"Did you know Celeste and my sister are best friends?" Caleb asks, his pinkie hooking with mine on the table.

Corm's features freeze. His jaw sets in a scowl, as he glares at me like my friendship with Saar offends him.

"Isn't your sister the famous supermodel?" the woman who came with Corm asks.

Caleb nods, and at that moment a group of servers swarms the place, quickly removing our plates and serving us the next course.

The conversation moves to other topics.

"Are you okay?" I ask Caleb.

"Of course." He shrugs, and his brush-off deflates me a bit. I guess I'm not a person he wants to confide in. But then he sighs and adds, "As good as someone can be when their father pretends they don't exist."

"Fuck him. He's an asshole, anyway. Nothing good happens when he actually notices a person."

Caleb whips his head to me and then laughs. "Fuck, you're refreshing."

"What are you talking about?" A smile tugs at my lips, his laugh contagious.

"You're the first person who didn't say 'oh, Cal, I'm so sorry.'"

I feign shock. "Oh my, was that supposed to be my line? Did you want me to pity you?"

"Shut up." He laughs, cupping my neck and pulling me in for a kiss.

It's just a peck, but it feels like the most significant show of affection between us ever. It doesn't come from physical need, from desire or temptation. It spawned from a completely different level of intimacy.

Keeping his hand on the back of my neck, he holds me only an inch from his face. He smells of whiskey, and something distinctly him. Heat swarms behind his eyes, but there's something else there too.

Affection.

Care.

Respect.

"Get a room, the two of you." Xander breaks the moment.

"Fuck you," Caleb hisses, but he pulls away.

I gulp down the first glass that I grab while I force my mind to find the rubble of my protective walls, and rebuild some sort of defense around my pounding heart.

I'm so distracted I don't even realize it's wine until the glass is empty. Shit. This won't go well with the two cocktails from earlier.

When another round of awards, and even longer speeches, start just before dessert, Caleb shifts his chair, getting closer to me.

He turns a bit, seemingly angling his body to have a better view of the stage.

"Have I told you that you're the most beautiful woman in the room?" His breath fans the side of my throat.

A delicious shudder ripples through me, pulsating between my legs. Jesus, he only breathed beside me.

"You didn't seem so keen on this dress—"

"Hush." He puts his hand on my thigh, the tips of his fingers sliding under the slit of my skirt.

"Who's Carly?" I scan around the table, but everyone seems like they're following the proceedings on the stage.

"It doesn't matter, but if you need to know, she's a nurse I dated briefly when my brother was in hospital. She was after my money, so I broke it off quickly, but I guess now I know she was after money, regardless of who the owner of the bank account is."

"She seemed adamant you married below your standards." I hate how petty I sound, seeking reassurance.

"She's several leagues below you, but do I detect a bit of jealousy, black swan?" His hand travels higher and I shift in my seat, my legs falling apart a bit.

I wish he wouldn't touch me, so I can find my confidence and wits. Why did I drink that wine?

"Please stop, Caleb. People…"

He leans in. "I need this, I need you to—"

"Then let's go—"

"Here, now, only you. Relax, and keep watching the ceremony."

My protest dies because his fingers graze my pussy. I stifle a moan, and Caleb lets out an almost inaudible rumble.

"Have you run out of all the underwear I bought you?" His voice is low, laced with need.

"No."

"Your pussy is fucking naked. Has it been like that all night?" he whispers into my ear.

The sensation of his fingers circling my entrance,

his thumb teasing my clit, and his words so close to my skin, short-circuits something in my brain.

"The easy access was a surprise for the ride home. Not for here."

He hums and plunges two fingers inside me, and I whimper. My gaze meets with Cormac's while Caleb casually puts his arm across my backrest, watching the ceremony over my shoulder.

Corm frowns, but luckily his companion leans in and tells him something that distracts him enough to look away.

Not that him looking is my only problem here. We've had sex in public several times already. But this is a new level of fucked-up. And somehow a new level of exhilarating.

"Hmmm, black swan, your pussy is so greedy. I love how you swallow my digits. Such a good girl, so wet for me."

I close my eyes, trying to tune out where we are. "Stop," I whimper-whisper.

His fingers sheathed deep inside me, he stops. A few beats, but he doesn't resume.

I turn my head to him. "What are you doing?" I hiss.

"You asked me to stop."

"Je vais te tuer."

347

He hums again, the bastard. "Talking French, black swan. Mixed signals here…"

"Bâtard."

He chuckles, but thank God he resumes his ministrations, edging me, and then slowing down. I'm a puddle of nerves and sensations.

At one point, I almost double over, masking it by casually bracing one of my elbows on the table.

This is so wrong.

And so right.

I don't know who this man is anymore. My fake husband is my real lover. He asked me to let him figure it out. But the more time he takes, the deeper I'm falling.

Caleb moves his hand in a leisurely tempo, and I clench desperately, chasing my release.

"Let go, Celeste." His words fan my nape, and I explode around his fingers, barely stifling a cry.

A thundering applause erupts around me, and I throw my head back, letting the remnants of pleasure seep through my body. Letting the audience reward—

What the actual fuck? I'm not on stage. The applause for the award of the night is only a bizarre coincidence.

But for a moment there, my mind lost its grasp on what's reality and what's make-believe. For a tantalizing moment, I didn't know who I was.

I was stripped down to bare sensation. But besides the physical, a genuine feeling blossoms inside me.

How am I supposed to play a role when the role morphed into real life?

Too real to pretend otherwise.

Too visceral to act superficially.

Too significant to maintain the sham.

I blink a few times while the clapping turns into a standing ovation. Dazed, my gaze finds Caleb's.

A satisfied smirk on his face, he ignores the mayhem around us and licks his fingers casually, his eyes locked on me.

Heat spreads up my cleavage into my cheeks. I attempt to stand up. Caleb jumps up to help me.

A ghost of a smile traces his beautiful face as he looks at me with adoration.

I'm hyper-aware of his hand touching my elbow. His eyes piercing through me. My arousal sticking to my thighs.

Something new passing between us.

It's confusing and overwhelming. It terrifies and enchants me.

I panic and turn to the table, and gulp down another glass of wine. Yes, a normal person would just deal with their emotions.

A mature person would have tried to have a

conversation. Why would I guess if he feels the same when I can just ask him?

Well, why would I ask him if I can pretend that my attraction is still purely physical?

Why would I do any of it if I can just flush it down with wine?

Because I'm scared.

I never had a ballerina's body, and yet I pursued dancing.

I came to New York, broken emotionally and financially, and I made it.

But now, for the first time in my life, I want something, and I'm too scared to reach for it.

Caleb puts his hand on my wrist gently to stop my guzzling. "Let's go home."

We don't say our goodbyes. We don't talk in the car or in the elevator. We just execute the exit strategy like we're running.

Away from these feelings, or toward them?

My head is swimming with alcohol, and my heart is galloping like a spooked horse as Caleb leads me up the stairs.

He opens the door to my room. This is the first time he's come in here. He's never once set foot in here before.

The energy between us is charged, but I'm not sure what drives it. I stumble and he studies me.

Merde. I'm drunk.

Caleb kisses my forehead, and I sway a bit. It's funny how I'm completely aware of the new energy between us, but equally unable to stand on my own feet.

He slides my dress down my shoulders and unzips the skirt part. The silk pools by my ankles. He kisses my temple and my shoulder. There is no urgency or heat in his touch or his kiss. His attention is similar to that peck on my lips at the gala.

Reverent.

Caring.

Affectionate.

He unfastens my corset, because I might have not worn panties, but that dress needed some control over my curves.

And it occurs to me that, while I've had sex with Caleb—a lot of mind-blowing, earth-shattering sex—and he saw my pussy or my breasts, he's never seen me naked.

I'm glad I'm drunk, and I wish I wasn't. Suddenly I'm self-conscious. I reach for his belt, just to occupy my foggy, unhelpful mind.

He circles his palm around my wrist and pulls it away. Gently.

Stepping back, he studies me, his gaze roaming around my body. "You're fucking gorgeous."

A gasp forms but comes out as a hiccup, and Caleb chuckles. It's then that my drunken mind tilts my axis and I stumble again.

Strong arms grab me, but instead of steadying me, Caleb hoists me bridal-style and takes me to bed. Effortlessly.

"I'm swooning here, pretty boy."

He laughs, lowers me to my bed, takes off my shoes, and throws the comforter over my naked body. What is happening?

"Good night, black swan." He kisses my forehead and leaves.

What the actual fuck?

Chapter 31

Celeste

I groan and drop my phone.

"Something wrong?" Caleb saunters into the kitchen, showered and bare-chested.

I woke up with a massive hangover. A glass of water and painkillers were waiting on my nightstand, courtesy of the man who took care of me last night. Who stirred feelings inside me, and left me void at the same time.

"Cora just texted me that the building where I used to have my dance school is available for lease again."

I'm conflicted about what happened yesterday, and my feelings jumble even more as my half-naked husband ambles over to me and kisses my temple.

"You look a bit green." He smirks.

"Va te faire foutre." I swat at him, but he catches

my wrist and pulls me to him, my body molding into his.

"I'm turned on even by your swearing." He captures my mouth, his hand fisting my hair.

All my conflicting feelings collide and explode again. I need to get off this roller coaster. We need to name this new thing between us.

His kiss is bruising and worshipping at the same time. The man is driving me crazy. He walked away from me last night, and he walked back toward me this morning, so naturally I don't know where I stand.

Or maybe it's just me who needs to discuss, label, name this. Me who can't simply enjoy things the way they are.

But that wouldn't be fair to either of us. Because as much as I tried to shield myself, feelings have snuck in, and he should know.

Because feelings definitely weren't included in our arrangement.

"Did you eat something?" He pulls away and tucks a tress behind my ear.

It's such a simple gesture, but fuck if it doesn't give me hope.

"I don't think I can eat."

"Well, as someone who has more experience with drinking, let me make you eggs and bacon."

My stomach lurches. "I don't think that's a good idea."

"Believe me." He chuckles and slaps my ass. "Sit and be pretty."

"Bâtard."

"If you want me to fix your hangover, don't speak French." He points to his underwear, grinning. And sure enough, I guess I do affect him.

With his impressive morning wood, he proceeds to make me breakfast, whistling.

"So do you miss it?" He moves around the kitchen with ease.

It's like watching porn and eating popcorn while doing it. Arousing and comforting.

"Miss what?"

"Your dance school. Why did Cora text you about it?" The muscles on his back contract with every move, and I would film this if I could do it in a non-creepy way.

"I do. I miss teaching. A lot."

"Why did you stop then?"

I let out a long breath. Not the conversation I hoped we would have, but he asked earnestly, so I don't want to push my agenda.

"I took out a loan to expand the space, and just as I finished with renovations and was about to hire other teachers..."

He turns from the stove. "Last year?"

"The plan was viable, and the client's interest was there. It would have worked, but my cash flow was dependent on my paid gigs in the clubs. When Charles van den Linden"—the man doesn't deserve to be called his father—"blacklisted me from work anywhere in the city, I couldn't keep up with the payments."

"And the loan?"

I look away.

"Fuck, Celeste, why didn't you tell me?"

"Because it's none of your business," I snap, embarrassed by my situation.

I recognize that his father's irrational vendetta against Caleb's sister-in-law was the catalyst for my failure, but it doesn't lessen the fact that I failed.

Frustration fills the kitchen while he prepares a plate for each of us. We sit beside each other at the breakfast bar.

"How much do you owe?"

"A hundred and fifty thousand."

"How have you been paying it?"

"From my paycheck."

I'm glad we're beside each other and I don't have to meet his eyes.

"Eat," he growls.

"Jesus." I shove a forkful of eggs into my mouth,

mostly to stop myself from lashing out. My indignation melts away when the perfectly soft and impossibly creamy texture hits my tongue. "These are really good."

"I'm not just a pretty face." He kisses my shoulder casually, using the words I teased him with before. It helps me to put my pride to the side.

"I should renegotiate the terms, though. Maybe you can help me with that?"

He turns to me. "You didn't talk to the bank after you closed the school? It's been a year."

"I know it's stupid—"

"But you're not stupid. You have a natural business sense, and I saw the books in your apartment. I don't understand."

"I have a bureauphobia," I blurt out.

Swiftly he swirls my bar stool and his, and I'm wedged between his knees before I can react. I brace myself for his laugh or doubt.

"The day of our wedding..." he says instead.

I jerk my eyes to him. He remembers my near panic at the courthouse and in the bank.

I nod, searching his face and finding compassion. I think.

"Thank you for telling me. Now, I'm going to take care of your loan, and you're going to accept it."

"I can't."

"Yes, you can, and you will. In return, you give Mia dancing lessons for as long as she wants."

"I already do that—for free, and with joy."

He pinches my hip. "Okay, unlimited access to your pussy."

I laugh. "Are you turning me into your personal sex worker?"

"I can afford it, since you didn't buy that airplane." He gestures to my plate. "Now cure your hangover, so I can fuck you nice and slow on this counter."

I snort, but get serious. When I asked for help, I wanted him to deal with the bank, or at least accompany me. "You don't have to pay my loan."

"I'm still going to do it. I wish I knew how much the school meant to you sooner."

I take another bite and almost moan. Fuck, how did I not know he makes eggs like a pro?

"Don't get me wrong, I enjoy the theater, but the school was different. Dance is joy, and I love spreading joy. It's amazing to see women and girls dropping their inhibitions, their image issues, their insecurities behind the door and experiencing freedom.

"Sometimes I wonder if it's just an ego trip. On the stage, anyone can replace me, but in my school, I mattered. I felt irreplaceable."

He studies me, tracing his fingers along my hairline, down my neck, over my shoulder. "You're irre-placeable."

* * *

LILY

@Celeste can you come to the bistro for a few candid pics?

What?

CORA

Lily's starting my social media campaign.

You can't afford me. LOL

CORA

Free lattes for life?

I'm already getting those! (devil emoji)

CORA

Exactly! You owe me:-)

Okay, I'll come in an hour

SAAR

I hate you all

???

CORA

???

SAAR

You're all on a different continent :-(

FaceTime later?

You're irreplaceable.

As a dancer?

As a teacher?

As a lover?

As his wife?

And why, suddenly, do I really want the latter to be true? Because the latter feels like the truth. Deep in my soul, I want, I need that to be true.

Caleb and I need to talk. I need to lay my cards on the table and tell him how I feel. There's always the risk that he might not feel the same. But I need to rip off the Band-Aid before I'm in too deep.

Merde. I'm as deep as I've ever been. There's no way I can protect my poor heart anymore.

"Could you maybe frown less?" Lily lowers her phone, startling me.

"Sorry, I was thinking about... a bill I forgot to pay." I swirl a spoon in the glass mug in front of me.

"No," Lily cries.

"What?"

She's been trying to snap a few candid but glamorous pics of the bistro's life, and I'm more distracted than helpful.

"We wanted to feature the beautiful layers of the latte." Cora sits beside me. "Why don't we take a break, Lil?"

Lily joins us. "No problem. I have other pics I can start with, but you, Celeste, with your looks, you're just so real and beautiful."

I grin. "Do continue."

We laugh.

"So how is Sanjay working out?" I ask.

"He's great, actually. I really hope he sticks around."

The door chimes, and I glance up and shriek. "No way. Why didn't you tell us?" I jump up and Cora turns.

Saar laughs and runs toward us. "I missed you, bitches."

"But your text..." Cora pushes off her chair.

"I tricked you. Surprise!" She cheers, spreading her arms above her head.

We all hug and squeal like teenagers.

Saar's blond hair is in a messy bun, and she doesn't take off her large sunglasses. Even wearing a simple white tee and black leggings, she looks like the super-model she is. "Who is that eye candy over there?"

"Don't you dare." Cora swats at her.

"Do you want him for yourself?" Saar teases.

"Yes, but not in the way you think." Cora rolls her

eyes, but she isn't really mad. This is just us, and it feels so good and normal to hang out.

"When did you arrive? Why didn't you tell us?" I ask.

"One of my jobs got canceled, and I just needed a change of pace. I'm only here for three days though. And I plan to sleep for most of them."

"What's up with the glasses?" Cora bumps her with her elbow.

"I partied all night and then decided it was time for home sweet home, so I'm a bit light-sensitive, shall I say?" She shrugs.

"Jesus, I wish I had your energy." Cora sighs. "Did you party with someone interesting?"

Saar snickers. "Okay, you wouldn't believe this, but the guy took me for dinner and then we went dancing. He was gorgeous, and I thought, this might be someone I could stand for longer than one night."

"Oh my God, the relationship cynic is thawing." Cora claps her hands.

Saar seems to have sworn off anything resembling commitment. I guess it runs in the family.

Last night's encounter with Charles van den Linden reminded me that the van den Linden siblings grew up with an example that didn't really show them what a healthy relationship looks like.

That they can be loving. Mutually enriching. Trusting.

But then I didn't grow up with such an example, and it didn't turn me off the idea of romance. Perhaps it's my mom's boasting heart that left a more lasting imprint than all the other stuff with my father.

"Hardly. No relationships for me. Listen to this, we're dancing and having fun and there are touches and we made out a bit... and then he licked my armpit."

I spit out the coffee I just sipped. "What the fuck?"

"What do you mean he licked your armpit?" Lily laughs.

"Exactly that. I was wearing a sleeveless dress, had my arms up dancing, and the dude leaned in and licked my armpit."

"By accident?" Cora sounds incredulous.

"No accident. Apparently, for some men, a female armpit is like a pussy."

"My dry spell has stretched for a while now, but I'm pretty sure I wouldn't orgasm if a man licked my armpit instead of my pussy." Cora shakes her head.

"To each their own kink, but I agree." Saar shudders.

We continue chatting for a moment before Lily pulls out her tripod again.

"Can I take a picture of you here? It would really help with Cora's marketing..." Lily fidgets.

Saar looks from her to Cora and then at me.

"Sorry, I know you came to have a break," Cora interjects after a beat of silence.

"Dude, are you kidding me? Of course you can take my pic. What's the concept behind it?"

Lily perks up and explains to Saar what she has in mind.

"I guess I'm dismissed as your model," I tease.

Cora's eyes shine with unshed tears. "No, of course I want pics of you too." She sniffles.

"What's wrong?" Saar turns to her.

"I'm just..." Cora wipes her cheek. "You're all so generous with your help. I'm so grateful."

"Oh, sweetie, believe me, having a pic taken here is nothing. Lily's ideas are great. And I'll repost. Don't sweat it." Saar pulls out the elastic and tosses her messy hair to the side. Of course, it looks like she styled it for hours. Effortless and real.

"Besides, I was promised free lattes," I deadpan.

"God, I missed you all. Even you, Lily, and your horrible coffees." Saar winks.

Lily rolls her eyes. "Seriously, will I ever live my barista skills down?"

"Never," we all say at the same time.

"You're evil." She pretend-glares at us, a smile on her face. "Not you, Saar, I'm grateful for your help."

"Don't even mention it. So what else is new?"

I tense. I haven't told Saar I've been sleeping with her brother. But of course, Cora glances my way, and it catches Saar's attention immediately.

"What did my brother do?" Saar groans.

I let out a long sigh. "We kind of got a bit involved."

She takes off her glasses, and I'm concerned about the red lines in her eyes and the deep shadows under them, but my heart hammers in my ribcage for a different reason.

I want my friend's blessing. Not that there's much to bless, or that she should have any say in it, but it still feels important.

"You slept with him?" She leans back.

I nod, the words lodged in my throat. Or in my mind, because I'm not quite sure what to say.

"So, the marriage is..." Saar's eyes dart to Lily.

"She knows," Cora confirms. "Do you guys need a minute?"

Saar shakes her head. "Obviously you're all in the know more than me. Stay." She turns back to me. "So the marriage is real?"

My shoulders fall slack. "It's complicated."

"Of course it's complicated. It's my brother. He never even commits to bringing a woman to his bed." Saar puts her sunglasses back on.

Bringing a woman to his bed. All the instances of our affair rush through my mind. I always assumed that

365

he had a public sex kink, and frankly, I didn't mind discovering it was mine as well.

But was it actually more than that? Not just a kink, but a deep fear of commitment? I'm just one of his women. A lay he doesn't bother to bring to his bed. Because in all of our encounters, he never has.

Last night? He wouldn't even stay in mine.

You're irreplaceable.

What a lie. I'm as dispensable to him as any other.

Chapter 32

Caleb

Celeste straddles a chair and, gripping the armrests, tilts her head back. I fist my hands, willing myself not to react, my palms sweaty and ready to touch her. To pull her to me. To kiss her. To own her.

Not that I could do it from the back row of the theater. I came to watch her rehearsal a few times. Staying in the shadows like a creep, but I couldn't help myself.

She moves around effortlessly, and so seductively. Frankly, the entire performance, not just her numbers, is racy enough to send my blood boiling.

It was kind of hot at first, but as time passes, it's purely annoying. I have half a mind to call Reinhard and have the show canceled.

Watching her today has a different flavor.

We haven't had a chance to speak since last night. Something shifted between us at the gala. Even before it.

Starting with her not-yet-fully-explained overreaction about her dress. Then my need to find her all night. To stand up for her to Carly. To protect her from Corm. To claim her at our table.

Fuck, that was so hot, and so fucking risky. The interaction—or lack of it—with my father, and Celeste's reaction to it.

When she stepped in, allowing me to find my composure after Corm's question. When she deemed my father an asshole. When she came on my hand.

It all collided into a potent cocktail of feelings, and I arrived at the conclusion that we can no longer pretend this is simply an arrangement. It's more.

But I saw it in her eyes, the moment she realized the same.

And when she panicked.

That's why I came here. She dashed away this morning because her friend needed her, but we need to talk. We need to own this fragile, but very real, thread between us.

But as her practice progresses, I'm getting more and more agitated. Because yes, watching her today has a different flavor, and one of the truly bothersome reasons for that is walking across the stage right now.

Why is today's rehearsal just her? No other dancers? Just Celeste and that idiot choreographer whose gaze on her doesn't scream colleagues. Fucking asshole.

Celeste stands up when he approaches her. He sits on the chair in the same position she just had and demonstrates something to her. Something that doesn't look nearly as graceful as her version.

She nods and they switch. As she tilts her head backward, he touches her shoulders from behind. She adjusts her posture, I think.

My mind stops processing the visuals at their face value, tainting the image with a bubbling outrage. Why is he touching her?

He moves his hand up her throat, tilting her chin further. She flinches and stands up, the chair toppling.

My legs move before my brain gets a chance to argue. "Get away from her." My voice booms through the auditorium.

The two of them whip their heads to me.

"Who the fuck are you?" the choreographer dares to ask. "You have no right to be here."

My legs eat up the distance, reaching the stage in long strides. With my hands, I find purchase at the edge of the wooden platform and jump up in one swift move, propelled by my anger.

"I have all the right to be here. I own the fucking

place." I put my hands into my pockets, savoring his flinch. My eyes find Celeste. "Are you okay?"

She nods, but then winces before she shakes her head.

"I don't care if you own the building. Get the fuck out of my rehearsal." The idiot steps forward, puffing out his chest.

Reluctantly, my gaze leaves Celeste. "I advise you to shut up right now. Don't you dare touch my wife again, because you'll not only lose this job but any other opportunity in this country."

Somewhere in the back of my mind, where the rage isn't ruling, I register Celeste's gasp. That doesn't stop me from taking a few steps closer to the idiot. "I strongly suggest you get out of here right now. No one touches my wife like you just did without consequences."

The echo of Celeste's heels fills my foggy mind, disappearing quickly behind the heavy black curtain at the back of the stage.

"You can't—"

I'm done with him. I need to be with Celeste. "You're fired."

I storm away, following Celeste's footsteps. I yank the curtain to the side and emerge in a hallway. I rush after her, calling her name.

She doesn't stop. She doesn't look at me.

Until she does.

And my heart stops and restarts in that moment.

Pausing in front of a door, she looks at me and I halt. Our gazes collide, tears pooling in her eyes.

The pain in her expression burns through me with a vengeance. I feel her suffering in my veins, deep in my bone marrow.

The oxygen doesn't hit my lungs. Something is really wrong. And while I don't know what it is, I know without a shadow of a doubt that I caused it. And the reasons, the logic, the explanation of my actions, are unimportant.

What matters is that she's hurt. And I want to burn the world to take that hurt away.

Celeste pushes the door open and disappears.

My shoes slap against the concrete, the sound almost obscene in the silent building. One leg forward. *I scared her.* The other one. *I hurt her.* Another step.

I scared her.

I hurt her.

My footsteps chant in my head, and it feels like a lifetime before I reach her door. I knock.

Nothing.

Leaning my forehead against the wooden surface, I stop myself from barging in, because something tells me I need to let her be in charge here.

But fuck, I want to break the fucking door down and demand answers.

Claim my right to console her.

Absorb her pain.

"Celeste." I knock again, and almost fall forward when she yanks the door open.

Stumbling at the threshold, I find purchase against the doorframe with my arm.

The tears are gone as she stands there in her comfortable wrap dress, the one she usually wears at her practice. Fuck, she's beautiful.

And clearly whatever her initial reaction was, she's found her composure. Now, she glares at me with venom.

It shouldn't, but it still gives me hope. Combative Celeste is one I know well. One I can handle. But there is no way I'm letting her wear that mask without explaining what hurt her earlier.

She doesn't invite me in, but she isn't blocking the entrance either. I glance over her shoulder. There is a mirror, a vanity, and a rack full of clothes. It's her changing room.

"You own this theater?" She puts her hands on her hips.

Shit, I forgot I blurted that out earlier. The thought of that asshole choreographer sends another jolt of rage through my veins, but I rein it in, forcing myself to focus on what matters.

"That's irrelevant." I push past her, knowing I might push her too far, too fast. But fuck, I'm not sitting on the sidelines.

"I don't need you saving me." She bangs the door closed.

I take that as a win. If she's willing to be with me in a close, confined space, she's willing to talk. Or at least to listen.

"He was touching you," I growl. Not the best opening, but a relevant one nevertheless.

"He was directing me."

"You flinched." It comes out like an accusation.

"You couldn't have seen that."

She steps away from the door, but also away from me. Turning her back to me, she faces the mirror and starts doing something with things on the vanity. Something that looks a lot like busy work to avoid me.

"Look at me, Celeste."

She keeps reorganizing the chaos in front of her. Grabbing a long bottle, she sprays around her head. Her hand circles around furiously and she misses most of her hair, the abusive mist hitting my lungs.

I clear my throat and demand, "Look at me and tell me his touch was innocent."

She flicks her gaze up, meeting mine in the mirror.

Instead of an answer, she glares at me, like I'm the villain here.

But she can't admit he touched her as a part of his work. Because I might have overreacted, but there was more behind his touch.

"That's what I thought." I scoff. "Isn't it enough you flaunt yourself half-naked in front of the audience several times a week? I don't need to watch some fucker groping you."

As soon as the words leave my mouth, I regret them. Fuck. Fuck. Fuck.

She doesn't turn, but her gaze cools. She lifts her chin. "Get out of here."

A frustrated growl lodges in my throat. I hang my head for a moment, but then I find her gaze again. "Celeste, I didn't mean… I'm sorry. It was a shitty thing to say, and I didn't mean it."

She laughs. "Didn't you? Like father, like son." She delivers the words with confidence, but her lips tremble, at odds with her determination.

If she kicked me in my balls, it would've hurt less. She looks down, and I consider leaving, to shield myself from the influx of feelings.

Feelings I don't want to name. Some of them undiscovered and scary. Some of them just plain nasty.

Celeste turns to face me now. Her hair dislodges

from the twist at the back of her head, and a sleek ponytail springs around, landing on her shoulder.

She's still put together and made up as always, but the bouncing tresses make her look more real. Almost exposed.

"I hate jealousy," she whispers.

"Maybe I wouldn't have to be jealous if... Never mind."

The coward in me roars its ugly head like it always does when a sign of commitment wafts my way. Goddammit.

How the fuck did we get here? I came today to take her out after her rehearsal and talk.

I wanted to tell her how this faux marriage has grown on me.

How I enjoy her company.

How she flipped my world upside down, showing me that not every relationship needs to be rotten. A transaction.

That I've never needed anything from anyone, and now I need her around. I still don't want anything from her, but I want to give her what she needs, what she wants, what makes her happy.

But I don't get to say any of those things, because somewhere between me entering the darkness of the theater and this painful moment, we unearthed something ugly and confusing.

"If what?"

"If you were truly mine," I bark.

"That's rich, coming from someone who can't even take me to his bed."

The words slap me into action before I can even consider the consequences. I eat the short distance between us and fist her hair, tilting her head toward me.

I half expect her to kick me, but when she doesn't... when she only stares at me defiantly, but full of heat, I pin her with my hips, lodging my leg between hers.

"You haven't screamed my name yet, black swan. Don't you dare pretend I'm the only one avoiding commitment. We're both guilty of keeping our walls so high we can't even see what's real anymore."

Her breath hitches. Her body still taut, she sags a little, and the suggestion of her pussy against my thigh alerts my cock immediately.

I pull her ponytail harder and lower my lips to her face. The familiar scent of flowers envelops me, fogging my brain like the aphrodisiac it is.

She whimpers and slackens more, her hands shooting up to grip my shirt. Like she can't hold herself up, but also like she wants to make sure I stay close.

I inhale a lungful, dragging my nose up her cheek. "I'm ready to demolish my walls. The question, black swan, is what are you going to do with yours?"

Chapter 33

Celeste

My hands clench his shirt like my life depends on it. Somewhere on the periphery of my fraught mind, I understand we have so much to talk about, so much to address, so much to apologize for.

But his declaration, his willingness to take the leap, overwhelms my senses, and I can't use my words. I can't find my voice. I can't formulate my fears and hopes into sentences.

Instead, I pull him to me and crush my lips against his, answering him with my affection. He startles, but doesn't hesitate for too long, accepting my kiss with passion and desire.

My sensitive pussy rubs against his thigh, lighting up little fires all over my body. Caleb groans into my mouth, one hand still tugging on my hair, the other finding my breast.

He scared me today with his display of possessiveness. He hurt me with his words of jealousy. He shocked me with his passionate admission.

But all of that is inconsequential. It's solvable. It's better than the game we've been playing.

Raw. Honest. Fiery.

That's what our kiss is, and that's what the argument leading to it was.

And while all the unanswered questions are still crying for attention, it's the closeness and the need to feel rather than understand that wins.

I yank at his shirt, but he grips my wrist. He pulls away from my face, but stays close.

Our gazes collide, and the world around us finds a break from its endless flow.

My breath hitches as I take in the breath he exhaled. In this beat of eternity right now, it's just us.

Two souls scared and courageous.

Two hearts hurting and soaring.

Two people falling.

The gentle, almost shy adoration in his eyes matches all I feel. The crease on his forehead mirrors all my hesitations. The subtle grin ghosting his lips tugs at the corners of my mouth.

He lowers his forehead to mine and traces my cheek with his knuckles. "Let's go home."

Weaving his fingers through mine, he steps back. I whimper, bereft of his touch, but know that a quickie in my changing room would set our relationship—no longer arrangement—back.

"Let's go home." I nod.

Caleb doesn't speak as he waits for me to gather my things. The theater is closed today, so we're probably the only two people here—

"What happened to Leon?" I shudder, recalling his touch.

"Who is Leon?" Caleb opens the door for me, and we leave the room, heading toward the back exit.

"The man you threatened moments ago. My choreographer."

"I fired him."

I stop, unsure how I feel about that. Leon touched me inappropriately, but I'm sure he'd have taken the hint if I'd had a chance to tell him to stay away.

There's also a pathetic girl in me with a distorted notion that Caleb's actions are romantic.

The grown-up me wants to make the point about not needing his saving.

The newly-in-a-real-relationship me decides there will be other battles to pick.

"I don't know how I feel about you being my boss,"

I say as we get to the car. "Hello, Peter." I smile at the driver and get inside.

"I've been your boss's boss for a year, and you didn't seem to mind." Caleb slides inside, wraps his arm around my shoulder and tugs me to him.

Like we've been doing this forever. Like we fit perfectly, and we know it. Like this is our new norm.

"For a year?" I turn my face to him.

I don't know what to do with this information, but he doesn't seem disturbed by any of it. "Yes, I got the theater last year when you needed the visa."

I blink a few times, our faces only inches away. "I couldn't get a job, so you bought me one? That must have cost you a fortune. And you didn't even like me back then."

He chuckles and kisses my forehead. "It worked out well." The nonchalance in his voice is infuriating.

"No wonder Reinhard hates me."

"That has nothing to do with me."

"A clear case of nepotism."

"You were not my wife back then, and you've more than proved yourself since. Frankly, that theater was barely surviving before you got on board. As far as I'm concerned, it was an excellent investment."

I shake my head and rest it on his shoulder. "You have been paying my paycheck for a year. That's—"

"Celeste," he growls. "Stop spinning that smart

brain of yours. I bought a theater, it's profitable now, no regrets there. You benefited, and back then it was easier than marrying you."

I jerk away. "I'm still your wife."

"Only because Reinhard is incompetent," he deadpans.

I gasp, but he laughs.

"He's incompetent, but his fuck-up got me the most beautiful, smart, accomplished, annoying, head-strong, stubborn wife. Not complaining in the slightest."

God, I love this man.

Shit, I love this man.

But maybe it's safe to love him.

"It's a good thing I didn't buy that airplane. You'd be ruined."

He laughs. "Fuck it. I'm buying you that airplane."

* * *

Three hours later, we're still stuck in the car.

"We could have just walked," I mumble, even though my legs and feet are sore from rehearsal.

"I'm sure it can't take much longer." Caleb squeezes my hand. He hits the intercom. "Peter, any news?"

"According to the radio, the accident included

several cars and pedestrians. We're stuck in a sea of traffic with nowhere to divert."

"Keep us posted." He releases the button. "We heard the helicopters an hour ago, I'm sure it's going to clear soon."

My stomach rumbles. "I haven't eaten since this morning."

"Wait here." Caleb opens the door and disappears for almost fifteen minutes.

What the hell? This delay feels anticlimactic after our conversation at the theater. By the time we get home, I'll want to stay in my room just from the sheer need to rest, my hangover still lingering.

The door swings open and he slides back in and places a box in my lap.

"Croissants?" I smile at him, and almost moan at the tantalizing steam coming from the box. Picking up one soft pastry, I groan. "They're fresh." I take a bite and actually moan around the flaky batter.

"Jesus, woman, stop those sounds before I have no option but to feed you my cock."

His voice is light and playful, but an undeniable need laces his tone.

"Let me eat in peace. We should have gotten something for Peter."

"I got him a sandwich."

"What about you?"

"I'm hoping you'll share."

I clutch the box closer to me. "Never." I slide farther from him, grinning. There's no way I can eat all five of them, but I can tease him.

"You'll let me starve?"

I pretend to think about it, but Caleb slides closer and pinches my chin, kissing me roughly and daring me with his hooded gaze.

"I guess I could share. I mean, you got me my favorite pastry."

"I know."

He snatches one and leans back. I cock my head in question.

"There were never croissants in my house before, so I concluded you love them. Is it sentimental?"

I don't know how to answer that. Frankly, I accepted the craving a long time ago without giving it much thought. "It's the weirdest thing, because I don't think I liked them that much in France, but I guess they became the stereotypical connection to the country that is no longer my home."

"Do you miss it?"

"Do you miss your parents?" I'm aware I'm stalling, but this conversation is a difficult one, even though it's time I shared and explained.

Caleb leans into the leather backrest, but he stays very close. Eyes trained on the dark partition in front of us, he sighs. "Since I learned about Mia, I hate my father."

His father ensured Caleb had no contact with his daughter or her mother. What if it was different? Would he be happily married to Reese?

A pang of unreasonable jealousy swarms through me. I don't say anything, because I can keep repeating the same mollifying words to him, but it won't help him. He needs to let go of that toxic relationship on his own.

Instead, I decide to bare a part of me that might show him we have more in common than we ever imagined.

"Me too."

His shoulders heave with another loaded sigh. "I'm sorry for what he did to you."

"Nothing compares to what he did... what he's still doing to you. But I was talking about my father." Bile moves up my chest as I remember the man.

I slouch into the seat, suddenly unable to breathe. Caleb turns his head and I feel his gaze deep inside me. "Your father?"

The confines of the car start closing in on me. I lower the window, and honking cars, exhaust fumes, distant music and a news anchor's voice infiltrate the small space.

Somehow it's easier to tell him about my parents

amidst the ruckus of Manhattan. "My father was jealous and controlling. He'd accuse my mom of flirting, make her change her clothes when he deemed them too revealing. He'd come to the theater where she worked and cause scenes.

"She shielded me from his wrath for most of my childhood, but when I was fifteen, he lost his job. He channeled his frustration into even more jealousy and control. I don't know if he truly loved my mom, and I don't know why she never tried to leave him. Or maybe she tried.

"He couldn't find work, started drinking then and became more aggressive, but never ever physical. Until..."

A shudder rakes through my body as I recall the night when I lost the most important person in my life.

Caleb pulls me to him, understanding that I won't be able to go through this story without his support.

"I was seventeen when he attacked me for wearing a slutty dress, but this time he accentuated his words with his fist. Mom intervened, but his rage was blinding and he pushed her away. She stumbled, fell, and hit her head on a coffee table.

"I left the country shortly after her funeral, and I vowed to always dress the way I want, and to never ever let anyone control me."

"I fucking want to kill him right now."

I chuckle humorlessly. "He's in prison, and he's not worth it."

Caleb holds me tighter and kisses the crown of my head. "I'm sorry."

"Me too. I've never told anyone. I miss my mom every single day."

"When I snapped about your dress and raged about the low-life choreographer..."

"It triggered me."

"Fuck, Celeste, I've never meant—"

I pivot to face him. "I know. That's the fucked-up part. I don't know why or how it happened, but I trust you. I trust that you wouldn't hurt me. Even today, when you lashed out at Leon, you first checked if I was okay. My father would have accused me of asking for it. But there are occasions when I can't control my reaction."

"I've never been jealous before. This is the first time I find myself acting before I can think. The need to—"

I put a finger on his lips. "Don't say anything right now. We're both learning how to dance together. I told you the story because I wanted you to see the other outcome of that horrible night.

"I came to New York, I built a business, I booked some damn good gigs, I met you..." My breath hitches at the last thing. "I could have stayed home, grieved, and blamed my father, but I chose to celebrate my mom and be the best version of myself, one that would make her proud."

"She'd be proud of you now."

I smile, warmth spreading through my veins. His praise truly is something I never knew I needed.

"Your parents will never be proud of you, Caleb, because they are selfish, narcissistic people. Don't let them rule your life. It's noble you're fixing as many of his mistakes as possible, but you need to look forward. He robbed you of the time with your family, but he can't rob you of it again. You're in control now."

He nods, and we stay still for several long moments. It's a stillness that deepens our understanding. That wraps all the hurt in kindness.

"I want Mia to spend more time with us." He looks at me with a question in his eyes. "Would you be okay with that?"

As his wife, he means. As the woman who isn't by his side only temporarily.

I smile. "I would love that."

Chapter 34

Celeste

I cling to him, practically asleep after the longest ride from work ever. The physical and emotional exhaustion coils around my bones. It also fills the air between us, like we both need to sleep off the past few months and wake up to a new beginning.

Or at least this new understanding between us. As I inhale the scent of him, I feel lighter and heavier at the same time.

Cal kisses the crown of my head. It seems like an automatic gesture, but it sets my heart fluttering every single time.

"Je suis tout à toi."

He groans and dips his head deeper, trailing my cheek and the side of my neck with his nose languidly.

I know I haven't told him I'm his in English yet,

and that's what he wants to hear so much. I'll tell him in the bedroom.

Oh God, I hope we're heading to his bedroom. Or mine. It doesn't matter, as long as he takes me to a bed. That's what he meant when he said he's demolishing his walls.

"Are you okay?"

Can he read my thoughts now? "Yes, just really tired."

We get off the elevator and step into the dark apartment, the only source of light coming from the dim spotlights around the floor. I shake off my shoes and walk to the kitchen, Caleb on my heels.

We drink water in a companionable silence in the kitchen before we make our way upstairs. I'm barely standing on my feet, exhaustion seeping into every part of my being.

He walks behind me but before I veer toward my room, he grabs my wrist.

"Where do you think you're going?"

My mind is buzzing with a latent headache, and it takes me an unreasonable amount of time to turn to face him. Or at least it feels like that, while the world swirls with me in my subtle motion.

What if everything changes once we share a bed? What if we don't enjoy the normal, so used to the wild and reckless way we usually have sex? Or worse, what if he realizes he doesn't like me in his private, intimate space and moves on?

He frowns and steps closer, crowding me against the wall. His breath fans my face. "What is it, black swan? Having second thoughts already? This isn't going to work if we both lean into fear."

Fuck, the man does read me already. But he's right. A part of me has this perverse need to discuss all the possible scenarios up front, so I can be ready for what might happen.

There is a much bigger part of me that recognizes that's not how life is lived. That I can't control the next minute.

But I can choose to enjoy it.

I can choose to believe in us.

So I choose.

He steps back, holding his hand out for me, and I take it. He kisses my knuckles and pulls me toward his bedroom.

He opens the door to what has been a secret chamber until now, and we step onto plush carpet.

"Cal..." Fuck, this can't be our first proper night. "I don't think—"

"Hush." He puts his index finger on my lips. "Let's just sleep."

He walks toward a dresser, taking off his cufflinks. He drops them into a mess of other personal items.

The room is sleek and modern, an elegant space like his entire house. Crisp white walls contrast with the dark accents and the chocolate-colored deep-pile carpet.

Draped in shades of brown, his bed is enormous, its masculinity softened with a casually strewn white throw.

A glass-walled bathroom in the corner draws my eyes. Why doesn't it surprise me that a man with a flair for exhibitionism has a glass shower as a key feature of his personal space?

I smile as a vision of his naked form there invades my imagination. That would be a sight to wake up to for sure.

Unsure what to do, I take a few steps in. My gaze travels to the artwork above his bed, and I'm thrown back to the memory of his first visit to my apartment.

The first originals of Andrea Cassinetti cover most of the wall in an asymmetrical pattern.

That series included a set number of drawings, and it seems only one is missing. The one I own.

My heart loses its rhythm and beats to the chaotic cries of my emotions. Part of *my* decor is missing from *his* personal space. The coincidence flutters in my stomach, tickling me with warmth.

"I don't think you should sleep in your dress." He breathes by my ear, startling me.

I pivot to face him. "I'm in your bedroom."

Making a sound that might be a grunt or a snicker, he snakes his arm around my waist and yanks me to him. "Don't make a fucking big deal about it."

Is there color in his cheeks? It is a fucking big deal, but I'm not going to argue that now. We're both tired, but we're both here. The significance of this step drapes around my shoulders like a veil of both dread and excitement.

"Do you need anything from your room?" He pulls at the string that holds my dress closed.

While I was studying his room, he stripped down to his boxers.

Fuck, he looks good. I step back to admire the perfect triangle of his torso. Our affair has been a series of stolen, passionate moments, or me ogling him in secret.

I take my time, tracing my fingers along his biceps while my gaze travels in appreciation.

He pushes the dress off my shoulders and it pools at my feet. We stand there for several heated seconds.

For once we're not rushing, the fiery passion replaced by something more potent. By intimacy that runs deeper than physical need.

"I'll go get my nightie." The words barely pass around the lump in my throat. I don't know why or when it got lodged there.

He unclasps my bra. "Do you need it?"

With one hand, he cups my breast gently, his finger brushing my nipple while he hooks his other hand into my panties.

"I can never fall asleep naked."

Maybe it's left over from the years when I covered my body because I hated it, or perhaps it's just a habit, but I certainly hate sleeping with all my curves and folds exposed.

Caleb squats and takes my underwear with him. He helps me step out of it and then shocks me when he leans in and kisses me between my legs.

It's a reverent kiss. A worshipping one. Just a brief touch of his lips before he stands up. The gesture steals my breath, and feelings I've never felt spread in my chest.

He gives my lips the same quick but adoring peck. "There's a first time for everything. Let's go to sleep."

I don't know if he's talking about having a woman in his bed or me sleeping naked, but it doesn't matter, because the amount of firsts tonight marks is overwhelming, regardless.

He hauls me into his arms bridal-style and carries me to his bed.

"Stop it, I'm heavy."

"I disagree." He throws it out there casually, but strictly enough for me to reconsider any comeback.

And what would I even argue? This man has only made me feel beautiful and desired.

After he slides beside me, he covers us both, positions me with my back to him and wraps his arm and leg around me.

I'm in Caleb van den Linden's bed. Probably the first woman to do so. The event is significant by itself, but it feels unique because we just lie here.

The remnants of the day rendered us motionless. Or perhaps the intimacy is too much for both of us to act on it.

Or I'm overthinking it because we're exhausted and should sleep.

But we don't. Sleep is eluding us. I wiggle and turn in his arms, facing him.

Caleb sighs.

"I can go and sleep in my room."

It would hurt, but it wouldn't at the same time. Who says we need to jump into everything tonight? We can build up to this real couple thing slowly. We've done it all backward, anyway.

"Don't you dare. I didn't just break my lifelong habit for a few moments with you here."

"But you can't sleep."

The room is almost completely dark, his face in shadows and still the most handsome thing I've ever seen.

"I'm savoring," he whispers, tucking a strand behind my ear. "Now stop talking and get some rest. This bed and my cock need to see some action soon, black swan."

* * *

A gentle stream of water infiltrates my foggy, sleepy mind. I stretch my arms, my fingertips brushing unfamiliar fabric.

Yesterday's events flicker through my mind, and I snap my eyes open. And the sight is fucking breathtaking.

My gaze lands on my husband's penis behind the glass, explaining the sound of water. Caleb stands under a waterfall in his shower, his arms braced on the glass wall and his head down.

Every single sinew, cord and muscle is on display. The whole image is a reward wrapped in sin. And then he lifts his head and looks at me. Scorches me with his eyes.

Oh my God, it's a good thing he never brings women into this space, because the amount of swooning might have detrimental health implications. That glass shower is God's gift to women. No, no, the current occupant is.

My heart rate spikes, and my pussy clenches.

Caleb smirks and fists his cock, giving it an aggressive tug.

I rub my thighs together, kind of grateful I'm under the sheets, because my visceral reaction is mildly embarrassing, and there's no bloody way I'm allowing him to see the amount of power he has over me.

We might have crossed the invisible border into a committed relationship, but I can't hand all the control to him.

That thought evaporates into nothing when he turns off the water and steps out of the shower. Bringing with him the scent of his soap, and something so carnal I almost whimper, he rounds the bed, devouring me with his eyes.

"Good morning, black swan, I didn't mean to wake you up," he drawls, not in the least sorry that he did.

But neither am I. "Good morning. Careful there with that package." I beckon my head to arguably the most beautiful cock I've ever seen. How does he even fit that thing inside me?

Wet as he is, he jumps into bed and somehow pulls the covers from me. "You be carefully reckless with it, darling wife."

"You're soaking the sheets."

He flicks his finger through my folds. "Soaked is what I'm after." He winks, a satisfied smirk on his face.

I giggle but yelp as he flips me around. In one swift

move, he positions me on top of him, straddling him as he grips my hips.

I freeze. I'm okay with my body, but this is my least favorite position, because it usually gets me thinking about all the extra folds plainly on display.

We fucked like this before, but it was always when I was fairly dressed.

"You're so fucking beautiful."

I don't know if his words are a response to my hesitation, but they come out with such conviction and honesty, I abandon my stupid notions.

I *am* fucking beautiful.

I reach between us and lift my hips, guiding him to my entrance. When an inch of him teases inside me, I pause. "We've never done this."

He studies me for a moment, his breath labored. "I'm glad I saved my bed for you."

Oh, fuck, that too. "I mean, no condoms."

His eyebrows jerk up. It's a slight jolt of surprise, but it's there. Like he's been reckless but never once unprotected.

"I'm clean and on the shot." I sink my hips lower and we both moan.

"How do you know I'm clean?"

I shrug. "I trust you, pretty boy."

A flicker of something dark flashes through his face, and he thrusts up and sheathes himself inside me, filling me, and drawing a deep guttural moan from me.

I circle my hips to adjust to him and start moving languidly. Our eyes locked, this feels the same, and dramatically different from any other time.

It might be the novelty of the environment, the newly forged trust between us, or just the lingering exhaustion from yesterday.

Whatever the reason, the result is cathartic. Transforming. Magnificent.

My orgasm builds and comes crashing down, faster and harder than ever before. Caleb cups the back of my neck and pulls me to him, seizing my lips in a punishing kiss. "That's my girl."

I don't have a chance to marvel in my high before he flips us, hikes my hips and drives into me again with such force, I leap forward on the mattress.

"Hands on the headboard," he growls, and I scramble to oblige without a thought.

Because there is no thinking this morning. There is only feeling.

Feeling adored.

Feeling safe.

Feeling ecstatic.

Feeling possessed by this man. Belonging to him. Loving him.

Pounding into me like he can't get enough, like he

needs to punish and reward me at the same time, Caleb pulls at my hair.

In the haze of my first orgasm, and the desire raking through my body and pooling in my core, my mind registers his voice, and a question that hits me raw and honest.

"Who do you belong to, black swan?"

Chapter 35

Caleb

I don't know why I need her to say it. It annoys me she hasn't yet, and it pisses me off that I need the reassurance.

I lean forward, bracing on my arm, while I tug at her hair again. "Who do you belong to?"

It's like I'm a man possessed, and her answer is the holy land I need to conquer. As if she didn't show me with her actions, her support, her presence.

"Just fuck me, would you?" she pants.

Turning her head, she snakes her hand around my neck and pulls my face closer. While her other arm holds the headboard, she manages to meet my lips in a sloppy kiss.

I drop her hair and straighten behind her. Gripping her hips, I pound into her like I can punish her for not saying the words. For being fucking stubborn and defiant. While I've known all along those are the qualities I love about her.

The room fills with our moans, our sweat, our bodies connecting. The sight of my cock disappearing into her awakens something primal in me.

"Fuck, Celeste, you should see how well you take me. Such a beautiful greedy pussy."

I'm channeling my frustration and my adoration into every thrust. Never have I invested this much into chasing someone else's pleasure.

Never have I had a woman in my bed.

Never have I imagined it might feel this natural with anyone.

But this is not just anyone. This is Celeste. The only woman that made it this far.

To my bed. To my heart. To my fucking soul.

The tingling builds at the base of my spine, but fuck, I need her to get there first. I snake my hand around and pinch her clit.

Her arms slide from the headboard, her head dropping into the pillow as she tenses and squeezes around me.

"Oh my God, Cal-Cal-Caleb."

Her chanting sends me over the edge and I roar as I spill inside her.

Claiming her.

Marking her.

Making her mine, finally.

My wife.

* * *

The evening sunlight streams through the windows, casting a warm, golden hue over my bedroom. Our bedroom.

Celeste nestles her head on my chest, and I hold Celeste in a tight embrace. Like my body is on board with her intrusion into my private space, but my mind still needs more proof she is really here. That I really let her this close.

We've stayed in bed today. Fucking. Laughing. Talking. Eating. The day has been floating in a lazy, but very satisfying way.

I don't think I've spent an entire day in bed since I was a teenager, and definitely never with a woman. My encounters have always been quick and selfish. Today, I'm doting on my wife, and the result is a new level of satisfaction.

I glance down at her, marveling at how peaceful she looks. There's a slight curve to her lips, a hint of a smile that hasn't quite faded all day.

Her eyes are filled with a warmth that makes my chest ache in the best way possible.

Is this really my new reality? This easy companionship, this effortless joy? It feels almost too good to be true.

Celeste catches my reverie. "What's that look for?" Her eyebrows quirk.

I shrug, giving her a lopsided grin. "Just thinking about how lucky I am."

She rolls her eyes, but her smile widens. "You sap."

I pinch her and she squeals, elbowing me. We roll around in a half-hearted fight, both of us laughing.

My laugh is the kind that comes from deep in my chest, the kind that only she can pull from me.

I settle on top of her, pinning her arms above her head. "I've never thought spending a day with someone doing nothing could be this satisfying."

"Obviously I'm great company." She grins, but then grows serious, our eyes locked in a passionate gaze, full of want and need and adoration.

The L word is on the tip of my tongue, but she speaks again. "I think we should plan a trip with Mia, take her out of the city for a weekend. Or maybe just the two of you should go away together."

That's not where I thought her mind went, but the fact that in this intimate moment, she thinks about my relationship with Mia... that she's never looked at my daughter like she's a burden, hits me like a potent drug. Unraveling me with the rightness of it. Of this.

I roll on to my back, taking her with me. "I'd need to talk to Reese about that."

"When was the last time you tried that?"

"Only back then, when Mia showed up. Her texts were short and aloof. Mia doesn't know the details of why I didn't know about her, and I'm grateful Reese protected her from that story, but she still doesn't trust me."

"Maybe you should try again. She must know from Mia that the two of you formed a relationship that is growing deeper. She might see it all differently."

She's right, but I've just forged a fragile bond with Mia, and if I'm honest, I'm scared Reese won't allow more, or worse, she'd curb the time we have now. "Frankly, sometimes it feels Mia is coming behind Reese's back."

Celeste jerks her head, her eyes widening. "Caleb, if that's true, you might lose her if Reese finds out. She's still young, and shouldn't traipse around the city like this. Where does Reese think she is?"

"I'm not sure. I'm not even sure if it's true. I tried to ask Mia a few questions to probe about the chances of meeting her mom, but she became all uncomfortable and I dropped it."

"Merde." She strokes my cheek, her eyes soft. "I'm sorry this has been so hard."

"It's gotten significantly easier since you became

part of the picture. We'd be still sulking at each other if it wasn't for you. Thank you."

She fidgets and slides down from me, pulling me with her, so we now lie on our sides facing each other. "Sometimes I worry I've been interfering too much. That you need some time alone with her."

"Don't worry, black swan, despite everything, there is no competition, I'll still buy you that airplane." I don't want any more serious, life-changing conversations today.

She rolls her eyes, but she understands my need to move back to the lazy and inconsequential. "You better."

I pull her closer. "Shit is happening too fast, catching me unprepared, but I have you to keep me level."

"And on your toes." She claims my lips. But when we come up for air, she dives back into another loaded topic.

"When was the first time you saw me?"

The question tightens my muscles. Out of all the topics she could have chosen, this one I'm sure will taint our current harmony. But we might as well clear the air.

I asked her the same question at her apartment before we got married, and she ignored it. I thought it was because she didn't remember, or just wanted to piss me off with her ignorance. But now she asked the question of me, so she must remember.

I remember very well.

"May ninth, ten years ago."

Her eyes widen and she sits up so quickly I almost roll off the bed. "You remember the date?"

I shrug instead of the answer, because this little detail is the least of my worries. The question is why she gave me a wrong number then. The only woman who has ever done that.

"It's not even your birthday and you remember..." She shakes her head.

"Why is the date important?" I sit up. Why are we even delving into something in the past that has no bearing on now?

"Because you remember it, and if it's not your birthday, or something else significant, why would you—"

"Because meeting you isn't something one forgets," I growl, suddenly annoyed.

At her for disturbing the easy flow from earlier. At myself for still remembering. At the memory that should have faded a long time ago. At my hurt ego that still resents her for giving me a made-up phone number.

She gapes at me for seconds that feel like several lifetimes. "Why didn't you call me then?"

I frown, afraid to ask my next question. Could it have all been a misunderstanding? "Why did you give me a wrong number?"

She opens her mouth and closes it. Again. And again, before she croaks, "I didn't."

"Yes, you did. I saved it, and had it for ten years, and unless you changed it, it's definitely not the number you're using now. I had to reprogram it when we got married."

She shakes her head and blinks a few times, her shoulders sagging. "Merde. I always thought you asked for my number and never called."

The realization that the wrong number had always been an accident gives me such a jolt of resolution, I pounce.

Celeste yelps when I pin her back against the mattress, covering her with my body. "Don't worry, black swan, now I have your number, so you can't escape me ever again."

Heat flashes across her face, her breaths coming in shallow bursts. "You remember the exact date you first saw me?"

"Yes, we established that. No need to repeat it," I growl.

She grins at me. "In case it wasn't clear earlier, I'm yours. Only yours."

"In case it wasn't clear, I love you." I lower my lips to hers.

She hasn't said it yet, but that doesn't matter. I know she feels the same.

It fucking sucks that the joy will only last for another week.

Chapter 36

Celeste

SAAR

I'm leaving today, but promise I can hang out with my niece and my sis-in-law when I return

It's a date. When are you back?

SAAR

Hopefully soon.

I have the interview today

SAAR

No worries, it's just a formality

I'm nervous

SAAR

You got this. I hope my brother is coming with you.

I should have known nothing could be this good forever.

The week after I moved into Caleb's bedroom passed in an unprecedented harmony. It's like that first night in his bedroom we exorcised our demons, unearthed our insecurities, and found redemption in each other's arms.

We're not perfect, but we are us. That's enough for now. The only blemish on the picture-perfect life we naturally embraced is the invitation for an interview with ICE.

Both Dominic and Caleb dismissed it as a formality. Isn't it strange it came this early? Are Cressard's connections really this powerful?

I pull out a simple brown shirt dress that hugs my breasts and flares at my waist, falling to my knees. Most of my clothes are still in the guest bedroom, because there was no time to move them.

My hair gets pulled into a simple chignon. With shaky hands, I apply my red lipstick.

I make another futile attempt at finding my watch, but it's nowhere to be seen. I've been looking for it since last night, but I must have lost it. The thought brings in tears, and a sense of foreboding.

My connection with... I shake my head.

It's going to be okay. I don't even have to lie. This

has become a real marriage. I've been repeating this mantra all morning, but it does shit for me.

I threw up twice already, barely making it to the guest bathroom because I didn't want Caleb to hear me. Who knew sharing a bedroom would have a disadvantage?

When I make it down, Caleb is in the kitchen. Dressed in a tailored navy suit, he looks perfect. Untouchable. In charge.

It hits me that if I get deported, I'm going to lose this man. It's probably a silly thought, but the weight of it pools around the crevices of my eyes, stinging.

When Caleb turns, his signature espresso looking tiny in his large hand, a tear rolls down and I wipe it angrily. Jesus, I'm such a mess.

He puts the cup down and rushes to me. "What's wrong?"

"Nothing, I'm just nervous." *And I feel even more freaked out because of my watch.* I don't tell him that. He's been eyeing me with suspicion for wearing it anyway. Probably wondering why I keep all three watches he gave me in their boxes.

He kisses my crown. "I'm coming with you, and Dominic will be there as well. It's a formality."

"You keep saying that, but just the idea of entering a government building makes me want to throw up."

"Which you already did, so there's nothing else to puke out." He winks, wrapping his arms around me.

I groan. "You heard that?" I bury my head in his chest.

He chuckles. "Can I make you a tea for the road?"

I shake my head.

"Or I can fuck you in the car on the way there to distract you." He takes my hand and leads me to the elevators.

"Can you be serious," I snarl, surprising us both. I pinch the bridge of my nose. "Merde. Sorry."

The elevator door opens. "Take it all out on me, black swan. I'm giving you a free pass."

I sniffle. Jesus, I'm such a mess. "Thank you."

"You can thank me later. On your knees." He winks.

"Caleb," I warn.

The elevator opens and we get into the car.

"Mia is coming this weekend. I'm going to call Reese today and see if we can go out of town," Caleb says.

"That's a great idea." I try to force myself to chat with him, but my mind remains frozen.

"I was thinking a theme park. Is she too old for it?"

I know he's mostly trying to distract me. We can easily make these plans after my interview. When my brain returns, and my heart resumes its usual healthy cadence. "I'm sure she'd love that."

A yellow cab brakes, barely avoiding a pedestrian. One man bumps into another, spilling his coffee. A young woman holding an umbrella balances a stack of folders as she enters a building.

Life on the streets of New York passes in its typical bustling nature, while we wait on what seems the longest red light.

"Celeste," Caleb's voice startles me. "You weren't listening."

I sigh. "I'm sorry. I don't know why I can't relax."

"Okay, enough of distracting you with words." Caleb hits the button and the partition rises.

Before I get my brain to string together a coherent thought, he drops to his knees, yanks me to the edge of the seat.

"Caleb," I protest.

"Shut up and be a good girl. We have just enough time to make you come."

I stumble out of the car, avoiding Peter's eyes. I know he can't hear us, but the amount of times we've raised the divider when he drives us is a bit embarrassing.

Caleb takes my hand and kisses it. "Ready?"

Strangely, his talented tongue distracted me for the ride, and it also relaxed me enough for the enormous knot in my stomach to soften a bit. I nod.

"Okay, wife, let's get you that green card."

We enter the gray offices that haven't seen an interior designer or a woman's touch in ages.

Caleb deals with an annoyed officer who sends us to the second floor, where we're supposed to wait.

My heart echoes in my temples as I follow him, while my breathing, my vision and my head feel like I'm submerged underwater.

My husband moves with confidence. I doubt he's ever been to a government office like this, but somehow he fits. Even wearing probably the most expensive suit in the entire building, he blends in.

We get to the second floor, where people of different races sit around, bored and grim, waiting in a long hallway.

Caleb squeezes my hand, and I force myself to give him a smile.

Merde, I have to nail it. If for nothing else than for him. He married me as a favor, and since then he's done more, so much more.

The least I can do is to go through this interview and get my stay in the US sorted out, so we can move forward.

"I'm good." I bite my lip and keep shaking my head

back and forth, as if that will lend credibility to my statement.

"I know." He kisses my temple, holding me closer. His phone buzzes. "It's Cressard."

Caleb lets go of me to answer, and immediately frowns. My heart rate spikes.

"Shit, Cressard, then send someone else," he hisses.

Dominic is not coming. I'll be at the interview all by myself. I squeeze my handbag, but my hand still shakes of its own volition. Stumbling, I slam against the wall, hoping for support while my knees go weak.

Caleb hangs up. He circles his hands around both my biceps, half holding me upright and half lending support. I think.

"It's going to be okay, Celeste. You'll be okay. Just answer the questions and then march out of there."

The oxygen is barely hitting the top of my lungs. "Where the fuck is he?"

"One of his foster kids needed... Never mind. He's not here, but it changes nothing. I'll be waiting here. You focus on that. Okay?"

I can't speak. I can't breathe. I can't think.

"Okay?" Caleb growls, his voice demanding.

It does the trick, and snaps me out of my spiraling breakdown. "Okay. He wouldn't be answering for me, anyway. But he has all the proof with him."

"He's taking care of that, don't worry. This is a

formality." He kisses my forehead, and I decide to believe him.

It's not like I have any other options.

His phone buzzes again. He groans and disconnects the call, but it lights up again.

"Sorry," he says and turns away. "What?" he barks into the receiver.

I watch him like a hawk, mostly to forget about my nerves, but it doesn't do me any good. His shoulders tense, and my stomach rolls immediately.

I clutch at my midriff as I brace my back against the wall.

Caleb hangs up, spitting a string of profanities.

"What happened?"

"Cormac got arrested."

"What? You need to go." I offer before I even consider what it means to me.

"I'm not leaving you here."

Gripping his arm, I force him to look at me. "Caleb, you reminded me a gazillion times that this is just a formality. Go take care of fucking Quinn. I'll be fine."

It costs me all my acting skills to sound confident. A part of me wants him to stay, but that is the scared and desperate part that needs a knight in shining armor.

The much bigger part is equally scared, but refuses

to be desperate. I know I have his support, and what good would it do for him to sit outside?

He shakes his head. "No way am I leaving you here. Especially with Cressard being a no-show."

"Caleb van den Linden, get the fuck out of here. You didn't start a company to have it fucked up now. What did he do?"

"I don't know... He's been charged with being drunk and disorderly." Caleb lowers his head, shaking it.

"Just go, Caleb, please. I know you support me. I'm stronger because of your support. And knowing I have it is enough. You don't need to sit here, waiting. Please."

He studies me, a war brewing behind his eyes. "I'm going to fucking kill him."

"Don't you dare. I'm getting my green card, and I want you around, not in prison." My smile stretches stronger than the feelings inside me.

His chest moves up and down, his Adam's apple bobbing in a similar rhythm. He eyes me like he can see inside me, like he can assess if leaving is a mistake.

So I lean into my performing skills and give him a smile, a genuine smile. "Go."

He shakes his head, contradicting his words, "I'll send Peter to pick you up. Call me the minute you step out."

"Stop ordering me around and go save your CEO."

* * *

I'm pretty sure I've been sitting in this office for at least three hours. The clock on the wall must be broken. No way it's been only five minutes.

Five minutes in which Officer Martinez introduced herself and said she'd get us coffees. She hasn't returned yet.

The air is thick with the scent of something sanitary, and something cinnamon-like. The sparse furnishings—a metal desk, a couple of mismatched chairs, a filing cabinet in the corner—do nothing to ease my mounting anxiety.

I fidget on the cold, hard chair, the sterile white walls closing in around me.

The door opens and I jump up. Martinez, a weary-looking woman in a gray pantsuit, narrows her eyes.

Merde. I'm already failing this. Nobody this nervous is innocent. I should just tell her about my bureauphobia.

Would that help me, or just make her laugh at my pathetic attempt to lie?

She puts a plastic cup in front of me before she sits beside me and puts on glasses. The fact she didn't take her own chair should probably comfort me, but it does the exact opposite.

I push my hands into my thighs, preventing them from bouncing.

Martinez flips through a file for what feels like another three hours, which is ridiculous, given it's a thin folder.

She glances up, her expression one of practiced indifference, as if she's seen too many cases like mine to muster any actual interest.

"Let's start with the basics, Mrs. van den Linden. When did you get married?"

The fluorescent lights above buzz faintly, casting a harsh glare that makes everything seem even more unforgiving.

My throat tightens, and I struggle to find my voice. "Um... we got married on..."

My mind blanks, the date slipping away. It's on the tip of my tongue, but I just can't grasp it.

She raises an eyebrow, and it sends panic surging through me. "I'm sorry, I can't... I can't remember right now."

"You can't remember the date of your own wedding?"

I bite my lip, fighting back tears of frustration. Maybe I can ask her to have this done over coffees in a coffee shop. I'd find my groove if we were anywhere else.

Memories of the night at the police station after my mom died fill my head, and I freeze completely.

"Mrs. van den Linden?" Martinez prompts me.

"I—I'm sorry. It's just... I'm really nervous."

If I expected compassion, I got a sigh. She looks back at the file. "Fine. Let's move on. Can you tell me where you and Mr. van den Linden have a joint account?"

The room feels smaller, the walls pressing in closer. I try to focus, to summon the information, but all I can think about is the ticking clock on the wall, each second hammering my nerves further.

"The bank... It's, um... I think it's... HSBC?"

She meets my eyes, her gaze steady but uninterested. "You think?"

"Yes, HSBC," I say, trying to sound more confident, but my voice wavers.

"Alright. When did you meet Mr. van den Linden's family?"

A wave of dizziness washes over me. I know this. I know the answer. But the words won't come.

She makes a note, her pen scratching loudly against the paper. "If you can't provide straightforward answers to these questions, it's going to be very difficult for me to recommend anything other than deportation."

Her words slice through me, leaving me raw and even more useless. I stare at her, completely paralyzed as she continues the interview that really becomes a one-sided conversation.

"How long were you dating before you got engaged?"

"When did you move in together?"

"Has he met your family? Were they here for the wedding?"

The questions are hammering down on me, and I try and mostly fail to answer. Or maybe I answer some?

I try to focus and remind myself my world is here, and I can't have my annoying anxiety prevent me from staying.

I can't disappoint Caleb, abandon the theater, leave my friends behind, and most importantly, I can't return to France.

Clenching my fists, I try to ground myself. "I'm sorry. It's just... this place..."

She eyes me, unimpressed. Closing the folder, she drops it on her desk. "Take a deep breath," she says, though her tone lacks warmth. "Let's try one more. How did you and your husband meet?"

I take a shaky breath, closing my eyes for a moment, trying to block out the oppressive room, the buzzing lights, the cold metal. "We met through his sister. She's my best friend."

Officer Martinez nods. "We can't proceed with vague memories and half-recalled details, Mrs. van den Linden. Especially in light of the fraud report we received."

Someone reported us? "I have a bureauphobia," I blurt out.

She stands up and rounds the desk to take her seat. "Don't we all."

Tears spill down my cheeks, despite my efforts to rein them in. "I love my husband."

I sound pathetic, and I hate how I said those words for the first time to this woman who just wants to close the case.

A knock on the door snatches her attention before she can laugh at my declaration.

She stands up and yanks the door open. "I'm in the middle of an interview—"

"And I'm Mrs. van den Linden's lawyer, Dominic Cressard. I'm sorry I got delayed." Dominic pushes inside without an invitation. "Officer Martinez, I brought all the documents to prove the validity of my client's green card application."

"Mr. Cressard, as of now, your client failed to reassure me of the validity of her marriage, and I'm afraid I don't have a choice but—"

Her phone rings and she sighs, picking up the receiver. "Martinez."

Dominic squeezes my shoulder and gives me a reassuring nod. While his presence lifts my veil of anxiety somewhat, I know I fucked up. *Especially in light of the fraud report.*

Martinez hangs up. "I see you have connections, Mr. Cressard." If she was indifferent during the interview, now she's pissed. "But I do my work with integrity."

Her words rip a gasp from me.

I bury my face in my hands, overwhelmed by a mixture of fear, frustration, and self-loathing.

I'm crumbling. And I don't know how to stop it.

Dominic helps me to my feet and marches out, while I follow in a daze. I'm going to be deported.

Caleb bought a theater to get me a job, and then he married me when that didn't work out. And I couldn't fucking answer a few questions to prove our relationship is real.

The looming separation shatters my heart into a million pieces. He can't leave his daughter or his business behind. I'll never let him do that.

I've lost him.

Chapter 37

Caleb

Pacing.

I've been pacing.

I've been at it for twenty minutes. Or lifetimes. How long does it take to come from the ICE offices? It didn't take this long to get there this morning, did it?

I pour myself another whiskey. Dominic texted me earlier. A message that didn't spark confidence. Something went poorly at the interview. And now the fucker isn't answering.

Celeste isn't answering either, and if Dom hadn't confirmed she was with him, I would have fucking broken her out of there.

I down the drink and go to refill it, but my phone buzzes. The amber liquid sloshes around when I drop the bottle to answer.

"What?" I bark at Xander, because he's the last person I want to talk to right now.

"Aren't you a ray of sunshine today?" Someone else clears his throat. "Right, sorry, I'm here with Declan."

"Be fast, I don't have time."

"We're in full-blown crisis mode and you have no time? Then maybe we shouldn't bother you." Declan delivers his words in his usual level tone, but after having spent some time with him, I can detect the edge to it.

Given that our CEO is splattered all over the media for his escapades last night, I don't blame him. Why does shit have to explode at the least opportune moments?

"If you had your brother on a shorter leash, we wouldn't be in this mess," I snap, ignoring the voice in my head reminding me that an argument is absolutely useless.

"What's up your ass?" Xander interferes. "This is not the time to argue about who can piss who off further. Corm has been released on bail, but as you know, the media is having a field day with this. We think you should step in as interim CEO."

I don't know what I expected, but it wasn't this. "Are we sure that's the right message to send to the stakeholders?"

"We talked to our lawyer, and to a crisis management consultant." Declan sighs. "Both suggested we show a united front and focus on ensuring the company runs without a hitch, and with crystal-clear focus. Xander and I agreed you have the experience and recognition to reassure our partners."

Declan's suggestion rings with reason, but before I have a chance to discuss it further, the elevator door opens.

Dominic and Celeste enter the apartment. She's still dressed and styled impeccably as always, but her steps lack her usual confidence, her shoulders sagging and her cheeks wet from tears.

In the background, I hear Xander and Declan talking, but my mind is consumed with one thought only. A rabid need, really.

Actually, two. Who do I kill? And how do I make her feel better?

"I have to think about it." I hang up, jeopardizing the future of my company. Inconsequential compared to the future of my wife. My marriage.

I quickly cover the distance between us and wrap her in my arms. She sniffles and lets me hold her, but she isn't leaning in. She takes the embrace, but her heart isn't in it.

I don't know what happened, but hopelessness burns inside my chest. A sense of foreboding washes over me. Like I'm losing her. Or I already have.

She steps back, and the loss of her closeness hits me with its sense of finality. What the fuck is happening?

"I'm going to get changed." She walks to the staircase, ascending like the queen she is, even in this broken state.

As soon as I hear the door click upstairs, I whip around. "What the fuck happened?"

Dominic unbuttons his jacket and drops his briefcase on the sofa. "We've got twenty-four hours to prove the validity of your marriage. Kind of ironic, since apparently the marriage *is* real now."

"What the fuck?" I resume my pacing as if that will help the situation.

Dominic sits on the sofa, the picture of nonchalance. "From my understanding, she panicked and couldn't answer any questions."

I look up to where our rooms are, warring between running upstairs to hold her and staying here to give her space to find her composure. Fuck, I want her to sass me, to bring out her wits like never before.

"She has a bureauphobia."

The fucking skepticism on Dom's face makes me want to punch him. He cracks his knuckles. "Regardless, this wasn't a routine interview. They got tipped off that the marriage is fake."

The information makes me stumble, like it hit me physically. "Who the fuck would tip them off?"

"I'm trying to find out, but that won't help us in the short term. Look, have her rest and lean into her acting skills tomorrow. I'll do my best to present the evidence, but if she can't answer simple questions, I can't guarantee anything."

My nostrils flare while my pulse speeds up. "What does that mean?" I grit out.

Dom shrugs, crossing one leg over the other. "I might get you off the felony charges, but Celeste will be deported, with a slim, almost nonexistent, chance of returning to the States."

My phone rings and I decline Xander's call.

I walk to the bar in the corner and pour myself another whiskey, only mildly concerned about the amount I already consumed.

Downing it, I smash the fucking tumbler against the glass banister. It helps about as much as the pacing. Zilch. Fucking nada.

I turn to the wall of windows. The view has always invited peace into my mind, but right now I only see the suffocating grid of concrete monotony. "I should have been there."

"It's not like they would let you hold my hand. This is on me alone."

I spin toward her voice. Celeste stands at the landing in black leggings and an oversized sweatshirt. I've never seen her this underdressed. Fuck.

She takes the stairs slowly, descending with resignation in her posture.

"We'll fix it all." My declaration is as desperate as it's a lie. As much as I want to fix it all, I have no fucking clue how.

She looks at me with similar skepticism to what Dominic rewarded me with earlier and walks to the bar. She pours two glasses and looks at Dom, who shakes his head.

Celeste passes me a glass and glances at the shards on the floor. She walks around and folds herself on the sofa, taking a sip.

Her every move reeks of despair, void of spark or any emotion. The fiery dancer I know and love is subdued.

It pisses me off, but more importantly it worries me.

"Will I go to jail?" she asks Dom.

I sit beside her and put my hand over hers. She recoils. Not visibly, but as soon as my palm touches her, she readjusts her position, distancing herself from me.

It might look like a natural move to make herself more comfortable, but I know she doesn't want me near her. I just know.

Why the fuck is she giving up like this?

"Highly unlikely. What is likely, with a fifty

percent probability, is that Officer Martinez will file a request for deportation. We'll fight it, of course. I'm going to call in all the favors now. You two go through your phones and find as many authentic pictures of your life together as possible."

He stands and picks up his briefcase. Buttoning up his jacket, he nods his goodbyes and leaves.

We both stare at the closed elevator doors on the other side of this cavernous room long after he leaves.

Celeste sighs. "I'm sorry."

I jump up to pace. Yet again. "You have nothing to be sorry about. Dominic will make sure we will prevent the worst."

"But we can't pretend the possibility isn't pretty fucking real. Dom said it's a fifty percent chance I'll have to leave."

"Then I'll leave with you," I offer immediately. Without thinking or considering the implications. That's what I'll do. I know that as much as I know I love her.

She stands up, shaking her head vehemently. Despite the situation, a jolt of hope courses through me at her reignited fire.

"You'll leave with me? What about Merged?" She puts her glass on the coffee table and marches to the kitchen.

I chase after her. "Fuck Merged." After today's negative publicity, Merged might be fucked already, anyway.

She opens and closes a cabinet, and then another one. "And what about Mia?"

I pause for the briefest moment, because my daughter does deserve consideration, but I'll figure it out. I will not abandon her. Or Celeste. I refuse to accept either of them being gone from my life.

"I'll have her fly to us every second weekend." It's a fucked-up solution, but I need to show her we can find a solution even if the worst happens.

She keeps banging the doors, opening and closing cabinets. "You'll have her fly to Europe twice a month. Don't be ridiculous."

I grip her wrist to stop her. "What are you looking for?" My words come out laced with harsh frustration.

Her shoulders slump. "Where are those stupid cookies?"

I enter the pantry and put the jar on the counter beside her. My phone rings, and I check the number. Xander.

"Do you need to take it?" She opens the jar and pulls out a cookie.

"No," I growl and disconnect the call.

"Is it about Corm?"

431

"It doesn't matter now."

"You should answer it." She takes a bite and drops the cookie to the counter, hanging down her head.

"Don't tell me what to do," I bark, and regret it immediately. "Sorry." I close the jar. "Do you want coffee? Can I draw you a bath?"

She chuckles, the sound laced with venom. "Stop being nice to me. Stop taking care of me. I know that you're used to fixing shit. But you can't buy my green card. You can't pay my way through that interview."

"But you haven't been deported yet, so why are you already giving up?" I punch the fridge, my knuckles almost cracking.

She flinches. "Because some of us learned to prepare for the worst. I need to regroup and buckle up for the worst possible—a very possible—scenario, and I can't have you hovering around me. It only makes this break up harder."

"We're not breaking up. What are you talking about?"

Her gaze meets mine, full of frustration and hurt. "You know what I'm talking about."

"No, actually, I don't. Okay, so you might get deported, but you're still my fucking wife." I pounce on her, cornering her. "And you may be scared right now, but don't you dare give up on us."

I pin her against the counter with my hips and cup

her nape. "Don't you fucking dare give up on us, black swan," I repeat, before I fuse my lips with hers in a punishing kiss.

A kiss full of frustration about our current situation. About fucking Cormac. About Merged. About this infuriating woman who built her walls on the way home from the ICE office like there was nothing to fight for.

She takes my lips, my tongue, my mouth, moaning, but then she pushes me away. "Stop it. Stop it. We haven't been together that long. Why are you making it harder than it has to be?"

Is she for real? "Because I fucking love you."

She sighs, closing her eyes momentarily. "I love you too, but let's be realistic here."

"Don't fucking try to diminish what we have," I bellow, and she winces. Fuck.

She loves me. She loves me. So why is she giving up?

My phone rings again, but this time it draws my attention because I recognize the ringtone. Only two people have a special ringtone on my phone. One stands across from me, mad and hurt.

"It's Mia."

I answer the phone.

The words that come from the other side of the line shatter my world for the third time in one day.

Every fucking part of my life went to shit on this glorious day.

"I'll be right there." I hang up.

"What happened?" Celeste asks.

"We have to go. She's in the hospital."

Chapter 38

Caleb

"I didn't know who to call." Mia hiccups, her arms wrapped around my waist. "Aunt Greta is working tonight."

I have no idea who her aunt is or what happened yet, but holding this scared girl—my daughter—takes precedence. The ride to the hospital was the longest half-hour of my life.

Right now, everything feels like an endless ordeal. Like I'm in flux, floating aimlessly, trying to put out fires, but I can't fucking stop the flames. They're licking mercilessly, burning me with hopeless frustration.

"I'm glad you called me. What happened?" I keep stroking her hair.

A quiet sob racks through her small body. "I found Mom on the floor in the kitchen."

Fuck. Fuck. Fuck.

I keep stroking her head, strangely aware that I've never needed to comfort anyone. Two important people are leaning on me, and I have no clue how to be here for them. How to make their situations better.

My gaze finds Celeste. She gives me a weak smile and a nod. It smooths the edges of my frayed mind, but I'm still at a loss about what to do next.

Reese never wanted to talk to me, so what's my role here? I should have tried harder.

As if Celeste could feel my inadequacy, she steps closer and pats Mia's back. "Let's have your dad find out what's going on, and when you can see your mom."

My hopelessness recedes as Celeste's words give me a jolt of purpose. Mia squeezes me before she turns to Celeste.

My wife wraps her arm around my daughter. "Let's get hot chocolate, and when we're back, I'm sure Caleb will know more."

Celeste pats my biceps, and her sad smile reassures me. Of what, I don't know, but as I watch the two of them walking away from me, I vow not to fail them.

It takes quite a lot of effort to get to talk to anyone, including waving around Benjamins, my paternity test results, and various threats.

By the time I finally get to talk to a young doctor

who is trying to stifle yawns, I almost donate an entire wing to the hospital.

It's what I learn that steals my oxygen, and makes me question every single decision—all of them cowardly—as a father.

"What's going on?" Celeste's warm hand on my shoulder brings me back to the bleak reality.

I turn to find her standing behind me, while Mia sips her chocolate on a seat a few feet away. My eyes dart between the two of them.

How does one's life go to shit in the span of several hours?

"Overdose," I whisper, knowing that it explains a lot and nothing at the same time.

"Merde. Is she—"

"She'll be okay." The words leave my mouth, but I know they're only a partial truth. "I mean, she's alive."

"Good." Celeste takes my hand and leads me to Mia.

I almost bolt, because I don't know what to do or say to her. Why the fuck is her aunt working tonight? Who even is her aunt?

I halt abruptly, and Celeste stumbles. Mia's head is down like she's staring into her cup. She looks much smaller in that moment.

It hurts looking at her, a girl that's the spitting image of me in a darker, more feminine, version.

A girl who courageously found me, and instead of my time and affection, I offered her my credit card.

A girl that has been—I'm assuming—living in less-than-ideal conditions, and I didn't bother to gain her trust enough for her to confide in me.

She didn't spell out her problems when she showed up in my life, but fuck, she showed up, and I...

"I'm like my father." A bitter chuckle gets lodged in my throat. My new personal low blurs my vision.

Celeste pinches my chin between her thumb and finger, forcing me to look at her. "You can wallow later. That girl needs you. You have the entire rest of your life to choose not to be like him, but you need to start right now. Because right now is what matters."

Fuck, I love this woman. The idea of losing her burns like acid in my stomach. Our unresolved conversation from the kitchen hangs above me like a sword of Damocles.

But my attention needs to be elsewhere. On another beautiful person who I grew to love without even realizing.

I sit beside Mia. "Your mom will be okay. She's sleeping right now, but they'll let you see her soon." I pull her to me and kiss the top of her head.

Her breath hitches with unshed tears. "Will you stay?" The vulnerability in her voice punches me in my stomach.

"Of course."

"Mia!" A woman's voice rings through the air, and my daughter shoves her empty cup into my hand and rushes over to the newcomer.

She's about my age, wearing a blue MTA shirt, and Mia wraps her arms around her similarly to what she did earlier with me. I guess I'm about to meet the aunt.

I stand, dunking my cup into a bin, and approach them gingerly. The woman frowns at me from above Mia's head.

"I called my dad." Mia turns her head to meet my eyes.

In a beat of silence, the air between us fills with my uncertainty, and by the look of it, a lack of trust on the aunt's part. Reese's sister glares at me.

"Caleb van den Linden." I extend my hand.

She shakes it. Thank God for that. Today has brought enough drama. "Greta Morgan, I'm Reese's sister. Reese didn't tell me you were in touch."

"Mom didn't know," Mia says quickly, and then covers her mouth like she could shove the words back inside. "I-I... Am I in trouble?"

"Of course not," I say.

"Little bit," Greta says at the same time.

I sigh, and Mia looks at me with so much remorse and anxiety on her face I want to wage a war to make her feel better. At this rate, I'd obliterate half of Manhattan with all the shit happening.

"Are you mad at me?" Mia looks down.

For the first time since Mia's call earlier, I'm sure of something, at least. "I'm not mad at you at all."

Her shoulders relax visibly, and it spreads an unreasonable wave of relief through my chest. It's lost in a sea of worry and unanswered questions, but it's there.

"Where is Reese?" Greta asks.

"Sleeping at the moment. We can see her in about an hour, when they move her from the ICU."

"Mia, can you wait while I talk to Caleb?" Greta's voice leaves no room for argument.

"I'll stay with her." Celeste joins us.

God, I'm grateful she's here with us.

Not only is she somehow present at every right moment, but she's not intruding. The silent support I never knew I needed. All while tomorrow's interview is hanging over our heads.

"This is my wife, Celeste." I introduce her to Greta.

As someone who never believed in marriage, the pride those words carry shocks me. But this is not about being married.

This feeling spreads to every corner of my cynical heart and mind, because I'm married to this woman.

Celeste leads Mia back to our seats, and Greta and I find a quiet waiting room that's empty, by some sheer stroke of luck.

"Reese is a good mother," Greta hurls at me the minute the door closes behind us.

Okay, I didn't expect this turn of conversation, but let's go with it. "Forgive me if I have a doubt or two, given that her—our—daughter found her OD'd on the floor."

"You have no right to judge her. Where were you for the last decade?" she attacks, stepping back from me like I'm a physical threat to her.

"I didn't know about Mia. But I think I have the right to pass judgment, given the current circumstances."

I don't understand what Greta's problem is, but fuck, I'm going to do everything possible to make Mia safe and comfortable. Loved.

"You can't take her away. Reese has lost way too much. I know you believe your money can buy anything, but if you take Mia, my sister won't make it." Greta's combative attitude wanes. She sags to an empty chair, her head hanging.

"My daughter didn't know me for most of her life, so I'm going to do all I can to make sure she has both parents well and present as much as possible."

Greta lifts her gaze. She studies me for a long

moment before she speaks. "Reese is a self-employed bookkeeper. After Mia was born, she used your father's money to get through school and got a CPA certification. She wanted a career that allowed her to work from home, so she could be there for Mia."

Greta stands up and paces the small space. "Everything changed a year ago when she was in an accident. Long story short, she became addicted to painkillers, and everything escalated from there."

From this short but efficient summary, I gather Reese is an admirable mother who became a victim of unfortunate circumstances. The knowledge offers relief and agony at the same time. "I had no idea."

"I don't understand how you found Mia—"

"I didn't. She found me."

I think of the texts from Reese, the ones that said she had no desire to see me. Those texts reinforced my belief that she was only after my money. But now I see the story is different.

"Reese lost her clients and their house. They've been living with me. She seemed better, and when the fridge got full again, I assumed that was the case. That she got some clients back."

I need to move, to process, to let out the simmering frustration. "Let's go back to Mia. She shouldn't be alone right now."

I don't wait for Greta, feeling like a caged animal here.

I don't have all the pieces yet, but even without the full picture, two things are obvious.

My daughter has more courage than me.

And I should have fucking tried harder to make our relationship legit. To find out how she lives on those days, during the long stretches of time, when she isn't with me.

I move with renewed determination, knowing full well that I can't fix any of those things tonight. I march back to the hallway, where Celeste sits with Mia's head in her lap, and it hits me.

In my efforts to fix everything, I didn't realize that sometimes all people need from me isn't my money, or me fixing their problems.

It's just being there for them. Supporting them. Or simply keeping them safe when they feel vulnerable.

Just like my wife is doing right now for my daughter.

I sit beside them, and Mia stirs, sighing in her sleep.

Greta doesn't join our little circle, but sits at the end of the row across from us, closing her eyes.

"You have a smart daughter. Thank God she decided to find you when she struggled the most." Celeste gives me a sad smile.

"I wish I'd accepted her the way she deserved."

"You got there eventually."

"But perhaps too late. If I'd cared about them better, I could have prevented this."

"You had your reasons—"

"Fucked-up reasons."

"You're here. That matters more than how you got here."

"I should have done more. I should have tried harder. I could have prevented this."

Celeste moves her hand from Mia's hair to my shoulder. Deep lines of exhaustion mar her face, her eyes swallowed by dark circles.

She gives me a weak smile. "You're here now," she repeats.

Fuck, she needs to focus on tomorrow, yet she's here for me and my daughter. But tomorrow is too important, equally important. And she needs a good night's sleep after today.

"I'm calling Peter to get you home. You need to rest."

She flinches at my suggestion, but immediately smiles. "Okay."

Fuck, why didn't I realize sooner she needed the comfort of our home? "I'm sorry—"

"No, Caleb, this is where you need to be."

She's right, and I'm right as well, she needs to get

some rest. But being right doesn't mean it feels right. Separating right now, considering our unresolved conversation from earlier, sends a sense of foreboding shuddering through me.

I watch her leave, her shoulders slumped, her head hanging. Even in her defeated, dressed-down version, she oozes elegance. My wife.

But it doesn't matter that she's mine, because her departure feels final.

Chapter 39

Caleb

Mia stirs and brings me back to reality. I don't even know how long I've been staring into the empty space where Celeste disappeared.

"Is Mom up?" She sits up.

"We have to wait a bit longer."

"Do I have to go to school tomorrow?"

I chuckle. "No, you don't." I smile at her. "The messages I got from your mom?"

She looks down, recoiling from me. Fuck.

"Mia, it's okay, I just need to understand." I take her hand and squeeze it.

"I found out about you when we were moving to Aunt Greta's. They argued because Auntie believed Mom should find you. But Mom didn't want to. I don't know why, but she wasn't doing well, and—"

"You did the right thing." I kiss the crown of her head.

"Do you think the 'thorities will take me from her because she's sick?"

Oh shit, I didn't get a chance to process a potential investigation into Reese's incident. "You mean authorities? Don't worry, you'll stay with your mom."

"But Mom said nobody can know she's sick because they would take me away."

Fuck. My. Life.

"Sweetheart, your mom needs to get better, and if she won't be able to take care of you while she does that, you'll stay with me. Nobody is taking you away."

She gives me the most hopeful smile. "I'd like that." Then panic crosses her tired face. "I mean, I don't want to leave her—"

"I know, Mia, I know. We'll help her get better." It's a vow, one I'll follow through on, no matter what.

Shit, I need to call Dominic Cressard to make sure Reese won't get into trouble for this. The hospital has probably reported her already.

Mia settles against me while I close my eyes for a moment, the events of the day running in a distorted loop in my mind. Fuck, I'm tired.

I pull out my phone and send a text to Celeste.

Good night, black swan.

I screen several messages from Xander.

"Will Celeste be okay if I'm your daughter for real?" Mia's voice sounds tentative.

"You are my daughter for real." I ruffle her hair. "Celeste will be delighted to have you around more. We both will, if your mom is okay with that."

Another bright smile hits me in the chest.

Mia fidgets, and then bites her lips. "Celeste looked sad today."

"Yeah, we've been having a tough day." I want to leave it at that, but then something prompts me to continue. "She's from France, as you know. We need to prove our marriage is real so she can keep living here."

Being honest and open with someone about an issue or a problem, not carrying it by myself, feels strangely liberating.

"But your marriage is real." The conviction in her statement is endearing.

"I hope the authorities see it the same way."

"I'll tell them." She looks at me with hope.

"I don't think that will be necessary, but thank you."

She slouches into her seat, restless. Shit, I wish I could take her mind off her mother, this endless waiting, or all her other insecurities.

I turn to her. "Actually, do you have any photos on your phone from any of our outings?"

She pulls out her phone and scrolls through. "What about this?" She points the screen at me.

Mia, Celeste and I are grinning in front of the smashing room, all of us still in goggles. I forgot the attendee took this picture with Mia's phone.

We look like a happy little family. A strangely formed one, but nevertheless real. I study my face and almost don't recognize myself.

"Can you send it to me?"

This was our first outing, and I was definitely faking my marriage and failing at the parenting gig back then. And yet, the genuine joy in my expression is undeniable. I don't think I have another picture where I look like this.

"Why are you smiling like this?" She cocks her head, studying me.

"Like what?"

"Like you found a treasure."

I look at my little girl and shrug. "Because I feel like I found one."

She leans into me and I hug her, giving her the support she needs, but equally getting some from her.

With a renewed energy, I decide to call Xander, and finally resolve at least one of the issues looming over my head.

* * *

At dawn, I take an Uber from the hospital, after I put Greta and Mia into another one.

Reese was transferred out of the ICU. To Greta's relief, I decided it's not the best time to waltz into Reese's life, but I stayed behind while the two of them visited with her.

That conversation will have to happen soon, followed by legal paperwork, so I can officially become Mia's parent.

All of that is a problem for another day. Right now, my focus is Celeste and today's hearing with the ICE officer.

I hope she got some sleep. I can't wait to wrap her in my arms and help her through today.

Checking my watch, I confirm I have time for one more important stop.

The Merged floor is eerily quiet at this hour. I walk around the glass-walled offices with a strange feeling of nostalgia, which makes no sense since this place is still very new to me.

Declan and Xander wait for me in our boardroom, the necessary paperwork laid out on the table. I certainly made Cressard earn his fees in the last twenty-four hours.

Declan leans against the wall and glares at me, not bothering to greet me.

Xander paces the room. "You look like shit."

"It's good I'm not here for a beauty contest, then."

Mindful of my wife waiting at home, I sit down and scan the documents.

"Are you sure about this?" Declan asks, a hint of a dare in his voice.

"Is your brother sober yet?" I hit back, just to spite him.

Pulling out a pen from my jacket, I scribble my name across the paperwork I never expected to sign.

But that's life. I don't have time to ponder the significance of the deed, because I have more important things to do today.

I stand and walk to the door. "If you'll excuse me, I have an important meeting in a few hours."

I walk out of there with mixed feelings, but I focus on what I'm walking toward.

If she gets deported, we'll move to Canada. That way we won't burden Mia with regular overseas flights.

But that's a huge *if* I'm not willing to entertain. I yawn as I step out of the elevator and into the penthouse.

The silence that greets me feels as eerie as the one I faced in Merged.

She must be sleeping still, and my exhausted mind is playing tricks. I shake off my wrinkled jacket and get to the kitchen.

Downing a double shot of espresso, I make my

way upstairs. I don't want to wake Celeste up, so I decide to take a shower in her room. Well, it's really a guest room at this point, but she hasn't fully vacated it yet.

She must have moved more of her things out though, because our room feels inhabited. That's good. She's where she should be. In my bedroom. In our bedroom.

I take a good half an hour under the pelting hot water, my muscles screaming for a good sleep. By the time I get out, the coffee kicks in enough for me to function reasonably.

I wrap the towel around my waist and pad across the hall to our bedroom. I close the door behind me with care, so I don't wake her.

When I turn, I blink a few times. The image in front of me slowly seeps into my weary, exhausted mind. But even blinking doesn't change the fact that our bed is empty.

It hasn't been slept in.

A thousand scenarios rush through my mind, none of them encouraging.

I'm immediately on alert, any remnants of sleepiness evaporating. Shit. She must have been so nervous, she couldn't sleep and probably left early.

I go text her, and realize she never responded to my message last night. I assumed she was sleeping already and forgot all about it. But it's not like her not to acknowledge the message after she woke up.

I dial her number.

Answering machine.

I dial again.

Nothing.

I dial three more times, scrambling to quiet the uneasiness spreading through my chest. Where the hell is she?

I call Peter. "When did you drive Celeste to the ICE offices?" Jesus, she must have been so nervous and scared.

"I didn't drive her anywhere since I brought her back home from the hospital."

I hang up without another word and dial her again.

Nothing.

Where the fuck is she?

We haven't been together that long. Why are you making it harder than it has to be?

She didn't. She wouldn't. Fuck.

I pace around our bed and call the concierge. "Did you see my wife leaving?" I bark.

"Good morning, Mr. van den Linden. I called a taxi for Mrs. van den Linden two hours ago."

"Where did she go?"

He hesitates. "Didn't she tell you?"

Oh, fuck the privacy.

"If you want to keep your job, you'll tell me where she went," I growl at him, hoping to God I won't need to strangle him for the information.

He clears his throat, but after a beat, he makes the right decision. "She went to JFK, sir."

I hang up and march to the bathroom. Her makeup bag is gone, and so are most of her toiletries.

Returning to the bedroom, I sink to the edge of the bed.

She fucking left me.

Chapter 40

Celeste

By now, I should have boarded my plane.

The constant, unending hum of the airport feels like a physical weight, crushing me. The plastic seat is as comfortable as a pebble in a shoe.

I clutch my boarding pass in my hand like it's a lifeline. It's not.

By now, I should have boarded my plane.

In case Caleb gets the crazy idea to come and search for me. He must be with Mia. That's where he should be.

By now, I should have boarded my plane.

On the way to Paris, a place that stopped being my home a long time ago.

The departures board flickers in front of me. If I don't stand up right now, I'll miss my flight.

The intercom crackles overhead, announcing flights and gate changes in a monotonous voice. It drills into my exhausted mind.

I close my eyes for a moment, but they burn just the same. From the lack of sleep and the sheer fatigue of my sleepless night. From the stupid tears.

But that burning is nothing compared to the gnawing ache in my chest. I open my eyes and finally stand. The red numbers on the digital clock in front of me flick, ticking another minute closer to my departure.

I have to make things easier for Caleb. I can't be the reason for him to face an impossible choice between me and Mia. Especially now, when she, and her mother, need all the help they can get.

That's why he sent me home last night. As much as it hurts, it was the right thing to do.

My hand goes to my wrist, and I sigh. I can't believe that, in the bleakest moment of my life, I lost the watch on top of everything.

When I arrived home, I flipped through the pictures on my phone to forward them to Dominic. Every snatched moment, every memory a reminder of my unexpected little family, brought a smile to my face, and tears to my eyes.

Caleb and Mia deserve as much time together as

possible. And his company as well, especially in the light of Quinn's arrest.

I wish I could be there for him through this period of his life, but there is no way I can perform any better today than I did yesterday.

The ICE office brought out all my illogical anxieties. It reminded me of that dreadful night at the police station in the seventh arrondissement when my mom died.

When, instead of condolences, I was hammered with questions and accusations. Or maybe it was just my perception, but it doesn't help me feel any better about my current situation.

I'd just get deported today, so I might as well save myself from further embarrassment, from painful good-byes and agonizing decisions.

I grab my carry-on, the handle cold against my skin, and trudge toward my gate. If I leave now, Caleb won't have to make the choice. It's the logical thing to do. It's the right thing to do.

So why does it feel so wrong?

The harsh fluorescent lights of the airport reflect off the polished floors, casting a cold, sterile glow over everything. The air is filled with the scent of fast food, turning my stomach.

I take a deep breath, trying to steady myself, but

my chest feels tight, and my eyes sting with unshed tears.

"Excuse me, do you know where the nearest coffee shop is?" A middle-aged woman with a kind smile and an unmistakable Southern accent interrupts my spiraling thoughts.

The normalcy of the question throws me off, and I blink a few times. "Um, I think there's one just around the corner to the left." I point vaguely in that direction.

"Thank you, darling." She yanks at her suitcase. "I can't function without my morning java. You too, huh?" She glances at my disheveled state, her eyes warm with understanding.

"Yeah, something like that," I mumble, managing a weak smile in return while trying not to think about Caleb's obsession with a good cup of coffee.

She pats my arm lightly. "Hang in there. New York can be tough, but it's worth it."

New York can be tough, but it's worth it.

This city, with all its challenges and chaos, has become my home. I belong here, with Caleb, fighting for our future, not running away to a past that no longer fits.

The harsh fluorescent lights now seem less intimidating, the sterile glow less cold. Like my mind clears of worries and anxieties, allowing me to see the colors. The brightness. The possibilities.

The scent of fast food becomes a grounding reminder of the life I've built in this city. I take another deep breath, but this time it feels more like a resolution than an attempt to calm my nerves.

Caleb's face flickers through my mind. His determined belief in our future, how we could get through this together.

He believes in us.

And I'm running away like a coward.

Merde. I turn around, and my legs that were barely moving now stride with a sense of purpose. The decision brings a rush of clarity that cuts through the fog of my fear and exhaustion.

What was I thinking?

Obviously I wasn't. I can't just disappear, leaving him to deal with the fallout.

He deserves better than that.

And I deserve to fight for what we have, not just give up at the first sign of trouble.

I dunk the boarding pass into a garbage bin and practically run toward the exit. The noise of the airport fades away, replaced by the pounding of my heart in my ears.

I need to get back to Caleb, to face this together, to tell him I'm not giving up on us. I need to get to the ICE offices on time.

As I exit the terminal, the humid morning air hits

me, a stark contrast to the dry coldness inside. My hair sticks to my forehead, and my dress clings to my sweaty skin, but I don't let that distract me.

It takes an ungodly length of time to finally get my turn in the taxi queue, but as I'm riding toward Manhattan, I feel lighter.

I make it to the ICE office fifteen minutes before my appointment. This time around, I don't allow myself to worry as I haul my luggage to the second floor.

I just need to see him. To tell him everything will be okay. It will be. No more running. No more hiding. No more faking.

Ever.

Dominic is leaning against the bleak wall of the hallway, looking like his usual confident and cocky self. "Here you are."

He frowns and takes my suitcase, looking over my shoulder. I peek down the hallway. Caleb isn't here.

My heart skips a beat. He must be with Mia still. My lungs constrict, making breathing really hard. Suddenly, the environment comes into focus, and gives birth to my panic. Sweat trickles down my spine as I realize I have to do this alone.

Well, not alone. With Dominic this time, but that only boosts the anxiety, because embarrassing myself in front of Martinez isn't novel anymore, but in front of Dom? Jesus.

"Where's Caleb?" we both ask at the same time.

Oh, he probably doesn't know about Reese being in the hospital. "He must be with Mia."

Dom frowns. "He went to fetch you at the airport."

"What?"

I fumble for my phone in my bag. I turned it off this morning.

It takes an unreasonable amount of time for the screen to light up, buzzing with notifications of about fifty missed calls from Caleb. Shit.

With shaking fingers, I dial his number, my heart pounding against my ribcage.

I don't register the ringtone before his voice comes through. "Celeste."

No one has ever said my name with such an agonizing mixture of love, pain and relief.

"I'm at the ICE office."

"Thank fuck. Is Dom with you?"

"Yes."

"I won't be there on time, but I'll hurry. Are you okay?"

His voice washes through me like the first warm rays after a storm. "I think so."

"Let Dom do the talking." I hear him say something to Peter, and then he comes back. "You fucking

461

scared me. I'm so going to punish you for this, black swan."

A shudder rakes through me. I deserve that. And frankly, his level of punishment rewards us both.

"Celeste van den Linden," Martinez's bored voice slices through the air.

"I have to go." I wish my voice sounded level.

"You got this."

* * *

My leg bounces as Martinez flips through the file Dominic prepared. I try to breathe and appear composed, but that ship sailed the minute we entered this gruesome office.

Though I must say that Dominic's energy is the exact opposite of mine, and it helps a bit. Not much, but it gives me a sense of safety.

Martinez's scrutiny of every single document and every picture takes an eternity. I almost wish she was asking questions like yesterday, because this silence is unforgiving and agonizing.

It lingers in the air, allowing me to think, which is counterproductive to keeping my nerves in check. I wonder if I'll be sent to jail before they deport me.

Will they detain me? Will I be able to say goodbye

to Caleb and Mia? What about Cora and Lily? My colleagues? Will I just disappear from their lives?

The thought of every single person who forms my tribe in New York lodges in my throat, restricting my ability to breathe.

I think of Cora's croissants, of the smashing room, of my favorite hair salon, of my walks in Central Park. I stifle a whimper, grieving even my closed dance school.

Dominic turns to me and frowns, but then smiles tersely. I don't know if he's just attempted to console me, but fuck his bedside manners.

Martinez puts down her glasses and bores her gaze into me, her expression tense. She then looks at Dominic, who gives her a blinding smile. Seriously, where is he pulling these reactions from?

She narrows her eyes and looks back at me. And before she even speaks, I know beyond any doubt that it's a good thing I came packed.

I only hope Caleb was serious when he said we'd figure this out, because it's an easy phrase to throw around before the grim reality takes shape.

Chapter 41

Caleb

Fucking traffic.

Never have I verbally abused Peter or my fellow commuters this much in my life. I keep sending texts to Celeste and Dominic, but neither of them is answering. I can practically feel the vein on my forehead straining with my pent-up energy.

I try to focus on the positive, but there is no fucking silver lining here. And the airport! What a nightmare. How do people travel like that regularly?

Why did she go to the airport in the first place? Was she really planning to run? Even though I know she didn't leave, chills cover my body.

She might have decided not to leave, but it's still not clear if she'll be allowed to stay. It doesn't matter. The where doesn't matter, as long as she's by my side. We can find a solution.

Peter finally pulls to the curb in front of the ICE offices, and I rush out without even closing the car door behind me.

Like this is the finish line of a marathon, a kick of adrenaline propels me forward. People step aside, and thank God for that, because my mission is unstoppable.

I need to see my woman. I need to see her now. Then we can deal with everything else.

How is it that in a span of a couple of months, I grew to appreciate this partnership, relationship, this marriage?

Somehow, without me fully making the decision, I stepped away from our agreement and became a married man.

For real. For better. Forever.

Ignoring the attendee at the front desk, I take two steps at a time.

"Excuse me. Do you have an appointment?" a frantic female voice calls after me, but I'm already bursting through the gray double door of the waiting hall.

A quick scan of the grim place confirms Celeste must still be in there. What was the name of that officer? I rush, reading the name tags quickly.

Martinez.

That's it. I push the door open, and the first thing I

register spreads pain through my chest, spiking my heart rate.

Celeste is crying.

Dominic stands up and is about to say something, but I stretch my hand to stop him.

"You can't do this." I look at a woman who must be Martinez. "This might have started fake. Perhaps a string of one-night stands. But it's way past that. Because casual is forgettable. And this woman is on my mind constantly. Whether I'm with her or away from her, it doesn't matter."

The officer widens her eyes, and my mind registers Dominic's voice, but I don't stop.

"She's etched on my mind, in my heart, and slowly but surely stealing parts of my soul. I don't remember who I was before her."

I turn to Celeste. "And I sure as hell don't want to meet myself after you. The only version of me worth being is the one I am with you."

Celeste blinks, her cheeks wet from tears. Fuck, she's beautiful.

She sniffles. "Cal—"

I raise my finger, because I have more to say. I don't even know where the words are coming from, but I turn back to Martinez, whose countenance has shifted slightly, a smirk on her face. Fuck it.

"If you deport my wife, she'll be taking pieces of

me with her. Vital, irreplaceable pieces. Because this marriage is fucking real. And my wife stays by my side."

Dominic swears under his breath. Celeste stands, a sob escaping her.

Martinez folds her arms. "Well, Mr. van den Linden, thank you for your unsolicited testimony. I don't appreciate the amount of cussing involved, so please control yourself next time. I'm going to gloss over your suggestions of faking this marriage at the beginning." She scoffs and clears her throat. "Because as I was just informing your wife, I find the presented evidence sufficient at this moment, and we'll proceed with her green card application process."

Several things happen at the same time.

A rock I didn't know I'd been carrying dislodges from my chest.

Celeste sniffles and giggles at the same time.

People in the hallway clap.

And the officer from the front desk comes in, panting. "You can't be here, sir."

I clear my throat and straighten my tie. Grabbing Celeste's hand, I turn on my heels. "We're leaving, anyway."

I nod and march out of there. As soon as we're in the hallway, I pull my wife to me and kiss the hell out of her.

"You're staying." I lower my forehead to her. "Why are you crying?"

"Because I'm happy." Her breath hitches as she holds onto my lapels.

"Why the fuck did you go to the airport?"

Perhaps this is not the time and place to unravel that. Perhaps it doesn't matter anymore, but the question leaves my lips before I can stop it.

"For a brief moment, I believed that it would be easier for you. For Mia and Merged. They need you here. But I couldn't do it."

"So you didn't return for this?" I reach to my pocket and pull out her old watch.

I almost forgot I put it there in my hurry to leave the house this morning, when the delivery from the watchmaker arrived.

Celeste stares at the now polished and repaired watch, her eyes blinking. She lifts her gaze to me. "I thought I lost it..."

"I wanted to surprise you. I didn't anticipate the shitty circumstances. I figured it's important, though." I take her wrist and clasp the tiny antique watch in place.

"But how?" She sniffles.

"Well, you didn't wear any of the watches I bought you, but you kept wearing this one, even though it wasn't working anymore." I shrug.

She sobs again, wiping her tears while smiling. "It's my mom's. I couldn't afford to repair it. You must have thought I'm crazy wearing it, but I felt stupid admitting it's value to you."

I pull her to me. "Who else do you want to be vulnerable with, black swan?" We stand there, frozen in an embrace, the stress evaporating slowly. "You couldn't leave."

I don't even know why I utter the last sentence, other than a desperate need for validation. For some assurance.

"I realized you deserve better than me running away. I realized I'd be leaving pieces of me behind. Vital, irreplaceable pieces of me, that belong to my husband."

Chapter 42

Caleb

"**R**eady?" Celeste weaves her fingers through mine.

Looking up at the tall building, I shake my head. "Not really, but I don't want to postpone this one more minute."

After the longest night and day yesterday, we slept like the dead, ignoring the rest of the world. I spoke with Mia twice, and I talked to Greta as well.

Dominic made sure the hospital report on Reese got lost somewhere at the police station. Nobody will bother her.

Mia confirmed Reese was awake and doing better, given the circumstances.

She'll be visiting her mom after school, so we came a bit earlier to have the opportunity to talk.

Holding hands, we take the elevator in silence. Frankly, I can't not touch Celeste every chance I get.

Funny how life so often gives us the exact opposite of what we're asking. And it's the best thing ever. She's the best thing ever.

In front of Reese's room, Celeste slips her hand from mine.

I frown. "What's up?"

"I don't think I should intrude. Mia is your daughter, and I don't want to make Reese uncomfortable."

"Mia is your stepdaughter, and this meeting probably will be all kinds of uncomfortable with or without you. I'd prefer you were there."

A smile brightens her face, and it hits me in the chest. I don't understand all the physical reactions I have in her company.

It used to be my cock reacting. Nowadays, my entire body reverberates at the sight of her.

"Okay. Let's do this." Celeste squares her shoulders.

I kiss her forehead. Another thing I can't seem to get enough of. These simple displays of affection. This time, though, I might have done it to give myself courage, to feel her support.

Not feeling ready at all, I push the door open. Reese lies in the bed, her eyes focused on the large window. I paid for a private room for her, which Greta accepted only after a heated discussion.

"Reese," I whisper. My throat is dry, and my voice is raspy, like I've just swallowed razors.

She turns her head and meets my eyes. Her skin is translucent, the deep circles under her sunken eyes giving it the only hint of color. Dark and unforgiving.

She sighs and lifts a corner of her lips slightly, but it drops back immediately like the tiny gesture exhausted her.

"Is it a good time?" I walk closer.

She nods, or rather, she blinks her answer. Maybe I was too hasty in pushing for a meeting this early after her incident.

"This is my wife, Celeste." Fuck, I'm really glad she's beside me. "I'm sorry we're meeting under these circumstances."

"Nice to meet you, Reese." Celeste steps to the foot of the bed.

Reese answers with another almost unperceivable nod.

I had played this conversation out in my head several times since we arrived at the hospital two nights ago. To be honest, I imagined it a few times since Mia showed up.

Standing here now, in a room with the woman who

brought up my amazing daughter, I'm not quite sure where to start.

"Greta told me you'd like shared custody..." Reese breaks the silence. "What about your father?"

The bitterness in her voice mirrors the bile rising in my stomach at the mere mention of him.

"We're no longer teenagers. He doesn't rule my life. I'm sorry for what he did to you and Mia."

Reese snorts weakly. "It's not like we would have driven into the sunset together. We were so young. At least he paid for my school and got me a head start."

"He also robbed me of a decade with my daughter," I snap.

Celeste puts her hand on my back, and my misplaced anger melts a little. But the idea of my father getting any credit, as Reese suggested, is nauseating.

"Look," I say, hoping to redirect the conversation. "My father has no say in this. You don't need to worry."

"I don't want Mia exposed to his brand of evil."

She talks about my father, but she might be including me in his kind of evil. "She will never meet him if I have anything to say about it. And I hope I can prove to you I'm not him."

She assesses me skeptically. "With money?"

"With actions."

She looks away, seemingly searching for answers in the large window. Celeste gives me an encouraging nod. It helps a bit, but the heavy feeling that I've failed this conversation persists.

"Mia told me she's been visiting you for months now. She seems happy to continue, so I'm not going to prevent that."

"I appreciate that."

"I'm not doing it for you, I'm doing it for Mia." Reese doesn't look at me, keeping her gaze on the window.

"I hope over time you can trust me more." What else can I say at this point? "I'd like to help out financially. I'm starting a trust fund for Mia, and opening an account for you—"

"I don't need your money." She winces like she caught herself lying.

"Yes, you do, Reese. And you deserve it. For choosing to keep Mia when my father paid you to get an abortion. For bringing her up by yourself, and doing such an amazing job. For all the times I wasn't there to help. We don't really know each other, and I know this must feel like a power trip to you. But it's not. Like you, I'm doing it for Mia."

Reese studies me with a tired gaze. I can almost see how my words slowly make their way through her pride and independence, and she reluctantly accepts them at face value. Not trusting me yet, but giving our family a chance.

Instead of acknowledging her decision to accept directly, she shifts her eyes to Celeste. "I hear you're a dancer, and you've been training with Mia."

There's a new softness in her face when she speaks about our daughter and her hobby.

"Yes, Mia is very talented and eager. I'm so glad she's back with her hip-hop crew," Celeste says.

"I have two left feet, so I'm not sure where she got it from." Reese pushes up off her hands, making herself more comfortable.

"Oh, I have an idea." Celeste grins and pulls out her phone.

She rounds the bed. Music starts playing, and she turns the screen to Reese, who plasters her hand against her mouth before she glances at me and back to the screen, giggling.

"What is that?" The music sounds familiar, and then it hits me. My impromptu street performance. "Where did you get that?"

Celeste didn't pull out her phone during that dance.

"Mia got it from one of the onlookers before we left." Celeste bites her lips.

"Mom, Dad." Mia runs into the room.

She gives me a quick hug and goes to kiss her mom.

"Hi, Celeste." She cranes her neck. "What are you

watching?" She registers it quickly, though. "Oh, isn't it great? Dad has moves." She tuts.

All three of them laugh and restart the video, giggling. At my expense. Ganging up on me. The three women who have become a permanent part of my life.

And I hope to make them laugh—even at my expense—for as long as possible. Because this is love.

"Okay, put it away now," I growl, and they all laugh again, but Celeste finally puts her phone away.

"Thank you." Reese looks at me, surprising me with her words.

My throat clogs up, and I don't know what to say, so I nod. I nod and hope she understands she can trust and rely on me. I nod to vow I will always take care of them.

Mia decides to stay longer, do her homework and keep Reese company, and we say our goodbyes.

"Oh, Celeste," Mia calls before we leave. "Are you staying in New York?"

"Yes, I'm staying."

"That's good." Mia beams.

Fuck, I love them.

We walk down the hallway, the harsh lights rendering everything into an artificial blue hue. I pull Celeste close to me, because it doesn't matter where we are, my life is brighter with her in it.

I glimpse an empty exam room and pull her inside.

She gasps as I pin her against the wall and lock the door.

In my peripheral vision, the life of the hospital continues behind the narrow glass pane in the door.

Here, only my need for this woman exists. I capture her lips, eating her protest and kissing her like a man possessed. Or obsessed. I'm both, and I don't fucking care.

"Caleb, what are you doing?" she pants when we come up for air.

I lean down and find the hem of her dress. "What does it look like I'm doing?"

"Don't you have to work? You already missed yesterday, and with Corm—"

"I sold my share."

Chapter 43

Celeste

I push him away. "What do you mean, you sold your share?"

A frustrated rumble comes with his sigh. Straightening, he abandons the delicious trailing of his fingers up my thigh.

I'd protest the loss if I wasn't utterly shocked by his revelation.

"I wanted to make sure I could leave with you, in case you got deported."

He searches my face for approval, or for something I can't name. But he doesn't seem his usual casual and carefree self with this admission. He fucking dropped his career because of me.

My heart attempts to flee my ribcage. "But—"

"Xander and Declan wanted me to step in as interim CEO because of the bullshit with Corm. I couldn't have accepted that, knowing I might need to leave only days afterward. Don't make a big deal out of it."

I'm completely speechless, filled with thoughts and emotions that range the entire gamut. When faced with a choice between me and his company, he chose me.

It's stupid and reckless. But it's so significant.

"It is a big deal, though." Tears pool in my eyes. It's a big fucking deal.

"Merged has been in my life for about as long as you, and I have no doubt in my mind that I'm left with the better of the two." His words leave no room for doubt.

My poor heart. I grab his lapels and pull him to me. Our teeth clash in a kiss that feels like everything. *Thank you. I love you. I trust you. I'm yours.*

We devour each other's mouths with urgency, like there's so much we need to accomplish with it, we can't ease up and savor it.

The kiss buries the past, clears any remaining doubt, and seals our future in the most explosive way.

It's a kiss like one that usually follows a proposal, or confirmation of commitment. But this union started with marriage, so we kiss to acknowledge its finality. The most brilliant finality.

"Have you just compared me to a financial company?" I admonish half-heartedly.

He chuckles and dips again to find his way under my skirt. "Oh, God, no. A company makes money. You only cost me." He smirks.

"Caleb," I hiss, half scolding him for his words, and half moaning his name as his fingers graze my underwear.

"So wet for me, black swan. Tell me, whose pussy is this?"

He's not even applying any pressure yet, just holding his fingers lightly over my mound, and my knees buckle. "Yours."

He pulls his hand away and wraps it around my throat before he kisses me savagely. "Whose mouth is this?"

"Yours."

I yelp as he whips me around, pinning me with his hips, my back to his chest. His hands cup my breasts roughly. "Whose are these magnificent tits?"

"Yours."

It's a ridiculous game, really. I'm saying what he wants to hear. What should concern me is how honest my answers are.

Because he might need me to feed into his possessive nature, but I'm his.

His to love. His to care for. His to argue with. His

to confide in. His to fuck. His to make love to. His to play with. His to laugh with. His to be vulnerable with.

His. His. His.

Caleb lifts my skirt. "Whose ass is this?" He squeezes both cheeks, probably leaving bruises.

"Yours."

"That's right, black swan, don't ever forget that." He rips my underwear off. "Hands on the wall."

I glance at the small glass panel as a nurse passes by and doesn't even look our way. Bracing myself against the wall, I bite my forearm as he fills me to the hilt.

We both moan as an overwhelming thrill takes over my body.

We might have upgraded to Caleb's bedroom, but it's still so satisfying to find each other in a public place.

That's who we've been from the beginning. That's the level of trust we showed each other before we even accepted our relationship.

The only difference is that I'm no longer in a role. I'm no longer playing my part.

I live it now with intense honesty.

LILY

One of my clients is hot (fire emoji)

CORA

I didn't know you ever met with them

LILY

I've never seen him, but his voice...

SAAR

Look him up online

Don't! Continue dreaming.

CORA

Don't encourage her dreaming about a man she can't have

I got a man I didn't want and I can't complain

SAAR

(puke emoji)

CORA

I need to get laid.

LILY

Me too

SAAR

This is officially the most depressing group chat

"Where are we going?" I tug at Caleb's arm, but he just strolls casually down the street. "I don't like surprises."

He laughs. "Didn't seem that way when I fingered you in the restaurant last night."

I roll my eyes. "Idiot."

"Keep up insulting me in that lovely accent of yours and I'll have to fuck you in a back alley here." He winks, but his eyes are darker, filled with want.

"Continue de rêver."

"Celeste," he warns, and I laugh.

"We will get arrested one of these days, Mr. van den Linden." I snake my arm around his waist, leaning into him.

The familiar street in Chelsea isn't exactly bustling with people, but our casual progress still upsets the flow of pedestrian traffic.

In the last four days since our first meeting with Reese, we seem to live in our own bubble, unaffected by the chaos the city bestows on its people.

With Mia spending most of her time with her mom, and Caleb being unemployed, I canceled my performances this week, happily passing them to my understudy. We need this time to enjoy peace after the turbulent few days we've had.

"It's a good thing Cressard is a resourceful lawyer, Mrs. van den Linden." He kisses the crown of my head and steers us to another street.

A wave of nostalgia sweeps through me. I wasn't really thinking about our exact whereabouts after Peter dropped us off, but now I wish we were elsewhere in the city.

I don't voice my concern, because there's still a part of me I'm not sure how to reconcile, or how to share properly.

"What's wrong?" Of course, Caleb picks up on my hesitation.

"My school used to be down there." I beckon with my head in the general direction.

"I know," Caleb says, and pulls me in that exact direction, crossing the road. "Let's go see it."

"I don't want to." I pull back, but he doesn't relent.

Stopping in front of the entrance I crossed so many times, he hands me a set of keys. I stare at them, frowning.

"Take them. They're yours." Caleb dangles them between his fingers.

"Keys?" My confusion is obvious in my lack of vocabulary. "Why are we here?"

Caleb sighs. "Jesus, woman, can't you just squeal with joy?" He rolls his eyes and unlocks the door.

"Why do you have the keys?" I don't dare follow him inside. I don't want to see the place I miss so much.

"Because you didn't take them from me."

"Caleb," I snap, and the bastard laughs.

"I got it for you."

"You rented this space?" I recall our conversation in the kitchen, but how and when would he even get it? For me?

"I bought it."

"Why?"

"You're kind of slow today, black swan."

"For me."

"Finally, you're catching up." He pulls me inside and leads me to the main dance studio.

The space hasn't changed much. There are some yoga mats in the corner. I think someone used it for pilates and yoga in the interim. The back wall is painted a hideous shade of red, but it still smells and feels like my studio.

"You bought this building for me?"

He nods.

"You're kind of shit at delivering gifts," I deadpan.

"Come on, it's not often I can make you speechless. Or frazzled. I had to milk the fuck out of the occasion."

He stands there, leaning casually against the mirror, handsome as sin. Entitled, perhaps, but kind as well.

This man keeps showing up for me in the most unexpected ways. "I love you."

"You can thank me on your knees."

I scoff. "I don't know if I want you to be my boss and my landlord, in addition to being my annoying husband."

"Oh, black swan, I'll be your annoying everything for the rest of our lives." He comes to me and takes my hand, placing the other one on my hip. "But I'm not your landlord. This building is yours."

He pulls me closer and starts swaying to nonexistent music. It's unreal how we find a rhythm without the beat, our moves synced.

I dance with him in the silence, soaking in the place and thinking about his generosity. *This is too much*, is my first thought, but I learned already that he lives by a different scale.

"Does this mean you won't buy me an airplane?"

He throws his head back and laughs, without breaking the dance. "I'm getting you an airplane, because I'm still traumatized from searching for you at a public airport the other day."

Now I laugh. "Such hardship, pretty boy." Our gazes collide, and the previous lightness gets heavy with desire. "I'm not going to run away."

"That's good, black swan, that's very good."

"Send him up." Caleb hangs up and turns to me, puzzled. "Cormac Quinn is here."

He gets out of bed and pulls on his sweatpants and a white tee. Completely disregarding my ovaries.

He kisses my forehead. "Get dressed."

"He's surely not coming to see me."

"Most likely not, but the idea of you being naked in the same space as him makes me want to kill him."

I laugh. "Possessive much?"

His expression darkens. "Celeste," he warns.

I roll my eyes and get my robe. It's concerning how his growling spreads butterflies in my belly. "Okay, okay, I'm getting dressed."

"Good girl." He winks and leaves.

I take my time getting dressed, knowing full well that those two need time to talk.

When I called Cormac Quinn two days ago, my attempt to talk to him proved two things. He's an asshole. No surprise there. And he's a smart business-man. Unfortunately.

I put on a white button-down blouse and a brown skirt and pull my hair into a bun. Stepping out of the bedroom, I catch Caleb's timbre.

They're still in the living room? I thought Caleb would take him to his office.

"I find it strange you'd come here out of the kind-ness of your heart," Caleb snorts.

"What can I say, we miss you."

"Bullshit. Why would I return to a sinking ship?"

"A bit of a PR nightmare deters you? We're thriv-ing, and we need you. We can find someone else, of course, but you brought in leads that would make us more money if you brought them to fruition."

I bite my lip and tiptoe to the stairs. I don't want to interrupt this, but I can't help but listen in.

"You could have sent Xander." Caleb walks to the bar and I step back, hoping he won't see me.

"I wanted to come myself, after I learned why you left."

Asshole. He wasn't supposed to bring that up.

"What do you mean?"

"Your wife has some damn good persuasive skills. If she ever decides to quit dancing, make sure we hire her."

I scrunch my face as if I could stop the words from coming out of his mouth.

"What are you talking about?"

"Oopsie. You didn't know she called me. My bad."

I step forward and walk down, the commotion drawing both men's attention. "Corm, so nice of you to visit." My words might have a polite meaning, but I don't hold back my sarcasm.

When I explained to him that my circumstances forced Caleb to sell his part of the company, I also asked him to keep my interference a secret. But what did I expect from him?

"Celeste, nice to see you. But I think I'll leave the two of you to enjoy your evening." He drops a folder on the coffee table. "Have a look and call us tomorrow. Good night."

My attention turns to Caleb. He studies me, his expression solemn.

Then, without a word, he walks to pick up the folder and flips through its pages. I stop at the base of the staircase, unsure if I should join him, worried I might have overstepped. Embarrassed him. That he might loathe my interference.

What man wouldn't? Shit. I wanted to finally do something for him, but I guess I should have thought it through better.

His gaze finds me again, and I falter.

"You talked to him." It's not a question, and that almost makes it worse.

I nod. "Yes. Is that an offer to buy back your share of the business?"

"No."

My heart sinks as I approach him and snatch the folder. Scanning the documents, I frown. "This is the sale agreement."

Caleb flips to the last page. Beside his signature are Xander's and Declan's, but the field for Corm's signature is empty.

"He wasn't there the morning we did this. It turns out he hasn't signed it yet."

He takes the folder from my hands, drops it to the sofa and pulls me to him.

"Are you mad I talked to him?" I lower my head, but look up at him through my lashes.

"I'm not happy about it, but when I look past that, I think I'm grateful. The asshole was waiting for me to come beg him. He came to gloat that I sent you to do it for me, but I guess now he knows that's not the case."

"I'm sorry, I couldn't bear that you left because of me. You deserve both. Merged and me."

"Oh, black swan, you're wrong. I deserve Merged, and thank you for nudging them for me. But I don't deserve you. I will, however, try to live up to that challenge every day. For the rest of my life."

Epilogue

Celeste

One month later

Thunderous applause erupts as the last beats of music fade away.

Caleb jumps up, clapping with the vigor of a proud man. A man who loves. A man who shows up for his loved ones.

"She was amazing, wasn't she?" He beams at me.

His joy is contagious, and spreads through me with warmth and familiarity. I laugh, because there is no other response for him right now.

I glance back at the stage in the school auditorium where Mia and her friends keep bowing, each of them

491

grinning and searching for their families in the audience.

She spots us in the third row. Probably because her father is towering over those around us, but also because he claps the loudest.

She sends us an air kiss and rushes off the stage with her crew, all of them giggling.

"They're all talented," Reese says.

"Mia was the best." Caleb's voice is full of pride and confidence, like he's stating a fact nobody should dare refute.

I lean into him, taking his hand. "They all seemed to have fun. Their joy comes across in their performance and touches the audience."

"Thank you for supporting her hobby." Reese looks away.

Over the last few weeks we've spent some time together, and while she's been attending therapy and a recovery program, her feeling of failure runs deep.

It's always the self-criticism that hits us hardest.

"Don't mention it." Caleb wraps his arm around my shoulder and pulls me tight. "I can't even take credit. It was Celeste who discovered Mia quit the crew. The rest was easy."

Reese's eyes glimmer with unshed tears. "Sometimes I wonder how things would have turned out if I'd tried to contact you sooner. I hope you understand what stopped me was mostly fear of your father."

"We can't change the past. Mia is in my life now, and I'm grateful for it."

Reese opens her mouth to say something, but Mia runs up to us, still buzzing with energy from the performance. "Did you like it?"

"Like?" Caleb hugs her. "I loved it, sweetheart. You were the best."

"You think?" She seeks reassurance, her face glimmering with sweat from the performance, but brimming with pride.

"You were amazing," Reese says, and the two of them hug.

"Congratulations," I say when it's my turn. "You guys rocked it."

We follow the crowd out as everyone disperses. "Did you like the routine? We incorporated all your suggestions." She bounces beside us.

"You made those moves even better." I pat her back.

"A celebration is in order, I think," Caleb suggests, as we spill out onto the hot street.

"Can we go for ice cream? Or burgers? I'm starving!"

Reese hesitates. "I have to head to my meeting." Her cheeks pinken as she refers to her group therapy.

"Oh." Mia covers her disappointment quickly. "That's okay. I'll eat at home."

Reese's face falls, and her eyes dart to Caleb. The moment would be ordinary, a mother seeking help from a father. But in their case, it's so much more.

They don't have a mutual parenting experience. They're still learning how to trust each other. Her unspoken request or question or whatever it is has its own significant meaning, and my heart hurts and swells at the same time.

"Let me say bye to the girls." Mia hops away to join a group of friends.

"We can take Mia for burgers, if you don't mind. She can stay over tonight. I know it's not our normal night..." Caleb says, and glances at me.

"Of course." I nod.

Reese bites her lips, her gaze moving to Mia. "I guess that would be okay, if Mia agrees."

"Thank you," Caleb says.

Reese blinks. "I'm sorry, it's just sometimes I feel I have nothing to offer her, and you'll woo her away from me. I know that's not what you're trying to do, and I'm being petty—"

"Stop it right now," Caleb warns. "You focus on your recovery, so you can be fully there for her. You'll always be the most important person in Mia's life. Your current circumstances might be shitty, but that doesn't diminish the great job you've been doing with our daughter."

Reese sighs, and gives him a shy smile. "It's a relief she has both of you while I get back on my feet. But sometimes it's hard to believe I'm not in it alone anymore."

"That's a good problem to have." Caleb smiles at her.

Watching their interaction seals my love for this man even further. But it also uncovers an empty spot I never realized I had. I look over at Mia, and wonder how it would feel to carry and raise children of my own.

I've never thought about that. We've never discussed it, since our union started as a formality, but suddenly the eventuality feels more like a necessary discussion.

Or rather, when we were still in an arrangement, he made it clear he never wanted any children. With anyone. And now I need to know if his perspective's changed.

"Do you want to stay with your dad and go for those burgers?" Reese asks when Mia returns to us.

Her eyes widen, excitement morphing her features. "Are you sure?" she asks, and then turns to Caleb. "Can I?"

"Always." Caleb ruffles her hair, and she scoffs.

Yeah, sometimes he needs to be reminded she isn't a little girl anymore. Even though in so many senses she is. Even though he missed out on time when she still was one.

"I'm glad I got to see you dance today." Reese hugs her daughter.

"See you tomorrow, Mom. I love you."

We pile into the car, the drive filled with Mia's excited chatter about her friends and their plans for the next performance. It's a simple, ordinary outing, but it feels extraordinary in its own way.

"Celeste?" She bites her lip, and looks at me with hesitation when we take seats at a quaint little diner near our building that Mia fell in love with.

"What is it?"

"The girls and I were wondering if you could maybe help us with more choreography?"

Before I get a chance to answer or even consider the honor, Caleb sits up straight and winks at me. "Mia, not only can she help you out, but soon she's going to reopen her school, and you guys can rehearse there."

"For real?" Mia's eyes widen. "That would be epic. Let me text them." She pulls out her phone and types at a mile a minute.

"I thought the building and the school were mine. Are you now booking the space on my behalf?" I grin, teasing Caleb while Mia is completely lost chatting with her friends.

"I'm only making sure you don't forget where your talent lies."

"Is that so?"

We grin at each other. I keep waiting for this ever-present joy to disappear, but so far it only keeps growing.

Mia drops her phone and dives into a menu. "Can I get a burger and ice cream?"

Caleb laughs. "You can have whatever you want. Tonight is your night."

We settle into a comfortable rhythm, eating our burgers and sharing laughs. I never imagined that our fake wedding would lead to this—a real family.

We finish our meal, and Peter picks us up. Mia dozes off against Caleb's shoulder on one side, and I squeeze his hand on the other.

"Caleb?" I meet his gaze.

His eyes darken as he brings my hand to his lips. "What is it, black swan?"

Oh my, the predator came out to play. A shiver of excitement rushes through me, and I almost abandon the topic I meant to broach.

He leans in and kisses me gently, careful not to disturb Mia. "What is it?" he repeats.

"I know you said you don't want children..." My

voice quivers, because shit, this is not something I should bring up here and now. This is not the place for a potentially challenging conversation.

Caleb's expression turns solemn, his features harden somehow. What if he says never? What does it mean for us? For this marriage?

A wave of nausea sweeps through me before he speaks.

"I've been on this quest to fix all my father's mistakes, which included marrying you. I always thought that his biggest mistake—the example he set to us as a father—was not fixable. That it fucked me up forever. But I recently realized that while he's a permanent stain in my past, I can't let him soil my future."

My lips curve up as my heart swells. How is it possible to fall for this man harder every day?

"And since I married a perfect woman, I want at least a dozen children."

I gasp. "A dozen?"

He cocks his head. "A half dozen?"

I snort, shaking my head. "Why don't we start with one?"

"Tonight." He seals the conversation with a demand.

Six months later

My mind lingers between darkness and light. I don't want to open my eyes yet, though I probably should. I'd planned on resting for twenty minutes, but my dreamless nap must have run long, guessing by the haze in my head.

I roll on to my back and stretch, waiting for the nausea.

Nothing.

I smile with relief. The first three months of my pregnancy were rough, with constant vomiting and a few emergency visits.

And while the fatigue from the first trimester still lingers, the nausea hasn't returned in the last three days.

I finally pry my eyes open and look around. The living room is dim, soaked in the darkness from outside. I sit up, the blanket Caleb must have thrown over me sliding to the ground.

My gaze lands on a note on the coffee table.

Peter will drive you to the party whenever you're ready. There's a gift for you on the bed upstairs. Wear it.
Love, Cal

Oh, the party. Why did the man insist on hosting a Christmas party at my school? I haven't even opened it yet. Besides some private classes, I wasn't able to fully immerse myself into the business yet.

I couldn't even continue with my performances because of my early pregnancy issues. I've stayed involved with the production, though. Especially after Caleb insisted on putting me in charge of the theater.

Reinhard resigned immediately after, which wasn't a surprise, but based on the sentiment among the troupe and the employees, nobody would miss him.

We found out it was Leon who tipped off ICE. Ironically, he revealed it himself when he showed up at the theater drunk, demanding his gig back.

Managing the theater my husband owns takes up all the energy that's left in me. Hence, I don't really feel like a party.

But I'm going to make the effort, because Caleb has been nothing but caring these past few months.

And while he's been trying to hide it well, he's also been quite worried about me. He deserves to enjoy a party, without me throwing up or falling asleep.

I trudge upstairs and gasp at the dress I find on the bed. The gift. It's the exact model as the wedding dress he sent to me, but this one is emerald green, to match my eyes and the festive hue of the season.

I text Peter that I need forty minutes and then get

dressed. With the color returning to my cheeks, I feel almost like my old self.

Peter waits for me downstairs and drives me to the school. Merde, I don't even know who will be there. I should have gotten more involved.

Well, I can still try to be a delightful hostess at a party that is officially mine—and Caleb's—but I haven't prepared.

The car stops in front of the building, and before Peter comes around to open the door, my gaze scans the building that has been a home for many of my dreams, and hopefully many more to come.

My building.

My school.

And while I recognize I wouldn't have gotten it back without Caleb's help, a sense of pride and thrill at what's coming descends on me.

After weeks of living in a stupor, I feel like I want to hit the ground running, and hire teachers and open courses.

The door swings open, and Peter helps me step out into the frigid winter evening. I pull my faux fur collar closer to shield myself from the wind.

"Have a nice evening, ma'am."

"Thank you."

"You got her here, great. Take the rest of the evening off, Peter."

Caleb rushes to us. Not caring about the temperature, he slipped outside in only his tailored suit.

God, the man is breathtaking. No matter how many times I see him, he steals my breath, and brings a smile to my face.

"You're going to get sick," I admonish.

"Hush." He kisses me. "How are you feeling?" Concern laces his face.

"I'm good. Sorry I'm late, I had a nap and it—"

He kisses me again. "Don't worry, you and our baby needed the nap. Let's go inside before my balls freeze."

"Oh, I wouldn't like that." I giggle as we cross the sidewalk and enter the warmth of the building.

Mistletoe and Christmas garlands decorate the door to the main dance studio. "Aw, you made it very Christmassy. And thank you for the dress."

He helps me out of my coat and hangs it up. "Let me see it."

I twirl around for him.

"Gorgeous." He yanks me to him and claims my lips. I immediately feel the outline of his hardness.

My all-day morning sickness has limited our sex life, and frankly, I'm relieved he still desires me.

I cup his erection, feeling a bit desperate suddenly. The world takes on new colors when one feels better. "Maybe we can skip the party."

He groans. "We can't skip this party. But we'll fucking sneak out soon." He points to a door to our side.

"That's a broom closet," I chuckle.

"That's our fuck closet from now on." He gives me one more punishing kiss, and then pulls me toward the sound of laughter and music in the main studio.

"I still don't understand why you didn't hire catering and hold this at our condo. Or in a restaurant."

"We needed a special place." He breathes by my ear, and I shudder. God, this man!

"A special place?"

I forget the question as soon as I enter the studio. The room has been transformed. A large table sits in the middle, surrounded by chairs clad in white silk with green ribbons matching my dress, that are all occupied by our people.

Caleb's brother Finn, and his wife, Paris. Saar, Cora and Lily sit beside them. Jose and Matilda follow, and the Merged crew is here as well. Corm, Dylan, Xander and Roxy. Reese and Mia complete the circle.

Everyone is chatting without noticing our entrance, which is great, because it gives me a moment to take the scene in.

The Christmas tree in the corner sets the atmosphere, but it's the elegant arch set at the front of the room that steals my attention.

Green and red fabric drapes around a wooden frame, adorned with Christmas decorations. Thick white candles flicker in large glass candle holders on the floor. It's breathtaking, but also... What is it?

I turn to Caleb with a question in my eyes.

He looks at me through his eyelashes. What is happening? It's really rare to see this man hesitating.

He leans in. "You know how our marriage hasn't been fake for a while now?" he whispers into my ear, and as always the warm timbre of his voice tickling my face sends shivers of pleasure down my spine.

"What are you saying?"

"The wedding was still fake, so I thought we should renew our vows." He takes my hand, and slides a beautiful diamond ring on my finger. "What do you say?"

I blink, my eyes darting between the ring, the room full of our friends, and my man. In Caleb, I found more than just a marriage. I've found a family, a home, and real love.

"What were you thinking? I don't have vows prepared."

"Just promise your obedience and we'll be fine." He winks.

"Je vais te tuer." I glare at him, but I can't hide my smile.

Caleb groans at my use of French, and then adds

504

another surprise to this wonderful day. "Je t'aime, cygne noir."

Thank you for reading A Temporary Forever. I hope you loved Cal and Celeste. Saar and Corm are next:-).

You can read Cal's brother story right now! Find out what happened when a beautiful designer, Paris, stole Finn van den Linden's coffee (what a meet-cute:-).
Read his story in RECKLESS BOND now!

Cal's lawyer, Dominic Cressard found himself in a fake relationship in this enemies-to-lovers romance:
Read RECKLESS DARE now!

*Crave more Cal and Celeste? Read about their Valentine's day in this **bonus scene** at www.maxinehenri.com/atf or scan this QR code:*

Also by Maxine Henri

Reckless Billionaires Series

Reckless Fate (Massi and Gina's Second Chance Romance)

Reckless Deal (Gio and Mila's Grumpy/Sunshine Bosshole Romance)

Reckless Hunger (Andrea and Ivy's Age Gap Romance)

Reckless Bond (Paris and Finn's Accidental Pregnancy Romance)

Reckless Vow (Brook and Baldo's Marriage of Convenience Romance)

Reckless Desire (Sydney and Hunter's Single Dad Romance)

Reckless Dare (Lo and Dom's Fake Relationship Romance)

Untamed Billionaires Series

Fall in love with the morally grey heroes obsessed with their women

Chosen by The Billionaire (Art and Violet's Enemies

to Lovers Romance)

Chased by the Billionaire (Ness and Rocco's Age gap/Innocent Heroine Romance)

Stolen by the Billionaire (Phillip and Lena's Forbidden Love Romance)

Tempted by Charlie (A Fake Relationship Novella)

Merged Series

A Temporary Forever (Cal and Celeste's story)

Corm and Saar's story coming soon

Book 3 coming in 2025

Book 4 coming in 2025

If you loved this book, please spread the word and leave a review. One sentence is enough to help other readers and make me very happy.

Author's Note

I loved, loved, loved writing Cal and Celeste and I hope you enjoyed their story as much as I enjoyed writing it.

I'm a curvy woman and I only recently learned to embrace my curves with love. Dancing has played a big part in it. I'm so grateful I can channel my life experiences into my characters. I hope the result is both entertaining and possibly inspiring for you.

This is my eleventh novel and frankly I still can't believe I have this amazing opportunity to share stories with you. I thank you from the bottom of my heart for joining me on this journey. You, darling reader, are appreciated and valued.

Thank you, Jessica and Emily at the HEA Author Services, for all your hard work whipping my messy manuscript into shape. Thank you, Dan, for finding mistakes when I thought I caught them all.

Thank you, JayCee, for the beautiful covers. I know I'm not always able to communicate my vision, but somehow we always get there. I appreciate your creativity and patience.

To my circle of trusted author friends (you know who you are), this gig is easier with you by my side.

To all my ARC readers, thank you for taking the time to read Cal and Celeste's story and helping me to spread the word and make this book a success. I really appreciate your support.

And circling back to you, dear reader, I hope I provided a satisfying escape, and that Caleb was a good fictional boyfriend to you.

I can't wait to share my next story with you.

Love,

Maxine

About the Author

Maxine Henri is a contemporary romance author who infuses her stories with steamy passion and complex characters. When she's not crafting stories that will have you swooning, she can usually be found sipping on a cup of black tea while reading a good book. Or traveling to new destinations.

Maxine believes that stories matter. They facilitate emotional journeys, inspire and entertain. And when it comes to books and fiction, stories are a great escape and probably the most beneficial addiction on this planet.

Her billionaire romances are the perfect escape, offering a taste of luxury and adventure. Maxine introduces heroes who may have a dark past, but are always balanced by a lighter side. And her leading ladies? They're strong, independent women who may be a little broken, but always find their way in life.

You can connect with her on any of these platforms:

facebook.com/maxinehenriromance

instagram.com/maxinehenriromance

bookbub.com/profile/maxine-henri

amazon.com/author/maxinehenri